By HARNETT T. KANE

NEW ORLEANS WOMAN:
A Biographical Novel of Myra Clark Gaines

PLANTATION PARADE:
The Grand Manner in Louisiana

BAYOUS OF LOUISIANA

DEEP DELTA COUNTRY

LOUISIANA HAYRIDE:
The American Rehearsal for Dictatorship

NEW ORLEANS WOMAN

New Orleans Woman

A BIOGRAPHICAL NOVEL OF
MYRA CLARK GAINES

By

HARNETT T. KANE

Doubleday & Company, Inc.

GARDEN CITY, NEW YORK

1946

TO

Annie Hirt Kane

There is nothing so powerful as truth—and often nothing so strange.

DANIEL WEBSTER—*Argument on the Murder
of Captain White*

Contents

Part One

THE YOUNG MRS. WHITNEY

CHAPTER I

FROM the drawing room, through the folding doors, Myra's rich laugh rang out. Colonel Samuel Davis, hero of the wars, the new choice of his people for their legislature, was a man who regarded himself as master of his household. He tried to ignore these unseemly sounds, but the peals went on. In his library at Delamore Place he listened with only half his attention to his callers, there to bid him good-by on his departure for his duties.

Yes, he nodded, it would be pleasant to work in the legislature. Yes, it *had* taken them a long time to reward him, he'd admit. Well, he had only done his duty. . . . Slowly the colonel's annoyance melted. His small blue eyes moved from guest to guest; his jowls rippled in a smile after a particular compliment. As his friends drained off their punch the colonel motioned to the servants to refill the cups.

Perhaps by accident, Colonel Davis stood close to the full-length portrait over the mantel which pictured him at the hour of his greatest glory, during the War of 1812. His stance majestic, he grasped a plumed hat, his sash red against the blue of his uniform. The artist had been successful in merging grandeur with corpulence, said some; but not, of course, to the colonel.

The narrow-faced D. W. Coxe, a long man in a long black coat, rose to propose a toast. From the next room Myra and her companion caught echoes of an oft-told tale: Samuel Davis's early life as a poor Delaware boy, his service as a sailor, his rise to the command of a French frigate, privateering against the English. Then, during the uprising of the slaves in Santo Domingo, the doughty young American had rescued the aristocratic Marianne Rose Baron Boisfontaine and her family; not long afterward he had won her favor.

"He's finally finished," Myra whispered to the youth beside her. But Mr. Coxe went on to tell how the colonel had lived with his Marianne in far-off, pe-culiar Louisiana, as a merchant, sugar planter, and captain of the port of New Orleans. Yet all this, the orator pounded out, had been only a preparation for the colonel's supreme moment, when he returned to Delaware and marshaled his people against the British at Lewes. He need not, said Mr. Coxe, tell them how the colonel defied the redcoats, sending their own ammunition back against them when they tried to make a landing; and he immediately went on to tell them. And now, eighteen years later, the colonel remained among them with his charming though regrettably frail wife and his lovely, vivacious daughter Myra. . . . Samuel Davis smiled and sipped, and he ceased to hear the ripple of the girl's voice through the doors.

Myra leaned back, her elbows resting on the ledge of the window seat. Behind her the late summer winds stirred the gold draperies; below the stately porticoed house on the hill lay the city of Wilmington in hazy outline. Her hair, a deep titian that seemed brown in certain lights, was lifted high on her head, emphasizing the air of independence, almost of queenliness, which, despite her tiny stature, struck those who met her for the first time. The firm cleft chin further reinforced this impression. Her eyes, long and deep, were a color between hazel and brown; they had a quality that implied a calm, good-humored appraisal of the world. The perfectionist might object that the eyes were too large and the red mouth fuller than many considered desirable; few would not agree that she was a woman of startling beauty. Not many who saw Myra ever forgot her.

Bending toward her was William Wallace Whitney, the man she had met three months before and had decided within five minutes that she would marry if she could.

A smile hovering about her mouth, she fixed her eyes on Will Whitney as he spoke. His countenance, like his figure, bespoke power, masculine and unashamed. Born to means, Will nevertheless seemed a kind of throwback to his grandfather's day, when men had to make their way under frontier conditions. His hands, the backs thatched with black hair, rested lightly beside him; his shoulders hunched slightly as he inclined his six feet three inches toward her. He was sprucely attired in a gray broadcloth suit; the fashionably tight trousers, strapped beneath the boots, bulged at the calves; and Myra wondered whether Will would not have been more at home in buckskin. Yet with all his size, and a certain awkwardness that accompanied it, Will had a quality of boyishness and gentle good humor.

They had been together frequently since that night of their

meeting at the cotillion. A visitor from his home in New York, he had been calling whenever he found the opportunity; and Myra, always direct, had helped to make the opportunity.

He was talking in jovial fashion, his smooth, sunburned skin flushing now and then. But Myra listened absently; though she tried not to show it, she was growing more and more disturbed. There was trouble ahead for her and Will—and the colonel.

The colonel lectured her frequently enough, sometimes with explosive force: she was forward; it hardly became a female to race about the lawn as she did, ride a horse with so little reserve, and—he grew beet-red at this point—express opinions. In Samuel Boyer Davis fidgety pride alternated with fumbling kindness. He blew hot, he blew cold, toward people and things; and now, she was afraid, the colonel was growing very cold toward Will.

His hand on her arm, his face suddenly grave, Will turned to the same subject. "The colonel—he doesn't like me, does he?"

"I don't——" She caught herself. Why deny it? The thing was happening that had happened several times before, when it had appeared that she was almost engaged. Samuel Davis had received the youth pleasantly enough at first; then slowly she had begun to observe premonitory signs, frowns and silences. Yesterday, when she mentioned Will's name, the colonel had glared.

Turning her face to Will's, she bit her lip. His words tumbled forth in a rush. "I have a lot to say. I know today's a bad time, but——" His collar seemed to be choking him; a lock of hair fell into his eyes, and he tossed it back with a nervous gesture. Myra waited, her heart beating heavily against the blue silk of her waist. Will dropped his eyes and was silent.

Then she stood up. Rising with her, he towered over her, stirred by the sudden intensity that he saw in her eyes. Her face had flamed. Just below her left ear lobe she had a tiny scar, a quarter inch long, normally unnoticed because it was only a shade darker than her clear skin. When she colored, however, the mark stood out against her cheek. She wasn't sure how she had got it; it had something to do with an accident in New Orleans. . . . Now it almost shone.

"Are you trying to say you want to marry me?" Her question was as direct as her gaze.

Will Whitney stared, and the hands that caught hers shook. "I thought it would be . . . Shouldn't I first ask . . . ?" His voice trailed off.

Gently removing one of her hands from his, she lifted it toward his chin. The ruffles at her waist touched his coat; a fresh, cool perfume—the perfume of her hair—came to him in waves. She said in a husky whisper: "*I'm* answering you, Will. And I can't stand on my tiptoes much longer!"

Her small, high-breasted figure was close to his. All at once his eyes, clear blue and sharp above his prominent cheekbones, widened, and she lost her breath as his arms reached quickly about her. He kissed her on the lips and then, hungrily, almost angrily, on the throat. A long sigh escaped her, and her hands wrapped themselves in the thick black hair at the back of his head. Suddenly he released her.

"I want to ask your father. Today." His voice was strained.

"Please," she murmured, her eyes wide in alarm. "Let me first . . ." She had little idea what she would do, but she had to keep Will from the colonel for the time being.

Down the hall the doors swung open, and Samuel Davis and the crowd started forward. A maid hurried to turn on the light in the hall; Myra and Will, separating, went to the drawing-room door. Bustling by, the colonel ignored Will. As he moved toward Myra, however, she whispered in the colonel's ear. He hesitated, annoyed at her request, then strode to the library with her. Closing the doors behind him, he raised his hand.

"Now, missy, first *I* have something to say to *you*. I don't like that damned whippersnapper Whitney. I won't have my mind changed either." The colonel swayed slightly. As the fumes of the punch swirled about her she held back her anger.

Instead she managed to say gently: "Can't we wait till you're home again?"

He was having trouble with his gloves, and she took his hands to help him. As she looked up at him through her long, reddish-brown lashes his face grew less set, and he nodded. "We'll see." But she realized more clearly than ever that it would be no easy matter.

Ten days later Myra glanced from the bay window in surprise as a stranger cantered up the driveway. The Irish maid,

Phyllis, her plump face alight with interest, ushered him in. "From the colonel, Miss Myra. Says he has to hurry."

Samuel Davis had left behind an important set of papers; he was sending her the key to his desk. Ordering a drink and food for the sweating messenger, Myra went to the cluttered desk and searched among the bills, receipts, and letters. Wasn't this like the colonel, who never remembered anything? If Marianne Davis weren't ill upstairs, she would know just where to find it. . . . Here was what he wanted. A few minutes later Myra had given the precious papers to the messenger. As she was tidying the desk a few words drew her eye: "I regret to hear Daniel Clark's daughter Myra is ill. I know you will care for her as if she were your own."

Her head jerked upward; in the mirror opposite, her face was that of a stranger. Perhaps this was a mistake, somebody else in the family. But no; there were no other Myras among the Davises. Like a dim light in the distance, a memory touched the edge of her mind. Some fifteen years ago a malicious classmate had informed her that the colonel wasn't her "father for true." Myra had asked Marianne about it. That evening the colonel had told Myra the other girl had invented the whole story. A few days later Myra had been enrolled in a new school; until today she had forgotten the whole incident.

Suddenly her heels were tapping up the stairs. In a moment the tired gaze of Marianne Davis, which had been fixed on the canopy of her bed, was shifted to her. Marianne's quick look of pleasure faded as Myra stepped into the light and the older woman saw her taut face. In silence Marianne scanned the note. She flinched as if she had been struck a blow. It had happened, the thing she had dreamed about a thousand times. Marianne put her hand to her eyes and sobbed the hopeless sobs of a defeated, aging woman.

Myra took Marianne in her arms and soothed her. After a time there was only the cheerful tick of the French clock on the mantel; Marianne lay on her side, her hands clenched.

"How . . . ?" Myra began, but Marianne's upward gaze pleaded that she be spared.

"Myra, I don't know what to say. So much of it I never understood. *Chérie* . . ." Her muffled voice was barely perceptible; as always, in distress, she reverted to French. "Ask your father

—the colonel." Though Myra patted her thin cheeks and said no more, Marianne went on in a broken monotone, almost to herself: "How many times I wondered if we were doing right. . . . It always seemed best . . . *'cré Dieu!'*"

Heavily Myra descended the stairs. So it was true. Then who was she, and how had it happened? Her real mother—was she dead, and had she wanted to give her up? Over and over the name repeated itself: Clark, Daniel Clark. She struggled with her earliest recollections: a house behind the emerald mound of the levee, a wide river flowing past; New Orleans, a blur of faces and foreign voices, narrow streets that sometimes smelled bad, and oddly different houses. It was all that came back—that and, of course, Colonel Davis, now easygoing, now forbidding, and the understanding Marianne. This man and woman whom she had regarded as father and mother, how was she to think of them now?

With a toss of her red hair she reached out for a sheet of paper, a pen, and a sandbox. She had promised Will to keep him informed of developments. Well, here in truth was a development. Addressing him at his home in Binghamton, New York, she set down what she had learned; then, more slowly, she added that she understood this put matters between them in another light; she would accept any course he wished to take. Folding the note, she rang for Phyllis. At her first sight of the girl the Irishwoman clasped her to her voluminous breast; now Myra could cry as she had been needing to cry for an hour.

In midafternoon of a damp and overcast Saturday a week later Myra tore open Will's reply. "Cannot see this makes slightest difference," she read. ". . . you, not someone who is or isn't Colonel Davis's daughter, that I want . . ." He would arrive on Sunday, to settle the whole matter with the colonel. Myra's face lost the stamp of pain that had been upon it. Her dark eyes glowed as she dropped into a chair to reread the message. She had hoped it would be this way, but how could she have known?

Then she heard the hounds outside. The colonel's carriage rolled toward the pillared entranceway. Preoccupied, he strode in, tossing gloves, stick, and parcels to one side, and was about to turn toward the stairs when Myra's figure caught his eye. An expression about her mouth, a certain tension, made him start. She spoke without preliminary. "I have to talk to you, please." She did not wait for a reply but walked to the side parlor. Before he closed the door behind him she asked her question.

"Who—who is Daniel Clark?"

His hand on the knob, the colonel wheeled about. A vein moved in his forehead; the words, when they came, were cautious. "A friend down in New Orleans. A long time ago." His eyes searched hers. "Why?"

"I'm not your child, am I?" Her hand worked at her handkerchief.

"You are! What fool bastard——"

He grew silent as Myra took the letter from her pocket. At the first glance his ruddy face became mottled, then seemed to dissolve into uncertainty.

"You've been under our care since you were ten days old. Doesn't that make you ours?" His eyes asked her approval. "Sometimes we wanted to tell you. But we'd had you so long."

Her expression softened; she bit her underlip. It was difficult, yet she had to continue. "Mr.—Mr. Clark—where is he?"

Samuel Davis swallowed. "He's dead." Myra blinked. What did she feel, sorrow or relief? She could not tell. The colonel, fists clenched, went on. "He was a merchant and landowner, very prosperous. Mixed in practically everything in New Orleans." Unsure what to say next, he observed irrelevantly, "His hair was red, like yours. He came from Ireland; I always thought you inherited your disposition from him, temper and all."

Myra found it impossible to manage a smile. Her face was brooding. "And my mother?"

Samuel Davis lowered himself upon one of the sofas, his hands hanging nervously beside him. "She was Zulime Carrière, a young Frenchwoman, a Louisiana Creole."* He spoke reluctantly, with an effort. "She was poor, and there was some trouble about their marriage. They were supposed to keep it secret till they could straighten out their affairs; at least that's what some said. We took you soon after you were born. Then, later, Daniel and Zulime quarreled; and when I left Louisiana you came with us. Daniel lost his money and died practically

*As generally used of someone in Louisiana, "Creole" means a white person. This meaning is followed throughout these pages.

bankrupt. . . . There were things about the whole affair we never understood." These last words, Myra realized, were the ones Marianne had used. Wearily she shook her head; there was something strange here.

"My mother. Is she dead too?"

The colonel went to the window, where he fingered the thick tassels of the curtain. "No," he told her finally. "She came North, after a little while, to Philadelphia, during the time we were living there. Then she went to France." Samuel Davis was impatient, anxious to be rid of the subject.

"When did she leave?"

"Oh, a year or two ago."

Myra's brown eyes widened. The Davises, too, had remained in Philadelphia until two years ago! During most of her life, then, her mother had been near her, and she had been given no hint. How did that happen, and why did they . . . ? Breathless, she poured out her questions, until the colonel waved his hand.

"It'll do you no good to upset yourself and us too over this. I've already told you all you ought to know. Don't worry that fine head of yours." Gruffly he caught her arms and kissed her cheek. Finding it damp, he shook his finger. "Come, missy."

Abruptly his face altered. "It's a good time for us to understand each other, too, about that fellow Whitney. You're not going to see him again." With that he walked heavily toward the hallway.

Myra ran after him; there were no tears now. The tiny scar below her ear stood out angrily against her flushed face. "Just a minute. I don't think we understand each other about Will. I want to marry him, and he's coming tomorrow to talk it over with us."

The colonel, turning livid, ran his big hand over his face. When he spoke, it was to curse Will and all the Whitneys. His wrath, as usual, served to calm hers; her face regained its natural hue, and her eyes grew cool. She managed to interrupt.

"And why shouldn't we get married? I'm over twenty-one!"

"Because I say no, God damn it! No! The sneak—he's after your money!"

"That's ridiculous. The Whitneys are at least as well off as
——"

His hand on the curved banister, Samuel Davis wheeled upon her. "After what I've done, when—when nobody else would have you!" She winced under his rage. "You won't see this man Whitney, that I warrant! Get to your room and stay there till I send word to you." In his frenzy his voice cracked. "And when Mr. Whitney comes he'll find a lively reception." He shouted, "I haven't forgotten my hand with a pistol!"

The threat might seem fantastic; yet she had known his fury to last for days, gaining as he nursed it. She recalled a white-hot quarrel in which he had been restrained only by the strong arms of two neighbors. His son, Horatio, had parted with him in anger and they had not spoken in years; and there were relatives in Louisiana with whom he would have no communication. . . . Unexpectedly he thrust her forward. "Up with you, God damn it!" She stumbled along the stairs.

Lying on her face across the bed, Myra rested her throbbing head against the sheets. The angry impulses slipped away, and her fears increased. A noise at the door made her jump; it was Phyllis, a finger to her lips. The maid brought word that only disturbed her the more. "He's downstairs oilin' his gun. Told Madame just like he told you, and more, 'gainst Mr. Will. Madame says she'll try to handle him and for you just to be quiet. But, 'fore God, Miss Myra, I'm afraid."

Myra straightened up. She understood at once what she had to do—get out of this house tonight and reach Will on his way. Her departure would probably bring a scandal at the least. The gossips would say she had chased after Will, and there must have been a reason. . . . Well, she'd chance their talk, and to hell with them. She took Phyllis's arm. The maid hesitated a moment, then nodded.

The upper hallway clock was striking ten when Samuel Davis mounted the stairs. His step sounded outside her doorway; hand on knob, he stopped. Myra fixed the last button on her tight-waisted gray silk gown and slipped beneath the covers. The knob moved; then the colonel changed his mind and lumbered to his room. Resting on her elbow, her heart pounding, she waited. Almost an hour later she crept along the darkened passage. At his door she paused; the only sound was the steady patter of rain against the windows. Myra's heart went out to the frail woman who lay a few feet away from her. If only she might let Marianne know how she felt about going under such circumstances!

Downstairs she threw on a cape and buttoned her heaviest shoes. When Phyllis, her teeth chattering, started with her to the back door they heard a faint howl.

"The hounds—they'll be baying at the first sound!" Myra cried.

Phyllis whispered reassurement: "I've tied 'em up, way at the back."

As they opened the door the wind lashed their faces, blinding them for a moment; violent gusts tore at their skirts. In the dark, slipping into puddles as they went, they felt their way toward the carriage. "I'll drive," Phyllis whispered. Suddenly one of the dogs was upon them, yelping. Almost at once a light went on at the colonel's window.

"Quick!" Myra pushed Phyllis onto the wet seat and jumped to the driver's place beside her. She hadn't ridden for years without learning how to handle animals. At the touch of the whip the horses started forward.

Lights shone downstairs; already someone was running across the porch. Through the slanting rain the front gates loomed ahead. If they stopped to open them they would probably be caught. "Hold on," Myra called to Phyllis through the noise of the rain. Under the whip the horses broke from a gallop into a run. At the gate they hesitated momentarily and then plunged through, leaving splintered wood behind them. The carriage tipped and made a turn that almost threw Phyllis out of her seat; and then they were racing into the curtain of water.

The night was almost pitch-black. Lightning now and then lit the landscape about them; in a crash of thunder Myra heard Phyllis's prayer: "Mother of God . . . Mary, deliver us . . ." She braced her own feet wide apart and lowered her head against the rain and wind. The water ran down the collar of her dress and up her sleeves as she clutched the reins. Her garments became wetter and wetter until at last she was soaked through to the skin and the water trickled along her body.

One of the horses slipped, and Myra leaped to the ground. Her hands trembling as she held the lantern against the wind, she made a quick examination. If his leg was broken they were really in trouble. But it was only a sprain. They could go forward, though it would have to be at a slower pace. A few minutes later the vehicle jolted far to the right and Myra was tossed violently against the rail. One side of the carriage had dropped into the ditch beside the road. The two women stepped down and sank to their ankles in thick clay. They looked at each other, despair in their eyes. From somewhere on the road behind them they made out the irregular beat of hoofs.

"Phyllis, your shoulder! Here, push with me. Pu-u-u-sh!" It was useless; the gumlike clay sucked at the wheel, and nothing happened. They tried again and sank back exhausted. The hoofbeats were nearer. Myra ran her palm across her face, wiping the water from it. Then in desperation she recalled something she had learned years before. Reaching into the carriage, she tugged at the velvet seat. Her small hands had always been strong; Marianne had once told her that her grasp was as powerful as a man's. Now she yanked out the seat and thrust it beneath the rear wheel.

"Push again!" They groaned and shoved, and still the vehicle did not move. "Try again!" It budged slightly; Myra's fingers ripped against a piece of projecting metal, but the carriage at last was moving.

Before she and Phyllis had seated themselves comfortably she had the horses under way. Yet now the others were close behind them. With a groan she used the whip. Her bonnet was a soggy, shapeless bit of cloth and whalebone, and she threw it away. Lips compressed, she bent forward; a turn was ahead, and as they wheeled around it her heart sank. The turnpike gate loomed before them, closed and locked! The keeper's house stood just down the road, but they could not wait. "Hold tight!" she muttered to Phyllis. The horses started to shy, then went straight through, leaving the barrier in shreds. One of the animals whinnied; the way lay clear ahead.

Midnight chimed as they rode wearily into Wilmington. Soon they were standing, spent and sodden, before a fire in the home of Myra's friends, the Grants. Bundled into blankets, sipping hot tea, they told their story. Mr. Grant relieved them of part of their burden; he would meet Will's steamboat when it arrived in the morning. As Mrs. Grant turned to Myra she stopped short: for the first time in twenty-four hours the girl was asleep.

The Grants closed the door behind Will Whitney. From the next room they heard Myra speak quickly, in agitation. Then her voice lowered and gave way to Will's deeper tones, and eventually there was silence.

In a few minutes the couple joined the Grants. "We'll be married today, as soon as I can get the license," Will told them. Phyllis ran to them, whispering a benediction, but they were interrupted by the doorbell. Into the parlor, brushing past the servant, came a begrimed Colonel Davis. Will stepped to Myra's side, catching her hand in his, and together they stared at him. Confused, his face working, Samuel Davis went to her.

"Thank God, Myra! We've been through hell, your mother and I. I thought you'd—you'd done something to yourself maybe. . . ." He dropped his head and went on. "We—I—I was wrong." Awkwardly, painfully, he was asking her forgiveness. Myra told him of their plans; she said she would like him to attend the wedding.

Silently Samuel Davis looked from face to face. His hands clenched, he walked to the window and gazed down the street. Then he returned to them: he was willing to agree to the marriage if Myra was sure it was what she wanted. "I'm sure," she answered steadily. Then couldn't they, if only for the sake of appearances and the family, have it at Delamore Place? And so it was agreed.

On a brisk September evening the crowds moved along the wide drive and up the porticoed entranceway. The colonel gave a last look around the ornamented reception room, conferred with the caterer—and then it was discovered that the license had been issued erroneously. The guests were startled when a messenger clattered away; they were further amazed when toasts were given in advance of the ceremony and the colonel announced that the orchestra would favor them with a brief concert, which lasted nearly an hour and a half. Finally the signals were given, and the colonel walked into the room in stately dignity, Myra at his side. The bride looked tranquil, and some said it was charming that everything—the couple's meeting and engagement and the rest—had happened so quickly and easily.

The honeymoon was a leisurely journey by water along the Atlantic coast and up the Hudson. Fall had arrived early in this year of 1832, and across the deck of their steamboat floated an acrid-sweet smell of burning leaves. As they walked together down the passageway Will decided he must carry her across the threshold of their cabin.

"Foolish, that's for the time we enter a new house," Myra protested.

"We'll try it then too," Will laughed. So light was she that he swung her about several times for good measure before he deposited her on her feet again. Half giddy, she clung to him, leaning against the hard strength of his chest. With a half-stifled exclamation he took her to him. As her head dropped back, her high-piled hair fell loose upon the crook of his arm. Beneath them the vessel's engines turned. The ripples of the water, reflected on the walls, danced crazily for a time; and then there was silence.

CHAPTER II

As THEIR carriage reached the outer gates of Whitney Place the doorway disgorged a mass of people over the wide steps and into the driveway. At once they were enveloped by Whitneys, bowing, smiling, gesticulating. After a moment a single figure rose above the hubbub. Will's father, Josuah, outweighed anyone Myra had ever seen—a man shaped like a pear, all globules of flesh, topped by a tiny head with merry blue eyes and heavy white hair.

Waddling up to her, the paterfamilias gave her a warming grin and kissed her hand. She had no time to say anything; Josuah Whitney was gently pushing, pulling, and easing her about from one relative to another: cousins, sisters, uncles, brothers, nieces, in-laws, distant Whitneys from adjoining settlements. Then she was taken into the arms of a surprisingly youthful woman who whispered that she was Will's mother.

Opinion did not remain undivided about the newest Whitney. Some of the aunts and cousins, seeing Myra at long intervals, asked pointed questions about her. "She's strong-minded," they were wont to say. "Too positive about everything." Others insisted she was "conceited, that's all." They did not understand or like the look of amusement that showed from time to time in her face, or that calm contemplation of things about her. Myra left few people neutral; they were quickly won or repelled.

There was that incident of the dance at Whitney Place, attended by all the local gentry, friends from New York City and elsewhere. One guest was a Frenchman who was headed West— a saturnine, long-faced man whose deep-circled black eyes gave the impression that he was noting and cataloguing everything he saw in curious America. He understood little English and Myra was one of the few in the room who knew his language. To the chagrin of some, Myra danced twice in succession with him.

Moving across the room at his side, she felt the currents of curiosity and suspicion directed at her back. Smiling faintly, the Frenchman asked a sudden question. "You, Mme. Whitney, you are not used to this life?" His well-tended hand swept the assembly.

"Oh, I'm new here, if that's what you mean."

"Not exactly, *belle madame*. I suggest you feel this mode rather strange?" He persisted, his probing eyes darting over her face.

"Why, not at all." She colored, and she knew he had discovered the small scar at the side of her face. "I find it . . ." She paused, her eyes moving over the musicians at the side, the children peeking over the banisters. "I find it different. But I'm accustoming myself to it."

He pursed his lips thoughtfully. "If Madame will permit another observation?" A curt refusal was on her tongue; then she checked herself: "Why not?" His black lashes blinked as he told her in a low voice: "The young madame gives the impression of—waiting. Oh, not today or tomorrow, but beyond that. And I don't imply that you are—well, impatient. Still— you wait."

Myra flipped her fan shut, but the quick, not unkind smile that illuminated the stranger's face made it impossible to be annoyed. As they rejoined the others her gaze had a musing quality. "Perhaps you're right, monsieur. Don't all of us wait, for something?"

"Some"—he passed his eyes along the line of elderly matrons —"some await death. You await—life. *Bon soir* and *bonne chance!*"

For the rest of the evening a tiny line remained between her brows, and the hand that played with her fan was tense. No, she was not happy here. Though she had fought against admitting it even to herself and she had difficulty naming the emotion, she felt, somehow, submerged. She found herself surrounded day and night by Whitneys, Whitney traditions, Whitney customs. The years stretched ahead; would she and Will know them as small parts of a Whitney whole, or would their life be theirs—with their own errors to make, their own gains to gather?

Nor was Will, she suspected, entirely satisfied. It was not a matter of discontent between them. She sensed, if she did not always see, his quick upward glance when she approached, the way his eyes followed her in a crowd. For her part, the mere sound of his voice in the hallway could make her skin tingle. No, it went beyond that. Months had passed since they had spoken of the time he would leave Binghamton, to establish himself in one of the cities. It was far from an idle hope. The family's wealthy cousin, Stephen Whitney, visited frequently, and he and Will discussed legal matters. Myra had faith in Will's ability. She had heard him argue before juries in Binghamton, watched him as he pounded home a point. Then he was no longer only another Whitney; he spoke for himself, confidently, powerfully. Once he had his opportunity, once he was free of the chains that held him . . . Having stated the matter to herself, she made up her mind. As she sipped her punch she planned what she would say to Will.

The eldest of the Whitneys were last to leave. Aunt Helen had watched Myra all evening; now, being bundled into her shawls within hearing of her odd niece by marriage, she was able to lean toward Will and stress her argument: "It's a question of stock, my boy—known family, known connections! When you want a good horse . . ." Without bothering to finish, Aunt Helen shook her wide shoulders and let herself be led out.

Myra turned to the stairs; the wound had been opened again. None of the Whitneys had been so pointed, but she knew they had been talking of her and passing about the story of her mysterious origin. Their silences, the way they avoided mention of Myra in their endless discussions of genealogy . . . Suddenly she realized that for months she had been resenting the continual recitals of Whitney connections, the traits of the children, the branches that this or that one might take after.

Only then did she become aware of something else in the back of her mind. In all her musings about moving to New York she had nursed an obscure hope that someday she would come upon people who had been friends of her mother or father. They could tell her the things she had to know. No matter how bad it might be, she would find out the truth.

As Will turned the knob of their door she went to him and smoothed back the rebellious lock of hair that had slipped into his eyes. "Will," she asked, "do you think we should stay here indefinitely? Time is going by."

At once he grew grave. Silently he rubbed his hand along the side of his face. "No," he said finally. "But Brother needs me. A lot of land cases——"

"How long will he need you?" Myra's look had a new glint.

"Maybe another year, maybe two. You know, dear, we aren't doing badly, building up a nice nest egg and——"

"But don't you want more than that? What about the world outside?"

"Please, let's not talk about it. Not tonight. You looked so beautiful downstairs"—his voice had grown husky, importunate —"I could've killed that Frenchman when I saw his arm around you." His big frame loomed over hers; his hands passed quickly over her. "Things wouldn't be as easy as you imagine. Maybe you'll feel easier when you're here a while longer. Let's wait and see. . . ." He sank down beside her, his dark chin resting lightly against her cheek. Slowly she nodded, as much to herself as to him. He took her to him, so quickly that a protest rose to her lips; then the impulse to repel him ended as abruptly as it had come.

She woke shortly after dawn, and her eyes ran affectionately over the rugged figure beside her. How tiny she seemed against his brown, muscled power. The early sun glinted over him, flecks of light catching in the crisp black hair of his chest. His face, beneath the arch of his arm, was gentle; at such times he reminded her of the kindly Mrs. Whitney. He grimaced, in a dream, and as he turned uneasily against her, her arm went protectively about him. He needed her in many ways—her certainties, her assurance. It came to her now that it must be she who reached their decisions.

The thought, as she lay there, was disturbing. How was she to know she was right in this present matter? They might be stagnating in Binghamton. Yet here, at any rate, was security for them, the known thing. Suppose the other course brought only unhappiness and bad times? What had Will said? She'd "feel easier" after she'd been here a longer time.

She stiffened. That part of it was true, all too true. With every month the two of them would sink deeper into the mold of "the family." A year hence she would be less discontented; a year or two afterward—who knew?—thoroughly satisfied. And of that she was afraid. Will stirred again, and her hand caressed his shoulder. They'd see. Yes, they'd see. Her finger was twined about a red curl just behind her ear—the bit of hair that Will, discovering her habit, had christened her "thinking curl."

Colonel Samuel Davis had always been an erratic correspondent. Unexpectedly there arrived, after a long silence, a five-page, meandering message. Going through an upstairs trunk, he had come upon a lot of her old letters. Out fluttered several handfuls of paper, an invitation, a program for a cotillion. Into her hand fell a receipted bill for a suit. But this was the colonel's; ever careless, he must have mixed some of his own letters with hers. Here was one in French; the writer was sorry to report misfortune, yet there was a matter he thought of concern to the colonel. . . .

She was about to put it aside when a line caught her attention. Her mouth slackening, she read: "I regret that our friends in New Orleans saw fit to suppress the last will of Daniel Clark, leaving his property to Myra, and substitute the earlier one. I continue to hold the separate property that Daniel once entrusted to me for the girl." The signature read: "Josef Deville Dégoutin Bellechasse, Matanzas, Cuba, 1820."

Despite the blaze from the hearth, she had grown chill. Her thoughts raced ahead. Then her father had remembered her after all! But why . . . Almost without thinking, she had tossed a heavy coat about her, slipped past a covey of nieces and nephews, and sped down the stairway. At Will's office she could not speak; instead she thrust the letter into his hand.

When he reached the final passage Will whistled. Running his hand through his hair, he swore softly. "This is hard to believe. But so was that first letter that told us who you were!" Then his face grew doubtful. "Still, it might be nothing. . . ."

At once Myra stood beside him. "Why didn't somebody let me know about this will, that the man says was stolen?" She found herself shaking his arm.

"Maybe they thought it would be best——"

"*They* thought! I had a right—I *have* a right to know!" As she went on, her flaming face startled Will with its intensity. "This property the letter mentions, could Colonel Davis have gotten it from him?"

Will took her hand. "Don't you remember, the colonel told us he got nothing at all?"

A new suspicion drained her face of its color. Certainly Samuel Davis had acted peculiarly in all of this. She sank against Will, clinging in a kind of desperation. Miserably he tried to soothe her. "Anyway, it's been so long. Wouldn't it be best not to get agitated, and let things——"

With a gasp she drew away. "No! I've got to know. Don't you see?" How could she believe anything that she'd been told about the affair?

In Will's face she read pain and puzzlement, as if he could not quite grasp these odd reversals. The sight calmed her. When she spoke again her voice was free of the last traces of emotion. "At least we can demand answers, can't we?" Her long brown eyes challenged her husband.

"Demand? From whom?"

"This man Bellechasse—and Father too."

Mechanically he nodded, and she walked toward the big desk. "If we get a letter written right now, we can make a sailing to Cuba this week, can't we?" He nodded again, then seated himself. At once she threw out suggestions. Would Mr. Bellechasse please to tell . . . ? Would Mr. Bellechasse make clear what he meant . . . ?

Then, in time for the next stagecoach, they prepared a message for Colonel Davis. The colonel must realize they did not doubt anything that had been told them, but . . . As Will wrote

on, her firm hand reached over to push into place the black hair
that curled along the back of his neck. He looked up and grinned;
the smile she gave him in return was meditative.

After more than a month passed and nothing further happened, Myra began to worry. Colonel Davis, at least, had had
ample time to answer. Finally she received a quick summons to
Will's office. A reply had come from Cuba. Tearing open the
elaborately sealed letter that had arrived in her name, she read
slowly.

For years I have hoped to hear from you . . . prided myself I
was one of Daniel Clark's closest . . . You have been the victim of
an injustice. . . . Your father wrote a will giving you his fortune;
several people saw it and heard him acknowledge it—and they can
testify to this. Then it disappeared under suspicious circumstances.
. . . Many things it is best not to put in a letter. If you decide to go
further, you will have to appear in New Orleans. In that case, may
I suggest you stop here on your way? . . . Yes, I still have the
property and shall give it to you. . . .

Mechanically Myra folded the letter, and they faced each other
in a long silence. Slowly she began to speak: "Do you realize
it? It means that, all this time——" Feet scampered along the
road; Will's clerk, panting, handed them a message: "Just in by
the coach." Colonel Davis had finally responded.

The colonel was uncertain and also resentful: he wished they
had consulted him before writing off to Cuba. But now it was
done. . . . When he received that letter, years ago, Bellechasse
was far away; there had been an argument with the executors,
and the colonel somehow had done nothing about it. A will was
admitted by the courts immediately after her father's death; it
did not mention Myra. The colonel was in the North at the time;
when he returned later to New Orleans he heard talk that Daniel
had made a second will. Still, the attorneys had advised him he
could never establish anything. "Also, as I told you before, I
was assured that Daniel's estate was *insolvent*." He must have
damaged his pen in underlining the word; he began again with a
new point. As to the Bellechasse letter, "I presume he refers to
the men who were the executors, R. J. Relf and Beverly Chew.
I have had dealings with them, not too happy. But nothing has

ever been proved against them; they are pillars of society in New Orleans." He concluded: "You have nothing to gain by stirring up unpleasant things, long forgotten, and better so. I strongly suggest . . ."

As they stood before the elder Whitneys old Josuah stirred in his big chair and his wife glanced quickly from Will to Myra. A small blue vein worked in the girl's throat; her lips were drawn tight. "Mr. Bellechasse says he saw the real will, and he and others can swear to it." She pointed to the letter. "And he talks about other suspicious circumstances!"

"But suspicious circumstances aren't necessarily evidence." Josuah puffed solemnly at his pipe. He didn't like this business, and his stolid face showed it.

"And this was more than twenty years ago." Will spoke in anxiety. "It'd be hard to prove——"

"That doesn't mean I—we shouldn't try to prove it."

Will subsided, and his father took up: "To go way down there to Louisiana"—he used the word as if it were a synonym for hell—"that would mean giving up everything you know, Will's work—your whole life for six months or more. For what?"

"To find out if I've been cheated!"

On and on the argument went. How could she let them know her agony of longing? She had to make this trip; there was the matter of that will, but beyond it stood other considerations. She would learn the truth about herself, how and why all this had happened. Whatever it was, she had to find it out.

Will remained beside his father, ill at ease, apprehensive, as the patriarch protested. The older Mrs. Whitney sat immobile, only her eyes shifting among the speakers. In particular she watched Myra, now striding back and forth, rapt and unwavering. Suddenly Myra faced her husband.

"I think I should go."

It was less an expression of opinion than a declaration of intention. Immediately her face changed; she seemed tired, as if she had ended a struggle. "If you think you have to stay here I'll go alone. I can——"

Josuah Whitney, rubbing his hand up and down the seam of his shirt, rumbled in surprise, "Come now, Myra. How could you, a female . . . ? How would you . . . ?" He ended by spluttering. Myra had not turned her head; her hands folded in front of her, she was staring up at her husband. Yet Will still wavered, and what she read in his face did not reassure her.

Then it was that Mrs. Whitney spoke. "I agree with Myra. You owe it to yourselves, both of you, to find this out." Her husband faced her as if she had committed an act of treachery. Before he could open his mouth she raised her hand with a determination that none in the room had ever seen in her. "Now, Josuah, the decision really isn't ours. They're the ones to make it." Her lips became a narrow pink line; she had said her piece.

Will's face altered. Quietly he told her, "All right, then, we'll go."

Myra's fingers tightened in his, and she asked, "When does another ship leave New York City for Louisiana?"

"Five or six days. That wouldn't be time enough. We ought ——"

"I'll be ready."

It was settled. The two men knew that nothing either could say would change the situation now. Myra exchanged a look, long and grateful, with Mrs. Whitney, who had understood.

CHAPTER III

THROUGH the scalding brilliance of the Cuban sun they bounced along the main highway of the tropical Spanish city. Their volante, a black vehicle like some magnified, thin-legged insect, jogged past stretches of whitewashed walls broken by ironwork projections; they crossed a stone bridge to behold the Bay of Matanzas, a spread of sharp and piercing blue, lightly rippled by breezes that sent Myra's hair flying upward. Soon, on a road that was a brown slit in a world of raging greenery, they were climbing in the clear bright air; ahead towered a blue-and-gray mountain range that dominated the countryside. Around a turn, like a paper toy, waited a small villa surrounded by soaring palms and squat groves of orange trees. It seemed a retreat in a verdant paradise close to the top of the universe.

The volante rolled to a slow stop. From the gallery stepped a lean figure, a white-haired man in a cream-colored suit, his wide hat in his hand. As she alighted Myra stood for a moment, half swaying against Will, her heart thumping painfully. Would she be sorry, after all, that she had made this long journey?

Josef Bellechasse came toward them, calling out a welcome in explosive, high-pitched French. *"Bon jour, bon jour.* It is good to meet you and your husband." His long sallow face, a network of fine lines, looked tired, yet the precise goatee moved up and down with a vehement life. The nose was aquiline, the lips narrow, aristocratic; but the eyes beneath the shaggy brows showed a warm, friendly blue.

M. Bellechasse led them through a shaded hallway to a breeze-swept rear veranda. From an informal garden, half swallowed in its many growths, there materialized a spirited, birdlike younger woman clad in a severe white silk gown. With a ringing exclamation Mlle. Bellechasse embraced Myra, then held her at arm's length. "Ah, beautiful, *hein,* Papa?" Her flutelike voice reached a high note. "Those brown eyes, how they remind you of *pauvre* Zulime!"

Josef Bellechasse set his head on the side. "Still, there's a bit more of her handsome father about her—hair the color of a brick, and that piquant look around the nose. Like the Daniel we knew in his happier days."

His look saddened, and suddenly his daughter was weeping in her handkerchief. In a few moments she recovered. "Women do well to cry at the proper moment; you must do it when you feel inclined." She nodded to Myra and blew her nose with a shrill honk. Suddenly an enormous parrot squawked madly at them from the side: *"Bon jour, bon jour!* Go to 'ell, go to 'ell." With an amused shrug M. Bellechasse explained that he had acquired the beast from a sailor and was trying vainly to raise its cultural standards.

"And now . . ." Mlle. Bellechasse clapped her hands, and the servant came forward with trays of fresh fruits, gravied meats, and a bottle of claret. Her father, as if he had been awaiting the opportunity, quietly handed Myra a bulky envelope.

"These will be yours, as your father intended—the deeds to some fifty lots of property in New Orleans." He paused. "I must explain. At the time, Daniel wished the transaction to be secret, and he gave them to me as if by direct sale. There is nothing to show they were not mine; Daniel, you see, trusted me."

Myra exchanged a quick glance with Will. Her eyes took in this simple house with its single servant, the once fine coat, darned at the sleeve, that M. Bellechasse wore. He must have had financial difficulties, yet he had never touched this asset, worth many thousands. Myra's eyes softened; here was a man of honor. After a brief silence, as they tasted the delicate foods, Josef Bellechasse began:

"I am seventy-three, my children—little time left. I shall tell only what I know." His voice was musing: "Daniel . . . Poor Daniel! A man with everything—then nothing. The world in his hands, and then only a sucked orange." A film came over his fading eyes. "I knew him from his first days in Louisiana. . . ."

M. Bellechasse, his waxlike fingers folded together, looked up. Overhead the birds made sweeping flights against the almost startling blue of the sky. He was reliving the days of his youth, the latter part of the eighteenth century, when the gold and scarlet of Spain's soldiers flashed in the Louisiana sun. "Here lay an empire—ready for the men who would take it." He spread open his palms in expressive gesture. Vast fertile stretches, from the Gulf up the Mississippi to the continent's heart, were largely untapped. "New Orleans—it was a little French-Spanish town in the curve of the river." The Creole shook his head. "We were ringed by swamps, we suffered floods, and sometimes we went hungry because Europe forgot us. But we were not barbarians! From France we brought our wines, our good furniture, our manners; we lost few of them."

Stroking his beard, he frowned at the memory of things he enjoyed no more. "The plantations up and down the river, visits *en fête,* soirees with court dress *de rigueur,* sometimes a duel beneath the oaks when two gentlemen could not agree . . . Our civilization had abundance, a certain joy, perhaps not least, tolerance." His thin nostrils flared. "Let some sniff, but we were not Puritans, and we were proud of the fact! We understood that life was meant to be savored, to be enjoyed for itself. Who was to say we were wrong?"

Colonel Clark, uncle of Daniel, had turned toward Louisiana as a place in which an ambitious Irishman could win fortune. The family had once stood very high in Ireland, friends gathered; Daniel himself proudly claimed kinship with the kings of an older day. By this time, however, the Clarks had suffered losses, and it was up to the colonel to restore their place. Prospering, he remembered the young man back in County Sligo. At Eton young Daniel had received a good preparation for a career; as soon as he was twenty he was summoned by his uncle. When they met again at the New Orleans levee the older man saw he had made a wise choice. The sturdy, handsome youth had a sharply appraising eye, the poise of a forty-year-old, and an eager charm. Quickly he demonstrated that he was one whom the proudest of Creoles could accept. Gay, urbane, he realized when to be free in manner, when to show proper reserve. Here Bellechasse waved a precise hand. "Daniel conquered the drawing rooms, and soon he was conquering in other directions. The older Clark had strategic connections; Daniel served as assistant secretary in Governor Miro's office, where he listened and learned, and improved on what he learned.

"Soon he was his uncle's agent, then junior partner; he knew how to master new methods of business as quickly as he did foreign tongues. As bold and untiring as any man in Louisiana, he went by horse or barge over plain and swamp and river, far up the Mississippi, into the Western territory of the new American states. Direct trade between the Spanish colony and foreign possessions, you know, was prohibited by the King." Bellechasse shrugged. "But the Clarks understood how to use their friendships." He and his uncle, as new subjects of his Most Catholic Majesty, soon entered into a business deal with General James Wilkinson, of the United States Army, to trade with Kentucky. Both Daniel and the expansive Wilkinson profited by these operations, but later Daniel was to grow bitter over the connection.

When he was thirty-two Daniel's uncle left him a fortune. The young Irishman was, however, not content; he saw it only as a foundation for his growing ambitions. Shrewdly Daniel guessed that the young United States would inevitably spread over the continent, and he acted accordingly. He bought land left and right, in New Orleans and beyond, along river and bayou. Men stopped him to ask if he were wise; he laughed and went on as before.

Then gradually Daniel shifted his interests. Natchez, up the river, became part of the United States; Daniel moved there for a time, and soon he was on excellent terms with the influential Thomas Jefferson and other Americans. He became an American citizen; he served as United States consul at New Orleans. Then he conferred in Washington City with Jefferson, now President; combining his own business with public affairs, he sailed for Europe to meet officials of the French and Spanish courts. Josef Bellechasse turned to Myra. "Ah, there was excitement about us in these years, the early 1800s. Perhaps you didn't know it, but Daniel struggled to influence Jefferson and others; he pictured the vast wealth of Louisiana; he sent letters, reports, and urged them to acquire it.

"Louisiana hung in the balance, a prize between nations—and not necessarily America's. The Creoles did like that last thought, let me tell you! To them Americans were barbarians, brawling Kaintucks, money-grabbing Puritans. And the Americans up North? They thought Louisiana a trap, nothing but wasteland, and a gumbo of people, all colors, all nations! For a while Jefferson was worried that Congress would turn down his Louisiana Purchase; and nobody worked like Daniel Clark to give him the facts to be used against his enemies. Jefferson won, and then on a winter morning of 1803—a day we never forgot—Daniel stood in the front rank of our Place d'Armes and watched the flag of the Americans as it rose in the breeze. Daniel cheered; we Creoles could only think back and cry a little."

Bellechasse, one of Daniel's close friends, had been commander of Louisiana troops under the Spanish. When Louisiana was in the process of transfer from Spain to France and then the United States, Daniel persuaded Bellechasse to take charge of the volunteer militia. Together the two friends helped maintain order in the days when many feared that the excitable populace might break out at any time in angry resentment. They grew more intimate than ever.

The boy from Sligo had become probably the leading citizen of New Orleans, one of the great merchants of the Mississippi Valley; his hand was in everything financial and political. He sent his own vessels up the Atlantic, to Mexico, to Europe. And he moved about in his own fashion, a little mysteriously, knowing much, telling nothing that he had no wish to tell. It was believed—and here M. Bellechasse lifted one of his heavy brows—

that Daniel had connections with privateers, such men as the
Lafittes of the Gulf. He lived on winding Bayou St. John, and
his villa was pointed out by some as a depot for the corsairs.
"But what of it?" The Creole gave an easy gesture. "Many
bankers and businessmen of Orleans had such affiliations. It
was another day from ours. . . ."

With the years Daniel gained in pride. "More and more he
must assume control of anything he touched, or he would have
no part of it. Perhaps he grew spoiled; things may have come
altogether too easily for him. I would not pass judgment."
Bellechasse frowned. "He was self-indulgent, and occasionally
he became a prey to flatterers, sycophants who hung about him.
There was a certain carelessness that grew upon him, a wild
Irish strain; he had to have his will, and when he failed he
stormed and sulked. Of this, more will come later. . . .
Eh bien . . ."

Bellechasse went on. "It was about this time, you know, that
the Aaron Burr troubles arose. You've heard that some people
tried to connect Daniel with Burr's schemes to split the West
from the rest of America?" Myra showed her surprise. "Burr
came to New Orleans with letters from General Wilkinson,
Daniel's old-time connection. Whatever Burr was after, whatever wild plans he had, he finally lost; but meanwhile he claimed
Daniel was one of his supporters. While Burr was moving down
the river, supposedly to take New Orleans, Wilkinson turned
upon him and armed the city against him. Ah, those were days
of excitement!

"Daniel and Wilkinson had broken by this time; and now
Daniel made charges that created a great sensation. He told
Congress that Wilkinson, while in the American Army, had
been a secret Spanish agent, for pay. The scandal that brought!
An investigation followed that cleared Wilkinson; but now
Daniel had drawn new and powerful opposition in Washington.
Daniel, he was never neutral in anything."

Myra sat up. For nearly an hour she had listened, her hands
tightly clasped. Daniel Clark had been no weakling; he had
not submitted, he had reached out to make things happen. The
words of Colonel Davis returned to her: "Myra, you're too
strong-willed. You want things your own way." At least this,
then, came from her father. It was something important for her,

something to cling to. She knew now that she had feared, all along, to find him a man without strength, a milksop, or only a drab and futile individual.

M. Bellechasse was speaking again. ". . . your mother, Zulime, Zulime Carrière. She was christened Marie Julie; Zulime was her Creole nickname, her *p'tit nom*. I don't think I ever saw a lovelier woman." In the face of the old aristocrat there glowed the memory of a rare beauty, undimmed through the decades. "You're a great deal like her. She stood about your height, Myra, and slim; but her hair was black, almost blue-black, straight, with a sheen to it—her skin, white without a hint of color. The eyes—they were yours. The Carrières had come from southern France, Provence; some claimed there had been a bit of Spanish, or perhaps gypsy, in the blood. Zulime looked it—quick and bright and impulsive, like you.

"When I first knew her family they had enjoyed happier days. The father was dead, the three girls were alone with their mother. They sewed, they knitted shawls for sale; one taught school. Zulime's first marriage was arranged, I am sure, to help the family." Seeing Will's and Myra's expressions, M. Bellechasse showed his own surprise. "You knew, of course, of Zulime's earlier husband?" He went on:

"While Zulime was in her early teens a newcomer arrived in Louisiana, Jerome, or Geronimo, des Granges—a curious fellow, big-boned, with a thatch of yellow hair. He was an easy talker, almost grandiloquent; he called himself a member of the old nobility of France, a victim of the revolutionists. Des Granges had letters of introduction; he called on many people, including Daniel Clark, and he received their assistance. Later . . ." The Creole made a sour face.

Soon after Des Granges met the Carrières he grew attentive to little Zulime. At first the family opposed, for he was twenty years older than the girl. Then, unexpectedly, when she was not yet fifteen, they were married at the cathedral. When Bellechasse beheld Zulime, a child in her white wedding dress, he wondered what the years would hold for her. . . . Des Granges set up a business, not the great one of which he talked, but an unpretentious shop on Rue Ste. Anne at its juncture with the Place d'Armes; the owner prepared cakes and served them with light liquors. Des Granges could not afford a slave; occasionally, then regularly, Zulime was noticed behind the counter. Stopping in from time to time, Bellechasse found that things were not going well.

"Des Granges drank a great deal, and tales rose of cheap intrigues with women of the water front. But Zulime had made up her mind; she would accept her lot, do as well as she could. I saw her as she folded her arms and watched the crowd in the store, and her face was calm—and resigned. There was a child, who died; then Zulime went back to the store." Josef Bellechasse looked hard at Myra. "You should understand that Zulime did everything to make a success of that marriage. What eventually happened was not her fault!" Myra, her eyes tense, nodded.

After a time Daniel Clark, wanting to settle one of Des Granges's overdue bills, entered the store. Later Daniel told Bellechasse about this first meeting with Zulime; no woman had so stirred him, he said. There had been stories that Daniel would marry this or that Creole belle; he had remained a bachelor. From then on he spoke repeatedly of Zulime, her beauty, her wistful air that piqued his curiosity. When he went back to the shop she served him gravely; she answered his questions with politeness, and that was all. Yet from her face, the way her eyes seemed to follow him, he suspected that she shared something of his emotion.

One of the Carrière relatives died in France, and the estate had to be settled. Des Granges offered to go, explaining that he could attend to matters of his own at the same time. With some reluctance the family agreed. "Soon after Des Granges sailed the Carrières heard startling news. Lying about in the water-front cafés, Des Granges had boasted that he had two wives, the other waiting in France for him. In a talkative mood he had given the details: she was Barbara Jeanbelle d'Orci; he had pronounced the three names with pride. They had been married in New York four years before he met Zulime; he told even the name of the church." Bellechasse shook his head. "None of us ever expected that the bigamist would come back to Louisiana. He'd used the Carrières' savings to get to France; he'd never be heard of again."

Daniel went to the Carrières; he wanted to marry Zulime. Her union with Des Granges was void, he told them, and he quoted authorities. When a man already wedded imposed himself on another woman the later marriage had no legal effect whatever. Zulime and her sisters hesitated; Daniel proposed that they go to New York and get the evidence; he would join them there. What happened next Bellechasse could not swear, but Zulime and her sisters, and in time Daniel himself, told friends the couple became man and wife. The wedding, however, had to be kept secret until Zulime obtained a court annulment of her connection with Des Granges.

Daniel, engaged in trading operations and state business as well, went on to Europe. The Carrières were startled when Des Granges suddenly came back—and the man had the gall, or the stupidity, to bring the other woman with him. Zulime at once filed charges of bigamy; there were investigations, delays, investigations, but finally Des Granges was declared guilty. Before he was sentenced, however, the friendly marshal permitted him to escape.

Meanwhile Daniel had provided a quiet home for Zulime along Bayou St. John. She had obtained the annulment, but still he insisted that their marriage must be kept confidential. "He was in the center of a violent political controversy," Bellechasse explained. "The first American governor, Claiborne, looked on him with a cool eye, and Daniel thought he was being passed over. Gradually he emerged as the leader of our Creole opposition to Claiborne. Soon he flung a triumph in Claiborne's face: he had himself elected the first Louisiana territorial delegate to Congress." The Creole's face flushed with his memory of these tempestuous days. "The governor challenged Daniel a little later; since dueling was against the new American law, they had to go outside the limits of Louisiana. Daniel rode a hundred miles; the sheriff raced to the scene and was just six miles away when the two men took aim. Daniel won; the governor sank to the ground, bleeding badly."

Zulime was waiting in tears for Daniel's return. The governor recovered, but hatred between the sides grew worse. Now again Zulime pressed Daniel for announcement of their marriage. She must wait, he told her; he would be ruined politically, for he'd have to shoot down the first man who sneered. When she persisted his temper broke, and Zulime left him and New Orleans forever. . . . Bellechasse paused.

The birds circled lower, crying to each other. Myra's eyes were on the ground. It was not a pleasant story; no wonder Mlle. Bellechasse had called her mother poor Zulime. . . . Softly Bellechasse defended his friend. "Perhaps I haven't done justice to Daniel. He had his pride, and I know he would have been destroyed in a moment had he told the truth." The Creole's gaze was kindly. "You'll understand better as you learn more about him, Myra."

"But me? How——" Myra began, and her voice broke. Stroking her hair, Will drew her against him.

"You were born a year or so before they broke up." Bellechasse's face had grown grave. "Daniel made the arrangements, in a friend's house in another part of the city. Zulime had agreed that she must give you up for a time; but when the moment of separation came she broke down and tried to fight the people who took you from her."

Myra lifted her face. Then her mother had wanted her after all! The knowledge came like a cool hand on a fevered face. How badly fortune had treated Zulime! And in the long years that followed, her mother had never been able to take her back. . . . The tears broke suddenly; Will leaned forward, caressing, comforting her. At last Myra raised her head again, and Bellechasse resumed.

Meanwhile the bluff Samuel Boyer Davis, retiring from his career as an enterprising privateer, had settled down in New Orleans and, with Daniel's help, was moving up in the world's affairs. At first Myra was placed with a coachmaker's wife, who was supposed to be her nurse; Daniel asked the Davises to look in from time to time, to see how Myra was getting along. The baby was growing thin and weak; the woman was neglecting her. Mrs. Davis took Myra, and the child quickly improved.

"For a few years Daniel saw you almost as often as if you lived in his house. As soon as he set eyes on you, I think, he fell in love with you. He called regularly; in the middle of the day he'd suddenly decide he had to hold you. He'd point to your red hair, the shape of your nose; he'd say you were Zulime's too, and then he'd be silent and thoughtful."

Myra was gazing at the green horizon. Back across the haze of two decades moved a vague wisp of an impression: a man with a head of bright hair, glinting as he walked toward her;

a man younger than Colonel Davis. She caught at another strand of memory. The pleasant man had brought her a pony, and the pony had shaken her to the ground. She had wept, and he had held a cloth to her cheek. Her finger touched the spot; that must have been how she got the scar below her ear! He had kissed her and told her: "If you want something hard enough, Myra, fight for it!" She had jumped back on the little animal and refused to be shrugged off; and that was all she could remember of her father.

Now she faced Josef Bellechasse. "The will?"

Their host became solemn. "In his later years Daniel made no secret among his friends that he had been married to Zulime. He referred to you repeatedly as his 'heiress.' We had no doubt that you'd inherit his estate." He frowned. "That involves another matter, Daniel's commercial connections. For years his partner in the North was D. W. Coxe."

Coxe, the strange, long-nosed individual who moved in and out of Samuel Davis's house, who had given the toasts that day the colonel left for the Legislature . . . The garrulous old man was supposed to be shrewd; in retirement he had considerable wealth. He had always asked her questions and somehow she had been suspicious of him, though she could never have said why. It was disconcerting to learn that the man had had a large part in her real father's life and that she had had no hint of it.

But meanwhile Josef Bellechasse was proceeding: "Daniel's connections with Coxe gradually became less and less important. He had befriended two young men, newcomers to New Orleans, R. J. Relf and Beverly Chew. Relf, I know, was a poor, frightened boy when Daniel befriended him; whatever he's become, he owes it to Daniel's kindness and favors. The two men were his clerks, then eventually his agents. He set up a firm in their name but *he* was the firm, capital, direction, and all."

In 1811 war with Britain was approaching, and finances tightened. Daniel heard that Coxe had fallen into difficulties; he arranged to leave by ship within a few hours. Calling Bellechasse, he spoke excitedly; although Daniel had practically ended relations with Coxe, the books might indicate that they were partners, and Daniel was afraid he would be pulled down with him. Also he was concerned over the possibility that he might suffer some accident on the trip; and so he transferred several properties to Bellechasse, to be held for Myra.

As his ship was about to lift anchor Daniel scrawled out an eleven-line document, a "provisional will," in his own words. It indicated that he was leaving his estate to his mother, and it made Relf and Chew the executors. But soon after Daniel left, Bellechasse met Colonel Davis and one or two others and learned that he had also given them great shares of his property for Myra's protection. Talking over the matter, Bellechasse concluded that the "provisional will" meant very little under the circumstances.

In Philadelphia Daniel cleared up his affairs. Returning, he took back the assets he had turned over to Davis and the others. There was now no need for the scheme he had followed to safeguard Myra against Coxe's collapse; it eventually developed that he had entirely different plans. However, he insisted that his friend Bellechasse keep the property he had given him: "it will remain a final safeguard for her," he told him.

Daniel was now a disturbed man. The war with Britain had begun badly; the enemy was at the Gulf, blockading all commerce. With cargoes rotted in the holds of his ships, Daniel retired from most of his affairs. "To add to his unhappiness, Samuel Davis felt he must go North to join the fighting, taking you, Myra, and his family with him. And so," said Bellechasse, "before you were six your father said good-by to you. It was a thing I would have preferred not to see, that leave-taking." Again Myra tried to think back. All that came to her was a lurching, grimy trip; the man with the red hair had faded away.

"Daniel had less than a year to live. He was only in his forties, but he had seen much, too much, of life. Now he spent most of his days in his house along the bayou. The thought of you, Myra, was his consolation and his hope. Early in the year 1813 he called me. He was preparing his final will; after a few bequests to his mother and sisters, the bulk of his property would go to you. He picked three close friends to handle the estate—Judge Pitot, Chevalier de la Croix, and me. Over and over he talked of the will; he worked among his papers, amounts due, lists of properties. Eventually, finishing it, he showed it to me and read it aloud. It recognized you as his proper child and went on with an elaborate statement of his holdings. The document was written by him, signed and dated, all as the Louisiana law required. It took the place of the 'provisional will,' of course; and it eliminated his subordinates, Relf and Chew, as administrators."

A few weeks passed. Calling at Daniel's house, Bellechasse was met by Relf, who said Daniel was too ill to see him. "Here was I, one of Daniel's intimates, being ordered away by a man who was practically a clerk!" Bellechasse exclaimed. "The upstart's manner became as offensive as his words; I pushed him aside. I found Daniel sitting up in bed, pale but able to talk. He chided me: 'How is it, Josef, you haven't been to see me since I'm sick? I instructed Relf to send for you.'"

" 'Relf sent no message,' I told him."

Silently Daniel pressed Bellechasse's hand. Fearful of upsetting his friend, Bellechasse left him soon afterward. In the hall he informed Relf that he wanted to help look after Daniel. There was no occasion for that, Relf replied; the doctors did not wish Daniel disturbed. "I grew angrier than ever," Bellechasse went on. "Still, I wanted no quarrel in Daniel's house. Before I left I made Relf promise to call me if any change came."

The next afternoon, having received no message, he went to Daniel's place. His friend had died hours before. After kneeling beside the shrunken figure, he walked slowly away. Near by stood the residence of Judge Pitot, who had also agreed to act as an executor. The judge spoke to him in bitterness: that Relf fellow had never told him, either, of Daniel's condition; and it was certainly strange the way things had turned out.

"What do you mean?" Bellechasse asked.

"You know the will disappeared," the judge told him.

"They said the will was found!"

"Ah, but not the new will!" the judge cried. "Relf brought out the old, provisional one, that we thought had been destroyed. And Relf said he knew of no other will."

The two men hurried to the third executor, the Chevalier de la Croix. His feeling exceeded theirs. That night they made a half-dozen calls in the hope that Daniel had left a copy of the will with others; they searched several safes in which Daniel had kept scattered possessions with friends. They found nothing. The funeral was the next morning, and half of New Orleans seemed to be at the cathedral—Daniel's slaves in long files, Creoles, Americans, even Governor Claiborne.

As they knelt a peculiar tension could be felt in the dim church; word had spread about the mysterious happenings. As soon as the body lay in the grave the Chevalier de la Croix went to court with a petition, saying he had "strong reason" to believe a second will had been made. Frequently, though the law did not require it, family notaries kept duplicates of such documents; De la Croix demanded that every notary in New Orleans be called. They came forward; Daniel had gone to none of them. "And so"—Bellechasse frowned—"Relf and Chew took over the estate."

Myra's strong hands had whitened. On Will's face was a cold, controlled rage that she had never seen before. He appeared to have forgotten her: "Then none of you made a real effort to get to the facts?"

"It all happened so suddenly. We thought it was too late, too——"

"Nobody assembled the evidence—what Daniel's friends would testify, what they saw, what he said?"

Bellechasse shook his head. Will strode back and forth, and his voice rang across the gallery, sharp and impassioned. This was the Will she had visualized in her hopes, strong and self-reliant, not the overcareful, hemmed-in member of the Whitney clan. He snapped out another question: "Yet several of you *saw* that new will?"

"*Oui*. Judge Pitot, the third executor, is dead, but Chevalier de la Croix is alive; and I can give you names of people who were with Daniel to the last and heard him say, till the moment of his death, that the will would give Myra everything!" M. Bellechasse was silent a moment; then he dropped his hands in a characteristic gesture. "The law, sir, seems sometimes delicately balanced to help not the just but the unjust. Relf and Chew had a free hand after that; and they have risen high in the world. Chew became collector of the port, and Relf nothing less than cashier of the state bank. In the business of New Orleans none ranks higher than the two of them."

Josef Bellechasse had ridden himself of a burden that he had held for more than twenty years, and a look of relief softened his countenance. After a moment he reached into his pocket and handed a letter to Will. "This came only last week from New Orleans." A Mr. Schaumburg, one of Daniel's creditors, had recently caused a little excitement by filing some kind of lawsuit against Relf and Chew over their handling of the estate.

Will slapped his hand against his knee. His eyes were afire. "This may give us a chance to intervene, to get a full investigation! That is, if you really think we should go into this and——" He glanced toward Myra, then ran suddenly to her side. She had half risen, then, her eyes rolling upward, fallen back in a faint. Mlle. Bellechasse darted forward with a cry and directed Will as he carried Myra to an airy bedroom. There she called for a bowl of water, medicine, a fan. Meanwhile she scolded the two men: "The *petite*, so much strange new intelligence, and the heat on that porch! *Assez*, go! I'll care for her."

In a few minutes, a look of restrained amusement on her narrow face, Mlle. Bellechasse summoned Will. "Ah, young husband, we have news for you!" She shook her head. *"Ces Américains!"* she murmured, and joined her father.

Puzzled, Will pushed open the door and found Myra resting beneath a mosquito net. As he went to her she regained her color, but for a moment her eyes were averted. Then, as if with an effort, she lifted her head. "Mademoiselle thinks it strange I shouldn't have told you. I said——" Of a sudden her words ran together in a rush. "I'm trying to say that I'm going to have a baby."

He swallowed, too surprised to speak.

"I knew it the day M. Bellechasse's answer came to Binghamton." She looked directly at him.

"But why—why didn't——"

"Because if I had told you we might never have come."

"Still, dear . . ." His hand went to his chin; his determination of a few minutes ago was disappearing. "Now, of course, we ought to go home. You should be resting——"

"We ought not, and I will not!" Sitting up, she shook her finger at him. "We'll go on as we planned. Don't you be a fool!"

Will, flushing scarlet, stared down at the sheet. Strong-willed as she was, she had hurt him. Instantly she took his head in her hands. "I'm sorry. But don't you see? It's for him—the baby—as well as me. It's for all of us." She pleaded; she had to make him realize that, since the moment she had known, she had been thinking of the child within her, the child who must not suffer the wrenching bitterness of the questions in her own mind.

Finally Will nodded. His face had another light, a reflection of her emotion. "Yes," he whispered. "Yes." Then he took her hand and lifted it to his lips.

Myra leaned toward him. "Is that all? You know, I'm not going to have the baby today!" Her mouth, half open, was a few inches from his; happily his arms went about her and they held together, breathless, wordless.

A knock sounded, and the two Bellechasses entered, a deepened sympathy in their eyes. In Myra's lap Josef Bellechasse placed a small object. He had had it prepared a week ago; now that he had met her, he said, he knew how inadequate it was for her.

Myra's fingers caressed a box of mahogany, rubbed until it had the sheen and feel of soft silk. The sides and top had been carved in a low relief of exquisite workmanship, Spanish in design yet touched with an Indian spirit. "The great bird at the front, he is a sign of good fortune," Mlle. Bellechasse whispered. Myra's eyes went from one to the other and she started to thank them.

"But, *chérie,* turn the handle!" Josef cried. She did, and the box played a Creole tune that she had never heard. The old man's eyes danced as he sang the words:

> "Ah, handsome girl with hair so bright,
> From what forge came such warmth of heart,
> From what heaven thy joy of face—
> From what angry god the fire in thy eye?"

He smiled, saying he hadn't known how appropriate it would be, with its "hair so bright"; nor, for that matter, the determination he had seen, once or twice, in those dark eyes of hers. Myra's face glowed. Despite what some said of him, Daniel Clark must have had his good qualities to draw and hold the friendship of a man like Josef Bellechasse.

It was now late afternoon. The other three turned involuntarily to Myra, and Mlle. Bellechasse spoke for them: "Wouldn't it be best if you stayed here a few days, resting, preparing yourself for your trip?" But by this time Myra was out of the bed.

"No. The ship leaves for New Orleans in the morning, and we'll be on it."

A few minutes later, after handclasps and kisses, they set off again in the volante. Seating herself, Myra touched the spring of the rich mahogany box, and the melody tinkled out: "Ah, handsome girl with hair so bright . . ." As the music reached the last line the smiling Bellechasse waved his hat and joined, with a laugh, in the words: " 'From what angry god the fire in thy eye?' " Behind him, through the house, came the squawk of the aroused parrot: *"Bon jour, bon jour!* Go to 'ell, go to 'ell!"

CHAPTER IV

USUALLY Myra awoke first. Now, long after dawn, she opened her eyes to find Will beaming down upon her. For a moment she could not remember where she was; she blinked up at the sunburst pattern in yellow satin that decorated the canopy of the four-poster bed, and the folds of mosquito netting that made it like a semiprivate room. Then she recalled that they had arrived in New Orleans late the previous night and gone promptly to sleep.

Though it was still March, every window was open and the air almost smelled of summer. She yawned. Leaning over to kiss her, Will ran his fingers through the rich red stream of her hair. Almost at once came a knock, followed by a voice crying something cheerful and unintelligible. Will sighed; at his response a middle-aged mulattress, her skin almost the shade of the tan Mississippi, strode in. In both hands she held a copper bucket of steaming water. *"Bon jou', bon jou'! Et il est bon, bon, oui!"* She pointed to the cloudless sky outside. After a *"Pardon!"* she returned with a silver tray bearing two tiny cups, which she set on a carved table beside them.

It was *café noir,* ink-black and powerful. Unprepared, Myra took a full swallow and choked. Will finished most of his cup, though he perspired under the impact. "Nice," he said, "but there's just too damned much *coffee* in it. Well, today I'll need the strength it's supposed to give." With that, he swung himself to the floor.

While Will scraped at his beard Myra sat before a delicate rosewood dressing table. Never had she been in so big a chamber; the pink plaster walls stood eighteen feet high, the doorways towered like works of architecture, the french windows were almost as imposing. Two red birds flashed in crimson streaks across the nearest window; from somewhere close at hand soared the strong, almost musklike scent of a flower, heady in the early morning. Below arose the cries of street peddlers: fish from the bayous, fruits and meats and seasonings for Madame's kitchen. A guttural laugh sounded near by; gurgling greetings were called across the court. In Delaware it would be called bedlam; here, she guessed, it was the beginning of a normal weekday. This was the New Orleans her father and mother had known, copious, easy. As she lifted her arms to drop the gray taffeta gown over her head her pulse beat heavily. She was not sure she would like this place; but each moment made her more excited at the prospect of venturing forth in it.

She dressed carefully for this day. Her full skirt billowed out from her narrow waist; a blue lace collar matched the trimming of her cushioned sleeves, and she carried a blue bonnet, to be tied beneath the chin. Downstairs Mme. Eulalie Montagnet awaited them. They had gone to her at the suggestion of Josef Bellechasse; the New Orleans of 1833 had no important hotels, and this was one of the few dependable boardinghouses that admitted women guests.

Madame, a tiny, narrow figure in black, her powderless skin a pale olive, looked at them with gray eyes that were faintly troubled. Her gentle, unpretty face reminded Myra of a collie's, intelligent and sad. Curiously for one so small, she spoke in a deep contralto that seemed to come from a point close to the ground. She opened a door; she had taken the liberty of placing Madame and Monsieur in the courtyard for their *déjeuner*.

Beneath a giant bush beginning to cluster with white buds their table waited. A bandy-legged Negro with popped eyes like yellow-streaked marbles gave them a roguish glance. *"Moi, je suis Dieu-Donné."* He grinned, looking like a kindly imp out of hell. Like a magician on a stage, he whisked out a platter of steaming food—first a deep omelette, filled with delicately muted onions, impregnated with greens, and covered with a fragrant red sauce; then broiled pompano, a delicate-fleshed fish from the Gulf; soft rolls, brioches, and *café au lait*. With each item Dieu-Donné leaned over and said, "Gaw' dam' good, *n'est-ce pas?"* It was almost his only knowledge of English; he spoke

French, but French with a difference—an African version, softened, edges broken, the Louisiana Negro "gumbo." After each course Will told him: "Gaw' damn good, *oui!*" and henceforth Dieu-Donné was theirs to order.

It was pleasant to linger here. Only now did they realize the plan of the house. It rose flush with the line of the *banquette* or sidewalk, a balcony jutting forth at the second-story level. The stuccoed brick, tinted peach, had faded into three or four different shades in the fervent sun and humidity. The building, narrow, three-storied, was built about a flagstoned court, its fanlighted doors and windows and balconies opening upon a leafy central garden. The brick wall at the rear made it a shaded island of perfumed quiet; a metal fountain, tinkling lightly, gave the only sound.

When Dieu-Donné approached a third time with the coffee urn, Will straightened up.

"Can't I go with you?" Myra asked.

"Do you want to be known as a brazen piece? Why don't you spend your time sewing?" Will jibed. In the hallway he kissed her and started off with a whistle, shoulders high, snug trousers sharply creased, dark blue coat flaring at the proper angle.

Myra turned back to find Mme. Montagnet on the curved stairway, sudden high spots of color on her pale cheeks. "*Pardon,* Mme. Whitney," she murmured. "I am a bit—*distraite.* Won't you come into the parlor?" There, as they sat before the marble mantel with its elongated gold mirror, Madame unexpectedly gave way to her annoyance. "Ah, those people upstairs." She let out a quick breath. "How can I manage my—my home if they behave this way!" Carefully she avoided the word "boardinghouse"; it took Myra several minutes to realize that the guests were far behind in paying their bills and that Madame lacked experience in handling such matters.

Only a year ago, doing a revolutionary thing that shocked relatives and friends, Madame had begun the operation of her establishment. Her husband, Télémaque, had been taken by one of the recent plagues, and the family had wanted her to give up the big place. "But we have been in this house since it was built after the last fire"—Mme. Montagnet shook her head—"and I will be here as long as *le Bon Dieu* will let me stay!" Myra found herself liking Madame from the start; that frail exterior, with its delicate nose and gentle gray eyes, concealed a firm will. In a few moments she learned more: Madame had been born a Montagnet and married a cousin, by whom she had no children. Though she looked much older than Myra, there was only two years' difference in their ages. Then all at once Madame apparently decided she had said too much to a stranger; she grew embarrassed.

Myra rose. "May I ask if you know anything of Daniel Clark?"

"Only a little." Madame was cautious.

"Where would he be buried?"

"The St. Louis cemetery, *certainement*. Nowhere else would a man of quality allow himself to be placed!" It was some seven or eight squares away; Myra, drawing on her gloves, prepared to walk. "But *non!*" Madame cried involuntarily. "People, they would take you for a fallen woman." Myra permitted Madame to call Céleste, the mulattress, who sent Dieu-Donné to find a hack.

As the cavernous vehicle rolled away she caught glimpses of other brick-stuccoed houses along the narrow streets. They stretched for square after square in connected lines, their façades broken only by galleries of ornamented iron, making designs that brought to mind black lace over a light-tinted fabric. New Orleans was French and Spanish and faintly Caribbean at the same time, a tropical town that dozed under the pressing heat of the sun. And Myra's nose and eyes suggested another reason why the Creole houses did not face the streets: the roadways were incredibly muddy, full of holes and deep gutters that held stagnant water and piles of overpowering refuse.

Sounds echoed about her: the roll of carts, the beat of drums outside the slave exchanges, the screeches of multicolored birds, an unseen baritone roaring an aria from a blacksmith shop. A Negress, her outlines those of a stone pillar, balanced a basket on her head. Two stolid, dusty Indians, man and wife, shuffled by in single file. When Myra's hack halted at an intersection a black man thrust flowers at her from a tray over his shoulders. "Vi-lets, madame? Cheap, cheap!" A drunken individual who looked like a fisherman slumped against a post; a grande dame murmured her resentment at the sight to the quadroon girl who carried her purchases. As they proceeded Myra blinked and sniffed and looked back.

"*Ici, madame.*" The driver bowed her out. The brick wall ahead was pierced by a gate. With her first step inside, she stopped short. Nowhere were graves as she knew them—only long, unbroken rows of vaults, three and four tiers high, with a few separate tombs here and there, heavy structures with pillars and templelike entrances. A phrase, hitherto meaningless, came back; these were New Orleans's "cities of the dead," all above ground because the water level rose so high.

When she found the sexton he scratched his head. "M'sieu Clock? Clock? He in a h'oven, yes?" He made Myra understand that "oven" was the term for the rows of receptacles, so like those in a baker's establishment. Then he recalled it: "Ah, Dan-i-*el* Clock!" He led her to a small tomb with a simple inscription. Before it a cracked vase held a bunch of wilted flowers. "Them from M'sieu Relf. Ev'y six mont', reg'lar." So Relf, about whom she and Will had wondered so much, cared enough to visit Daniel's resting place. The sexton rubbed his beard. "But 'e jus' tell us to put 'em on, long time 'go. Never come, him. Humph!" As he hobbled off, it was evident that the sexton was no admirer of M. Relf.

This, then, was all that remained of the glory of Daniel Clark, once beloved of New Orleans. He lay alone in his forgotten grave, in a city that at the end must have been strange and foreign to him, as strange and foreign as it suddenly appeared to her. From her throat she took the violets she had bought and placed them before the tomb; slowly she sank to her knees and prayed for the man who had been her father.

Sweat poured down Will's chest and in trickles along his itching legs. Hours had passed, and he had found nothing. First he went to the water front, threading his way among barrels of molasses, pushing past stevedores as they argued over cotton bales. Eventually he ferreted out a flyspecked office, the headquarters of Mr. Schaumburg, who had filed the recent suit over Daniel's estate. The sullen assistants, sorting flour kegs and aromatic boxes of preserved fruits, did not know where their employer was.

Next on his list came the name of a person over whom he and Myra had speculated: Pierre Baron Boisfontaine, brother of Marianne Davis. Myra had heard little of him; vaguely she recalled that he and the crotchety colonel were not friends. At the doorway of a building that was almost a replica of Mme. Montagnet's a Negro in livery reported that Monsieur was "over the lake" and would not be back for "five, six day, maybe."

Will frowned. The following name was the Chevalier de la Croix, one of the executors of Daniel's second will; here certainly would be an important person to see. Far below the settled area the carriage rumbled toward the suburbs. They approached a raised house of the ornamental type, white, deep-galleried. Iron gates hung ajar; they halted at the end of a drive before a curved double stairway. A Negro attendant—very courteous, very correct—took Will's hat and led him down a wide passage to a shadowed room. Will lowered himself gratefully upon a long sofa, rich in ornamentation, faintly outmoded; along the hall he heard an exchange of voices. The butler returned. He was sorry, but M'sieu de la Croix was not well, he could see no one; would M'sieu Whitney leave a message? Will's anger snapped; he wished to consult M. de la Croix on matters concerning Daniel Clark and Daniel's daughter. He would be back.

Returning to the Place d'Armes, the old parade ground in the city's heart, Will halted uncertainly near the cathedral. The breeze was strong beneath the three bell-shaped towers, the central one soaring above the others. Through the open doors came a low chant and the ancient scent of incense and burning tallow; against the white altar a resplendent figure lifted the chalice. It had been near this spot, Will reflected, that Daniel Clark stood for the ceremonies transferring Louisiana, and——

He heard his name called. A neat, stooped man with a blond pompadour took his arm. After a moment Will recognized him: Albert Ainsworth, a cotton factor, who had called at Whitney Place. Ah, Will must join him for a little refreshment. They entered an oblong café, filled with tables at which men chatted and gesticulated in six tongues, and before long Will found himself drinking another cup of coffee.

Mr. Ainsworth snickered as Will gave a summary of his difficulties. Ho, that was not the way to proceed here! One sent a letter, asking to see the other individual a week hence. Then, after an hour of polite conversation and many sips of coffee, they might approach the subject. When Ainsworth first arrived, he had run about like an—he apologized—an American. Now he behaved like a Louisianian. Anyway, what brought Will here?

"Well, my wife and I——" Will sensed it would be wisest to feel his way a bit further. "Oh, just an inheritance, not sure ourselves just where we stand." After a few guarded remarks he brought up the man Schaumburg. Did Ainsworth know him?

"Slightly." The cotton man made a gesture of easy dismissal. "A small wholesaler. Hardly heard of him till he filed a suit all at once against Relf and Chew. A wild thing. Made some stir, but nobody takes it seriously. Relf and Chew, you understand, are pretty high here, with their banking connections." His shrewd eyes passed reflectively over Will's face. "A thing like that could be suicide for a man in Schaumburg's place." His expression invited Will to go further, but Will decided against it; and he declined Ainsworth's suggestion of yet another cup of coffee. As they parted, the cotton factor reminded him that he must bring Myra to call on the Ainsworths, any time soon.

A final address remained on Will's list. Josuah Whitney had mentioned the brothers Greer and Lucius Duncan, commercial lawyers; Josuah had once had dealings with them. Behind a paneled doorway on Chartres, the main business street, a thriving establishment was in operation. After waiting a few minutes Will was led to a pair of desks, side by side. Two gray-haired men, lean and alert and carefully expressionless, shook Will's hand. One indicated a chair.

"I'm here," he began, "in the interest of myself and my wife, Myra Clark, daughter——"

He stopped in astonishment; the two men had stood up. One looked uncertainly at the other, who gazed steadily at Will, mounting anger in his eye. "It so happens, young man, that my brother and I are intimate friends of Mr. Relf and Mr. Chew— and their attorneys! We've already been annoyed by ridiculous allegations about this estate. We have nothing to tell you, nor will our clients."

"Except this." The older brother spoke up suddenly, his voice trembling. "You'd better be certain of what you say!"

A sharp retort rose to Will's lips. "I'd advise you and your clients to keep your threats until you're injured." This remark almost started him on a chain of others, but he slammed his hat down about his ears and pounded out. Damn it, he'd played a fool this time! Still, could he have realized who the Duncan brothers were?

He knew now just where he wanted to go. He headed into one of the massively arched Spanish structures next to the cathedral, the old Cabildo. In a cavernous room he sought out the clerk of the probate court. An assistant listened impassively as Will asked for the succession of Daniel Clark. "What is your interest?" he inquired.

"That's none of your concern," Will told him. "I needn't remind you that these are public records."

They stared at each other; the clerk's eyes fell. After another wait he returned with an armful of records. Will's pen raced, leaving angular writing across his first sheet, then another and a third. After a time, however, he dropped the pen and riffled through the records. This was strange, but here it was. . . .

At a side desk the clerk also worked, filling seven or eight separate sheets with brief, identical messages. Then he addressed them to men whose office addresses were evidently very familiar to him. He snapped a finger; the slave nodded at his whispered directions and gave a bow after the final words: "See that every damned letter is delivered before dark!" Will's pen scratched on.

A new fury possessed Will as Myra met him at the door. Shedding his coat, he threw himself on the bed; then the words came in a passionate flood: "It's astounding! Twenty years have passed since Daniel died. The law requires that any executors end their work within twelve months; they got one brief delay, but they've never finished. Year after year they've kept on selling Daniel's property—without legal authority of any kind!"

She started to speak, but Will, rising on his elbow, sped on: "More than that, the law says sales must be at public auction, after full advertisement. Practically everything has been done at private sale, without anyone to check; and you know what abuses that can mean! By law, all transactions require separate court orders; these men didn't go to the court for approval, in advance or afterward. And the law is damned clear on something else: within a year or two at the outside limit they *have* to file a complete inventory." He pounded the bedcover. "In twenty years they've never done it!"

Myra caught his arm. "But under that 'provisional will' wasn't Daniel's mother supposed to get everything?"

"Yes." His eyes blazed. "Instead she got practically nothing. A few thousand instead of millions. She and the rest of Clarks, all women, stayed up North. These fellows had a free hand. When you think——"

The mulatto woman rapped; a man was downstairs to see them. In the parlor a bright-mannered individual, with a face like a pink apple fringed in yellow hair, bounded up. "Mr. and Mrs. Whitney? A delight, a delight. Charles Schaumburg, Charles W. Schaumburg. I can guess what you're interested in, all right—that suit of mine." He bubbled on. "I've had more excitement over this—too much for me and my digestion." He paused. "The case? Oh, it comes up the end of this week. Of course you can look at my documents. Brought them with me."

While Mr. Schaumburg's words ran ahead Will and Myra scanned the petition. As a dissatisfied creditor, the merchant cited several facts that Will had found; then, to Will's delight, the document touched upon the missing will. Relf and Chew did not, "as they would ostentatiously have it believed, possess the full confidence of Clark at the time of his death. . . . With the utmost caution Clark had kept Relf and Chew unacquainted with the existence of a second will—not surely from feelings of friendship and confidence." Doubtless, it was added, Clark had allowed the earlier will to remain in Relf's possession to keep him in ignorance of his changed plans, "as if with inspired forecast, he wished to save his estate from the administration of his *soi-disant* friends." The paper was carelessly drawn, lacking in details; still, it would provide Will and Myra with their opportunity.

Will turned to their caller. "You wouldn't object, would you, to asking for a delay of a few weeks, so I could gather evidence of my own?"

Mr. Schaumburg gave him an apprehensive glance. "Oh, I couldn't! The judge was very stern; he said he'd permit no delays. Mr. Relf and Mr. Chew are aggravated already, and some of the witnesses are getting restless. De la Croix, for instance."

When Will told of his fruitless call on the chevalier, Mr. Schaumburg's countenance became pinker, and his eyebrows drew together. "Please! We mustn't upset him before the trial.

He's hard enough to deal with as it is. Keeps saying he wants to be fair to both sides and—well, he's always suspicious that somebody is questioning his honor."

"Look," Will began, "the only way I know to fight a case is to fight it with all the——" Then he gathered that his man was growing huffed. Will caught Myra's look, and she shook her head. Mr. Schaumburg was a fool; they'd have to work as hard as they could and hope for the best.

On the morning of the hearing Myra and Will arrived early. About the grim courtroom a group of attendants made vague motions with their dustcloths, until the size of the task seemed to appall them and they gave up. The sight of Myra in the room, sitting boldly beside her husband, made a stir. She knew that every male eye was upon her, appraising, evaluating. The fact that the expert glances were approving ones made her feel no less on display. She pulled the lace upward at her throat to hide the beginning of her well-defined bosom and tried to think of other things.

In swept the effervescent Mr. Schaumburg, followed by a striking-looking Frenchman, with heavily chiseled features and abundant, gray-streaked hair, who might have been any age from thirty-five to fifty-five. The latter stepped forward, took Will's hand, and kissed Myra's. He was Pierre Baron Boisfontaine, just arrived from the country. He focused his snapping black eyes on Myra. "Of course you don't remember the times you sat on my knee!" Then he became earnest. "I have a great deal to say to the two of you. We'll have to meet after this—this proceeding." His lively face darkened; he shared Will's opinion of Schaumburg and Schaumburg's putty-faced attorney. (Will, dismayed after his first interview with the fellow, had given up any attempt to co-operate with him.)

The courtroom doors swung open to admit the impressive Duncan brothers and, with them, an oddly assorted pair. In the lead marched a short, slim man, immaculately attired, his thinning grayish hair carefully in place. The face, much lined, had no strongly defined features except the pale blue, slightly protruding eyes. "Relf," whispered Boisfontaine, and Will and Myra did not conceal their interest. With him came Beverly Chew, an individual who, as Myra told herself, might have been submerged in any company—pale, long-nosed, almost bald. Though considerably taller than his associate, he was obviously dominated by him. His air, in contrast with Relf's assured manner, was diffident; as he walked he seemed almost to apologize for himself.

Pierre Boisfontaine bowed coldly to the two men. Chew looked embarrassed, then returned the salutation with a slight inclination of his head; Relf went by without a flicker of recognition. Taking his seat, the senior partner folded his arms and gazed sternly forward. So this was the individual who was at the heart of it all, thought Myra. The face was rounded, the nose more or less regular, though short, the lips thin and narrow. Seeing him on the street, one might pay him little heed. But as she studied him she recognized a certain chill and steady power, a rigidly controlled strength of will. Here was a man who would leave nothing to chance, for whom all life would go according to plan. Now he was elaborately ignoring Myra and all the others opposed to him. A muscle, working intermittently in the back of his neck, gave the only hint that he was under tension.

The judge ascended the bench. The case had hardly begun before Will and Myra, and Boisfontaine beside them, were groaning to themselves. Schaumburg's attorney fumbled and blundered; the Duncan brothers were as casual as they were expert. After a string of minor witnesses Pierre Boisfontaine was called. Myra leaned forward; so, unexpectedly, did Mr. Relf.

Yes, Boisfontaine declared, he had been one of Daniel's intimate friends. "He said repeatedly he would leave Myra the bulk of his estate. During his final months he made a new will, with papers giving information about all his holdings, and deposited everything in a small black case. Once he showed me the case and put it in a trunk—in his downstairs office at his bayou home." Relf's stare was growing harder and harder.

"I was there when Daniel passed on," Boisfontaine continued. "During his last hours he talked again of Myra. The will, he said, was in the office below his bedroom. I heard him tell Lubin, his Negro confidential servant, that as soon as he died Lubin must take the black case, containing the will, to M. de la Croix. He reminded Lubin just where he would find the case."

Myra hardly breathed; her hand was pulling at the unregenerate "thinking" lock behind her ear. This was strong new evidence, of a sort that Josef Bellechasse had been unable to offer them. Carefully, with a side look at Relf, Boisfontaine went on:

"Mr. Relf had been moving in and out of Daniel's bedroom all that day. Shortly before Daniel died I saw Relf take a bundle of keys from the armoire. One of them opened the black case in the downstairs office. Then Relf went below and sent the servant Lubin somewhere——"

"Where?" The elder Duncan shot the question.

"I don't remember that."

The attorney bowed, as if he had made an important point.

"Then Relf came forward with the old will instead of the new one. We were astonished. We felt sure——"

Duncan slammed his fist on the table. "Will the witness confine himself to the facts!"

Will writhed; Schaumburg's lawyer was letting Boisfontaine suffer needless badgering. Why didn't he help him, protect him against these tactics? Boisfontaine resumed: "We were certain the will had been withheld, because——"

"I object! I object!" Duncan was shouting. Still Schaumburg's man did nothing. Pressing his cross-examination, Relf's attorney obtained a statement that Boisfontaine had never heard Relf's integrity "called publicly into question." Myra whispered, "But that means nothing at all!" Will nodded helplessly. At last the witness stepped down. He had not been allowed to tell his full story; much of its effect had been lost.

At the back the crowd parted; the Chevalier de la Croix had arrived. A frail, dark-haired man with faded and deeply circled eyes walked slowly forward. Myra inspected him as he rested his veined hands on his ivory-tipped cane. He looked, somehow, withdrawn, as if he had had his fill of the world and wanted only to be at rest. This was the man her father had chosen as one of his most trusted associates, who had been so certain Daniel's will was suppressed that he demanded a court search.

The chevalier took the stand. His voice was calm; *oui,* he had agreed to be an executor of the estate. About two weeks before Daniel's death he had talked with him in his downstairs office. Daniel was sealing up a packet of papers—his will and other documents—and he wrote slowly across the outside: "To be opened in case of death." Daniel cautioned him he must say nothing about this to Relf and Chew.

A light burned in Myra's eyes. Will's fears about the old man's touchiness and remoteness had been for nothing, then. De la Croix was giving fine corroboration for their side. Yet Lucius Duncan appeared little disturbed. Leaning forward, he asked politely, "What was in this supposed new will?"

The chevalier's gaze swept the room proudly, almost imperiously. "I know nothing of its contents. I never did."

"Might not the will of 1811, which Mr. Relf brought forward, have been the same that Mr. Clark placed in the case?"

"Perhaps; I have no way of knowing."

How could De la Croix say this? Certainly his words were contradicted by his own actions at the time. Why, after twenty years, was he testifying this way? Will's brow wrinkled heavily; Pierre Boisfontaine's black eyes had a new and different sparkle as they fastened on the chevalier's face.

"Now, monsieur." Attorney Duncan stepped forward. "Do you regard Mr. Relf as a man who would do away with a will?"

"Definitely not!" The dark head shot up. "I've always considered him a person of extreme honor. He has served as cashier of the state bank through one administration after another, almost from its founding. I myself was president of the bank a few years ago. Recently when I went to France I named attorneys to represent me here; in case of their death I appointed Mr. Relf as a substitute. I would hardly have done this had I thought him a destroyer of sacred documents." Now the chevalier was glaring.

Myra pressed her hand against her throbbing throat. Almost everyone in the room sensed that some further stroke was on its way. It was not long in coming.

"When Daniel Clark mentioned the girl Myra to you, did he discuss her status?" Attorney Duncan's eye was intent.

"He did. He told me"—the chevalier raised his voice, as if to leave no doubt of what he was about to say—"that she was his bastard child."

And now at last the impeccable R. J. Relf deliberately shifted in his chair. Admitting for the first time that Myra was there, he looked directly at her, his blue eyes cold and inquiring, as if some repulsive creature had been brought forward for inspection. Others in the courtroom turned toward her; a mumble of voices rose, and several men stood up to see her better. Slowly

Myra's head sagged. Her face, which had first gone crimson, drained of color. Those words were like a whip cracked across her face; and this man said her father had used them! She felt for a brief moment that she was in a hideous nightmare. But this was happening about her and to her, while the world snickered.

Only gradually did she become aware of a pressure against her arm. It was Pierre Boisfontaine, seated between her and Will. "Courage, Myra," he whispered. Then he added, "Myra Clark!" Like a challenge came his use of the name that the others were trying to deny her. She lifted her head, to gaze steadily forward for a moment. Then she turned her face to meet that of Richard Relf and all the others, and she did not falter. As the blood returned, the needlelike scar stood out against her cheek. Her long brown eyes flashing, she stared directly at the Chevalier de la Croix; in them were defiance and contempt. Studying her, Pierre Boisfontaine saw a firm set of the jaw that he had not noticed before.

Years earlier he had watched another jaw tighten in exactly the same fashion. It had been Daniel Clark's, on the morning he started off for his duel, to the death if need be, with Governor Claiborne of Louisiana.

CHAPTER V

THROUGH the undeveloped lower areas of the city rolled the Boisfontaines' carriage. It passed thinning lines of weatherbeaten frame houses, farms, and dairies maintained by industrious Gascons, who waved gaily as it went by. The two Boisfontaines glanced again at the younger couple opposite them; Myra managed a thin smile, then returned to her thoughts.

Will had given up his efforts to revive her spirits. Her fingers were cold to his touch; though the sun beat through the window, her lips had grown only slightly less wan. Eyes dulled, holding herself rigidly against the cushions, she was wishing hopelessly that she were anywhere except in Louisiana.

When the judge had dropped his gavel on the preceding day,

with a casual dismissal of the whole affair, an almost irresistible impulse had come to her to run blindly through the audience. As she turned away Pierre Boisfontaine seized her arm and Will's and whispered: "But this isn't the end of it! Those blunderers, Schaumburg and his man . . . so much they didn't ask or let us tell!" Seeing her weariness and the blurred look on her face, he proposed that they go with him and Mme. Boisfontaine the next day to spend a week at their plantation, downriver from New Orleans. Myra, still half dazed, nodded, and they made their way out.

At Mme. Montagnet's, Will quickly put Myra to bed. Sitting beside her, he reasoned softly. After all, their side had been sadly handicapped. They had a great deal still to find out about this matter. It wasn't hopeless; Pierre Boisfontaine had more to tell. . . . Myra thanked him and looked away. Her eye stopped on a picture near the window—a little girl's portrait; and the sight of it was another hurt. Her baby, taking shape within her —would he grow up with this stain? Again she saw the sallow face of the aristocrat De la Croix and heard his clipped words: "He said she was his bastard child." With that she gave way to twisting sobs. At first she repulsed Will's efforts to comfort her; in fury she cried out against what had happened. "God, how I wish I'd never heard of this!" Then she collapsed against him.

She slept little that evening. Repeatedly a dream came to her, a dream of surging flight, high in the air over mountains and valleys. Then she was back at Delamore Place, as a child, with a younger, sweet-faced Marianne Davis at her side. They played together on the lawn, and she lay beneath the trees on the crest of the hill. But then out of the sky dropped something dark and horrible; she did not know what it was, but there was malevolence about it and it moved closer and closer. . . .

With the first light of morning she was up. The scratching of her pen awakened Will, and he pushed aside the mosquito bar. Bent over the desk, she was writing a note to the Chevalier de la Croix: In the name of her father, with the hope that he would remember the friendship of Daniel Clark, she was asking him to see her. She wanted simply to hear what he recalled, in his own words. Wouldn't he receive her?

Despite Will's protests, she was firm. She had to make this effort at least. The Boisfontaines were not due for several hours, and she wanted to go to the chevalier with the letter. Again Will demurred, but not long afterward they rode together through the iron gates of the De la Croix residence. The servant stayed away from them only a few minutes before he returned with a firm message: Monsieur sent his regrets; Madame had heard everything he knew.

Now, as the Boisfontaine carriage gave a jolt, Myra succeeded in rousing herself. They were leaving the main road for a passage to the east, bordering a narrow waterway. Delicate, feathery willows trailed over the silvered bayou, like women washing their hair by the water's edge. Handfuls of red blossoms, fallen from a bush, floated in the wind; cows stood to their knees in the tranquil water, munching at rushes, unconcerned with the geese that swam among them. Over it all hung the somnolence of afternoon.

Toward them advanced a procession of ox-drawn carts and wagons laden with straw and vegetables. Solemn men walked with their stout-framed wives beside the carts. They bowed their dark heads; brilliant Spanish eyes flashed greetings, and they went on. These, Pierre explained, were Canary Islanders, transplanted to Louisiana during the years of the dons. Bringing their cattle with them, they had given their name to the vicinity of Bayou Terre-aux-Bœufs.

The shy Mme. Boisfontaine looked thoughtfully over her fan, her high cheekbones rising above the braided black edge. "You should not feel entirely unfamiliar with this scene," she told Myra. "Over there was where Colonel Davis' house stood." Only tangled weeds remained. There was a dull ache in Myra's breast; so that, too, was gone. . . . The place had changed greatly since then, Pierre pointed out. More and more sugar growers, finding lands taken elsewhere, were venturing here. Now they displaced the Spanish cattle and vegetable growers, who moved slowly out toward the lowest reaches of their bayou, where it approached the Gulf. There, necessarily, the Canary Islanders were resorting to fishing and trapping. "You see before you," Pierre observed with a wry glance, "the advance of one culture, the retreat of another. The change isn't always for the best." He waved his hand. "This, in any case, is what we've done to show our civilization."

They were at the edge of the Boisfontaine plantation. As the carriage turned to the side they passed under a white archway; a double line of live oaks curved into the distance. At once they were inside a tunnel of half dusk, still, cool, and touched with a sense of mystery. Each tree rose like an aged, twisted giant holding arms high into the air; the branches met overhead to form a canopy of intertwining green and brown. From it hung curtains of gray moss that scraped lightly at the top of the vehicle. Then all at once, in a sun-splashed clearing, there lay before them the proud whiteness of Bon Séjour.

For a moment the plantation house seemed tiny; but that, Myra realized, was only because of the towering trees. A wide brick basement supported a main floor of wood, with a gallery around the four sides. Squat brick pillars, below, gave way to tapering colonnettes that met a down-sweeping roof. About it grew a controlled abundance of trees and bushes, oleanders and jessamine, sweet olive and the sharp spikes of the Spanish dagger. To each side a *pigeonnier* lifted its peaked tower; the only sounds were the low cries of the birds and the whispering of a group of house servants, bowing at the front stairway.

Through a maze of curtseys Aimée Boisfontaine escorted Myra to rooms made ready for her and Will. As this was a rural place, she found a greater informality than would have been the rule in a Creole city mansion; yet the mahogany and rosewood pieces stood even taller, and the doors and windows rose more imposingly, than in New Orleans. Quietly Aimée took Myra's hand. "And now we follow a rite at Bon Séjour. On arrival, a swim in our bayou." Myra hesitated, until Aimée, less diffident than she had been at first, encircled her waist. "Come, *chérie*. The men will go in together—later of course."

The bathhouse squatted half on land, half over the water. As Myra donned her full-length water costume the older woman made admiring comment: "What fine legs, and such breasts!" With a smile Aimée noted that it was a well-formed husband Myra had too. "You must be very happy, yes?" Myra wondered what Colonel Davis, who upbraided her for "forwardness," would have thought of such frank appraisal.

At the water's edge she drew back. It was motionless, dark as a brown wine, altogether unlike the swift, clear streams she knew. With a laugh Aimée pulled her forward, and she floated. Then something scaly touched her arm, and she shuddered.

"Only a shrimp." Aimée smiled. "He may be one that the women will catch for your supper." The bayou, still warm from the sun, covered her soothingly, protectingly, and she gave herself to the enjoyment of it.

"See, *chérie*," Aimée told her, "don't let the first look of a thing frighten you too much." Aimée swam a few strokes away, then returned, and her face had sobered. "Myra, I was a friend of your father's. Don't accept without question all the things they'll say. He had his faults; he was a man and—and standards were not the same. If only things had worked out a bit differently for him and Zulime . . ." A gleam touched her delicate features. Aimée Boisfontaine was one of those who had been close to Daniel Clark and had found him a decent, good human being.

Several of Myra's gowns had been laid out for her, and a girl was there to assist. She chose the newest—a flimsy green silk, unusually tight in the waist, wide-sleeved, deep-cut at the throat. She piled her hair high on her head, where it gleamed in the candlelight like tongues of flame. Then, following an impulse, she selected two full red roses and pinned them at the low neckline. The gold mirror told her the color had returned to her cheeks; in her eyes the flecks of light were dancing again. The quick glances of the two men as she joined them in the drawing room showed her she had succeeded.

The meal, served on a rear gallery, was aromatic and richly blended. The bayou provided raw oysters. "Most people along here would rather cook their right arm than a good oyster." Pierre grinned. The countryside also yielded the contents of the succulent gumbo, a combination of shrimp, crabs, bits of ham and herbs, served over rice; and the plump duckling, almost lost in a thick brown sauce.

By unspoken accord they avoided for a time the matter that was in the backs of their minds. The Boisfontaines chatted of earlier days on the plantation; of the time Daniel had been here and made a Parisian think he was a native of France because his accent sounded so precise; of the neighbor who wanted to challenge a Yankee for saying Boston smelled better than New Orleans. Out of the garden rose several scents, one, then another dominant for the moment. From close by came the ripe pungency of the small, conelike *Magnolia fuscata,* reminiscent, in more concentrated form, of the tropical banana; and just over their heads hung clusters of lavender wisteria blossoms, like the faces of silent children in the shadows.

After the frozen cream and cheeses and coffee they moved to the front lawn. There Myra knew a repose of spirit that had not been hers in months. The edges of the hanging moss lifted with the wind; a short way off a shaft of moonlight picked out one of the statues, a marble Summer, cornucopia in her hand. Like the mythical figure, all life seemed arrested here, caught in its moment of fullest ripeness. A thought came to Myra: would a place like this—many like this—be hers, were justice done? Quickly followed another question: this child of hers and Will's —would it, too, be cheated? More and more the baby was in her mind.

As if he read some of her reflections, Pierre let out a long breath and tossed his cigar to the half-moist earth. "We owe this"—he indicated their surroundings—"this and much more to Daniel Clark. Daniel was the benefactor of our family. We Bois-fontaines lost everything, you know, during the uprisings in Saint Domingue. Marianne, my sister, met Samuel Davis and they went to New Orleans, where Daniel made him a protégé. I followed, and for a time I looked about, restless and unsettled. I was skilled in one thing, the handling of sugar cane; it was not easy to get a foothold.

"I met Daniel, and we liked each other. He asked me if I'd take over one of his holdings; in time I was managing them all, Sligo, Havana Point, Desert, Houmas, and the rest. As the years passed we grew closer. All of us heard about him and Zulime, of course. But Daniel seldom spoke of her to me until just a year before his death, when we were riding about the cane fields. I think he was close to tears; suddenly he was telling me of the thing that had been preying on him." The two men lit their cigars; for a moment twin flames lit up the circle. In the illumination Myra's face was an intent white oval, slashed by the lines of her mouth.

"On the day we talked Daniel explained that he had met Zulime years earlier, as Mme. des Granges, and had fallen very much in love. But there was that bar between them. I'd always been told Zulime hadn't been happy with Des Granges. He was" —Pierre's mouth twisted—"poor stuff, always in trouble, one kind or another. Eventually he left the city, and the French section soon rang with the story—from the fellow's own foolish mouth—that he was a bigamist. . . . *Eh bien.* At this Daniel went to Zulime, and she took a trip North with her sister and found someone who'd been present at Des Granges's original marriage. Daniel persuaded her there was no reason why she shouldn't accept him now, and a priest joined them in a ceremony in Philadelphia. It took place in a private home, and Daniel thought that, for discretion and for political reasons as well, the event must be kept secret until Zulime's connection with Des Granges was officially annulled." Boisfontaine lifted his shoulders. "Zulime, naturally, was the victim of this arrangement. Still, I'm certain from everything Daniel said, and my knowledge of him, that he planned eventually to make the announcement. But to go on . . ."

Zulime was about to have her child, and Colonel Davis arranged for her to use one of Pierre's houses. Before long Zulime had to give up Myra. Here Boisfontaine's voice thickened. "It was a hard thing; but, as Daniel told me, he persuaded her it was for the best. Someday she could take you back." Myra winced; once more pity swept her for this woman whom circumstance had treated so harshly.

More and more Daniel called on the Davises to see Myra and play with her. Meanwhile, though Pierre did not know the details, Zulime obtained some kind of court recognition that her union with Des Granges had been entirely void. But by this time certain of Daniel's friends were at work. He stood at the peak of his success—Louisiana's delegate in Congress, a great social figure. They told him her station was below him; he would hurt himself through such a mésalliance. Daniel still hesitated, and Zulime, desperate by now, went to Philadelphia to get the record of her marriage to Daniel.

"She couldn't find it. No publication had been required by the Pennsylvania law and no civil registration; the priest who performed the ceremony had gone to Ireland, where, it appeared, he had died. Zulime was told she had no rights, or at least could prove none. That, I suppose, was the cruelest thing that happened to her. After a time"—he opened his palms—"she was married again, to Dr. James Gardette."

"Without"—Myra gripped the edge of the chair—"without getting a divorce from Daniel?"

"Could she get a divorce without a record that she had married him?" Pierre asked compassionately. In the silence that followed, the creak of a wagon sounded along the bayou passageway. Will spoke up, and there was quiet admonition in his voice: "This would mean Zulime's union with Dr. Gardette could be questioned. But if we show she'd been properly married to Daniel, *that* wouldn't be affected!"

Myra passed an agitated hand over her face. What an involvement her mother had created! Pierre, drawing on his cigar, shook his head: "Before he died Daniel told me he was willing to announce that he and Zulime had been married. He wanted to correct his mistakes; he was ready to let the gossips sizzle in hell. But how could he do it, then, without making Zulime liable to prosecution? Dr. Gardette was still alive.

"About two weeks before his death I was in Daniel's office, at his house, with De la Croix. Daniel brought out a black case with a packet in it. This was the interview De la Croix described on the witness stand. But it happened differently!" Pierre's black eyes smoldered, and he talked with furious emphasis. "I remember what happened as clearly as if it were an hour ago. Daniel told him, 'De la Croix, this is my last will. You've consented to be *Myra's executor and tutor.* You'll do what you promised?' De la Croix nodded." Pierre leaned forward, pointing his cigar. "Then Daniel declared, very distinctly, to De la Croix and me, *'I've given Myra all my estate; there's an annuity for my mother and a few extra legacies.'* "

And yet De la Croix had taken oath that he knew nothing of the will's contents. Will spoke sharply. "You're very sure of that?"

"I'm ready to swear to every word of it—and also what followed. After a week or so I came into the city again. Daniel had grown worse, and he asked me to stay near him. Through all his last day he referred to you, Myra; about an hour before he died your name was in his mind. He turned to Lubin, his servant, and asked him: 'You'll be sure, now, to carry the black case to the chevalier?'

"Relf was in and out of the room during all this time. Toward the end, as I managed to tell the Court, Relf took the bundle of keys in Daniel's armoire and went downstairs. Before long Daniel rolled on his side, and it was over. Lubin, much excited, whispered to me that he'd followed Relf, seen him enter Daniel's office, and heard the door lock. After a few minutes Relf left by another entrance." Pierre scowled. "Within an hour Relf was back at the house with the notaries. He brought out a document —the earlier will."

A cloud passed over the moon. The marble Summer merged with the blackness of the shrubbery; the silvered water of the bayou disappeared beyond them. Myra felt suddenly that she and Will were alone in an alien world, rich and burgeoning and hostile.

During the days that followed at Bon Séjour Myra alternated between gray pessimism and reviving hope. These new facts of Pierre's—her eyes brightened as she and Will ran over them. Yet Zulime, driven by her own hurt or despair, had married a third time, while her union to Daniel remained in effect. Or could they prove that second marriage to Myra's father, after all? . . . The Boisfontaines insisted they must try not to think too much about the case. Someone was coming here in a few days, a friendly woman who had nursed Myra; Aimée mentioned a name they could not place. Meanwhile they could enjoy a few diversions. They rode along the twilit avenue of the trees; Will rowed Myra about the bayou. The lazy days merged into each other.

Soon they were inspecting the cane fields, touching the tiny yellow-green stalks that thrust themselves a few inches above the ground. The weeds, like everything else, grew too quickly in this mealy ground; the Negroes worked over the rows in the fervent heat. Will and Myra visited the sugar mill in which the men would eventually push the heavy purplish stalks into the jaws of the machinery. Myra's eyes followed the long lines of slaves, agile and young, middle-aged, bent and elderly, whose sweat produced the wealth on which so much of Louisiana thrived. Their many lifetimes of little-rewarded labor had made possible much of Daniel Clark's possessions. And now she and others were fighting over the right to these possessions.

As their horses jogged at the bayou edge Will pointed his whip. The water beside them was deepening, acquiring a stronger current as it neared the Gulf; the land on both sides had narrowed. Only a short distance off began the marshes, endless expanses of gold and green, threaded by thousands of interconnecting passageways. They were passing a file of unpainted houses, fashioned from ends and bits of old wood, topped by straw-pale palmetto thatching—the homes of the Canary Islanders. The front of each residence was hung with animal pelts, strings of red and green peppers, and occasionally a bird cage. They could feel many pairs of eyes watching from cracks in the batten windows.

From the last house a burly, barefoot fellow with an enormous round nose came pounding toward them. His rough-bearded face cracked apart in a smile. "My-ra!" he boomed. He whirled back toward the house. "*Sí,* it is Señor Clark's lil one, all right!" Out of the doorway moved a timid line, a mother and ten or eleven children. As Myra dismounted, the father rubbed his hand on his trousers and thrust it out. "Estevan Perez, at you' service. The Davises and Daniel, they was my good, good frien'. An' you, I carry you too many time', and change you' di-per too!"

The children giggled, and Señora Perez hissed to Estevan to mind his tongue. "You mus' come in," Estevan urged them. "Daniel, he know my place well, from fishin' trip' and lot' o' good time'." He changed his expression, and moist sympathy shone in his eyes. "Now I hear they try say you born on wrong side the blanket!" Señora Perez, with a violent glance at her husband, helped Myra forward.

Directly before them on the mud floor, half lost in the dim light, sat an ancient woman with curved nose and stringy white hair. Her fading eyes stared until one of the grandchildren whispered who Myra was. Then the fantastically wrinkled face broke into a grin. "We know Daniel down here, *sí,*" she shrilled. "Kind fellow, him, always doing for people. Them next door they wouldn' be on two feet today if Daniel didn' bring 'em food. That other, what got to be sheriff—who were 'e, when Daniel found 'im sittin' on 'is fish net'?" With that she sank back; during all of their stay her eyes were fixed on Myra's face.

As they accepted glasses of strong red wine the younger Señora Perez came forward, a small object held reverently in her hand—a crucifix of ancient wood, exquisitely carved, polished to a high degree. "It was Daniel Clark's," the señora told her softly. " 'E gave it to us, once, after Estevan save 'is life in the Gulf." Estevan looked abashed. "Now we think you should have it." Myra's eyes filled. Seldom had a gift so affected her.

And it had belonged to her father; at last—her heart beat as she told it to herself—she had something she could know he had touched. She kissed Señora Perez, and slipped the crucifix inside her bosom.

Suddenly the grandmother motioned to Myra. "Go. She got sight into future," whispered Estevan. Myra wanted to refuse, but there was no way to do it. As she bent over, the crone caught her wrist, and the grip was like a man's.

"I do this for Daniel." She poked a bony finger at Myra. "Do not take it for joke!" A dark glare came into her yellowed eyes. "If you wan' easy life, thing' you like, *go back home!*" She spat out the words. "You mus' make choice, now, soon. If you stay, you not have pleasant time. Suffer, cry, many time', many time'. You lose much, much—thing' you think you never do without!" Then the señora's face grew kindlier. "Yet don' despair; in end, you win. Not ev'ything, but main thing, thing you wan' mos'."

There was no other sound in the crowded room. Will approached, and the señora swept him with her glance. "I no see you with 'er in day' ahead. No! She alone!"

Myra backed away, and Will led her out into the sunlight.

As they returned toward Bon Séjour beneath the double line of oaks a servant ran forward. "Mam'zelle Aimée say can you come in garden, yes?" In a moment they stood before a tight-lipped, emphatic little woman in a fussy gray dress; she looked narrowly at them, then jumped up and planted three precise kisses on Myra's face, one on the forehead, two on the cheeks.

"Mrs. Smyth," murmured Pierre. The visitor, resuming her seat, shook her fan at him and took matters into her own hands.

"Sit down, you young ones, and you, too, Pierre. I can explain this to poor Myra better than you. Now listen"—she pointed to the Whitneys—"and you may learn something. I was Mrs. Harper, Harriett Harper, before you were born. I married Colonel Davis' nephew, and we were living with the Davises. That Sam Davis—there's a one for you. Never knew what to make of him, still don't! Some say he's his own worst enemy, though I've heard other folks claim the credit! Well, where was I? Oh! . . . By the time I got to Louisiana, Des Granges had skipped, and ten people assured me the miserable fellow was found guilty of bigamy in some sort of court action. You hunt for *that,* son," she directed

Will. "Daniel Clark himself said it, and he also told me, without ifs or ands or buts, that he married Zulime, up North." She nodded several times, like a hen pecking at the air.

"Well," she resumed, "just before you came to us I had a child of my own. I've had seven." Myra's look must have shown the spinsterlike Harriett how surprised she was at that statement. "Haven't I? Haven't I?" Harriett demanded of the Boisfontaines. "Anyway, Myra, I thank the good God I could suckle you as I did, when they took you from Zulime. Not that that father of yours made it any easier for us to raise you. Extravagances, lace gowns, foreign-made rattles! Do you know, before you were five, he sashayed over with a personal slave for you. She got in our way, and I sent her back!" It was not difficult to visualize this honest, peppery character defying Daniel or anyone else.

Perhaps because of the service she did in nursing Myra, Daniel was always grateful to Harriett; they remained close friends until his death, she went on. He called on her just before he left hurriedly for the East, when he made the "provisional will" naming Relf and Chew. On his return he told Harriett he would discard that document; it had been made to meet a situation that no longer existed.

In his last year or so Daniel talked more and more to Harriett about Myra. He was making a new, final will. "I remember especially one thing he told me—'I'm making a Bill of Rights for my child.' He also said something else I can't forget—'I'll never give Myra a stepmother.' He had very little to say in those days about those two, Relf and Chew," she sniffed. "What he said wasn't good, I can tell you. He'd learned that they were more interested in themselves than in him; they'd played their part in getting him to break up with Zulime, carrying tales and spreading rumors and all that. Anyway, he told me he'd advised Bellechasse, Pitot, and De la Croix all about his plan to recognize you, and the three said they'd look after you.

"Ah, the confidence that man had in De la Croix—more, even, than in the others. He was making him your tutor; he was laying out a plan for your education in Europe and America, under De la Croix's direction. The chevalier knew so much about France, and this and that; he'd watch so well over you!" Harriett's eyes glittered. "Well, I'll tell you more about him later."

She paused. "As for that will, not only did I *see* it, I had it in my hands overnight, and went through it again and again! Daniel came to my house when I was busy and left it there. He gave a two-thousand-a-year annuity for his mother. Lubin, his faithful servant, was to be freed and given his support. And, of course, it declared you his proper child. It's as if somebody carved it on my brain, and no one on earth could make me tell a different story!"

Myra wanted to hug the prim little creature, but she feared a rebuke. A servant approached; spying her, Harriett adjusted her shawl about her sloping shoulders with an exact motion. "If you don't mind, Aimée, I won't have any of this coffee Célimène is bringing. Might there, by some remote chance, be tea in this house?"

Célimène snickered as she deposited the tray. "Right 'ere, Mam'zelle 'Arriett. Always trys to remember a lil pot for you." Célimène, however, handled the foreign concoction as if it were a poison.

A few moments later Harriett looked up from her tea, hesitant for the first time. "Maybe you haven't heard of this, but I'll tell you before others will. Zulime had another child." Their eyes opening wider, Myra and Will leaned forward. "Actually" —Harriett shrugged—"I suppose this has little or nothing to do with you; still, they may try to lie about it and use it. A girl named Caroline was born to Zulime a few months before she married Daniel. Zulime and her sisters said definitely she was Des Granges's, born within eight months after Des Granges went to Europe. And this I have without argument—Daniel himself called her Caroline des Granges. He left her a little annuity in his second will, under that name.

"The child was born in Philadelphia, not long after Zulime arrived to hunt proof of Des Granges's bigamy. Some months later, as you know, Daniel and Zulime married, and the child stayed in the North."

"What's happened to her?" Myra blinked.

"Caroline has lived a very quiet life, I suppose. None of us ever saw her. She stayed in boardinghouses, on a farm, and in Philadelphia. Daniel started out by looking after her; then his mother helped, and when she died she left a little to Caroline. Last I heard, the girl had married, up East."

Myra looked blank. Yet another fact, important to them, had

been kept from her. And the girl Caroline, too, had been resid-
ing near her for years, without her knowledge. She wondered
about this Caroline, as she was to wonder about her many times
again; then she turned back to her coffee.

In a moment, after she had swallowed a warm rice cake, Harriett's lips pursed. "Another thing, and I'll say this if they skin
me for it! You know De la Croix came out, fine and loud, to
demand a search for the lost will. And now he's changed his tune.
Why? Well, mighty soon, mighty soon after Daniel was in his
grave, several of us noticed that De la Croix became very
friendly with Relf and took a nice supply of Daniel's Negroes at
a low rate from the estate, and other favors too! They got
awfully close, that pair."

Myra and Will looked swiftly at Pierre Boisfontaine. The
older man inclined his head. "I've heard there were business connections between the two after Daniel's death. Beyond that . . ."

There was a long silence. Then Will asked a question that had
been on his mind for the past hour. "The property that Daniel
left—what would be its value today?"

Pierre wrinkled his brow. "Well, values change from year to
year. Much of it has gone up enormously, because Daniel bought
shrewdly. But I'd say that if Myra were to receive what was due
her it would be worth . . . oh, some twenty-five or thirty million dollars. About one third of all the property in and around
New Orleans."

Harriett choked over her tea as if it were indeed Creole coffee.
Myra and Will stared at each other; they were beginning now to
understand some of the forces against them. Célimène passed the
hot cakes.

CHAPTER VI

SETTLING again in the city, their first act was to equip themselves
for a longer stay. Old Josuah Whitney had observed that they
might have to be in New Orleans a whole six months; Myra
feared it would take longer than that. Summer had come with
a vengeance, while they were dressed for a far cooler scene. They

conferred with the amused Mme. Montagnet and returned with attendants and heavy bundles.

Later, hanging his two soft, cream-colored suits in the armoire, Will grunted. "Wearing one of them is like being a little undressed," he told her; "so comfortable you feel guilty." With a cigar in his mouth, he said, he could parade like any planter from up the Mississippi; and he stalked about to demonstrate. From her place at the mirror Myra smiled. She, too, felt odd. Her close-fitting gown of scarlet brocade, severely simple, cut to a new low point, was an innovation.

When she told Mme. Camille that, with her red hair, she thought the dress inappropriate, the modiste cast despairing eyes at the ceiling. For some, *oui;* but the shade of Mme. Whitney's curls permitted a pure, vivid hue like this; and Madame's white throat, the quality of her bosom, they cried for this costume. Myra had succumbed; now she knew she had never appeared quite like this before. Watching her, Will told himself the same thing. Was it the calm interlude on the plantation or, perhaps, the coming of the child that gave her this added warmth, this quality close to radiance? She had fully recovered from the recent blows; he suspected she had an inner vitality, an elasticity that he could not match.

As a finishing touch she applied a bit of pink cream to her full lips and then, half guiltily, smeared some on her cheeks. When Will grinned Myra protested, "The Creole women do it; look at Aimée Boisfontaine!"

He drew closer. "This Louisiana will ruin you, Myra. One peek, and Binghamton would call you a hussy for sure. But I'm not complaining about the effect!"

Soon they were talking rapidly of the things they must do as they dug into the case. Will's enthusiasm outdistanced hers; he didn't see how they could fail if they got together the evidence to back what Bellechasse, Boisfontaine, and Harriett Smyth had told them. Why, if only someone had tried in the first place!

"Look here," she told him. "I want to do part of this—a lot of it."

He made a grimace. "Anything reasonable, and legal, my dear." When Will joked she knew his spirit was up. As they went on, with suggestion and countersuggestion, both grew earnest. Despite Will's sanguine hopes, there were difficult tasks ahead. How to reach facts long hidden, how to prove what they felt certain was the truth, when people were strongly inclined not to believe it?

As Will left for the day she went to her own tasks. The previous night they had read with anxious interest a new letter from Josef Bellechasse. Her heart skipped a beat at his first line: he thought he knew where she might find Zulime; a friend had just told him she was living near Bordeaux, with one of her sisters, while the last sister was somewhere in Mississippi. He suggested several persons who might help locate the Mississippi place. Finally he had recalled someone, a Mme. Benguerelle, who was supposed to have strong information about Des Granges's bigamy. Perhaps Myra could find the lady in New Orleans. Once again Myra blessed the old man for his help.

She hurried through letters to the persons he suggested. Then she addressed a message to the girl Caroline, about whom she had just heard from Harriett Smyth. She hoped, she wrote, that Caroline would join with her in this effort to do justice to the name of Zulime Carrière, their mother. Would Caroline write to her, whatever she thought about this? . . . Then she turned to the last and hardest letter, the one to her mother. She tore up several efforts before the words sounded natural. Only recently, she wrote, she had learned who she was. She hoped someday to see her mother and talk over the matter with her. Meanwhile could Zulime set down some of the facts for her? As she folded the note, Myra offered up a prayer. How much more she wished to ask—things she could not set down on paper, perhaps not put to Zulime at all. . . . She left the house.

It had just stopped raining, and the streets were lakes. She discovered why New Orleans called its squares *islets;* they had become literally that. As her carriage rolled on, Myra gazed out pleasantly, inspecting the low-arched buildings, watching the crowds. At one corner a handsome young Frenchman stepped forward, beaver hat in hand.

"Pardonnez-moi, mademoiselle?" He wanted to know if they hadn't met before. Myra's face wrinkled. "Perhaps New York or Philadelphia?" The stranger smiled. "Perhaps either. Does it matter?" Lifting his brow, he opened the door. Startled, Myra slammed it shut. His dark face flushed. "So? Then Mademoiselle shouldn't give an appearance of amiability that she doesn't have!"

Almost instantly Myra's strong hand reached out and slapped him across the cheek. Amazed in his turn, the Frenchman stood stock-still, the mark of her five fingers outlined across his olive skin. A dangerous sparkle came into his eye, and then it faded, to be replaced by a satiric grin. At once she ordered the driver to proceed. Certainly, she thought to herself, she could have handled the situation with greater finesse. What she had done might have brought on a duel with Will. Well—she clamped her lips together—hereafter she'd keep her good spirits strictly to herself!

An unexpectedly familiar face loomed a few feet away. It was her foster brother, Horatio Davis. They had not met in years; knowing of his estrangement from the colonel, she had thus far hesitated to approach him. The tall youth had become an impressive man, barrel-chested, strong-chinned, a dignified figure beneath his high hat. Stopping the carriage, she called to him. Gravely he moved to the gutter edge and took her hand.

"No, I can't ride with you. Yes, I heard you'd come to New Orleans, and why." A firm line of annoyance formed from the end of his nostrils to a point below the lips. Then his composure vanished, and he bit off the words: "You know that what you're here for is useless. You can no more prove what you claim than —than I can jump to the moon!" Passers-by craned their necks; quickly Horatio quieted. He went on more coolly, "Don't you understand the impression you're making? Think of my reputation, the way——"

"Then it's your reputation, not mine, that concerns you, Brother Horatio!" Myra's curls trembled as she shook her head. "You don't care that people lie and cheat——"

"For God's sake, can't you understand you're heading against everything that counts, every interest——"

Myra put her hand on the door. "That's all you have to say to me?"

Horatio stood there on the banquette, looking fiercely into her face until she signaled to the driver. For hours afterward she remembered the expression.

There was surprise, too, when Will walked into the court offices that morning. Attachés exchanged glances; everyone had been certain the trouble over the Clark estate was finished, and good riddance. With a slight gesture of disdain an assistant brought out the records. After a few minutes Will stood before the chief clerk. "At least four or five of these papers have disappeared since I was last here."

"Indeed?" The light-lashed eyes had a mocking note. "What proof have you for such an accusation?"

"What I've seen myself."

"I'm afraid that wouldn't be evidence against the reputation of this office." The mocking expression had changed to defiance. Will knew he had been defeated, at least on this count. With a curt nod he went back to the table; without letting the papers out of his sight, he penned a message and summoned a passing black man. Returning from her trip, Myra was soon at his side. He had divided the papers into two piles, and she applied herself promptly to one of them. Her appearance here drew quick attention. A woman in such a place—where men worked! Other attendants poked their faces in the doors, until Will looked up. He had taken off his coat; the sight of his husky shoulders, muscles outlined beneath his sweat-dampened shirt, removed their smiles.

At midday they chose to forego their meal; by closing time they had a full working summary, with notes. Will handed the clerk a sheet. "For your reference, here's a list of every document now in the collection. If any are missing the next time, I expect to call on the judge. And good day to you."

Just outside the building Will was halted by a swarthy, hulking individual. Though his countenance showed signs of excesses, the man was obviously one of great physical power. "Whitney! You!"

Handing Myra their notes, Will asked her to walk ahead. As he faced him the man cried in a surly voice, "You're beginning to make a nuisance of yourself, you hear?" He grabbed Will's arm. "You're a damned outsider, coming here to disturb things with that woman of yours——"

His words were interrupted by a fist against his mouth. Bleeding heavily from the lip, the fellow landed a heavy blow against Will's shoulder. Myra stood back. The crowd thickened; she knew she must hold tight to the papers in her hand. Over the heads of the men she saw the sleeve of her husband's coat. His fist connected squarely with his opponent's chin, and the big man went crashing to the banquette. Will pulled him up by the lapels;

he could not speak. As the stranger rubbed the blood from his face he gave Will a glare of hate. Will shoved him back against one of the stuccoed arches, then spat in the gutter and led Myra away.

Mme. Montagnet, their tiny, deep-voiced landlady, gazed in dismay at Will's rumpled costume and the dark bruise on his chin. She had never discussed their case with her guests; it was a matter beyond her concern. Now her mouth trembled; such a thing in the house of a Montagnet! Then suddenly her face changed; without a word she brought warm water, bandages, and an antiseptic. Still not inquiring about the cause, she folded her arms over her narrow chest and made an observation. "New Orleans, it is not a tranquil city. A person must watch out for himself." From a resting place in the hallway she drew forth a long cane.

As she pressed the catch a narrow blade appeared. She thrust it into Will's hands. "A man seldom has to use his sword cane. Just let him carry it; people will know." For the first time they had concrete evidence that Madame liked them. Will protested; it was too valuable a thing to give away. Madame shrugged. "My husband Télémaque, he used it for years. Twice he saved his life because it was in his hands. What use has a widow for a sword cane, I ask you?" With that, she left.

Will made the cold, precise weapon flash through the air, and winked. The day hadn't gone altogether badly; at least they'd been able to hit back, hard.

The next day, and every day after that, they took it for granted that Myra should accompany him. They had so much to do, so much to find. . . . Hunting, sorting, copying, asking questions, they worked steadily, often until late in the evening— so late that Mme. Montagnet, bringing coffee, would deliver a lecture to the effect that even the young needed rest. Despite their peculiarities the Creole was warming to them by perceptible degrees. On one such evening Myra thought of Daniel Clark's Negro Lubin, and asked her: "How would we go about locating a Negro who lived here years ago? A slave."

Eulalie Montagnet's eyebrow raised. "Find the master, certainement."

"The master died."

"Then you might as well look for one black bean in a bushel-ful."

When Myra told all she knew of Lubin, Madame said she would inquire. Two weeks later she approached them at the breakfast table. "I have a bit of intelligence for you." They lowered their forks. "The *nègre* Lubin, he has not been in the city since long years. When M. Clark died Lubin did not get his freedom. He had to stay on at the warehouse with M. Relf. Then they accused him of steal——"

"But Lubin was my father's trusted servant!"

Madame made a gesture of deprecation. "I say only ac-*cuse*. And him a *nègre* . . ." In silence they finished the meal. A little later Myra's finger, tracing through records of sales, stopped halfway down. Lubin had been sold by Relf and Chew, with a parcel of others, to an upriver plantation owner.

"Why don't we write?" she asked.

"That would be foolish. Slaveowners don't like outsiders tampering with their property."

Finally she convinced Will, and they dispatched a note to the master, a M. Fortier. A reply arrived within a week. By a coincidence the family had just been talking of old Lubin; he had died not quite a month ago, after having been with the Fortiers a full nineteen years—an admirable servant, skillful, respected. When he first came, there had been a few difficulties. Lubin had complained that someone (M. Fortier did not recall the details) had "tricked" him; he had been promised his liberty, then denied it; there was also trouble because his wife, who had been with him a long time, had been sold away. One never knew, of course, how much credence to give such stories. At the beginning Lubin had tried to kill himself, then he had run away; it had been necessary to have him whipped once or twice. After that he settled down.

Will took a sheet of paper marked "Lubin" and drew a long, straight line through it. Myra shuddered. Her father's faithful worker, whom he had attempted to reward with his liberty! They had missed him by a few weeks. How many others were they losing to time?

Her fingers touched the wooden crucifix that she carried inside her waist—the only thing that she had of her father's. Once more she thought of Señora Perez's prediction; much as she wished to, she could not put it out of her mind. *Would* she win in the end, as the old woman had said? But would she first know suffering and pain, more pain than she had ever experienced? Then the old woman had told them—how had she put it?—that Will would not be there. Could it be mere foolishness, a crazy crone's mutterings?

"What is it, dear?" Will's look was worried.

"Nothing—just cobwebs in my head." She smiled, or tried to, and went back to work.

One day soon afterward her finger paused again, at the name of De la Croix. This was the business deal between him and Relf and Chew, only three months after Daniel's death. The chevalier received seventy-five slaves for a payment of eighteen thousand dollars.

Will's lips puckered. "Must have been mighty poor grade." He checked the list: "Flibo, Meroke, Dorian, Janin, Phoebe . . ." But no, most of them were prime hands, between twenty and forty years old; they should have fetched far more, tens of thousands more! Here was something else: Daniel's contract for digging the Canal Carondelet had been transferred to De la Croix, who had received five thousand dollars of Daniel's estate for accepting it. Will spent a day of inquiry; when he returned there were sparks in his normally calm blue eyes. "That was a very valuable contract. De la Croix should have paid for getting it!" Such were the transactions between Relf and the man who had changed his mind about Daniel's will.

Only slowly did they come to a full realization of Daniel's vast holdings. He had foreseen that New Orleans would grow upriver and beyond, into the far outskirts, the old outlying plantations. He had sensed that sugar and cotton would skyrocket with the years. Discovering a particular piece of ground on their map, they stared hard. Formerly it had been wasteland at the edge of the French city, and along it, on Daniel's property, Daniel and Colonel Davis had operated a ropewalk. Now it was Canal Street, dividing line between the French and American sections, thickening with shops and offices. Many were certain that Canal would become New Orleans' main street and the richest property in all Louisiana.

"Don't you see"—Will's voice rose—"if we establish your claim the heart of the city is yours—and also all those acres of the finest residential ground, and the plantations too. If we ever get a judge to listen . . ." Myra stirred; it was a breathtaking prospect. So many people, so much land. One third of all New Orleans, including Canal Street!

Early that summer, as they prepared to leave the court offices for the day, Myra skimmed over an inconspicuous document—the will of Daniel's mother, who had died some years after her son. Myra's eyes fixed on a sentence: "Further, I do give, devise and bequeath to my granddaughter, Myra Clark, natural daughter of my late son, the sum of two hundred dollars, to purchase a jewel as a remembrance of me." A stricken expression crossed her face as she showed it to Will.

The street noises, the rumblings of cotton drays and cries of food hawkers, were suddenly louder. Quietly they walked out. "Natural daughter of my late son . . . Natural daughter . . ." Had they been spending all their time in pursuit of a mirage? The meal was a dreary one; Dieu-Donné, responsive to all their moods, grew solemn with them, and Eulalie Montagnet watched sadly from a distance. Upstairs they faced each other in the twilight.

"Myra——" Will began.

A knock summoned them to the door. There, all flounces and ribbons, beneath an overpowering hat, stood tiny Harriett Smyth. She shrilled a greeting and raced on: "And how goes the case? I'm in from the country and had to find you. Hope I'm not—— Why, my dears, what is it?"

The story of the day's discovery was quickly told. Harriett could be a good listener when, as sometimes happened, she had no desire to talk herself. At the end she wagged a thin finger at them. "I could've told you something like this would happen. Don't you children realize the opposition just got there first? Daniel told me he never advised his mother about you; until he could announce the wedding, he wouldn't do it." Her voice sharpened. "Remember, the family were never here; whatever Relf and Chew told them they took for gospel. Doesn't the record show that?" She lifted an angry chin to Will, and he nodded. "And look at that provision in the will—a small jewel, a token. Myra, you were about fourteen then. You'd been in the same city with Daniel's mother for years. She'd probably never heard of you till the end. It looks to me—and I'd tell God himself—that this was suggested to her, for a reason!"

"You mean to——"

"To blacken you, in case you ever acted obstreperous. The way you're acting now, my dear!" There was triumph in Harriett's shiny face.

"Of course," Will spoke slowly, as if debating with himself, "this really isn't a mortal blow to us. Mrs. Clark's statement would have no value as direct evidence; it would be her opinion, based on what was told her. Someday"—his face became sterner —"maybe we can put some people on the stand and find out just how this happened."

"And I hope, young man, I'll be there to watch 'em squirm!" Harriett's chuckle sounded over the apartment. They joined her, and outside Dieu-Donné brightened up as well. Ascending the stairs, Eulalie Montagnet also smiled. They seemed such nice people, these Whitneys, in spite of what they were doing. She sighed as she wondered how her good mother would regard her —harboring a woman who went into court with a case! Shaking her head, she made her way to the shrine in her room.

Eulalie's husband Télémaque looked down upon her from the wall—a beaming face perched atop a stout man's body, the drooping quality of his oversized mustaches contradicted by the merriment of mouth and eye. He had one hand inside his coat, like a goodhearted Napoleon; the other held his sword cane, happily unconscious that it had since passed to an American, and a Yankee at that. The portrait hung near the altar; the taper threw a wavering reflection on Télémaque, and often it looked as if his lips and fat cheeks were moving. Often, too, when Eulalie rose from her prayers, she appeared far from dolorous. She had been communing with her Télémaque as well as the saints, and she had found the right thing to do next.

The dead husband was almost a living member of the household, observing, judging, available for a bit of advice. Not a day passed without a reference to him: "Télémaque would not like that, no." Or "Télémaque, how he must be sighing tonight, for a crawfish bisque like this!"

There were not many bright points in Eulalie's life. "Ours is a declining family," she once told Myra in a burst of low spirits. Word had arrived that Tante Clarice had succumbed after a

long siege of "the nerfs," some kind of emotional disturbance.
"Our people, they came here in almost the same boat with Bien-
ville, just two years later," she explained. "But now . . ." One
by one the Montagnets were fading, dying as old maids or
marrying and failing at their duty—a single child, a mere pair,
nothing at all to show. Today they were clerks, holders of one or
two small, declining plantations on Bayou Lafourche. Eulalie's
house was, in fact, one of the most tangible of remaining
Montagnet assets. Yet all, male and female, had united in resentment of Eulalie's shame in taking boarders.

"No Montagnet ever did such a thing," Cousine Eliska
bristled. "At our plantations a room was always in readiness for
any passing stranger. Papa would die before he accepted a franc,
I tell you."

To this Eulalie responded, "No Montagnet ever starved either.
Maybe your papa would rather die than take an honest franc for
services rendered! For that matter, I notice that none of my
family objects to borrowing from me, taking dollars that I earn
by disgracing them, yes!" This brought tears and more recrim-
inations. Yet it was true; operating on a narrow margin as she
did, Eulalie was helping to support the other Montagnets. It was,
of course, only "borrowing," even if it involved the use of Dieu-
Donné and Céleste. They always returned the servants, at any
rate, Eulalie told Myra.

Will and Myra saw few of their fellow boarders. Almost all
were French—elderly couples in from Bayou Teche, an occasional male from up Red River, bourgeois families who were not
of the city Creoles. They came and went; sometimes they paid
promptly, sometimes slowly or not at all. "Why don't you call
the police?" Myra asked when Eulalie sighed over the last group.

"The police?" Eulalie's thin nose rose as if she had discovered
dung in her parlor. "Police have never been in this house. Ah,
how could I live when word got around, I ask you?" Myra had
no answer.

A messenger in livery, tiny basket in hand, appeared before
Myra, obviously on a social errand. He took out some fifty
notes; would Madame pick hers? Myra was amused; because
the slave could not read, the recipients would know about their
fellow guests in advance. The notes were sent by Aimée Bois-

fontaine; she and Pierre were to leave soon on a visit to Europe. As Myra might have heard, when most Creoles died they wanted to be buried along the Mississippi or in their other home, France. At any rate, could she and Will come the following Thursday night?

The streets about the Boisfontaines' town house were lined with carriages as they arrived. The many-paned doorway glowed with light; from inside came a buzz of voices. Aimée's uptilted glance at Myra's new red brocade gown convinced her that the modiste had been eminently correct. Along the hallway a dozen pairs of eyes fixed upon her, and several conversations were interrupted. A younger Boisfontaine took them in charge. Myra, always a social being, luxuriated in the scene—the velvets of the draperies, flowers and soft carpets, hundreds of candles in girandoles, the gurgle of wine falling into crystal glasses.

As she and Will moved from one grande dame or dignified seigneur to another, they heard names in a pleasant confusion: Soniat-Dufossat, Jaubert, Avart, Trépagnier, Lemonnier. Everybody was talking; it was a rapt, volatile crowd, enjoying the Gallic art of good conversation. Pierre Boisfontaine, shining in his evening elegance, whispered his compliments to Myra. She knew suddenly that with the possible exception of a sleek, oriental-looking brunette in a white shawl she was the handsomest woman at the party. At the last minute she had discarded the light face coloring she had tried; now, warm lips parted in excitement, she had no need of it.

In a moment she drew up short before a young Frenchman with an oddly familiar face. He bowed; Mlle. Boisfontaine introduced him, Philippe d'Abadie. Myra's head jerked upward; it was the one who had mistaken her expression that day! A mischievous light danced in his eyes; his mustache bristled. At Myra's side Will frowned, the beginning of a suspicious flicker in his gaze. But they exchanged only polite inconsequentialities. As she and Will started away M. d'Abadie raised his hand and touched his cheek, on which her fingers had been so boldly outlined that morning. Quickly, so that he would not see the answering laugh in her eye, she turned away. She was grateful to the man, anyway.

They almost bumped into two late arrivals. Will recognized Mr. Ainsworth, the stoop-shouldered broker whom he had met on his first day in New Orleans. With him walked his wife, a petite ash blonde with observant green eyes.

"You've never kept your pledge to bring this lovely young thing to see us," the older man chided. Will promised to remedy the situation.

"Sunday night?" demanded Mrs. Ainsworth.

"Sunday night," Myra answered.

Soon they were approaching a short, slender man, at least seventy years old, with a lightly hooked nose dominating a massive, gray-white head. An intent group surrounded him, and he was speaking solemnly, waving his hand back and forth. "Chief Justice François Xavier Martin, you know, of our Supreme Court," someone whispered. "The judge that's the historian too. A triumph for Aimée; he practically never goes out. First time I've seen him at night in ten years." The crowd parted for them; impatiently the judge stopped his discourse, squinted his heavily circled eyes, and thrust out a diminutive wrinkled hand. They had to guide their hands to his; he was nearly blind. After a bare nod he picked up the lecture. It dealt with Louisiana law. "Noblest of the nation in its origin . . . supreme wisdom of the Latin race, stern but just. Sternness, you know, is of the necessity." He paused. "You're from New York, Whitney, and a lawyer, I've heard. What's your opinion of these matters?"

Taken by surprise, Will was silent a moment. The old man's tone was that of an annoyed uncle; he seemed to be defying Will to say something intelligent. "I think, sir," began Will, "that a little understanding, a little mercy, aren't bad qualities."

Awaiting just such an answer, the judge pounced. "Ah, these debilitating philosophies! Where would we be——"

A servant interrupted with a plate. Dropping his talk, the justice attacked his food with savage energy. Bits of jellied meat dropped to the collar of his shabby suit, worn longer than most clerks would have been willing to keep it. Finishing, he gestured for a second plate, received it, wolfed through it with unabated fervor, and ended by using his bread to wipe it clean. "He likes food as much as money," a neighbor whispered to Myra. "Watch, he'll be telling us about thrift."

The monologue resumed. "Stability, honor, thrift—the basis of our well-being. Where would they be, Mr. Whitney, under a soft-headed system of laws?" In a moment he made a joke; he threw back his heavy head, his mouth fell wide open, but no sound came forth. Up went the head twice again, always in silence. Meanwhile Myra was learning more about the judge himself. "Once he gets his hands on a dollar he's never been known to give it up. They say in nearly twenty-five years on the bench he's saved every penny he made. . . . What does he do with it? Just keeps it. No pleasures, no wife, no expenses. His passion is his bank account." Myra was puzzled; eventually she discovered that most of Louisiana regarded with awe and amusement the eccentric chief justice and student. Having known stringent poverty as a boy, Martin had never forgotten the experience; the rules of his life were harsh.

"And how, Mr. Whitney," the judge rolled on, "does your Anglo-Saxon law treat such matters as—as bastardy?" He pointed a finger. "In Louisiana we give it the short shrift it deserves. No bastard"—his dim eyes swept the group—"can inherit anything, under any circumstances. Isn't that just? Mustn't we protect the basis of our society, the family?" Myra's eyes lowered. His choice of subject, the way he was turning in her direction—did they mean anything? She mustn't be oversensitive. . . . In a few minutes she managed to get Will away. His fingers caressed her upper arm in a message of reassurance.

They became separated; she found herself in the middle of a group in the main parlor. As she talked she grew aware of a flurry among the women in the hall. The shawled, oriental brunette left them and approached Myra. She smiled brightly, too brightly; her slanted eyes had an expression almost feline. "Mme. Whitney," she cried in a voice more than normally loud, "you mentioned you'd spent your early years here?"

"Yes," Myra responded in a tone weaker than she had planned.

Reaching her, the woman put her hand on Myra's. "Who was your mother, dear?"

A pool of silence widened about them. This was to be it, was it? Myra's eyes passed up and down the inquisitor, and her words came clearly. "Zulime Carrière. Perhaps you've heard of the Carrières?"

The lady ignored the question; she had one of her own. The fingers on Myra's arm tightened; she would not have been surprised to find them clawed. "And your father?"

"My father was Daniel Clark." Myra's cleft chin lifted; she surveyed the room as if in defiance. Jeweled hands, carrying cakes toward half-opened mouths, stopped in mid-air. Mustaches twitched as one pair of elderly male eyes met another.

The shawled beauty dropped her hand and gave Myra a slow smile. "Thank you, Mme. Whitney." Through an ice-like wall that seemed to envelop her Myra managed to nod in return. The circle of silence spread through the room and into the next.

Suddenly an elderly deaf man turned to his neighbor and cried out: "Daniel Clark, *il n'était pas marié!*"

The words rang out. They were taken as a signal for a nervous outburst of conversation. Several older women had decided by this time to make their disapproval clear. Myra found herself the target of a barrage of hissing exclamations; she caught occasional phrases: "And in polite society! . . ." "No shame . . ." To Myra's further horror, the two women who had been beside her quietly disappeared, leaving her alone in a group of red-faced men. Her eyes sought wildly for support.

Then Aimée Boisfontaine, only a touch of pink on her broad cheekbones betraying her excitement, came to them. Adroitly she started the conversation. "Cenas, we have forgotten cakes for Myra. One of you other men, fetch some wine for all of us!" With a skillful movement Aimée maneuvered Myra from her conspicuous position to a group of empty chairs at the side. Will joined them, giving her icy hand a reassuring squeeze; he managed a smile and an answer to one of Aimée's questions, but his face was quickly grave again.

By unspoken agreement the party was breaking up, long before the scheduled hour. A few came forward to bid Myra and Will adieu. Most of the others walked stonily past; they wore a look that Myra had once described as curdled gentility. Stiffly the small figure of François Xavier Martin appeared before her. The chief justice gave a cold bow. "Madame, if you do not mind my opinion—you have no case. You had best give up these— these ideas of yours." Without waiting for a reply he walked to the door. Then he had known all the time who she was!

Unexpectedly her gaze crossed that of the sharp-eyed Mrs. Ainsworth. For a moment the cotton factor's wife seemed not to know what to do; then she gave a chill inclination of the head.

Though it was a minor thing, after what had happened, it went deep.

As the door closed on the final guest Aimée turned back to the room, where Myra stood in the middle of the polished floor. She dropped her fan. "I—I'm sorry, Myra. . . . I had no thought . . . If only . . ." She stretched out her arms and took Myra into them. Two of the servants crept about the chamber, picking up crushed flowers, snuffing out the half-melted candles.

In their carriage Will reached over without a word and lifted her into his lap. Her head against his shoulder, she remained silent, rocking slowly back and forth. There might be other occasions like this, worse perhaps; she winced. Then in a moment a memory returned, a day out of her dim childhood: The red-headed man had comforted her when the pony threw her; but then he had shaken a finger and said, "If you want something hard, Myra, fight for it!"

She straightened up, and her voice regained its firmness. "Do you realize, Will, why a lot of those names were familiar tonight —vaguely familiar?" He stared at her in the dark. "Avart, Lemonnier, and the rest. You'll find most of them in the records of the succession. They're the families that have the property— our property." She gave a laugh that ended in a sob. "I'm looking forward, more and more, to getting back what belongs to me!"

As they prepared to leave the house the next day a mulatto brought a message. Mrs. Ainsworth had just remembered another engagement which she had for Sunday night; she was sure Mr. and Mrs. Whitney would understand. Will tore the note into pieces and tossed it in the fireplace.

That same day Myra dropped her pen as she came to a notation that had hitherto escaped them. Years ago one François Xavier Martin had bought a fair-sized property from Daniel Clark's estate, through R. J. Relf and Beverly Chew. A woman's voice rang in her ears from the preceding evening: "Once he gets his hands on a dollar he's never been known to give it up."

Judge François Xavier Martin of the Louisiana Supreme Court would be the final authority to pass on her claim. Will gave a low whistle.

CHAPTER VII

THE first of September arrived, but no leaves turned red or brown, and few fell from the trees in New Orleans. Now and then came a fresh breath from the fringing bayous; generally it remained as stifling as August, and Myra suffered from the humid heat as never before.

Her time was near, mid-October. She and Eulalie Montagnet had worked over her dresses, letting out waists, fashioning deceptive folds; eventually, however, it was evident to even the most careless observer that the child was well advanced. Though Will thought she should give up her visits to court, she continued to work at his side until the Creole landlady, reddening delicately, suggested that perhaps it would be best if Mme. Whitney stayed inside. . . . Eulalie Montagnet repeated the tale of the New Orleans belle who loved the opera so well that she went until the very last moment; and then, halfway through the performance, she caught her husband's hand. *"Cher,* I'm afraid I cannot wait for the ballet!"* But that—Eulalie lifted her shoulder—had happened in a *loge grillée,* slatted against the public view; anyway, it was only a story. . . . Already, she insisted, Myra should do nothing except rest in bed, think pleasant thoughts, and drink sugar water. The latter was the deep-voiced Eulalie's specific for almost everything from *"les nerfs"* to rheumatism and heart failure.

Myra compromised. She would stay home but would give her attention to their case. Her strong hands would not be idle. She sat at her *secrétaire,* listing, filing, bringing clarity out of the chaos of seven months of record making. Before long she was arranging summaries of all their documents; as Will shaved in the morning he outlined his day's plans to her. She searched out the pages he wanted, she noted points he was to hunt.

Once, when Will asked for a long file, to check the size of a plantation, she had the answer ready without looking: "Three thousand acres, in St. James Parish, twenty-five buildings, including slave quarters."

His brow furrowed. "How did you know that?"

She pushed a strand of hair from her eyes. "For you, Will, this is one case out of many. For me, it's *mine*." Thoughtfully he nodded.

She kept up her flow of letters, seeking contact with anyone who might know about the case, hunting information, names, dates. A message arrived from the Whitneys. The family were delighted about the baby, but they expected Will and Myra to have it where every proper Whitney should be born, in Binghamton. Colonel Davis's letter on the subject opened with sentimentality; her eyes skipped. By this time, he hoped, they had decided to give up their vain dreams; only pain could come. . . . He had just played chess with D. W. Coxe, who sent regards. That Coxe again! Someday, Myra told Will, they must see Coxe and talk with him.

There was still no reply from her mother. Had Myra's letter gone astray? Or—and she thought more and more of this—did her mother, after all, care so little? Will was growing restless; he had been basing his hopes on the certainty that before long he would be in touch with this central figure. Replies came to several notes by which she had tried to locate the Mme. Benguerelle mentioned by Josef Bellechasse—the individual who had information about Des Granges's bigamy; they were polite, but the correspondents could not help. No answer of any kind had arrived from the girl Caroline, her half sister, of whom Harriett Smyth had first told her. By this time Myra was certain she would never hear from Caroline. Harriett, in a recent letter, had passed on word that had come to her. Caroline had never been happy about the treatment that she received as a girl; she resented Myra and the better fate that had been Myra's, and she wanted nothing to do with her or her litigation. Myra sighed.

Yet Will continued to make progress. He was acquiring friends—several younger lawyers, one of the United States postal assistants, an amiable keeper of archives. They made suggestions and dropped casual bits of information. Relf was not a favorite among many who came in contact with him—especially those he regarded as beneath him in business or social rating. With the enlarged position of his later years, he maintained rules of association as precise as his dress and demeanor. From several whom Relf had treated with hauteur Will learned, for instance, that Daniel Clark's sisters were in poor circumstances.

Though supposedly entitled to large shares in the estate, they had received little or nothing. Old Mrs. Clark herself had had a difficult time before she died; Daniel's sister in Ireland was dependent on contributions from friends. Will shook his head; it all added up to an interesting picture.

For Myra the approach of the child was slowly pushing aside her other concerns. When she awoke her first thought was, How many more weeks, how many days? She lost her first annoyance at her ungainliness; she accustomed herself to sitting in a side position at the escritoire. Alone for hours, she passed her hands over her body; she had company, her child.

She and Eulalie came to know each other better during these days. Myra was not long in discovering that the establishment was operating on an even thinner edge than they had suspected; a few dollars less a week, and Eulalie lived close to terror. Once Myra found her on her knees, washing the parlor windows. The Creole crimsoned. "My Télémaque, how he must weep when he sees me now," she said, and rubbed her long, thin nose. The next time he made their regular payment Will increased the amount. "Ah, *non,* that is not right," Eulalie protested. Only when he assured her it was still less than most other places charged would she accept it, and then with misgivings.

Eulalie's family called regularly, to give her advice, reprimand her, and borrow from her. Myra caught glimpses of them— lean, fierce individuals with a certain Montagnet look, a sharp profile, long upper lip, air of impatient dignity. They walked stiffly, as if afraid of contamination by the untouchables that Eulalie permitted here. As they left, Eulalie's face was usually white, the muscles of her throat in a tight knot. Over and over they urged her to give up the boardinghouse and sell the place.

One morning there appeared not the usual one or two Montagnets but a delegation, five in an angry row. Eulalie faced them, apprehension in her eye. "Tante Eulalie," began Edmond, one of the younger members, "do you know the identity of these Americans"—as Edmond used the word it was a reproach— "that you're harboring?" Solemn at nine, Edmond had gained additional gravity with the years.

"Why——"

"We've heard the woman claims—boasts—that she's Daniel Clark's daughter. And you know——" He checked himself;

even to a widowed aunt there were things a Montagnet could not say.

"And I know what, Edmond?" Eulalie for once did not drop her eyes. She stared him straight in the face; more than that, she was staring straight in the faces of Etienne, Auguste, Elégeas, even the bald and bearded elder, 'Ti (Petit) Gilbert. There followed an uneasy pause; Auguste's eyes sought Elégeas's; Etienne nodded earnestly to Edmond.

"Have you finished, all of you?" Eulalie's chin trembled, but her eyes did not waver. "Then listen to me. I know what Mme. Whitney is—a fine woman, yes! I know what she stands for, what she is trying to get—justice. I know all her story, and I believe every bit of it." This was not entirely true; Eulalie still had a few misgivings about Zulime Carrière, but suddenly she could not admit them to her family. "If we turn against her because some things she says are—unpleasant, we should not be proud of ourselves!"

The men exchanged anxious glances. To think that Eulalie, of all the Montagnets, should talk so wildly, almost like one of those American women who expressed their minds on any subject! Elégeas, of the button nose and doleful eyes, rose. "We have also been pained by a certain astounding story. Some are claiming you have taken to doing part of your own housekeeping."

Defiantly Eulalie almost shouted: *"Oui, oui, oui!"*

'Ti Gilbert, his nervous hand almost massaging his hairless head, fixed his gaze upon her. "First a boardinghouse, then strange people, then housework too. I cannot think how we will break the news to Grand'mère Azéma!"

"Then for once say nothing. Keep it to yourself!"

This was family desecration; no Montagnet conceived of the day when he would not go to Grand'mère Azéma with the tiniest development. Eulalie knew her remark would be repeated to Grand'mère, with variations and elaborations, fifty times during the next few days. 'Ti Gilbert was backing away. "The family will not take this latest *grotesquerie* in good spirit. I'm afraid they will no longer regard you as a true Montagnet."

"Then tell them they need no longer ask money from me like true Montagnets! And *bon jour* to you!" Eulalie, almost weeping, flung out her words, then folded her arms on her agitated breast. As they slammed the door she ran quickly to her altar. She apologized to the saints, and to Télémaque as well, for her manners; but for the spirit in which she had made her remarks, she assured them, she was not ashamed—even that part about Grand'mère Azéma. Grand-père Sosthène, Azéma's late husband, always said Azéma thought herself God's wife and right-hand man! As she straightened up Eulalie felt much better. She had been hearing some talk of this thing called emancipation; she believed she knew now what it might feel like.

The next day was a restless one for Myra. Before retiring that evening she and Will sat together in the shadows behind the ironwork of their balcony. They watched a silent world of black and silver—the moon's gleam on the tile and shingle roofs of the French section, an irregular panorama of plateaus and triangles. The stars hung low; in the distance along the levee they could make out the tips of pale sails against the darkness. A light went off in the locksmith's shop down the street, then another near them. A man strolled below, using his pole to put out the street lamps. From the gardens about them rose a breath of night-blooming flowers, pungent in the warm air. Myra, her night robe around her, had let her hair fall loosely. Its dark cloud touched Will's uncovered throat, and he curved his body so that she could fit herself into his arms. As she sighed luxuriously they heard a carriage roll up, then steps on the banquette.

With a crash their door was flung open and three heavy-set men pushed in. They heard a cry: "There!" Myra, stepping into their room with Will, recognized the speaker as the individual Will had beaten that day in front of the Cabildo; she saw the same bloated face. As she watched, the man's companions leaped to Will's side. Caught by surprise, clad only in his nightshirt, he nevertheless fought hard. The thin garment was half torn away in the struggle; then he was being held to the floor and his hands roped behind him.

"What the devil is this?" Will shouted as they pulled him to his feet.

The leader, a cigar between his lips, grinned. "Just the deputy sheriff, Leander Blasco, and my men. Come to get you, Mr. 'Merican lawyer." He held out a paper that Myra caught up—a document calling for the arrest of William Wallace Whitney, on the complaint of R. J. Relf, for unfounded, libelous utterances damaging the reputation . . .

"It's a real warrant," Will told Myra. He managed to wheel on the intruder. "But why a sudden arrest, late at night, without a chance to arrange bond? In any other place——"

"To hell with all that!"

"My wife, in her condition . . . Can't you——"

"God damn it, you're coming with us, now! You'll find out what happens to Yankee meddlers!"

Will, his arms helpless behind him, tried to shake the man off. Blasco reached out and punched him in the mouth. Will dropped against the door, his lips bleeding; the others forced him forward down the stairs. Eulalie Montagnet, her face gray in fright, ran to Myra as she stood swaying on the landing. By the time Myra stumbled to the head of the stairs the carriage had rolled away. Her voice echoed down the empty hall.

In the carriage Will found himself wedged between the two assistants while Blasco sat opposite him and leaned forward. The man was trying to goad him—into what? "God damn you, you bastard, mother-loving Americans! You son-of-a-bitching——" The salt taste of his own blood, dripping from his lip, made Will cautious. The flood of insult continued, with variations; across the half-darkness Will looked steadily into Blasco's eyes. His silence stirred his captor to new annoyance. As the carriage bumped along Blasco moved closer, his knees against Will's bare ones. With a sudden ferocity the deputy pounded both fists into Will's stomach. The moan that followed made Blasco's aides guffaw. Another pair of heavy blows and Will sagged. One of the men caught him by the back of his hair and pulled him toward the cushions again. When the carriage rode past a street light they saw his stomach rise and fall against the shreds of his garment. Blasco was half standing in the carriage; his heavy boot lifted, then shot up, into the groin. A high shriek of pain came through Will's clenched teeth. Between throbs of torment Will found he had bitten through his lower lip.

"You Americans, you take anything, *hein?*" Blasco was demanding. Will's head hung down on his chest; his mouth twisted. "Say something, God damn you," yelled the deputy sheriff. "Look at me! I'll make you!" As Will pulled himself upward with an agonized effort his tattered nightdress fell open, exposing his powerful chest. Blasco motioned to his helpers; they thrust Will's head far back, so that his torso was arched outward. Blasco took a long draw on his cigar; the red end glowed. Then slowly, as if wishing to prolong the act, the man reached out and pushed the instrument into the flesh. There was a tiny hiss of burning skin and hair; Will's body wrenched violently, then went limp. The cigar had been snuffed out; Blasco took out a match, relit it, and thrust forward against one nipple, then the other. The performance went on and on, into the armpits and against the ribs, the face and then between the writhing legs. . . .

Meanwhile Myra dressed quickly and in desperation. "Who— who can I see?" she demanded of Eulalie.

The Creole wrung her hands. "Somebody with influence, somebody that——"

Myra's head rose. "The Boisfontaines! They're still at Terre-aux-Bœufs for a few days. I'll have to go right now."

"But—but the way you are! You'll injure yourself!"

"I've got to think of Will. I won't get hurt, I know I won't."

"And at this hour!" Eulalie fretted. What an excitement this would cause among the Montagnets—police and everything else; she tried not to think about them as she went on. "You couldn't get a hack to make the long trip."

"Then your old one. The horses are still here."

"It hasn't been used in months; and I gave up the coach-man——"

"Then Dieu-Donné."

"What will I do for service in the morn——" The look on Myra's face stopped her. "*Bien!* We'll manage without him." With startling alacrity Eulalie routed out the chattering black man and helped him with the vehicle; just before he and Myra went forth Eulalie whispered to the slave, "*Vite, vite!* M. Whitney, he is in trouble!" The Negro's eyes popped wide at this, and he cracked the whip.

They raced through the lower city, then along the highway paralleling the Mississippi. Carefully Myra braced her awkward body; she had hoped to sleep on the way, but she could not. She twisted her hands as she called to Dieu-Donné to speed up; her fingers touched the crucifix of her father's, which she had thrust into her dress at the last moment, and she prayed. The horses were going too fast, she knew; at that, the trip felt agonizingly long. She could not shake from her mind the cold rage that she had seen in Blasco's eyes.

Once or twice they made a wrong turn, and she moaned to herself. The clear night, the moon's rays covering road and trees in a wash of silver, seemed to mock at her misery. Rolling beneath the oaks, the carriage brushed the hanging folds of moss, as on the last trip to Terre-aux-Bœufs. But now the strands that dragged across the top were like fingers grasping at the vehicle. An owl beat its wings on the door, and she thrust her hand against her mouth to silence her cry.

At last, in the first gray-pink forewarning of dawn, they rode between the rows of oaks, along the cool, tunnellike passage, and ahead stood the white outlines of Bon Séjour. Never had any sight been so welcome. Padding forward, wrapped in his robe, Pierre listened without interruption, then told her he would be quickly with her. While he dressed, Célimène was dispatched to see that a carriage was prepared with fresh horses. Aimée, appearing in a moment, pressed coffee upon Myra and urged her to stay at the plantation. "You'll strain yourself, and then you know what'll happen."

With a deliberate motion, Myra rejected the thought. "I still have six weeks ahead of me. Will needs me; nothing will happen." Nor could she force herself to lie on the sofa as Aimée proposed, even for a few minutes. Sitting on the edge of it, she tugged steadily at a strand of her hair; there was no Will here to reprimand her.

Pierre Boisfontaine, neckpiece awry, drank his coffee standing up. Dieu-Donné, insisting that he be allowed to return with them, scrambled up to the carriage seat. Aimée gave her a fervent kiss, whispered, *"Bonne chance, p'tite,"* and they were on their way.

By midmorning Pierre had obtained a note from the superior judge, a friend. It fetched the sheriff, a stout, stolid individual with a carbuncle on his cheek, who admitted them through the prison gate. Pierre asked Myra to wait outside; she shook her head, and her eyes were firm. A consultation of attachés followed; then an attendant led them across a barren courtyard to the entrance of a line of cubicles. For a moment, at her first sight and smell of the building, Myra almost succumbed to nausea. The stench was of urine and human offal, of long-sweated, rancid garments and lice-ridden bodies. Stone walls drained a grass-green slime; tiny windows admitted streaks of light, barely illuminating floors lined with refuse. A man, bloated with some disease, rolled on his side, and a stream of yellow vomit poured out of mouth and nose. Myra stumbled toward the last cell.

There she could not suppress the cry that rose to her lips. Will lay on the floor, breathing heavily. He was naked, and his face, his torso, most of his body down to the ankles, had been burned and cut. His eyes seemed lost in a blue-green swelling; his lips looked like ripped flesh. Myra dropped to the wet floor and threw her coat over him. He stared blankly for a moment, then managed a grin. "No tears, madame. I'm all—all right." He said no more; she realized that only by strong effort could he keep himself from whimpering. By this time Boisfontaine had found a doctor. "First, a cigar for me," Will demanded. Myra went to the slit of the window, and while the doctor probed, Will smoked away. The tobacco's effect was soothing; he had something on which to bite when the pain tore at him.

The doctor swabbed and bandaged and then brought the report: "Three ribs broken, a badly sprained leg, deep cuts and bruises and"—he dropped his eyes before hers—"a number of interior injuries. He has a strong constitution. Still, watch him."

The sheriff looked sheepish. This had happened before he arrived, madame; the men said M. Whitney struggled something fierce. Myra lowered her head; she was afraid to speak what came to her tongue. She smiled at Will. "No tears." Pierre arranged to have Will brought into the sunlight, where she sat beside him for hours. Over a low wall, in the women's section, they were inspected by a group of harpies—unruly whores, besotted brawlers, who screamed first at the silent man, then at Myra. "Lady, he got you in a fix, but you sure came back at 'm!" "He gotta marry you now!" After a while, disgusted at the lack of response, the women retired, with anatomical suggestions to the two of them.

In the meantime Pierre went to work. When he saw the bond fixed for Will's release his face clouded. Thirty-five thousand dollars! He'd never heard of so exorbitant a figure. Pierre himself pledged twelve thousand; calling on a cousin, and using a great deal of persuasion, he obtained another five thousand. The day was gone. Returning to the prison, he told Myra; she blanched but thanked him.

The next day Pierre again gave up everything else for this new task. Two men agreed to contribute; then, finding that the case involved Relf and Chew, they withdrew. No banker, no cotton or sugar factor, would help. Hearing the word, Myra slumped in her chair. Pierre called on the judge who had signed the order; he could not bring himself to repeat that dignitary's comment that Myra herself ought to be confined in jail with her husband. Still Pierre continued to try.

A week dragged along, a second began. Will improved, but only slowly. She was up before each dawn at Eulalie's, swallowing a quick breakfast under Dieu-Donné's anxious eyes; she was with Will until dark, when he was taken back to the green walls. Though she watched she saw no more of the deputy Blasco; it was hinted to her that he had the favor of higher-ups and was used only for "special jobs."

When the inmates discovered that Will was a lawyer he was surrounded by a woebegone circle—debtors, anxious for advice. Some were in prison because they owed as little as twenty dollars. According to the rule, a debtor must be held no longer than ninety days—provided he repaid the cost of his "board and lodging," which might run more than triple the original amount. If he could not do so he stayed on, increasing the total "bill" with each day.

One such fellow prisoner, Victorien Badeaux, had been sent here for a few dollars, but he had already accumulated a liability of a hundred. An excitable rooster of a man, he asked Will again and again whether he would ever "see free." He was a former fisherman from Bayou Lafourche, a descendant of Canadians who had come to Louisiana in great bands during the preceding century. During a year of bad times he had come to the city, opened a cake shop, failed, and, to his amazement, ended behind bars. A "Cajun," as the term was beginning to be used, Victorien was half naïve, half cynical; while he knew many things that astounded Will and Myra, his credulity about others appeared no less amazing.

At one moment he would launch into a tale of water-front amours that would have done credit to a French Casanova. "An' w'en they fin' that man sank in the river, wid big rock in 'is middle where 'is gut' once be, ev'body, they know. 'E been playin' wid his las' udder feller's wife, yes! But who they can blame it on, I ask? Hard to pick one man outa every husban' in the Third Municipality!" Then, a few minutes later, Victorien would talk of the simple bayou life that he had left, among the crab nets and fishing boats, with tiny sugar-cane patches at the water's edge. He had a family of eighteen brothers and sisters on two houseboats, and he spoke nostalgically of the leisured existence they all enjoyed: rollicking country dances, fishing fleets, family *rassemblées* or reunions. Yet when Myra asked Victorien if he wanted to go back home he gave a mirthless laugh. "Me, I like the city." He grinned like a wicked cherub. Gradually they were adopting Victorien, or perhaps he adopted them; in any case his drolleries helped pass the days.

Arriving one morning, Myra was met at the gate by Victorien. "'Allo. 'E not feeling well," the Cajun told her in a mournful tone. "Lot of people got fever." She hurried through the stinking corridors to the room at the end. His brow flushed, Will lay restless on a filthy bed. Through the hole of a window Myra saw the tops of the cypress trees in the adjacent swamp; she shuddered every time she passed the mosquito-filled place with its shallow water like black ink. Now she remembered a saying she had heard at the court: one way to wipe out the whole criminal population of New Orleans was to let it stay a little while in Parish Prison. Down the hall a door clanged, and attendants shuffled past, carrying a twisted body.

How she got out of the place she did not know. She found herself inside a carriage; the driver was impatiently clicking his tongue. Again her eyes met the high line of cypresses above the swamp. "Mr. Relf's office," she called.

Knees trembling, holding her coat about her ungainly body, she hurried through a paneled doorway. God help her, she must succeed. The clerk took her name and returned promptly. Mr. Relf was not in, ma'am; the youth went back to his ledgers. Myra started out, then whirled about and pushed open the door. Seated at his desk, R. J. Relf looked up at her with his pale blue, bulging eyes. There was nothing in his small, expressionless features to indicate that he even saw her; he remained silent, his precise hands upon the papers before him. The room, with no item out of position, reflected the man, his costume spotless, the last thin hair of his head in place.

"I've come to ask something from you," she began. He made no reply. Still standing, pushing the damp red hair from her face, she rushed on, describing Will's condition and the fever epidemic at the prison.

Before she had finished, Relf lifted his well-manicured hand. "Madame, I've brought certain charges. The law's course——"

"But the law isn't taking its course! He hasn't been tried. That bond, it's enormous. It's——"

"The matter's with the courts." The tone, like the words, was unconcerned.

As he turned away her hand touched his sleeve. "Please! Daniel Clark did a great deal for you. If you had any affection for my father——"

A red flood suddenly passed over Relf's pale face. "Your father? I'm not convinced you're Daniel's child, legitimate *or* illegitimate! Perhaps a—a natural child"—he made a gesture of disdain—"and perhaps born of Zulime Carrière. But as for Daniel——"

Myra pulled back, eyes blazing, her scar glowing against the dark flush of her face. "You hate me, don't you? The sight of me reminds you of what you've done—the things you'd like to forget!" Her hand was beating against the back of the chair.

"Madame, your conduct is unladylike. . . ." He waved his hand as if to remove the offensive sight from his eyes.

"You do what you've done, and you object to my *manners!*" She was close to hysteria.

Cool again, Relf opened the door. "I don't want to hear any more of this tirade."

At once her own rage disappeared. "One more thing. If my husband dies you'll be responsible. And I'll come back, Mr. Relf, and kill you." Her voice was calm, almost matter-of-fact. "This isn't a threat. It's simply a statement of what I'll do." As the clerks blinked up at her she walked across the wide room to the street.

Eulalie Montagnet bustled into action in her kitchen, collecting, wrapping, tossing out directions. Dieu-Donné and the mulattress Céleste scurried about, lifting jars into the carriage, shoving aside the cat, gathering bottles and, not least, an ample mosquito net. A little later Myra and Eulalie made their way past the prison guard and into Will's cell. The many cases of illness and the fear of contagion had prevented even the usual perfunctory cleaning; the smell was like a slap in the face. Cockroaches crawled all about them; a rat slipped from one of the untended beds. With Victorien Badeaux to help her, Eulalie lifted the half-conscious Will, tossed aside the foul bedclothes, and replaced them; over him went the bar, held up by strings to the ceiling.

Rolling up her sleeves, Eulalie tossed bucketfuls of water over floor and wall, killed roaches, and mopped. Once or twice she thought of the Montagnet clan and the new storm that must be impending; her lips drew tighter and she worked the harder. Myra tried to help, but Eulalie put her in a chair. "Think of yourself too," she ordered in her deep voice. "Whatever you do here, do it sitting."

Pain darkened Will's clear eyes; his brow was like a hot stone, and his newly healed lips were cracking. Angrily Myra wiped the tears from her eyes; reaching over with a firm gesture of her capable hands, she tore away Will's linen and washed his body. Even through the thick walls the climbing sun made the cell stifling. Still she had to keep Will well covered, rub his skin and apply warm clothes—anything to make him perspire.

Close to delirium, Will shifted from side to side. "Case next week . . . Ask judge if he can't . . . Myra, don't look so sad." His mutterings told of his unspoken fears that she would be hurt by the setbacks, his agitation that she would suffer, and, too, his own nagging doubts. "Can't prove . . . Maybe other lawyers could do better . . . Got to try harder . . ."

Eulalie interrupted him with precision, filling his mouth with a mysterious black brew, adding a little lemon juice to help keep it down. Myra sank her head in her hands. Had she been wrong in urging him in the case as she had? Suppose they finally lost it all? Suppose—and this thought pursued her—suppose Will never got up from the narrow bed? . . . When night came Myra refused to leave. The warden shook his head. Ma'am, it was against every rule; they had to lock the cell, and she'd be there with seven men, pickpockets, murderers, crazy people. "I'll

still stay," Myra told him. Eulalie hurried in with an extra bit of
equipment—the sword cane. Returning to the cell for the evening, several of the inmates cursed at the sight of Myra; others
grinned. "When they roll that carcass out, deary, don't forget
I'm here. . . ."

Little Victorien Badeaux, the sword cane in his hand, was
standing before them. "Anudder word out o' you' God-damned
dirty t'roat', and I slit you from gullet to navel!" A snicker came
from the back; Victorien swerved around, and the men quieted.
They remembered what had happened to a river boatman who
had harassed the Cajun; he had gone home to Kentucky minus
an eye and with a permanent limp. Through the long night Victorien sat up in his bunk, sword cane before him. Once Myra
glanced up to find lines of cockroaches moving in the moonlight
from the ceiling along the strings to the bed; the top of the bar
was a crawling mass. She shrieked when she reached for a bottle
of quinine and touched a sluggish rat. Two others, silhouetted
against the window, watched her in curiosity.

Will's condition fluctuated; the fever ebbed, then it flared.
Myra was shocked to see how his flesh was losing much of its
firmness; his ribs showed through his scarred chest. All about
them men were dying, six and seven and eight a day. Guards
deserted their posts, and no visitors called; all New Orleans
recognized this as a pest spot. For another ten days Myra stayed
within the prison walls. She could discover no facilities for bath-
ing, for cleaning her teeth; there was a single loathsome women's
privy. Her dresses became sweat-ringed, her eyes grew bloodshot
for lack of sleep, and her hair, untended, turned lank and stringy.
Everywhere she met evidences of vermin. The men scratched at
their beards and armpits and stomachs and drew forth objects
that they inspected and cracked. Unclean, odorous like the rest,
Myra eventually realized that she, too, had attracted the para-
sites. But she had made up her mind; she would not leave her
husband alone in this charnel house. Now, at least, he was better;
though his injuries had told on him, the doctor conceded that,
with continued attention, he would recover.

Then the scrawny Victorien Badeaux, her helper, took sick.
Myra put the sword cane beside her, took out more linens, and
began to care for him. She must do double duty now; and she
swallowed additional cups of Eulalie's coffee. Through all of the

nights she managed to keep awake, though she was often peril-ously close to the slumber of complete exhaustion. Perhaps it was the nearness of death and the knowledge that this woman might save them if they were the next to fall sick that deterred the men about her in the cubicle. At any rate she went unharmed.

The sheriff touched her arm, and she jumped. Pierre Bois-fontaine came hurrying in. "Good news at last. You and Will, you know, are citizens of New York. My lawyer appealed to federal court, and the whole case is transferred; you can leave now."

In the early morning light Will was watching them and under-standing. He managed a thin smile. As she went to him he re-proached her with an attempt at his former lightness. "No tears, Myra. No tears." As he said it his own voice broke.

After a minute or two she whispered to Will, and he nodded. She walked to the sheriff's side; they wished to pay Victorien Badeaux's expenses, to obtain the debtor's release when he was better. The Cajun, rolling over on his side, tried to raise his arm. He succeeded in getting his finger to his lips and threw her a small kiss.

At that moment, with a moan, Myra sagged against Pierre, and he caught her before she fell. In his arms he took her to the carriage where Aimée Boisfontaine waited. At her first glimpse of the contorted face Aimée cried out, "Quick, it's begun. The baby——" Myra, whimpering, her face glistening with beads of sweat, was tearing at the cushions of the seat.

An hour later, as Aimée and Eulalie stood at the doctor's side, the child was born. A healthy squall broke through the cloth in which the squirming object was held. Wiping his face, the doctor spoke judicially. "A bit premature, but sound—and strong, I'd say. Look at that red hair. She'll be as healthy as her mother."

Myra moved her head. "A girl. That's nice. But this will dis-appoint Will, won't it?" Eulalie started to say something, then checked herself. "Still, we have time. . . ." Myra's eyes, tired as they were, had a glow. Signaling to Eulalie, she forced a smile. "You didn't believe me, did you, when I said he—she wouldn't come till everything was ready? . . ." Her head fell back, and she slept.

CHAPTER VIII

FOR both Myra and Will the doctor advised rest and milk, slow walks and thin broth. Eulalie Montagnet, with a firm nod, added her own recommendations of well-stocked gumbos, gravied shrimp dishes, and, eventually, visits to the opera. For several weeks neither patient left house or courtyard. Myra's strength and color returned more rapidly than Will's; his weight remained low, his skin drawn tightly across his high cheekbones. They sat in the garden with the baby by the hour.

At the beginning they talked little, drinking in the sun and bright air of early fall. Frequently they dozed, and woke to find the light changed, their bodies crisscrossed by shadows from the balcony ironwork above them. Then they moved and lay back once more. And over and over they talked of the child, whom they promptly called Rhoda, after Will's mother. Myra could never forget Mrs. Whitney's deft intercession, which had shifted the scales in her favor back in Binghamton.

Myra luxuriated in her motherhood, in the small pink form beside her, dependent on her for the fulfillment of all its wants. She knew a physical delight as Rhoda pulled weakly, then almost savagely with her lips at her mother's breast. Myra watched as the child nestled against Will when he picked her up, and held tightly with her fist to his big finger. Shafts of light, slanting across the courtyard from the high walls, outlined Myra's face; though still weary, it showed a serenity, a new contentment. She had regained her beauty; her heavy brown eyes, with their lashes that sometimes seemed red, were calmer than Will had ever remembered them. Her hair, dropping over her shoulders, was a circle of flaming color. One of her first chores, as soon as she could manage, had been to wash her curls; only then, she said, could she feel rid of the accumulated grime of her stay in the prison.

Peace lay about her like sea waves. Her life was complete here; she, her baby, and her husband were together on an island of their own, behind barriers of brick and greenery and their private contentment. The days went by in changeless rhythm. The rain dropped in cascades at the windows, the roof steamed, and the sun rose again.

Then all at once Will asked if Myra wanted to see what the rest of the world was like, if it was still there. Her pulse quickened as she dressed; had she ever thought a mere trip outside would mean so much? She grew sadder at the sight of Will's shrunken chest; but when he slipped on his trousers, three inches too big at the waist, the two of them burst into laughter. From an upstairs window beside Rhoda's cradle Eulalie watched them as they left. Looking up at her Télémaque on the wall, she asked him if they didn't look like a fine young couple.

Walking slowly, they picked a path toward the river. All roads led to the levee; the water front echoed to the rolling of barrels and the piling of cotton bales on the open wharves. They inspected the steamboats, with their curved lines soaring arrogantly over the oily water, their sets of twin smokestacks ruling everything about them. Lines of men and women were crossing gangplanks, inquiring about the departure. Urchins screamed, comparing the *Memphis* with the *Annabelle*.

It was boom time, Will reminded her. Louisiana rolled in a prosperity such as neither the Creoles nor the first American newcomers had anticipated. The nation was pouring its wealth down the great river—flour from the West, hides, whisky, mules, pork on foot, freshly killed, salted, or smoked. Sugar planters, cotton growers, wheat growers apparently had one goal: the city in the river's bend. For nearly five miles the stream was lined by packets, ocean-going vessels, flatboats, arks of every shape and size; and still men fought for additional space. "New Orleans is gonna be the biggest city in the world 'fore it's done!" a merchant was shouting to a cotton factor as they passed; it was not difficult to believe him.

Will's eye caught a name painted on a pile of produce. It was that of a man who held twelve thousand acres claimed by Myra. From then on they listened as clerks called out other produce and their destinations. "They might almost be reading a list of Daniel's holdings," Will murmured; silently she nodded. In a few minutes they found themselves near a private steamboat landing; the vessel was ready to start. Evidently it bore a group of merrymakers bound for a visit to a plantation below New

Orleans. Under an overseer Negroes were lifting aboard hampers of wine, delicacies in bottles, and piles of game birds. A tinkle of laughter came to their ears; glasses in their hands, a circle of men and women were drinking a toast on the deck.

At the edge stood the owner, giving final instructions for the departure. They recognized M. Avart, a glittering figure at the Boisfontaine party of last year. His eyes met theirs, and he looked through them. The vessel pulled away, trailing a thin spume against the sunlight; in a few minutes it was lost in the brown distances of the Mississippi. The name of Avart was one of the most conspicuous in their files; his estate, among the great ones of the Mississippi, had once been Daniel Clark's. They left the levee to return home.

They stopped before a double file of Negroes, chained loosely together, in the charge of a heavy-boned, sweating trader in flesh. At the corner the bedraggled row stood silently in place. Two or three feet away waited a haggard young brown woman, with a baby half asleep in her arms, the marks of tears striping its face.

"Look, it's hardly older than Rhoda," Myra whispered.

The woman, catching the words, turned pleadingly to them. "Buy me, please, buy me!"

The trader hurried up, suspicion in his eye. "You want the whole lot?" he shouted at Will. "All of 'em or none!" Will was impassive. "Then no tampering!" the man yelled, and started the line moving again. The black woman, staring back at them, nearly fell to the ground. The baby in her arms was crying.

"Will," asked Myra, "isn't there a shorter way home?"

A little later they sat together beside Rhoda's cradle. Myra saw again the bales of cotton, the hogsheads of sugar that might have been—that should have been—hers and their baby's. Her fingers touched Rhoda's soft reddish hair, and in her ears echoed the spiteful words of the Chevalier de la Croix, the sneering remark of R. J. Relf: Perhaps Myra was born of Zulime, but he hardly believed she was Daniel's daughter, "legitimate *or* illegitimate." Her child was stigmatized no less than that black baby she had just seen, for whom the world's gates were shut; and Rhoda would remain stigmatized until the mark against her had been removed.

Fondling the child, Will's hand touched hers. "I think we're ready to go back to the case, don't you?" he asked. She nodded. Their interlude in the shade had come to an end.

Once again she moved between courthouse and home, working over records while Will added to them. Before long he applied himself to the matter of Jerome des Granges's conviction for bigamy, which they were assured had occurred in New Orleans back in 1803. The keeper of the archives met him with a question: was that under the Spanish period, which lasted most of the year, or in the last part, after the Americans came? "Under the Spanish," Will replied with certainty. But the Spanish records proved to be mere flimsy fragments; the bulk of them had been taken by departing officials. "Where would they be now?" Will asked. Madrid, maybe, or Mexico City, or Havana—or lost forever *peut-être*. This was a bitter disappointment.

"Still," Myra told him, "something may happen to help us prove there was a conviction. So many people say it happened. . . ."

Meanwhile she turned to the problem of the mysterious Mme. Benguerelle, to whom Josef Bellechasse had referred her—the one who knew about Des Granges's bigamy. Myra had a "feeling" about her; the greater difficulty they had in locating the lady, the more certain she grew that the search had importance. She asked Eulalie if city directories were printed here. *"Oui,* for several years," the Creole answered; she had all of them to date. Quieting Rhoda, Myra ran through the pages. Only in the earliest publication did she find a M. Benguerelle.

Eulalie's interest in the case was increasing by the day; it was she who proposed that she accompany Myra to the address. No one there had heard of the Benguerelles. Eulalie went to the next house with her, and then to others all about the neighborhood. One woman thought the whole family might have been wiped out by yellow fever. Ah, *non,* those were the De Lauréals, another answered.

Several householders showed suspicious faces to Myra, *une américaine.* Had Eulalie not been along, doors would have been slammed. At the last cottage a white-haired matron nodded with marked reserve. *Non,* she couldn't help. Somehow Eulalie turned the conversation to food, and the two women exchanged recipes for stuffed crabs. Then the matron remembered: Mme. Ben-

guer*elle,* they meant? Eh, that poor thing, how she had had bad
times with her husband dying that way in a convulsion! The last
they heard of her, the widow had moved to the country. Maybe
Abbeville, somewhere in the 'Takapas country. That, Eulalie
explained in her deep voice on the way home, was the French
prairie section of Louisiana, "filled with cattle and Cajuns." As a
city Creole, she adopted a patronizing air toward the Cajuns. In
any case Myra now possessed a clue.

As they approached the house again Eulalie received a shock
of her own. Her Tante Burdette was walking toward them with
umbrella, shawl, and market basket. She lifted her mourning veil
—she had been in mourning now for twenty years—to greet
Eulalie; then she sighted Myra and dropped the netting with an
abrupt motion. Angrily she stalked past Eulalie, uttering not a
word; at the corner she headed in a direction away from the
market. Eulalie understood well where Burdette was going: to
Grand'mère Azéma. Eulalie had stepped further into the shadow.
Myra wondered why Eulalie snorted, then started to talk over-
brightly about the new contralto at the opera.

New Orleans' brief, damp winter arrived. The thermometer
showed forty degrees, yet the penetrating cold felt far worse
than that would indicate. Overnight the stately rows of poinsettias that lifted their scarlet faces below their window became
withered, headless stalks. But the evergreens maintained their
same friendly luxuriance, and soon the bite went out of the
wind. For days at a time, through December and January, Myra
sat with her papers in the sun-washed courtyard while young
Rhoda fixed solemn blue eyes on her.

As they went over the records one afternoon Will suddenly
shoved them forward and sat staring glumly. "They tell us a
lot"—he frowned—"but not enough. Any fool can tell they've
been picked through. We have only what they think it won't
hurt too much to let us see. These can't be all of Daniel's papers.
His letters for instance; he must have exchanged thousands; we
have a handful."

"Well, let's demand them!" Myra's hand slapped down, so
hard that Rhoda looked up with a cry. Myra ran to her, laughing, and Will joined them. As the baby sank back, pacified, they
returned to the desk. Will's pen raced across the page; when he

came to the word "demand" he underlined it and winked at Myra.

After a dozen revisions they finished a petition to the probate court. Hearts pounding, they pushed through the crush of people before the Cabildo; this was an important moment, the filing of their first direct action against the enemy. It called on Relf and Chew to produce Daniel's real will, to bring forward every record, paper, and letter found in Daniel's office and house, and finally to tell exactly, item by item, what they had done with the Clark estate.

Coldly the attachés took the petition. At once Will and Myra felt a new wave of hostility against them. Stories had been spread. There was the man, Whitney, that got himself kept in prison three weeks. And her—did you know she threatened to kill Mr. Relf and Mr. Chew and their whole families? Yet thus far most Orleanians, even when the peculiar Whitneys were pointed out, paid little heed. It was all farfetched; nothing would come of it. Just ignore the two Yankee adventurers. They'd go away.

That seemed to be more or less the opposition's policy. If Will expected a direct answer he was quickly enlightened. First the distant heirs of old Mrs. Clark had to be served, in Pennsylvania, Missouri, Mississippi, and Ireland; the judge had to name attorneys to represent them, and he did so—the brothers Duncan. Months went by; the Duncans reported difficulty in reaching the heirs and asked patience. The court, Myra told Will irritably, had been very patient already. Exasperated, he finally filed a motion, calling on Relf and Chew to present the papers without further delay. After a few weeks the judge signed the order; a date was set. When the day arrived nothing happened; the Duncans were out of town.

The Duncans returned; after weeks spent in getting other affairs in order they agreed to appear. They still did not produce the papers, but came to argue. Will complained. "Your honor, the court has already ordered the papers brought in!" The judge's look indicated that the young man was, alas, impetuous; he suggested a new date to go into the whole thing. With a groan Will agreed. On that morning the Duncans strode in, again without the records but armed with an answer.

After further study, the attorneys announced, they concluded that most of the documents sought by the Whitneys must have been among the "private papers" of Daniel Clark. These had never been inventoried; they must have been lost or destroyed by dampness.

Will, his face livid, jumped up. "Why *weren't* they inventoried? Who decided what should have been inventoried and what shouldn't?"

Lucius Duncan looked bland. "There's a customary procedure in these matters, my dear sir."

"Yes," Will snapped. "But there's also a customary procedure in honoring a dead man's last will, and *that* wasn't followed!"

Mr. Duncan passed his eyes disdainfully over the rude "American." The judge frowned. Mr. Whitney should not indulge in such insinuations, if he pleased.

"But, your honor, I'm not insinuating these things. I've charged them, in so many words!"

The judge lifted his spectacles. The young man was tiresome. "Case continued."

Winter melted before spring, the precocious early spring of these alluvial lands. A few weeks later Myra greeted Will at the door of their apartment. "Anything wrong?" he inquired. She shook her head, then smiled hesitantly. He was alarmed; Myra seldom faltered about anything. He cupped her cleft chin and saw a tear in her eye.

She sniffed, "I didn't want to cry. I wanted to say it—well, simply. I'm going to have a baby again."

Will enveloped her quickly and fiercely. He'd work harder than ever. This was enough to make him go out and challenge every damned man in New Orleans, one after the other! At that moment Myra's body grew taut beneath his hands, and she stared up into his inquiring face. "This time there'll be no mistake. It'll be a boy!" If will power meant anything Myra would manage it.

Spring gave way to the flaming summer of the semitropics. In the courtyard, beneath the ripe red and yellow blossoms, Rhoda crawled on her blanket, thrusting fat fists toward the flower beds, gurgling when she saw the big-toothed Dieu-Donné, accepting Eulalie as a substitute if Myra had to leave. The Whitneys enjoyed hours of wandering about New Orleans in the slow-falling evening. They walked by Congo Square, to drink sweet beer while they looked on at the Negro dances. They visited the bird shops, filled with tropical imports in strange feathers, or sweet-voiced blue captives from the bayous; they stopped for sherbets sold by proprietors who knew no word of English.

Regularly they stood about the Place d'Armes for the parade of fashionable and unfashionable, the belaced and berouged, the torn and dirtied: richly clad Negro women of light color, "*placées*," kept by white men of wealth and taste; priests, hunters with skinned frogs slung over their shoulders, stout Germans in ill-made garments, Norsemen whose light hair and eyes looked oddly out of place, a few Turks, Malays, Scotsmen, and Mexicans. Myra liked the casual spirit, the high humor of the crowds. To her the city seemed more childlike than wicked, pagan rather than venal. Sometimes she could not tell just how she felt about New Orleans, for her emotions changed from day to day.

Crossing Canal Street one morning, they chatted together until Will spied a short, rather stumbling individual with a worn black hat. Almost instinctively Will put out his hand to help him. The ancient shook his head with petulance and drew away. Only then did they realize it was François Xavier Martin, chief justice of the Louisiana Supreme Court. They could not be certain he had recognized them; but they had been the only people near him, and they knew his hearing to be extraordinarily keen, his memory for voices phenomenal. It was difficult not to conclude that the crotchety old fellow had shown once again what he thought about them.

At the beginning of the mild fall they read in the *Courier* of a "gala performance" scheduled in the American section. They bought tickets and thought no more about it until, at the door of the tent, they discovered what it was—a dog matched against seventy-five rats, "New Orleans size," a "contest to the death"; afterward a tiger set loose against a bull. They stopped there; it was one phase of New Orleans life they would not investigate.

As they turned away an excited figure bobbed toward them. Victorien Badeaux, the Cajun debtor, explained that he had resumed his cake selling.

"Why don't you go back to Bayou Lafourche, where you'll be out of trouble?" Will asked with an effort at sternness.

"Ah, the country—wonderful," Victorien agreed with a laugh that broke his face in half. "Me, I always like it. But New Orlean', that got the interes'!" His eyes sparkled. "In country you fish. In city thing' happen."

Myra sighed, and Victorien winked archly at Will. A saucy girl, about sixteen, walked by and made a pert behind in Victorien's direction; it was not difficult to guess what Victorien found so absorbing in New Orleans. Quickly Will changed the subject.

"Damn, but I glad to see the bot' of you," Victorien murmured. "I look, but nobody tell me where you be. I got informations for you." They remembered that Victorien had been the prison gossip, repository of all news and rumors. Now he hurried on. He sold cakes to clerks in the lawyers' offices, and he had been hearing things. Putting a stubby finger to the side of his nose, he whispered, "Those mens Relf and Chew talkin' about somethin' big-big they gon' do agains' you. Somethin' bad, from yo' own fambly." It was all he knew.

Solemnly Victorien shook hands and returned to his cake selling and other activities. On their way home they wondered whether to give credence to the little man's talk. When Dieu-Donné met them with a letter marked Wilmington, Myra felt a premonitory twinge.

It came from Marianne Davis. She was writing without the colonel's knowledge; she had thought this new trouble would pass, but it was only growing worse. What had happened was this: the newspapers had printed stories about the filing of her case in New Orleans, and people had made unfriendly remarks about the colonel. Where had he been when her rights were taken from her? The New York *Evening Sun* ran an article reflecting on him; he wrote an angry reply. People agitated the colonel, asking him questions on the street; he was talking increasingly against Will, saying that Will encouraged Myra to make a fool of herself and also of him, the colonel. . . . Myra and Will stared; could there be a connection between this and Victorien's rumors?

Another matter, equally important, was puzzling Myra. Her mother had never answered. Did it mean so little to Zulime that she would maintain a blank silence? Try as Myra would, a fear recurred. Perhaps, then, some of the things they said . . . Each time, furiously, she cast aside the thought and felt ashamed. Now, with this new word, she spent many sleepless nights; when she dreamed, it was of terror and flight, of Daniel and a dark, faceless figure, her mother Zulime.

Arriving in court a little later, Will walked casually to the record book, then bit his lip. Relf and Chew had applied for authority to take a statement from Colonel Samuel Boyer Davis in Wilmington. Only recently, they said, they had been informed that he possessed facts flatly contradicting claims made by the Whitneys. A friendly fellow attorney sidled up to Will: Relf's office was very much excited. Relf had received an urgent letter from a man named Coxe, who had had a talk with a Colonel Davis and reported Davis willing to be examined by them.

After that Will had difficulty in concentrating on his work; he had to go home and talk to Myra. He had hardly arrived when Eulalie joined them, and her face was a warning that she had more bad news. Pointing with a nervous finger, she handed him a copy of *L'Abeille*. Mr. Relf had taken up his pen to refute certain misstatements; he wanted it known that he and Mr. Chew had had a difficult estate to handle, had done only what was proper, and so on. Then, without apparent emphasis, Relf struck hard. As for the allegation that Mrs. Myra Whitney was Daniel's proper child—even her guardian, Colonel Davis, had never made that claim. Once, in fact, Davis had filed an action asking that she be given an allowance as the illegitimate daughter of Daniel Clark; and the New Orleans court had refused to grant it.

Myra put her hand to her mouth; her hands had become cold. Anxiously Will argued, "This is only Relf's side. I'd have to see the evidence before I believed it." Secretly he was disconcerted. Was Colonel Davis turning against them, as it appeared? Before both of them passed a rush of confused reflections, impressions they had hitherto suppressed, questions that suggested themselves with insistence. Bellechasse, Boisfontaine, and the others had always looked odd and made cryptic remarks when the colonel was mentioned. . . . He himself had been so evasive. Why had he shown such anxiety for Myra to remain ignorant of who she was? Had he ever gotten anything, money or property, that should have gone to her? Or—was it true that she was illegitimate, and the colonel knew it all the time?

Slowly Myra spoke. "It's up to me to ask him for the full

story. I've already waited too long to do it." After a moment she took up a sheet of paper and began a careful note. Had Daniel ever said Myra was not his lawful child? Had the colonel really filed such a document as Relf claimed? What part did D. W. Coxe play? When Will called out several more questions she shook her head. "Anything beyond this," she told him with an effort at a smile, "would strain the colonel's temper—such as it is."

October passed into November. The new baby was due late the following month; Myra must remain about the house, and she was glad of it. The happenings of recent weeks made her anxious to be back in the island of isolation that had been hers for a time. The colonel must answer her letter satisfactorily or . . . She tried to turn her mind from the alternative. Little Rhoda lay pink and plump and fragrant before her; the dimpled face responded to every familiar sound. For a time Myra was able to forget most of her other concerns and concentrate upon the child.

But a sudden cold spell meant that the baby had to stay indoors, and she grew cross. Myra, once more awkward, carrying the heavy new weight before her, had her own moments of unreasoning annoyance. Once, when Will did not respond immediately to a question, she tossed her comb to the floor and broke into tears. "You—you care more about the case than you do about me!" she cried, and sank her face against the baby's long robe. In Will's arms she apologized. It was simply that she was worried; nearly a month had gone by since they had dispatched the message to Colonel Davis. In silence they watched the wind as it swept the leaves across the dim winter courtyard, and then Will returned to his desk.

Poor Will; he still showed, in his eyes, in the set of his shoulders, the effects of those shattering weeks in prison. He never discussed them, or the man Blasco, but the libel case against him was still pending. With an effort she went to the armoire; she and Eulalie had to let out several more dresses. Before her lay the flowing brocade—her major extravagance in New Orleans. She had had that one opportunity to wear the elegant creation, at the Boisfontaines' reception. She suspected it would be a long time before they would be invited to a similar event. She dropped the dress into a drawer and banged it shut.

As Will prepared to leave the house she called out: "Didn't you bring some lawbooks when we came from New York? Let me see them." Pulling on his shirt, he glanced inquiringly at her. He'd heard that women in her condition had whims. Well, she'd had very little time for that the last time, had she? He complied. For several days she said little; the baby remained on one side of her, the pile of books on the other. Then she asked questions: a mandamus, how did that work? Where would she find material on inheritances?

Soon she was frowning. "Why, a lot of what's in these books doesn't apply to New Orleans at all!"

He touched her under the chin, and a glint came to his blue eyes. "That, my dear, is an observation I can second!"

After a time Myra asked less and talked more, sprinkling her conversation with legalisms; she was at the late freshman stage, when a little learning became a heady thing. Will thought her new interest a good thing; it took her mind off other matters. Only Eulalie did not approve. To her it was hardly natural for a woman to be behaving that way at such a time. Will grinned. "Eulalie is worrying that the *bébé* will arrive with a petition in his hand, demanding his right to fresh milk!" Eulalie crossed herself. *Dieu Seigneur,* if Grand'mère Azéma heard that . . .

The doctor, phlegmatic for a Creole, was not entirely satisfied. There were a few—a few physical involvements, he was afraid. The last birth had come somewhat hurriedly, a little prematurely, hadn't it? More important yet, Madame appeared a bit *distraite*. She must not be agitated.

Christmas came and went. For the Creoles, Eulalie explained, the day was mainly a religious occasion. The true time for holiday pleasuring had always been New Year's, *Le Jour de l'An.* On the latter morning, in the city and among the plantation people, children would gather about holiday trees for gifts from Papa Noël, the big-bellied visitor in red and white; throughout the day families would visit from house to house. "Ah, the New Years I have enjoyed!" Eulalie told Will and Myra. "One year Télémaque and I, we went to thirty houses and still had some left on our list." But things were sadder now for her and the other Montagnets. She could think kindly of the family even if half of them no longer wanted to speak to her. On *Le Jour de l'An* all who had differences were supposed to shake hands and make a new start. Eulalie sent out word that if they wished to call she would have coffee and eggnog for the Montagnets.

Early that morning Eulalie carried in a tiny tree, a pretty trinket, and set it up near Rhoda's cradle. The baby gurgled and reached for the gay red hangings. Her mother's face had no spark of response; it was a grim New Year's Day for Myra. Her skin seemed swollen. The new baby was overdue; twice already they had thought the time had arrived, but the pain had gone. Now Myra lay on her back, her breath coming quickly. Will moved nervously in and out. Eulalie, sitting beside her, counted her beads and kept an ear cocked for the Montagnets at her doorbell.

Dieu-Donné waited in the kitchen, the bowl for the eggnog freshly polished, the cream and liquor, cinnamon and other ingredients at hand. One o'clock, then two, then three. Céleste went to the door; no note there, no hint from the Montagnets. *Certainement,* Dieu-Donné murmured, somebody was coming? Céleste shook her head; white people could be very peculiar. Upstairs Eulalie's mouth was held so tightly shut that it whitened. Well, let them stay away.

The baby snored, and the coal settled in the grate. Then, of a sudden, a stifled cry broke out from the bed. Myra tried to sit up and fell back. When Eulalie caught her arms Myra threw them off.

"Will! Will! Please——"

With a peremptory gesture Eulalie shoved him aside. *"Le docteur.* He said to call him quick. Waste no time now!" Leaving hat and topcoat behind, Will clattered down the stairs; Dieu-Donné abandoned the empty eggnog bowl and found a carriage. The doctor lived far across town; Will gave the driver an extra coin to spur him.

At the doctor's house the dark maid shook her head. *"Il n'est pas ici!"* Like everybody else, the doctor was on a round of social calls. Scowling, Will took down several addresses and ran back to the hack.

At the first residence Will waited feverishly at the end of a queue of men and women, all crying playful greetings to each other as they approached the threshold. Greens and poinsettias draped the doors; ahead was the buzz of a hundred or so voices in conversation, a hum of music, the emanations of perfumes and mixed spirits. Men were tossing canes and beavers to one side, women removing gloves and pelisses and scarves. The host, puzzled at Will's expression, had difficulty in understanding him. The refreshments, monsieur, were straight ahead. Oh, the doctor? Gone a half hour ago.

Before the next house Will learned that the doctor's carriage had just rolled off. At the door of the third the servant grinned. *Le docteur* was over there somewhere. Will was intercepted by an affable young man, who sought to steer him to a pair of smiling girls. Past an enormous silver bowl from which a foaming mixture was being ladled, Will pushed toward a group of men about the whisky bottles on a sideboard. He saw, or sensed, lifted eyebrows. Let them call him anything they wanted, American barbarian, lout, vulgarian . . . At last, there the man was. Recognizing Will's drawn face, the doctor let out a sigh. He reached for a second glass, thrust it into Will's hand, and guided him forward. As he donned his coat the doctor took his last sip. Only when they were inside the carriage did Will realize he still held his own glass. "Down with it," the doctor ordered. Will swallowed.

The doctor was still at work two hours later. As Eulalie hurried in and out, Myra's whimpers echoed through the building. At the half-opened door Will caught a glimpse of Myra's contorted body, and Eulalie slipped past him with a lament: "The *bébé*, it will not come. *Sainte Vierge, Sainte Vierge!*" Before she went back she knelt, her apron to her eyes, at her altar.

In the silence that followed, Will heard the opening and closing of doors in the neighboring houses. Streams of men and women moved in and out on New Year's visits, laughing, exchanging greetings and good-bys, while snatches of music spilled into the street.

Downstairs the bell rang; a slow, steady step ascended. Will looked up into the face of Colonel Samuel Boyer Davis.

"Colonel! I'm glad——"

"You mayn't be glad when I'm finished, you bastard!" In a rage the colonel pulled out the letter they had sent him, and threw it in Will's face. "You're responsible for this—this quizzing! You take our daughter from us, fill her head with wild stories, bring her to this hellhole of a city——"

Will's hands tightened. Unthinking, he lashed back. "You fraud! Myra wouldn't be here, trying to get her rights, if you'd looked after them the way you should! You have a hell of a nerve and a hell of a lot to explain. And now you're playing with the other side, aren't you?" His face was twisted in bitterness; he realized suddenly that he had been shouting.

Samuel Davis had turned crimson to the roots of his white hair. He raised his hand and slapped Will across the face. Just as he did a wild cry reached him, and Eulalie ran out. *"Messieurs, messieurs,* are you crazy? She's heard it all, and she's so bad off ——"

For the first time Samuel Davis knew that Myra lay in torment a few feet away. A call, low and weak, came to him. Pushing open the door, he stumbled to her side. Her hand, moist with perspiration, was clutching at the sheets. He caught it, and she stared at him through her pain.

The two men stood together at her side. She gave them a brief look of satisfaction, and the colonel sank to the floor, burying his head against the pillow. Then she was racked by agony again, and the doctor looked up. *"Messieurs,* will you go outside?"

In the hallway the father and the husband sat down; now they talked quietly together. In the middle of their conversation a squall broke forth, and Eulalie came to the door, her face wet but beaming.

"It's another girl." Her eyes went to Will. "She says she's sorry."

CHAPTER IX

OVER the rooftops poured the winter rain, silver streaks changing direction with the wind. Along the canyonlike street iron balconies dripped steadily; the big metal key before the nearby locksmith shop swung back and forth, back and forth. With an anxious glance at the clock, Myra settled against the pillows.

She had prepared everything with care for Samuel Davis's first visit since New Year's Day; already he was an hour late.

Eulalie had produced a Creole *déjeuner,* full-scaled and abundant. The silver with the Montagnet monogram, brought from downstairs, shone in the reflection of the fire. The coffee urn, misted by the brew within, sat cheerfully on the table near the bed. Over Eulalie's shocked protests Myra had diluted the brew to meet the colonel's taste; regardless of New Orleans standards, matters had to go well today. Finally Will had been well cautioned; he and the colonel having already exchanged apologies, there must be no further hostilities. At the edge of Myra's thoughts moved an uneasy fear. By the time this meeting was over their case might have collapsed.

The bell rang three times, imperiously, and the colonel stamped upstairs, to stand dripping from beaver hat to muddy shoes. A hack driver had tried to rob him because the day was wet; he had told him to be damned, and walked. Eulalie ran in; the colonel would not only die of pneumonia, he would also ruin her room. Come with her! The tiny woman's deep voice rumbled. Mutely, recognizing for once a superior determination, the colonel obeyed; soon he stole back, enveloped to his chin in a lavender blanket. (At least, Will told himself, Davis couldn't stalk out in a rage.)

The colonel took his pastel bulk to the bedside. Julia, the new baby, yawned and thrust a tight fist at him. "Just like her father," he mumbled to Myra, who took care to regard the remark as a witticism. Dieu-Donné entered with the platters, his eyes bulging at the man about whom he had heard many tales. Outside he whispered to Céleste, "Look' jus' like a fat fella in pink, 'im. Do 'e always dress like that?" Myra had remembered the colonel's taste for broiled fish at breakfast, and omelette and liver; Eulalie had added warm rolls, brioches, fresh fruit, a bowl of preserves, and pitchers of cream. An hour later the colonel purred. After a third cup of coffee—best he ever tasted in a French house, anyway, he assured them—he leaned back. The moment had arrived.

"First off"—he belched politely—"if anybody claims I'd testify Daniel didn't marry Zulime, he's lying. As I said to you, Myra, I couldn't swear he *did.* Talk came to me about a private marriage; Daniel himself never told me anything to make me think a marriage didn't take place. That's all I know about that."

He looked at Myra, and she was certain he was telling the truth. His anger kindled. "I never authorized anybody to tell Relf how I'd testify. I met D. W. Coxe on the street, and he asked a lot of questions; now I know why he was so curious!" Will's heart rejoiced; the opposition had overstepped itself there.

Settling in his chair, the colonel went back to his earlier days, his first meeting with the ambitious young Daniel; his sailings as captain of Daniel's vessels; his transfer to New Orleans, where Daniel had set him up in several businesses. From time to time the colonel had heard of Zulime, but he considered this none of his business. Then Daniel had requested him to arrange a place for Myra's birth, and eventually Myra was taken into the Davis household.

Here Myra, her own child at her breast, asked in a low voice, "My mother—did she come to see me at all?"

For a full minute Davis hesitated, staring into his cup. These things—things he had never planned to tell—were hard to say. "Yes," he finally whispered. "Every chance she had. Daniel was afraid there'd be too much attention if she came openly; she called late in the afternoon or at night. She brought gifts and clothes she had knitted, and Marianne told me she cried and cried over you." He fell silent, uncertain how to proceed. Myra's eyes moistened; a part of her burden of doubt and hurt was slipping away. Those stories that Zulime had been hard, and cared nothing about her, they weren't true after all! The flicker of the fire, directly opposite her, was reflected in her face; slowly it took on a softened, dreamy quality.

The colonel resumed. One morning, when Myra was about five, he met Daniel on the street. The merchant was in an agitated mood, on the eve of a sudden trip North. Having heard that his partner Coxe, in Philadelphia, was embarrassed by bad speculations, he was afraid his own fortunes would suffer, and he wanted to protect Myra. He gave Davis property valued at thirty thousand dollars; then, a few days later, a letter arrived from the Balize, last stopping place at the river's mouth. Writing hastily, Daniel forwarded a message to General Hampton of Houmas plantation; in case of mishap to Daniel, Hampton was to give Samuel Davis various large notes for Myra's benefit. Then in Philadelphia Daniel thought yet again of Myra, with a third directive to Davis—a packet with titles to still other properties, all for her. When he returned, however, Daniel took them all back; he had other plans.

"Then he told me you'd receive his full fortune." The colonel nodded firmly. "You'd carry on his name and his ambitions. You'd be an important woman; you'd travel and enjoy a splendid life. Sometimes we thought he was a little extravagant in his talk; every year seemed to increase his affection for you." Then the war with England began, and Colonel Davis felt he must go North. When he told Daniel he intended to take Myra with him the two men quarreled. Daniel wished to take Myra; the Davises, too, wanted her. "But we'll give her up if you're ready to announce her as your child," Davis told Daniel. By this time, however, Zulime had gone North and married Dr. Gardette; Daniel could not have claimed Myra as his daughter without starting a great deal of gossip. They argued back and forth; after a time Myra's father, calming, admitted that perhaps it was best she continue for a while with the Davises. Before they left, Daniel gave them as much as he could readily spare in those unsettled days—a small fund of two thousand dollars to be kept in a bank, the interest to be used for Myra's education. He would send more from time to time, to add to the nest egg. And they said good-by.

But no further word arrived from Daniel; within a year he was dead. Colonel Davis was now fighting in the war; he did not hear of Daniel's death until months had passed. Hastily he wrote to business friends in New Orleans. Their replies eventually arrived: no, Daniel had made no mention of a child in his will.

"We didn't know what to do, Marianne and I." The colonel leaned toward her, his hands pressed together, almost as if he were begging for her understanding. "I was far away; nobody mentioned Daniel's later will. All I knew was that Daniel had said he'd make you his heiress. Relf and Chew, as a matter of fact, told the city that the estate was practically insolvent. Then, while I was still in uniform, I received a court notice. Relf and Chew were suing me for the two thousand dollars Daniel had provided for your education. I wrote right away, explaining that the money was being held in a bank, accumulating interest for you; I told them I was sure they had too much respect for Daniel's memory to do this.

"They acknowledged my letter, and they went ahead and claimed the money, these friends of Daniel Clark!"

The colonel slumped in his chair; through the silence that followed the rain beat in new fury against the window. And so had gone the last dollars that Daniel had managed to put into Myra's hands, or within her reach. There were few things that the methodic Mr. Relf had forgotten.

As Myra stared into the fire Samuel Davis resumed. Not long after the Davises settled in the East a woman knocked at the door. It was Zulime, now Mrs. Gardette. "She asked to see you, Myra, and how could we refuse?" the colonel asked. "She called several times, and kissed you and played with you. Once, when she said good-by, she became almost hysterical. We got frightened finally." After a moment—the memory was harsh—he added, "We never forbade the house to her. She must have sensed how we felt; she stopped her visits for a time. Then suddenly she was back, with a proposal that was like a slap to us. She wanted to—to take you."

Myra's hand gripped Will's until it whitened. Her lips opened, but no sound came. Then her mother had tried to get her, and she'd never been told of it!

Slowly Colonel Davis shook his head. "Myra, Myra, you don't blame Marianne and me, do you? Zulime had two children by Dr. Gardette, and stepchildren to care for. How would you have felt if we had suddenly told you you weren't ours and given you to a strange family? When unfriendly people asked questions, how would Zulime have explained you?" His hand, outstretched toward her, fell. "And also—you must know this—Zulime was never practical; she never thought ahead. Everything considered, weren't you better off with us? Even she finally agreed and we didn't see her again for months."

A silence followed. Myra, her handkerchief to her eyes, averted her head. Awkwardly the colonel resumed. "Then one day I was walking on the street with you. I saw Zulime and started to turn the other way, but she hurried over. I was frightened; suppose she said something to you, something she shouldn't say? But she didn't; she only touched you and looked hard at you several times. After we said good-by I took you to the corner. Waiting for the carriage to pass, I glanced back. Zulime was still there, staring after us. She stood on the sidewalk, her hands at her sides, just looking."

The colonel's face, seeking Myra's, had an expression of dull pain. "You don't hold what we did against us, do you? It was for your happiness. . . . You remember the schoolmate that ran to you one day with the story? It was a good thing Marianne was with me when I heard; I could have gone out and strangled the sniveling thing. We managed to change schools, but I was always afraid other people would tell you. Maybe that was one reason I hated to lose you—to Will or anybody else." Once more Samuel Davis held out his hand, and now it trembled. Myra took it and nodded, seeing again her mother, standing alone, watching as she walked away.

Samuel Davis's face hardened. "And this brings me to one of the things that decided me to come here—the way R. J. Relf has twisted the truth." Will looked up sharply. "After the war ended I took up my affairs in the East. Then I heard rumors, vague stories that Daniel had tried to recognize you, Myra, before he died. I returned to New Orleans for business reasons. Bellechasse had gone to Cuba, the Boisfontaines were then in France, but one or two people told me what they suspected. When I tried to speak to Relf and Chew, I found that these two book-keepers had risen high in the world. Once I had given them orders; now they haughtily refused to discuss the matter. I talked to several attorneys and turned the case over to a man I once called my son, Horatio." The colonel's brow clouded; his differences with Horatio had not grown less bitter with the years. "I wanted Relf and Chew to produce in court every paper or record regarding you.

"Well, I went up Bayou Lafourche for a few weeks, to handle a land transfer. When I got back I found a suit had been filed in my name—but not the suit I wanted, not by any means! Horatio had gotten along with Relf and Chew; I suppose they told him what they wanted him to believe. In the petition he called you Daniel's natural daughter. When I saw this, I wanted to thrash Horatio. I'd never used any word like that; Daniel had never said it. I had the suit recalled."

Will jumped up. "But Relf says the court passed on the claim and rejected it."

Samuel Davis handed him a paper. It read: "Withdrawn at request of petitioner."

Will looked up, a bright new light in his eyes. "This puts a different face on the matter. No judge would pay much heed to a statement supposedly made by somebody who immediately withdrew his claim. Relf's lawyers must have told him that; but here he is, using the document out of court, knowing it had been recalled. . . ."

There was a long pause. Myra leaned forward, her face searching. "Father, you wouldn't mind testifying to what you've told us?"

Samuel Davis fidgeted. "Myra, this is all hopeless. Why don't you come home, to quiet and peace, and forget this scandal, all this dirtiness? But—well, if you call me I can't answer anything but what I've told you, can I?"

Myra's eyes went to Will. The colonel was their witness; and his story would help a great deal.

As he left the postal offices a few weeks later Will frowned at the object in his hand—a letter, much handled, with foreign markings, from Bordeaux. In a moment he was hastening home. On this first bright day of spring Myra sat on the floor with the two children, Julia kicking her stockinged feet as she lay in the middle of a cocoonlike covering, the year-old Rhoda crawling on a blanket, her industrious fingers exploring the folds of the cloth. Without a word Will sank beside Myra and placed the letter in her lap.

For a moment it remained there, untouched. Rhoda waved her hand and gave a loud gurgle; Will reached over for her while Myra, fingers shaking, ripped open the envelope. He steadied her hand and together they read her mother's message.

MYRA, MA CHÉRIE:

How often have I wondered if I could hope to address you so! Your letter came several months ago to my cottage in the country, after being delayed in the town. There is much to tell, much to ask.

Long ago I became convinced that your rights, and mine, would never be recognized. They worked very skillfully, our enemies; I can hardly believe anything will be done. However that may be— for months my son, my sister Sophie, and I have found no happiness here and have thought of going back to New Orleans. It now appears we should be there in a few months. At least I shall have the joy of seeing you before I die.

Myra touched her glistening eyes. It was a sympathetic message, and generous; yet there was that hopelessness, that acceptance of defeat: "I can hardly believe . . . Long ago I became convinced . . ." Still—and here her heart lifted—she would meet her mother at last.

Their mood of uncertainty had passed; Will chuckled as he described how the impeccable Relf's face had fallen when Will and Colonel Davis walked into court together, and the way Relf froze when the colonel, his arm around Will, gave that dignitary a deep, wordless bow. The brothers Duncan had scurried out of court after their client; the Duncans, Will was certain, had a lot of explaining to do to Relf! Myra's rich laughter rang out. Dieu-Donné, working over the pots, began to talk cheerfully to himself; in the hall Eulalie nodded to the picture of Télémaque. It was the first time, she informed him, that she had heard those two in such a humor since she didn't know when. She felt so pleased she took Télémaque off the wall and rubbed his face for him. Back in place, he, too, smiled happily upon the world.

After agonizing delays a hearing came up before the state probate court, for the recognition of Daniel's second will. They went back to the courtroom that Myra well remembered. There was the same smell of stale tobacco and unventilated halls; bored attendants made weak motions at the same worn furnishings, with what must have been the same dusty rags.

Opening proceedings, the judge narrowed his expressionless gray eyes. This case had been hanging fire long enough; he would countenance no further obstructions, no useless quibbling. To Will's astonishment the brothers Duncan murmured agreement. But they had been responsible for all the delay!

"Now, as to this matter of the papers that Mr. Whitney is anxious to see . . ." The judge's upper lip buttoned firmly over the lower. Before he went further they knew what he would say. He had examined the various statements; it appeared that Daniel Clark's private papers had been kept in another room, an office below the bedchamber, in a trunk—the trunk in which Mr. Relf had discovered the will of 1811. But these papers remained there and were not inventoried. How, then, the judge asked, were they to know what *had* been in the trunk? As to what had happened to the papers since then . . . That, too, was a question. Messrs. Relf and Chew said they were not in their possession, that they must have been lost, or perhaps destroyed by the moisture of this climate. Benignly the judge glanced up. "Can the court compel them to produce what is missing or taken by dampness?"

And now—the judge opened his hand—the case must go on without further delay. Will rose, a stunned look on his face. "But we've expected all along that some of the papers, at least, would be brought forward. This—this is a blow; we need a little time to prepare——"

The judge's face was stony. "Ah, but the other side is ready, sir! For a long time the character of one of our respectable citizens, Mr. Relf, has been involved in this controversy. Simple justice requires that it be settled." Relf, arms neatly folded, staring ahead as usual, made no sign that he heard anything. Suddenly Myra hated the man more for this affectation of unconcern than for anything he had done.

"And now"—the judge pursed his lips—"Mr. Whitney wishes to have a will probated. Will he present the will?"

"But——" Will stammered. "But it's been taken. That's why we're here, to tell——"

"Ah, how can we recognize a will that isn't before us?"

The attorneys Duncan rose. "We move for a verdict of nonsuit." Nodding, the judge blew his nose, as if in relief that he was rid of a nuisance. Will dropped back, and Myra put her hand over his. There had been no hope for them in this court from the beginning.

In her parlor Eulalie listened to their slow footsteps. She understood what that meant. And this morning, when they left, she had shared their eager expectancy. *Eh bien* . . . She had prepared a special dinner for this event. But, she sighed, a bouillabaisse, with twelve kinds of fish, it was still a bouillabaisse with twelve kinds of fish. As a dessert she had concocted a brandy-and-fruit combination that Dieu-Donné would ignite at the table: at least the babies would have a nice show.

From her cradle Rhoda crooned in delight at the steady blue flames that darted before her. Her parents smiled. "Eulalie, you've outdone yourself," Myra told her. But Eulalie knew they had forced themselves to swallow the rich mixture; as for her bouillabaisse, she could count at least a half-dozen of the fish that neither had touched.

Dieu-Donné came to the door. Victorien Badeaux was below,

wanting to speak to M. Whitney. Solemnly the cake seller shook his benefactor's hand. A thousand sorrows; what had happen' was enough to make a saint cry, yes. It wasn' that he hadn' made plen'y of hard prayer' for their side! . . . He had come running over because two people just told him M. and Mme. Whitney had given up and were going back to the Yankee states.

"Tell them they're a little early," Will snapped out. "No call for buzzards till the animal rolls over," he added very quietly. It was a saying from his boyhood; until this moment he had forgotten it. With a broad smile Victorien hurried away; Will started back to Myra, a whistle on his lips. Halfway to the door it faded.

Myra had gone to the outside gallery. Outlined against the tracery of the ironwork, in the shadows left by the street lamp, she awaited him. It was she who broke their silence.

"What do you think?"

"I don't know." He spoke deliberately. "We've never been able to present our full case."

"We've never had a hearing, full or otherwise!" Her voice quivered. "Still, we lack so much we ought to have—proof of Des Granges's bigamy, the record of Zulime's marriage to Daniel . . ."

Will lit his cigar, and a feather of smoke twisted upward, carried by a puff of wind toward the river. A pair of horses, drawing an unseen vehicle, clopped down one of the side streets. Will resumed: "And you know you've heard no more from your mother. Five more months, and not a line."

Myra said nothing. Doubt and apprehension were again gnawing within her. Perhaps Zulime had reconsidered; or—her heart skipped a beat—could something have happened to her? Yet, for reasons that she could not name, she was certain Zulime would come. Will spoke again, and though his tone was casual, she realized at once that he had been considering with care what he had to say.

"I picked up another letter at the postal office. My practice up in Binghamton seems to be suffering. Father asks whether it's worth while to stay here and sacrifice what's certain for—well, a gamble. You see, the way things are going, we're not accumulating any income for ourselves and the children." He puffed hard. The high outlines of the cathedral rose against the moon, and a bell tolled in the distance.

Myra's heart thumped. "Will, there's another matter. A baby —again." Quickly she added, with an effort at humor, "A boy this time; I know it."

Will drew her against him on the bench, and his voice was husky. "Wouldn't it be better to have him where the family is? Wouldn't it be best for us all if we went back?" Then his excitement diminished. "Besides, we really ought to be considering our finances." When she looked toward him in surprise he hurried on. "Oh, nothing serious. We have enough in the bank to last us another year or so at the least, and I suppose we could borrow from the family. But——"

"You know I've some money of my own, and the property Josef Bellechasse gave me."

Drawing her hand to his lips, he kissed it gently. "No, I couldn't go through yours after my own. Anyway, maybe we've done all we can. Why shouldn't we go home, at least temporarily, and see what develops?" He stopped; Myra was staring steadily ahead. Before them the dark was illuminated by yellow-green sparks, the flicker of darting fireflies in the evening. On the banquette below, a sailor was walking with a graceful girl from the market section. Unaware or careless that others watched, the couple embraced. A man in a light suit walked tactfully around them; the lovers did not notice. On an overhanging balcony a soft hand broke off a white rose and dropped it below. The sailor caught it; the girl placed it in her hair.

After New Orleans, Binghamton would be a drab place. She made herself listen to Will. "We'd take up where we left off . . . things just as before." Her breath caught. "Just as before" —that meant the same slow engulfment by the family, the same submergence of Will among the other Whitneys. He had changed during these years in New Orleans; he had struck out for himself. They hadn't always been happy, but the mistakes at least had been their own. Once they went back, she was certain it would be forever. Yet if Will were determined she realized she would go with him.

Will moved closer to her and talked of the new baby, the child that was on its way. His head dropped on her lap; slowly, caressingly, with her fingers she followed the line of his strong features, the beginning of the dark hair high at the temples, the place where it curled behind the ears. He stirred, and she felt that what he was now to say had, like his earlier remarks, been pondered in advance.

"On the way home," he began, "I got a hint, an indirect one, that if we dropped our case, completely, they'd forget the libel action. I didn't——"

Myra's voice took on a deeper note, one of barely restrained rage. "So they're willing to bargain? Maybe they think we'd bring a stronger suit next time!" She drew his head up until she made out his eyes in the dim light. "Will, we'd be leaving here beaten, admitting their lies! The people who did this would go along just as they've been going, taking what's ours." Another thought stopped her. "My mother's coming back home. Now they'll taunt her on the street. We helped bring this up, when people had almost forgotten, didn't we?"

Restlessly, her skirts rustling against him, she walked to the balcony edge. "And our children! How could they escape the mark? Sooner or later they'd be told their mother was a—an illegitimate——"

CHAPTER X

WITH their bedside coffee Dieu-Donné brought a less palatable object, a limp sheet of legal paper, just delivered. Will gave it a hasty look and swallowed the beverage in quick mouthfuls.

"Well, pressure's tightening. Relf's libel suit comes up in a month."

"So soon?" Myra's eyes darkened in apprehension, and she took slower, thoughtful sips. Timidly she asked, "What would the penalty be?"

"He's asking twenty thousand dollars in damages. They might charge me that and give me as much as six months in prison." The pupils of her eyes dilated in fear. She remembered his previous three weeks in that hideous place near the swamp. Will, about to swing his long legs over the edge of the bed, slipped back to her. "Don't worry too much. We've had the thing transferred to federal court, you know. Anyway, we don't want it hanging over us while we get on with our own case, do we?"

It was good to hear Will confident again, thinking of the forays that lay ahead. She watched as he poured water into the wide white bowl at the dresser and cast aside his nightshirt with a habitual gesture of impatience. On a quick impulse she hurried to him and kissed him softly on the cheek. Surprised, he dropped the soap and pressed her against him, holding her within the protective arch of his great frame.

After a minute she disentangled herself. "Remember, just a month before court."

With a slap at her beruffled backside, he pushed her away. "You started this, baggage!"

In a moment, rubbing his chest, he called out, "I'll need your help, practically every hour of the day. Will you get out Relf's petition and Bellechasse's . . ." As Myra worked at the desk Will hummed a "gumbo" song of Dieu-Donné's. Along the street below, in the yellow sunlight, the *marchandes* were calling out the excellences of their blackberries and crawfish; a liquid Negro laugh came from the courtyard. Rhoda woke and beat against her covers, waking Julia, who screamed angrily. As she went to the children Myra smiled. This was another day, wasn't it?

When Will saw the first name on the opposition's witness list he clicked his tongue. D. W. Coxe, eh? He'd been collecting a lot from the record about Coxe; it would be interesting, mighty interesting, to have him on the stand. At least they wouldn't still be wondering what Coxe had on his mind or up his sleeve. The word went along Lawyers' Row on Chartres Street that Coxe was to be Relf's major witness.

The same day brought a note from Josef Bellechasse in Cuba. He had just recalled an old trunk in which he had stored several letters from Relf. He hoped to find them and send them by the next boat. Even if they weren't important Myra and Will might want to see them. The kindly old man had become one of their most loyal friends.

The weeks hurried by. No further message arrived from Bellechasse; bad weather in the Gulf delayed all vessels on their way to New Orleans. On the morning of the hearing none had been sighted down the river, but Victorien Badeaux promised to watch for them.

Nervously Will and Myra entered the court. The judge was a round, pink man wearing thick-lensed glasses that made his eyes look like tiny blue balls. With his first words they realized he was able and impartial; his firm voice made it clear to both sides that he would tolerate no foolishness. Soon the crier shouted, and from the back moved the bent figure of Mr. Coxe. The blood-less face turned; the long nose pointed, knifelike, in several successive directions. Myra was taken by surprise when, advancing directly to her, he lifted her hand. "Miss Myra, I regret the need to appear here. But after all, we both want only the truth, don't we?"

Myra, a sense of disquiet growing within her, nodded silently. What was this man's game? Certainly he must know she felt, at the least, suspicious of him. As he lingered, ignoring Will, she suddenly understood something of his purpose; he was demonstrating for all to see that he was a kindly, disinterested person. Her face showed what she thought, and Mr. Coxe left. Taking the stand, he surveyed the room with a look that combined humility and a desire to please.

D. W. Coxe, aged sixty-six, was a gentleman. A mole below his nose moved up and down as he spoke. Yes, he'd known Daniel for years, intimately. Daniel, alas, had fallen into financial difficulties in his later days. If it hadn't been for the skillful management of Relf and Chew he hesitated to say—oh yes, he mustn't express opinions. Humbly he apologized.

Mme. Zulime des Granges? Yes, he had known her. He met her at an early date, way back in the spring of 1802, when she came to Philadelphia and gave birth to a child called Caroline. "On the very day Caroline was born I took her from the lady, at Daniel's direction." He nodded, still serenely.

Myra and Will exchanged startled glances. This was different from anything they had heard about Caroline.

Greer Duncan strode forward. "Did the woman object when you took her baby?"

"Not at all." The blandness did not diminish.

"Did she ever see Caroline after that?"

"She never saw her again. She never made an effort to see her. Although eventually she and Caroline lived near each other, she had no interest in seeing her."

Myra stared at her hands. He was picturing Zulime as a callous, unnatural mother; he was making it look as if she went to Philadelphia only to have the child and then get rid of it. Coxe continued: "Daniel Clark arrived in Philadelphia after the child was born and promptly went on to Europe. As soon as she was able to travel she returned to Louisiana." After that Mr. Coxe saw that Caroline was provided for in a nursing home, then a boarding school where she gave services in exchange for lodging, and eventually on a farm; since then Caroline had married. "And that's all I know"—Mr. Coxe's gray eyes blinked—"about the illegitimate child of Daniel and Mme. des Granges."

Will stepped forward. "Did Daniel ever tell you Caroline was his child?"

Coxe looked at him for several seconds. Crossing his thin hands on his stomach, he answered, "I don't recall, but was there any need, under the circum——"

"Did Daniel tell you it or didn't he?" Will's eyes flamed.

"I'd say, to the best of my knowledge——"

"Yes or no?"

"Well, no." Mr. Coxe, no longer so kindly, gave Will a glare of annoyance.

Will went on.

"In his last testament of 1813 Daniel called the girl Caroline *des Granges*. How can you explain that?"

Mr. Coxe, regaining his composure, looked sadly at the questioner. "Ah, I'm acquainted with no such document. I know only the will of 1811, which the courts fully recognized, under the able executorship of Mr. Relf and——"

Will slapped his hand on the desk; the judge leaned forward, pink cheeks quivering, to caution Coxe. "No discussion, please. Simply give an answer."

Gazing steadily at the witness, Will resumed. "Several people swear that Zulime was convinced her marriage to Des Granges was void, and became Daniel's wife in Philadelphia at this time. Do you know of the wedding?"

"I certainly don't! I don't believe it possible, in view of the unlimited confidence between Daniel and me"—he emphasized the words—"that Daniel would have married in Philadelphia, or anywhere else, without informing me of it. And, I might add, without inviting me!" When a titter arose in court Mr. Coxe peered forward in annoyance.

Will pushed deeper. "Did Daniel at any time tell you he wasn't married to Zulime?"

Mr. Coxe's pale face flushed. "He never said anything to lead me to think he *was*." Taking a long breath, he went on. "To my knowledge, Daniel had no other child besides Caroline. He never acknowledged Myra Davis to me, never said he was even acquainted with her. I'm convinced he would have told me of Myra had he been"—the gray eyes swept the court—"had he been certain of it."

Myra's face flamed to her temples. He was following the same line Relf had taken, using the bitter words that imputed a gutter morality to her mother. And this man had taken Myra's hand in friendship a moment ago; he had visited in her home, dined at the Davis table! Now he continued: "There was never any question among those who knew the Davises that Myra was their child. When her marriage was announced she was called Myra Davis. I've brought a newspaper clipping of that event, which I offer in evidence." He had forgotten nothing.

Attorney Duncan cleverly brought him back to Myra's mother. "Did you see Zulime des Granges again?"

"Several times, in 1807. She had had a quarrel with Daniel and came East to inquire into reports that Daniel was engaged to another woman."

Myra's head jerked up. "The rumors were true." Coxe nodded to the court. "They involved Miss Louisa Caton, granddaughter of Charles Carroll of Carrollton." Blandly he elaborated. "Mr. Carroll was, of course, one of the signers of the Declaration of Independence; the lady had a reputation as a beauty—quite a catch."

Will interrupted. "Was that 'engagement' ever announced?"

Mr. Coxe gave Will a wary look. "Well, not publicly. It hadn't gone exactly that far——"

"Was there even an understanding with her family?"

"I'd say no; matters hadn't progressed, but he gave me to under——"

"Then it *wasn't* an engagement!"

Mr. Coxe stared at Will, violent animosity in his eye. He started to reply, then clamped his lips. Will, nodding, told him to resume his story of Zulime's return to Philadelphia.

"Well, she called me to her lodging place and complained of Daniel's desertion. She said he had"—again that pause—"promised to marry her and hadn't done it."

"Promised?" Will almost shouted. "Are you certain of the word?"

"Very certain. Then she said that since Daniel was engaged to another woman——"

"Just a minute! Who told her he was engaged?"

"Well, I did."

"Precisely! Go ahead."

"She said that in such a case she felt herself free to marry once again. A little later she did." He leaned forward, another paper in his hand—the marriage certificate of Zulime and Dr. Gardette. "I thought the court might be interested," he murmured. "And that, sir, was the last contact I had with this Zulime, nee Carrière, alias Des Granges, alias Gardette!" The mask of benevolence had been dropped.

The judge pounded on the bench. Again Mr. Coxe apologized, and Will turned to another point. "Did Daniel ever tell his mother about this girl Caroline, or his daughter Myra?"

Mr. Coxe paused a moment; then, putting finger tips together, he shook his head. "No."

"Then who did?"

"I think it was I."

"Then *you* advised Mrs. Clark that Caroline was his illegitimate child?"

"Yes." Mr. Coxe bowed, but his tone was less definite than before. Myra leaned forward in her chair; she was certain that Coxe was wishing, somehow, to be spared these next questions.

"Who helped Daniel's mother make her will?" The words crackled.

The witness's mouth formed the words: "I did."

"Didn't you, then, suggest she mention Caroline as Daniel's natural child?"

"That's—that's so. I thought she should do it, to be fair."

Will drew forth Mrs. Clark's will. "This document also names Myra as Daniel's illegitimate daughter." Coxe nodded, blinking his eyes several times in quick succession.

"Yet you've just said you knew nothing whatever of Myra as Daniel's child—that you were sure she was the Davises' daughter!"

"Well . . ." Mr. Coxe's slow swallow could be heard several

feet away. "Well . . . by that time I'd heard claims about Myra; and—and I thought the old lady should know about them."

"Then it *was* while she was acting under your counsel that Daniel's mother named Myra as an illegitimate?"

Coxe's eyes darted about the court. "Why, Mr. Relf told me there were some statements——" He went no further; he seemed afraid that he had already said too much.

"Exactly!" Will slammed his fist down. "Mr. Relf worked with you in all this, didn't he?" The witness was silent; against his pasty white face his lips had turned almost blue. "Yes or no, yes or no?" Will demanded.

"I acted in consultation with Mr. Relf, if that's what you mean. I knew how well he was taking care——"

"Please, just answers!" Suddenly Will rapped out a sharp new question: "Now, do you have an interest, direct or indirect, in this matter?"

Mr. Coxe's face grew mottled. "You imply that I——"

Lucius Duncan moved up, protest on his tongue; before he could speak the judge leaned over. "It is a legitimate point."

Coxe glanced at Duncan, then replied shortly, "No."

"Yet"—Will waved several papers at him—"the documents filed by Relf and Chew show you made claims for hundreds of thousands against the Clark estate!"

"Yes, but these have been settled! Six years after Daniel's death Mr. Relf and I cleared them up."

"Meaning you took great tracts of property and money from Daniel's estate?"

"Obviously!" A reedy edge had come into the voice.

"Fine." Will nodded briskly. "Now, if Mrs. Whitney's case is upheld, don't you know that these acts of Relf and Chew will be rejected and you'll have to return it all to her?"

"Perhaps." There was a slight curl of the lip. "If you make good these ridiculous——"

"Then the answer is that you do have an interest?"

"If you put it that way, yes."

Will had won. "And while you were garnering this little fortune, do you know how well the heirs of Daniel Clark were faring under the old will of 1811?"

"I—I know of them."

"Are they well off?"

"That word, sir, is a matter of definition."

"Then I'll define my meaning. Isn't it true the Clark family has been in poverty?"

"I've heard so." The last words were barely audible.

A buzz of conversation rose in the court. The brothers Duncan looked uncomfortable; even the stoic Relf was scowling. It had been a long day, and the judge adjourned court. Myra saw that Will, after his masterly climax, had grown very tired; his back sagged, and his shirt and even his coat were dark with sweat. On the way home they talked together excitedly. Will had made Coxe look very weak at the end, Myra pointed out. But some of the things the man had claimed stuck in her mind—Zulime's supposed statement that Daniel had only promised to marry her, and his story of the girl Caroline.

Will spoke angrily. "Of course their reason for emphasizing Caroline so much is to blacken you, indirectly. But Daniel and Zulime were married long before you were born, and the question of Caroline really has nothing to do with you."

Nodding, she told him, "And Coxe didn't offer a single bit of evidence that they weren't married. All he could say was that he didn't think they were."

Still, both of them realized that what this enemy had said against Zulime was dangerous to them, unless denied or explained by Zulime herself. Arriving home, Myra asked anxiously if there were any letters; when Dieu-Donné shook his head she turned wearily away. Will knew she was thinking once more of her mother; his mind, however, was concerned with the matter of those letters that Bellechasse had promised from Cuba.

Late that evening Victorien Badeaux came to the house. The Cajun had just watched a small fleet of Cuban vessels as they swung round the river's curve; the weather had finally improved, and they arrived in a body. Will thanked Victorien; returning to Myra, he gazed from the gallery toward the Mississippi. On the sweep of the spring floods the vessels were riding high in the moonlight. It was nearly midnight; Bellechasse's letters, if they had come, would probably be delivered sometime tomorrow, wouldn't they? If they did have any value, he suspected it was too late to use them. Will yawned and tossed his cigar over the rail.

Inside, he yanked off his neckpiece. As it fell to the floor he stood silent a moment; then he leaned over and put it on again. A half hour later he was walking past a drunken soldier at the wharf's edge. The first of the Cuban vessels turned out to be the wrong one; he tried two more before he found what he wanted. Back home, sweating after his exertion, he shielded the gas jet from Myra and the children and prepared for a quick scrutiny of the several enclosures. At the first glance he straightened and read more slowly. A little later he threw off his shirt and searched for note paper. As the night's heat settled over him he ripped off his undershirt. When three o'clock rang from the cathedral he was still working. Myra got up and went to him. Her hands on his wet shoulders, she leaned over and read with him.

The next morning Will rose before the court to offer evidence that would, he declared, place several matters in a different light. All of it referred to the fifty lots of ground along Bayou St. John that Daniel had entrusted to Josef Bellechasse for his daughter Myra.

As the audience stirred Will spoke in quick, staccato sentences. Just a year after Daniel died R. J. Relf wrote Bellechasse in Cuba, asking that he turn over all of the property. Bellechasse replied that he'd be happy to do so—providing the transfer showed the property was to go, as Daniel wanted, to Myra and no one else. For more than a year Relf was silent. Then suddenly he wrote a second time, asking an outright transfer of the property—without mention of Myra. Once more Bellechasse answered that he'd give up the property, but only as Daniel had provided. To show his good intentions he sent Relf a power of attorney, substituting Relf in Bellechasse's place for the purpose.

"Several more years passed," Will observed, flipping to the next letter. Wishing to clear up the matter, Bellechasse wrote Samuel Davis. Davis answered: "I sincerely hope you have not given any authority of this kind to Relf. If he can take the property he will not fail to do so, and it will be lost to Myra." Davis had just been to New Orleans, where he had failed to obtain anything for Myra; and Davis now added: "Relf has positively denied having any knowledge of this matter (the bayou lots), and pretends to have received no power of attorney of any kind!"

Grins spread over many faces in the crowd; it enjoyed these little evidences of the tactics employed by the correct Mr. Relf.

And now Relf wrote again to Bellechasse, with a rather different demand. This time he admitted he had received the power of attorney, years ago. But he wanted Bellechasse to change it and give half the lots to Relf, for the girl Caroline. This Bellechasse thought he could not do without abusing the confidence of a dead man. Yet, if it were felt that part of this property was really due Caroline, Myra herself might be willing to agree to a division. Let Relf send a sworn statement to this effect from Myra and her guardian, Colonel Davis.

"But"—Will leaned forward—"Myra was then about sixteen. She had no idea she was Daniel's child—and it's evident Mr. Relf had little wish to see her so informed! So Mr. Relf subsided for a time. Then, lo and behold, there came still another letter to ask Bellechasse to violate Daniel's trust—from none other than Mr. D. W. Coxe." The merchant squirmed uncomfortably as Will went on. "Mr. Relf had again changed plans. In Relf's behalf Coxe demanded that all the lots be given up to Relf and none kept for Myra. Bellechasse called it what it was—'an astonishing request'—and rejected it, finally."

Will sent the letter spinning across the table and picked up a last one. "Here, may it please the court, is another interesting statement by Bellechasse: 'On the very day of Daniel's death I acknowledged to *Relf,* De la Croix, Judge Pitot, and others that this property did not belong to me but was pledged to Myra.' So we see that back in 1813 *Bellechasse told Relf all about Myra* and her father's attitude toward her. Yet now, many years later, Relf says flatly he knows nothing about Myra and has no reason to believe she is Daniel's child—legitimate or illegitimate!"

The crowd sat up. Will whirled about, his gaze passing from Relf to Coxe. "It isn't an idyllic picture, is it? Here was Myra, unaware of the existence of this property; and here was Relf, working year after year to talk Bellechasse into giving it over. As for Mr. Coxe, this worthy, high-minded man"—his scornful eyes flicked over the pale face—"here's the individual who assured us he had no interest in these matters. Now we find him intervening, becoming a partisan in a scheme to take away what a father left his child!"

Will sat down. From the Relf followers came scattered hisses, from others laughter and applause. Myra's head was high, and her eyes shone with a fierce joy. Never had she seen Will as he had appeared during the last hour, dominating everything about him, triumphant conviction ringing through his words. This was the Will Whitney she had hoped to see, the Will she had known could emerge.

The judge ascended the bench to give his verdict; Will stepped forward and waited. The judge stared through his thick glasses, his applelike face quivering slightly as he began to speak. "I must agree with Mr. Relf's attorneys," he declared, "that the statements of Mr. Whitney call for judicial investigation. These are serious charges, reflecting on a well-known individual of our city. On the other hand"—he cleared his throat—"Mr. Whitney has presented a striking collection of evidence, calling for full consideration." He balanced, he analyzed, he evaluated. At last, glancing to each side, he declared, "I therefore pronounce the defendant Whitney—guilty."

Will's hands went quickly white, but he did not unfold them or change his position. Myra pressed her fist over her breast; for a minute she thought she would suffocate. Could they afford heavy damages—or would it be worse?

The jurist was mumbling something. The courtroom grew silent to catch his words. "I therefore sentence you"—he rubbed his chin and permitted a quizzical expression to cross his face—"to pay a fine of one dollar."

Eulalie Montagnet stood at the door, smiling over the children's heads. Immediately behind her, not less triumphant, waited Victorien Badeaux.

"A kiss, *chers!*" cried Eulalie. She gave quick congratulations on both cheeks, then broke into half-hysterical tears.

Victorien, too, burst into speech. "*Le Bon Dieu,* he know' what the right side is now! I have intercede' with five pow'ful saint'—friendly one', not the stuck-up kine. And you see what happen?"

They faced one another, breathless, bright-eyed. Then Eulalie gasped, "Ah, so much *fla-fla,* I forgot! Victorien, he came over with news of his own."

The Cajun, aware again that he was the bearer of valuable tidings, straightened up. "You' *maman,* Zulime, she back!"

Myra's face was suddenly blank. Will went to her side, and Eulalie and Victorien quietly left them together. A tight knot formed somewhere inside her; she knew she had turned panicky. Would she be sorry now when she did meet Zulime?

The bell rang, and Myra ran to the door. Her countenance a white mask, she tore open the note that a Negro held out to her. The message, in a woman's hand, was badly scrawled, as if written under the prod of a hasty decision. Could Myra call on her tonight or perhaps tomorrow morning? Zulime gave an address on Rampart Street.

Myra faced the messenger. "Tell my mother I'll be there in an hour from now."

CHAPTER XI

THE house on Rampart Street, one of several in a row, had a worn look of dimming prettiness in a faded frame. Single-storied, brick with a cracked yellow stucco covering, it sat even with the banquette. Beyond a wooden gate an alley led to the garden. There, among ropelike vines that climbed over the walls, two women walked, their pale dresses gleaming against the final light of day. A red bird flashed from the roof to the crepe myrtle bush that dropped foamy clusters about the cistern, and one of the women stirred nervously.

Inside the third Carrière sister knelt at a *prie-dieu*, her hands clenched before her. The taper, flickering in its glass cup, outlined a slender figure in clinging black. The hair, tightly wrapped, was deep black, bluish in its overtones. A rush of words, in a voice thick and impassioned, came from the lips of Zulime Gardette.

When a knock sounded she quickly bent her head for an additional prayer, then pushed open the front door. Myra Whitney, her daughter Rhoda in her arms, looked up. As the two stared in silence Myra tried to speak but found that no words came. Then suddenly she stepped toward Zulime and kissed her on the cheek. Catching her hand, the older woman pressed it almost convulsively to her lips.

After a time Zulime spoke in accented English, her voice vibrant. "They said it would be best if I—if I didn't try to see you." Through long black lashes she fixed her gaze on Myra, and then she asked humbly, insistently, "You don't hold that against me, do you?" When Myra shook her head Zulime's eyes filled; it was almost a minute before she could go on. "Long ago I told myself it wouldn't do to think any more about New Orleans and all this. Your letter came as a shock; for weeks I looked at it, trying to decide how to answer it. And for hours after I arrived here I walked up and down, telling myself I must write you— and not daring to do it."

Myra felt the desolation that lay behind the words. At the same time she was touched by the loveliness of this woman, with her warm, almost childlike expressiveness. Like an echo down a corridor, she heard Josef Bellechasse's remark, "There was a glory about her," and she understood what he meant. Streaks of gray could be traced in Zulime's hair; the eyes had shadows. Otherwise the beauty was unmarred: white skin without a touch of color, half-petulant lips, a retroussé nose that helped give the air of youth. Yet it was above all the eyes—heavy-lidded, of a luminous brown—that caught and held the attention. All at once Myra realized that, despite the differences in coloration, there was a marked resemblance between her and Zulime. These were Myra's eyes, and the face was almost Myra's, with a pensive quality, as if the years had left their mark of suffering.

Zulime asked, "What can you hope to do about this, Myra? Isn't it too late?"

"No! That's why I'm in New Orleans. And I need your help."

She saw Zulime draw into herself, almost cringing. "Would I have to—to testify?"

"I'd think so."

"Ah, 'cré Dieu! There's so much it would be hard to say to the world!" Zulime's hand trembled helplessly; there was a catch in her warm voice. "I've been a fool, several times in my life. Nobody did more to injure me than I myself." She paused. "Still, I haven't been the things they've claimed. You believe that, don't you?" Her eyes were entreating.

"Of course." Myra pressed Zulime's hand. "But with you away, they've been able to say almost anything. Can't you tell me how things did happen?"

Zulime seemed not to have heard. With a forlorn smile she reached out for the child. "She looks just the way you did—red hair and all. Daniel's red hair." She glanced up shyly. "They let me have you, you know, for nearly two weeks. Myra, you're more blessed than you realize. You have a husband you love, and your children." Rhoda's dimpled hand tightened on Zulime's wrist; after a long wait the older woman began to speak of her childhood.

"We lived only a few islets from here"—she pointed—"in a house even tinier than this. Papa died early; with three little girls, Maman had a hard time. Relatives helped; there was talk of trying to place us in a convent, but Maman wouldn't hear of it. Better the Mississippi River, she said. She was sure *le Bon Dieu* would send us a deliverance."

Then a tall, light-haired man from France, not unhandsome in a gaunt fashion, was introduced to them. He was called Jerome des Granges, and he and Zulime's mother talked of the old days and old families. He represented himself as an émigré of highest descent, victim of the *sans-culottes* of Paris. For a time, though it was out of fashion, he went about with hair powdered. He paid increasing attention to Zulime; when she was fourteen he wanted to marry her. In those years such an early union was not remarkable; and what a family decided a mere daughter would not oppose.

"Maman thought it was a solution; what could I say?" Zulime shook her head. "I had had visions of romance; I forgot them." Holding the child to her, Zulime walked restlessly around the room. "Jerome was a strange man, not vicious, but moody, dissatisfied with the way life treated him—and weak." Though he spoke of his great plans, eventually he was forced to open a small shop to support them, and on borrowed funds. Soon, over the protests of her family, she stood beside him at the counter. He had the ceaseless attention of his creditors; when things grew unpleasant he turned to the bottle, and many nights Zulime dragged him to bed.

Zulime's face clouded. She had a child, a boy, who lay in his grave within a week. Becoming bored with colonial life, Des Granges itched to revisit France, where he would look into his "interests." An uncle of the Carrières died unexpectedly in Bordeaux, and they were advised to send a representative to see that they obtained their fair share. By this time Zulime's older sisters had also married, but neither husband wished to leave his business. Jerome announced that he'd be happy to go if they provided a purse for the trip. The sisters began to gather funds.

Zulime remembered, too well, that day Daniel walked into the shop—tall, imposing, in a hot temper. Zulime, her own anger flaring, promised the handsome Irishman that her husband would meet his obligations. Daniel asked for sherry and remained an hour at his table; his eyes never left her. Within a week the young merchant was back. He complimented her on the cakes; she dropped the tray, and the two leaned over to pick it up. Flushing, she excused herself. Here Zulime winced. "For the first time I knew I had been—awakened by a man. But I was married. . . ." After a pause she resumed.

"The marriage was going more and more badly, though. Stories came to us; Des Granges was drinking heavily, consorting with water-front women, mulatto street girls. The family wanted me to leave him; Père Antoine, the cathedral priest who was our good friend, reasoned with him. For a time Des Granges sobered and things went better. But then he was restless to go to France; he said he'd take what money we had and borrow the rest." In April 1801—how well Zulime recalled the clear, balmy day—he sailed for France. At the river landing she waved to the vessel until it rounded the curve. With a deep sigh she returned home.

Soon she found people grinning, gazing at her with odd expressions. A tart-tongued housewife asked a puzzling question: "How do you like sharing your husband?" Immediately afterward an older friend came in, Mme. Benguerelle. At that name Myra looked up; it must be the same person Josef Bellechasse had advised her to find! Zulime was continuing. "My face must have shown how I felt. When Mme. Benguerelle asked me what the trouble was I put my head on her shoulder and cried. Now, she said, she could tell me the story that was spreading over New Orleans. Just before he left, Des Granges had been boasting that he had another wife in France and was going there to be with her. 'That's not true,' I told her. But Mme. Benguerelle shook her head; unfortunately it was."

Not long before that, it seemed, Des Granges had passed the Benguerelle house. Drunk and voluble, he spied her husband and insisted on joining them. His words shocked them; they gave him coffee and he quieted. Then, however, he confirmed most of the things he had been shouting to them. Yes, he had another wife, alive today, Barbara d'Orci. No, they hadn't been divorced, just drifted away from each other; but he'd had a letter from Barbara, and things would be all right again.

Closing the shop, Zulime called on Père Antoine and told him the story. He listened carefully, nodding his shaggy head; then he advised her that if this were so her marriage to Des Granges was not binding—"void from the beginning." "Still, child," he warned, "you must get proof." A few days afterward she left Des Granges's house to live with her sister Sophie. Such was the situation when a carriage drew up one day, several months later, and Daniel Clark asked permission to speak with the family. Des Granges was gone, his bigamy well known, Daniel pointed out; he himself had received a letter from the man, then nothing for months. Like everybody else, he doubted that the fellow would ever return. Daniel went to the point—he wanted to marry Zulime himself.

The sisters sat speechless. The Carrières, they knew, were at least as good as the Clarks; yet they had suffered reverses, and Daniel was the rising man of New Orleans. Still, they had no written evidence of Des Granges's earlier marriage. . . . The meeting ended in uncertainty. Daniel called on the Carrières again; several more months passed without word from Des Granges. The fall of 1801 approached, and Zulime was to have a baby again.

Involuntarily Myra's head lifted; her mother, hands twisted in her lap, guessed her thought. Reddening, Zulime dropped her eyes. "The child was Des Granges's," she whispered. "He had known before he left. . . ." Unexpectedly Daniel came to her. Why didn't she and one of her sisters go East and get the proof they wanted? Daniel had business there; he would join them later and they could be married. Eventually the Carrières agreed. To Zulime, Daniel talked of the years ahead—travels to Cuba, France, Spain, the great world of which she had only heard.

Zulime and Sophie found the church in New York at which Des Granges had married the D'Orci woman; a number of the people at the rectory had vague recollections of some such ceremony. But the old priest was away, and the register of earlier

marriages could not be found. The sisters were advised that one
or two residents of Philadelphia had been witnesses on the occasion. They went to that city, but their search was interrupted
when, late in December, Zulime gave birth to the baby Caroline.
She and Sophie remained in Philadelphia nearly six months, caring for Caroline during that time.

Myra stared. "But Coxe testified that Caroline wasn't born
until spring of 1802, and he said he took her from you the day
she was born!"

Zulime's eyes widened. "Lies, all of it! That man, how we
know him! Wait. . . ." Giving the child back to Myra, she sped
to the rear. Shyly her two sisters re-entered with her. Rose, the
oldest, stood there, plump and kindly. Sophie, the middle one,
was an angular woman with sharp intensity of feature and
manner. They shared a family look, a soft beauty of a Latin
quality. The newcomers took Myra's hand with gentle murmurs,
then sat, astonished, while Zulime told them of D. W. Coxe's
statements.

"*Sale bête!* How he can live without being struck down by
God!" Sophie gave a shrill cry, her eyes dancing in anger. "He
never saw us then. It was not till five years later that the man set
eyes on us, and he knows it. When we eventually left Philadelphia the child was nearly seven months old, and we placed her
under the care of a matron and nurse. Later Daniel told us he
had this Coxe take general supervision; all the rest of it this man
has concocted!"

The quieter Rose blinked. "Why should he tell such things?"

Zulime's nostrils flared. "Because he wants it to look as if
Daniel and I were never married—for his own reasons." With a
sigh she resumed.

"In the meantime, during that same spring in Philadelphia,
Daniel came to us one morning, flushed and smiling. With him
he brought Dr. Gardette, a witness to Des Granges's marriage to
Barbara d'Orci." The doctor remembered the circumstances; of
course he'd swear to them. Daniel turned to Zulime: so now they
could be married, couldn't they? However, he thought it best to
have a private ceremony; they should not announce it in New
Orleans until Zulime had filed a court action against Des
Granges. Taking her to him, Daniel asked her, "You do want
to marry me don't you?"

Here Zulime made an odd little movement of her lips. Her eyes had a look of remembered pain, but with it an expression close to defiance. "I have no regrets for that part of it, Myra. Even had I known what would follow, I think I'd still have said yes. More than anything else, my life has meant"—she raised her chin—"Daniel Clark."

Quickly she gave the details. "We were married by a priest in a house Daniel rented for us. Sophie attended, and also Mr. Connolly, an Irish friend of Daniel's from New York, and M. Dorsier, of Louisiana, the other witnesses." Zulime was only twenty-one. This time she and Daniel remained together only a few weeks; business complications called him to Europe in August. Zulime, planning to return to Louisiana, wanted to take the child Caroline with her, but Daniel argued that it would be best for Caroline to remain in Philadelphia for a while. If Zulime appeared with Caroline there would only be talk. So, for the second time, Zulime acceded to Daniel's wishes.

Just before she left Philadelphia, Zulime received an excited letter from New Orleans; and here the placid Rose took up the narrative: "I was buying my vegetables at the market when a friend whispered to me—Des Granges had arrived again, with a woman called D'Orci!" Getting back home, Zulime and Sophie went to the authorities; long delays followed, but at last Des Granges was found guilty and escaped.

Meanwhile Daniel had also come home. He acquired a villa for Zulime along Bayou St. John, a raised building, thickly grown with vines that made it a perpetually cool retreat. Daniel provided the furnishing of a small castle: marquetry tables, delicate rosewood, mirrors reaching to the ceilings. About the house stood groves of oranges; on warm nights they walked together beneath the sky. Lights blinked on the vessels that moved noiselessly near them between the bayou banks; otherwise they lived alone in a world of their own fashioning.

Louisiana seethed with excitements. New American laws had gone into effect; the governor, Claiborne, made Creole teeth grate. Daniel had become a leader of Claiborne's opposition, and the other side struck at him with every kind of charge. Daniel told Zulime he still hesitated to reveal their connection; she understood, from Sophie and others, that people were whispering about her "visitor," commenting on the rich house of a woman who had been a storekeeper's wife. Yet what Daniel wished, Zulime would do.

"I was happy for a time." She smiled. "In many ways Daniel proved to be a good husband. He had his faults—he loved flattery, he wanted his way in everything—but the first years of our marriage were good ones. Daniel was gone a great deal, in Washington, on visits to the Indies. I waited; I told myself it would be only a little longer."

During one of Daniel's absences Sophie brought amazing news. Des Granges had again crept back to Louisiana; he sent a message, demanding money. Zulime hurried to two attorneys that she knew; they filed several actions against Des Granges; finally, in the year 1806, she obtained an annulment of her connection with Des Granges. At last she had done what Daniel wanted.

That same year saw Myra's birth. As Zulime told of the episode the memory hurt. "When they took you away Daniel promised you'd be returned as soon as the marriage could be given out. Now, though, he was the territorial delegate to Washington, higher than ever, and further into politics. It was true, as he told me, that the attacks against him were getting worse rather than less violent. But all my fears, all the doubts that I had pushed to the back of my mind, came forward. Gradually I sensed something I hadn't realized before. Certain friends were working on Daniel, suggesting that he get rid of me and ally himself with some woman of rank and wealth. One of these people was Relf; another, I suspected, was Coxe in Philadelphia. I'd never yet met Coxe, but I gathered a few things from Daniel's remarks.

"Now these men tried new tactics. When he came back from Washington, Daniel rushed to me one night, swearing bitterly. Hadn't I been at the opera the other evening with a certain man? I cried and denied it. I'd hardly left the house when he was gone; nobody could point to a single wrong act that I'd committed. He stormed away; soon he had gone East, and rumors reached us that he was being seen with certain women of society. In particular I heard the name of Miss Caton, of Philadelphia."

Zulime's face had a look of pain. "She was a beautiful young girl, Miss Caton—rich and talented, and very high in social affairs. She belonged to a crowd that Daniel was seen with in those days, in Baltimore and other places. People were full of talk about her and her sisters—their magnificent toilettes, their goings and comings. Eventually, several years later, I heard she became the Duchess of Leeds. . . . But now everybody said that Daniel was courting her and that she approved of him."

Zulime and Sophie talked over the matter. There was one thing left for her to do—go North, see Daniel, and appeal to him for the last time; if she failed she must get the record of their marriage and publish it. She owed that to Myra and to herself. With Sophie she went to Philadelphia. While her sister rested at their boardinghouse she had herself taken to Daniel's hotel. As the driver drew up she saw Daniel stepping into another vehicle. Pulling the veil over her face, she asked the driver to follow him. In the growing dusk she sat back, trembling, until they approached a mansion on the outskirts. There she waited.

A few feet away she could hear music, the voices of men and women as they moved about the drawing rooms. In a few minutes a familiar male figure appeared at a balcony, bearing on his arm a girl in a glittering gown. They were together a long time; finally, hand about her waist, Daniel led Miss Caton back to the party. Zulime dropped her head.

The next morning she and Sophie went to the church of the young priest who had joined her to Daniel. The housekeeper shook her head; he had sailed back to Ireland, poor boy, in sad health—years ago. Nobody had any idea where he was, or whether he was still alive. No, there were no records for that year. Zulime and Sophie, growing anxious, consulted each other; the witnesses, Connolly and Dorsier, where were they now? Neither had seen M. Dorsier in years; he was no longer in Louisiana. Mr. Connolly, of New York? They did not know even his first name.

Some time earlier, when they had talked of going East for another purpose, Daniel had given them a letter of introduction to D. W. Coxe. After a tense week Zulime sent it to Coxe. He called on them, and from the first his light eyes indicated disapproval. Zulime went to the matter at hand. Would he give Daniel this message: Unless Daniel announced the marriage she would do it herself. Coxe shrugged; it seemed rather unlikely, he observed, that people would believe such a statement.

But, she assured him, Daniel *was* married to her; he once told her he'd informed Coxe himself of it! Mr. Coxe asked a single question: could she prove it?

"We stared at each other. Then he made a suggestion: why didn't I consult an attorney? He sent one to me. The lawyer told me I couldn't establish the marriage." She groaned at the memory; through all of a cold Sunday she sat in her room at the boardinghouse, trying to absorb these successive shocks. Where should she go now? She had no wish to see New Orleans, a place that meant only heartbreak to her. She had a little money left; later she'd see how she felt. The strong-minded Sophie prepared to go, though with many misgivings. She reminded Zulime that she needed someone with her; the youngest sister had always been dependent on the family. This time Zulime was firm, and reluctantly Sophie said good-by.

For weeks Zulime stayed close to her room. Then, as she walked near her boardinghouse, a friendly face loomed up, that of Dr. Gardette, strolling with his young daughter. They chatted, and she complimented the child. The widower asked if he could come to see her. Some time afterward she told Dr. Gardette her whole story. Daniel's unwillingness to declare their marriage—did that mean it had no legal value? By abandoning her and planning to marry again, hadn't Daniel released her from any obligation to him? Dr. Gardette sympathized; everything that he heard from her made him bitter toward Daniel Clark.

"Perhaps I wanted to show Daniel I didn't care; I don't know. . . ." Zulime frowned. "But I had become fond of Dr. Gardette. He was a good, decent man, and kind. My little fund was almost gone. Anyway, when Dr. Gardette asked me to marry him I agreed."

Sophie slapped her hands together. "If I had been with her it would never have happened! *Pauvre* Zulime, how many times have I told you, you think with your heart? When you did that you gave those villains the thing they could always use against you!"

Zulime, chin in hand, made a wry movement that Myra recognized as a mannerism. "*Oui*, of all my mistakes, this was the worst. But for twenty-three years I was a faithful wife to James Gardette. . . . I hope God will not be too cruel to me."

After a moment Myra asked if Zulime had seen the girl Caroline again. Her mother's face fell. "Caroline . . . When I went back to Philadelphia I tried repeatedly to see her. At first it was impossible; the guardian told me Mr. Coxe did not want it. I insisted, and several times I threatened to go to court. Finally they let me call now and then. But by now she was growing up, and they had been telling her things about me, harsh things. Once when she was in her early teens, living far out in the country, I wrote that I'd be there a few days later. I made the trip. When I knocked they told me she'd 'forgotten' and gone out. They had defeated me there too."

And this was all that she knew of Caroline, the dull, pathetic waif who had lived out her childhood in dim corners—on an obscure farm, working for her keep in a boarding school. Myra wondered for a moment whether she would ever meet this half sister from another world.

There was a long silence, and Zulime unclasped her hands. "I have some consolation. At the end, I was told, Daniel regretted as bitterly as I did the wreck we had made of our affairs; and he died trying to do the proper thing for you, and convinced he had done it. But Relf has won, hasn't he?" A look of fear came back into Zulime's eyes. "You understand, *chérie,* how I've felt about testifying to a great deal of this?"

Slowly Myra nodded, but the excitable Sophie jumped up. "Me, I have no worry. I'll answer everything they ask, and if they don't ask I'll tell them!"

Surprisingly the old, gentle Rose concurred. "When you wish me I'm ready too."

Myra, the hope lifting suddenly within her again, saw them through a mist of tears. Going to the two older sisters, she kissed them, and then Zulime. She and her mother clung together, Zulime weeping quietly to herself.

There was a noise at the door, and a young man entered. At once Myra knew it was James Gardette, a thin-faced, sensitive boy in his early twenties. He eyed Myra with abashed curiosity; awkwardly he shook her hand. Then he smiled and said that this was less difficult than he had anticipated. James explained that he had just finished his medical studies in France, and hoped to get a start in New Orleans. He had heard a great deal about the city, and about her as well, he added. "You're beautiful—

like our mother," he told her simply; and her heart went out to him.

CHAPTER XII

FOR hours the next morning Will and Myra and the Carrière sisters sat together. Will's introduction to Zulime was a difficult moment for both of them. They stared at each other in momentary embarrassment; Zulime's white fingers toyed nervously with the chain at her throat. Like most men on meeting her, Will was almost overwhelmed by her rich, soft beauty. Quickly he went to Zulime's side, kissed her hand, and, still holding it, led her to the sofa.

Then he and Myra listened intently as the sisters spoke. He covered pages of notes, and he asked questions: who else had been there, did they have the letter, where had Zulime been when that happened? Finally, with a tired exclamation, he dropped his papers. They had gone as far as they could at this time, and the meeting ended.

Back at Eulalie Montagnet's, Will sat in his chair for a long time, silent. At last he lifted his eyes to Myra's. "There'd be plenty of people, of course, who wouldn't accept the story in its bare outlines; but it's impossible to listen to them and not be convinced they're telling the truth." His face had grown very earnest. "As for Zulime, there's a quality of—of plain goodness about her, and honesty. I don't think she has a malicious streak in her." Myra, her eyes glowing, slipped over to him and, standing behind his chair, clasped her arms about his shoulders.

"She was foolish, pretty foolish," Will went on. "Maybe it took courage to do what she did; maybe it was weakness, or just a matter of too much faith in others. . . ." He let out a breath. "How I'd like to put her on the stand and let her tell it from start to finish!"

Myra stood before him. "But an opposition lawyer—what he could do to her! The way Daniel dominated her in everything . . . and then her marriage to Dr. Gardette. We may understand how it happened; we can sympathize as Zulime talks to us. Still, to force her to say it in a courtroom . . ."

"Actually"—Will spoke reflectively—"the wedding to Gardette has nothing to do with our case; it wouldn't affect her previous marriage to Daniel. And about the girl Caroline— whatever some may claim about it, she was born within eight months after Des Granges left Louisiana; under the law the baby would be Des Granges's unless there was undisputed evidence to the contrary."

"But," Myra persisted, "you remember how careful Coxe was to try to show the baby *wasn't* born until four or five months later. His whole story is arranged to prejudice a court against her. . . ." She paused. "Anyway, I think Zulime would collapse on the stand if we tried to make her testify."

Will was silent. "Yet you know the other side can call her any time it wants. She's come back, within the jurisdiction of the court!"

Myra's eyes narrowed. "I wonder if they'll want to . . . if they'll dare. She might tell a few too many things for their comfort." Will suspected that she was right; but they might try it nevertheless.

There was much new work to be done. Every name that Zulime provided, every hint of a source, had to be followed. Successful days alternated with discouraging ones. They spent weeks tracking down an elusive record, only to find it had nothing they wanted. They decided to devote time to another, less promising matter, and came upon supporting material that took their breath.

But basic information eluded them. Try as they might, they could uncover no more clues to Mme. Benguerelle, whose story would buttress theirs at a vital point. Then Zulime gave them the approximate dates of the several annulment proceedings that she had brought against Des Granges in the civil courts. They went to the older archives and asked for the index of 1805 and 1806. The clerks looked amused. "No index—you'll just have to look." Thick dust lay over everything, untouched in months. After a short survey Myra dismissed Will; she wanted to concentrate on this task herself.

From Eulalie she obtained rags and a duster. There ensued a half day of intensive cleaning, carried on over the angry objections of the staff. By that time she had the section in usable condition; and now she went through the documents, one by one. There were heavy gaps, and hardly a record was complete. She found nothing, but she went back over them all, on the chance that she had made a mistake; then she tried the year 1804, then 1807. Only then, discouraged, her eyes reddened after long concentration on the fading papers, did she give up. As in so many other instances, they could only wait and hope.

Will and Myra went steadily back and forth between their place and the house on Rampart Street. Their original constraint had disappeared; Myra was becoming closer and closer to Zulime. Gradually, hesitantly, Zulime was beginning to call at the Montagnet house. On one of her first visits, entering Myra's room, she halted for an inspection. Ah, that bed could only have come from a plantation; nowhere else did they need them so big. The dressing table—she hadn't seen such a piece since . . . Zulime grew silent, and a stillness fell over the room; the memory must have been distressing. Poor Zulime, Myra told herself. She had spent a great deal of her life on the outside, looking in at others.

A message arrived from Will: would Myra sort out several records for him? The children started to cry, and Zulime reached into the cradle, discovered the trouble, and handled Rhoda and Julia with a sure touch. Eventually she asked, "Would you mind a bit of advice, *chérie?* Those small bumps on Rhoda . . . a *tisane,* brewed from a mixture my *maman* used, will make them go like that," and she made a flying gesture. She and Myra talked quickly of youthful ailments and digestive systems; they shifted to Myra's own childhood—the care the Davises gave her, her illnesses, her school troubles.

"And Mrs. Davis," Zulime inquired, "she was a good mother to you?"

"Yes," said Myra. "Yes." She would never forget the gentle Marianne.

"Then I'm glad." At this Myra went to Zulime and kissed her. As she did she wondered if many women in Zulime's place would show such generosity of spirit toward one who had replaced her.

Will returned, and soon he and Zulime were deep in conversation. Myra watched them happily; the two had struck up an immediate friendship. It was a brilliant day, the air as sweet as a light perfume. Couldn't they go for a ride about the city? Will objected that he had his work, but in a moment he agreed. Zulime, Myra sensed, was a bit fearful of exhibiting herself about the city. Once or twice Myra had felt that her mother was almost hiding in her house; and she had made up her mind to do something about it. Now Zulime herself seemed about to make an excuse; then, with a slight shake of her head, she concurred.

At first, as the carriage pulled away, Zulime was constrained, and Myra made small talk. Then Zulime roused herself, and soon she was absorbed in the scenes about her. She clapped her hands in excitement, and another New Orleans opened before Will and Myra. This café—it had been the favorite of refugees from Saint Domingue, where the poor, impoverished things sang songs and challenged each other to duels and sometimes died of broken hearts. Over there had been a ballroom where Zulime once attended a gala dance; it broke up because a Creole heard an American use the word "frogs" in describing a meal, and thought he meant Frenchmen. Here came Chartres, the old commercial thoroughfare of New Orleans and—she saw suddenly—three empty buildings in a row. Businesses were moving to Canal Street; Daniel had always said the city would develop in that direction. . . .

They were not passing unnoticed. An ancient Frenchman recognized Zulime and bowed with a sweep of his beaver hat. A woman squinted, then made ostentatious display of the fact that she was ignoring them. The latter experience was repeated several times; Zulime carried it off well, without tension in her glance, without tightness in her smile. As they bade good-by Zulime caught Myra's arm and held it briefly. *"Merci, merci,"* she whispered. Zulime had known the purpose of the trip.

After some hesitation Eulalie Montagnet came to Myra. Would Mme. Gardette and her sisters come for coffee later that week? Her steady eyes did not reveal the struggle that had preceded this decision; Eulalie could well guess the upheaval that this news would cause in the Montagnet hierarchy. . . . The little party was a major success. Myra and Will sat at the side while the four women talked furiously, zestfully, nostalgically. Did they know about the cruel Mme. Ventura, who was poisoned by her slave after a particular mistreatment? Was it true there had been a charivari because the rich Widow Dufaux had caught up a young man for a husband; and had they really been serenaded for twelve hours, until she sent the boy out in his drawers, to pay off the crowd? Seldom was there one speaker; two and three and sometimes four cried out all at once, eyes flashing, tongues tripping.

When the afternoon ended, with Creole cherry cordial, Myra realized that Zulime's cause had acquired an ally. No longer did Eulalie look to the side when Mme. Gardette was mentioned; no more did she flash odd glances at Myra when the name arose. Thereafter Eulalie argued the case with warm enthusiasm, at the market, in her progress along the banquettes. Several older Creoles, after such sessions, paid calls on Zulime, renewing old friendships; and the Carrières were more cheerful than they had been in a long time.

Myra did not know of the consternation among the Montagnets. Eulalie was sponsoring that woman; the daughter had been bad enough, but the female herself! It was a disgrace before God and the Montagnet ancestors. Grand'mère Azéma delivered an ultimatum. Until Eulalie stopped consorting in that fashion Grand'mère's door was forever locked against her. Eulalie sent word that she would cross that threshold only when Grand'mère sent her an invitation! Thereafter additional Montagnets sniffed when they passed. One, Eulalie learned, was including her in her prayers—as a delinquent whose soul was in danger.

With Zulime and her sisters as frequent guests, the Whitney ménage had a new lightness of spirit. Will joked with the high-strung, witty Sophie; he grinned when Tante Rose called him *"mon fils."* Young Dr. Gardette joined them occasionally, and his sharp Gallic humor added to the animation of their days. James mimicked the older type of family doctor, with his fifty bottles of medicine in a bag; the best remedy for most New Orleans illnesses, he told them, was his own prescription—water, soap, and a shovel to clean the gutters. He had a good measure of that trait of Zulime's which Will called human-kindness. He would make a good doctor, he and Myra assured one another; he would also make a good man.

By imperceptible degrees Zulime became the center of their activities. She told Will, and frequently Myra as well, that they must not spend all their time on the case. She led them and the children on short trips about the surrounding country, to the outlying *faubourgs,* for exploration of the levees; to the American section where the houses were well spread out, not bunched as in the French part; and over the shelled road to the lake, for shrimp-and-fish dinners in restaurants on stilts above the lapping water.

Zulime's gestures were doll-like; she could hardly utter a sentence without a movement of her hands. When she sat in a big chair in a billowing dress, a blue bow at her throat, she looked not much older than Myra herself. Yet a pensive knowledge shone occasionally from her heavy brown eyes. Once when Myra protested a statement Zulime's laugh was wry. "Believe me, *chérie,* I know. Don't forget, I was a wife at fourteen!" Again she could be discerning. "Myra, how have you learned so much in your sheltered life? It was different with me. Perhaps, though, it isn't good to find out things through your own mistakes, is it?" Then, chin in hand, she would muse over her earlier years.

Myra, she said over and over, had a quality Zulime admired above everything else—something she must never lose—her determination. Even she herself—Zulime made a *moue*—was acquiring a bit of it from her daughter. At first, Zulime added, she had been sure the case was hopeless; now she no longer felt completely pessimistic. Here she gave Myra a long glance. "And I suspect, my little one, that you've had more to do than most people realize with interesting our Will in this matter, and keeping him interested!" Again Zulime had understood.

When Will and Myra, on one of their Sunday trips, stretched out in the grass along the levee to watch the clouds, Zulime studied them. How youthful they seemed, how unmarked by life! For them matters appeared all-fixed, all-certain. Might neither of them, Zulime whispered, suffer reversals to shatter their balance. That night she added a prayer to those she always addressed to the saints. She asked that God be kinder to Myra and Will than He had been to her and—she added after a pause —Daniel.

Half turning from the mirror as she dressed for another of their rides together, Myra asked Zulime a question. In her fingers lay the carved crucifix, gift of the Perezes of Bayou Terre-aux-Bœufs. Zulime, a curious expression on her face, asked, "May I see it?" When she received it back Myra noted that Zulime's hand was shaking. From her pocket Zulime drew forth an identical object. "Daniel gave it to me on the day of our marriage," her mother told her in a low voice. "He came with armfuls of gifts, jewels and flowers. Then he took this out and kissed it, and me. I've never lost it; it's the present I remembered most."

Starting for the door, they were met by Dieu-Donné with a letter. As Myra tore it open a newspaper clipping fell into her hand. A name stood out: "MARIANNE BOISFONTAINE DAVIS . . . quiet passing . . ." Myra sank against the sofa, and grief suddenly engulfed her. Marianne, the selfless and uncomplaining, had been dying up there, month by month. . . . Marianne, who had taken care of her, heartsick and helpless . . . Now Marianne was in her grave, and already the first flowers had faded upon it.

Without a word Myra dropped her head into her hands. Zulime reached out and took Myra to her. "Now you have me," she told her daughter. "You have me."

"I think we've done as much as *we* can." With a long sigh Will set a heavy file of documents on the chair beside Myra. "I've traced everything as far as I can go, but——"

"But what?"

"Well, no matter what we offer, I'm afraid the probate court of Louisiana will ignore us. Remember the last time?" Hands folded beneath his coattails, Will was pacing past her, almost scowling in his thought.

Myra's hand tugged at the curl behind her ear. Several minutes passed in silence; then she was beside him. "Remember something else—what we did in the libel case? We went to the federal government. We're citizens of another state; we can——"

Will checked himself. Then, catching her by the elbows, he smiled. "Why not, damn it, why not?" His voice rang out, and the children began to laugh and gurgle in response.

A week or so later, standing together, they handed in a new and formidable document. They had vastly extended their charges. Now they accused Relf and Chew of fraud in taking possession of Daniel's property; they demanded that every person who had acquired land and other holdings from the two men return them to Myra. Carefully they listed every such person they could find, and warned that they would list others when they learned of them. And they went further: they claimed also the annual interest that had been accumulating on this property over the past two decades, every item of rents and profits that had gone to these people—just as if Myra, the rightful owner, had held them all the time.

Eulalie Montagnet gave a grunt when she glanced at the documents. *"Mes enfants,* what an excitement this will cause! The people you are suing—but it is a blue book of Louisiana!" She did not overestimate the proportions of the furore that spread quickly over the city and state. Receiving his court summons over his bedside coffee, M. Soniat-Dufossat blinked and forgot the ritual beverage. The agent of the Chevalier de la Croix, pulling open the notice, slammed down his desk and wrote hastily to his principal, almost ripping the paper as his pen tore off the words. Stephen Henderson, better known as "Old Moneybags," tugged at his neckpiece, then yanked so hard at the bellpull that it came off in his hands. Mme. Avart, her jeweled hand dipping her roll delicately into her cup of chocolate, asked her husband what this rigmarole meant, and dropped her roll when he told her.

Through all the week and the weeks that followed, notes sped from lawyers' offices to factors' warehouses. The bulk of the inquiries was forwarded to Messrs. Relf and Chew. Demands were made, meetings held, ultimatums issued to those dignitaries. To them all the two men gave assurance: these matters were well in hand; they had only to watch Relf and Chew and follow them in their defense.

A new judge occupied the federal bench. A date was set, and Will and Myra appeared in court to face a mass of richly attired, frowning opponents. The latter's attorneys stepped briskly forward. First, since many of the defendants reported that their native tongue was French, they insisted they must be given the charges in that tongue. Will's heart sank; practically all of them read English. And what an enormous expense of translation and printing would be involved! But the opposition had not finished: Will and Myra must provide them with documents "of every sort" mentioned. Yet Will and Myra had no way of getting most of these records; these people were the very ones who had them! Certainly, Will whispered, the judge would not grant these arrogant demands, made obviously to halt them at the start. The judge cleared his throat; in a firm voice he did exactly that.

The next point was to be taken up in a few weeks; suddenly Will grew worried over this as well. In suing, he had asked that the subject be considered as a "matter in equity," to be heard without rigid restriction on evidence. "Equity" was an old institution under English law. In the United States, from early days, cases had been heard in this fashion. Yet, as his attorney friends pointed out, the old Code Napoléon of Louisiana, based on the Latin law rather than the Anglo-Saxon, had never recognized "equity"; cases had to be taken up under the strictest rules. If this course were followed most of the Whitneys' best material would be ruled out.

Will was insisting that cases could be heard in equity in the Louisiana federal court. Ever since Louisiana had been admitted to the Union there had been confusion on the subject. In Louisiana state courts the old Code Napoléon was still followed; in Louisiana's federal court no real effort had ever been made to adopt liberalized American rules for a case of this kind. Years ago, back in the 1820s, a Federal law was adopted declaring that equity procedure would be in effect in all states—including Louisiana. But nothing had happened. And now the judge ascended the bench again. Mr. Whitney was wrong; the matter must be tried under "existing practices of the state of Louisiana." That meant, Will fretted, that Louisiana was in the United States but not a part of it.

He had other matters to concern him. Under the Louisiana law the other side must reply directly to their charges within three months at the latest. On the day the three months ended Will and Myra went to the court. No, no answer yet. After a few weeks Will was back; then again after another few weeks. Nervously he filed a motion asking that the other side be made to answer as the law provided. The judge said he would consider this request.

Weeks went into months. At length, his face set, Will asked the judge if he were ready to require the opposition to reply. This time he received a frozen glance. "I've decided not to grant your request. That's all." The clerk, sitting beside the bench, lifted his pen to set down this action. The judge leaned forward. "That's not to be recorded." The clerk's glance made it evident how strange this procedure seemed to him.

Will's eyebrow went up. "At least you'll permit him to report that I did apply."

The judge shook his head in growing annoyance, unconcealed for the first time. "Again, that's all, young man," he rapped out.

Baffled, Will consulted other attorneys. They could only suggest that he push ahead in the case as best he could; eventually he would be able to apply to the Supreme Court in Washington and ask it to straighten out the point—and the judge. Summer recess arrived; wearily Will and Myra continued to comb through the records. Sitting beside him, she noticed his drooping shoulders, the muscle that twitched beside his mouth when he was tired. When he came in one night Zulime called Myra aside, and together they ordered him to bed. Yet early the next morning he was hard at his tasks again.

By this time Myra had to stay close to their rooms; the third child was very near. Deftly Zulime and Eulalie Montagnet administered teas, quieted Julia and Rhoda, and helped look after Will. The summer was the worst they had known in New Orleans. Will plodded through mornings and afternoons during which the air grew stifling; Myra fought her nausea, her temptation to indulge in temper. Meanwhile she worked over documents as she sat up in bed. She was growing disturbed that Will had so little to say; discouragement had returned again.

She tried to ignore his depression and talked brightly of other subjects; through days when she wanted to scream, and evenings when the perspiration made rivers between her breasts, she struggled over the case. Then, late on a June night, when the watchman was putting out the street lights, she lowered a handful of papers. "Will," she murmured, "make a separate file of these, please." He went to the desk; before he had time to comply she called out in anguish, "Go for the doctor!" By this time she lay moaning in agony.

Summoning Eulalie, Will raced toward the doctor's house. There they were sorry; the *docteur* had been summoned to a down-river plantation. In anguish Will ran back home, to ask further directions. He found a circle of agitated women at the door; over Myra hovered Zulime and a man—young Dr. Gardette.

James Gardette showed no hesitation. His voice was calm, his touch sure; when his aunts chattered too much an authoritative word hushed them in a second. Eventually, taking a respite, he stepped outside with Will. Twin channels of sweat were pouring down his dark, well-molded cheeks, into the tuft of hair at the base of his throat. The youth's fingers did not tremble as he lit their cigars.

"She isn't in such pain this time," Will told him with a heavy breath.

"No." James shook his head. "I'm using a little drug—something new from Paris. Some say women ought to be allowed to suffer, but . . ." James's shrug showed what he thought of such medieval opinions. Suddenly he recalled his recent conversation with them about the overuse of drugs, and he flushed. "This is different," he explained. But a cold chill ran along Will's back. Suppose this—this experiment was wrong? Suppose the boy was killing her?

He turned to protest, but a thin cry summoned James back. Agitated, Will walked up and down the hallway, until at last he sank on the top stair and leaned against the wall. He almost leaped to his feet when a hand touched his shoulder.

"Is she . . . ? Is it . . . ?" he stammered.

Zulime took his fingers and drew him forward with a quivering smile. "Myra wanted me to hurry out and tell you," she said softly. "She promised it would be a boy this time. It is."

Now they had three small digestive systems to watch, three voices to listen for in the night. Myra caught herself referring proudly to "my family"; relaxing in the courtyard, she basked in her motherhood. The boy, healthy, lusty-lunged, received his father's name. Zulime and Myra called repeated attention to the remarkable quality of the baby's eyes, his hair, the way he already recognized his father's walk.

With Zulime and Eulalie at her side, Myra gave up everything else for her maternal chores. Rhoda, now an expert toddler, went exploring along the flower beds in the courtyard and ran to Dieu-Donné when a turtle came dragging after her.

Julia, singing to herself, found her cradle sufficient for her wants; and little Will's soft eyes fixed upon his mother, the source and boundary of his universe. For the present she found it good to be only a mother.

July came and ended. The heat approached its fiery peak, but Will continued to work against time. One morning *L'Abeille* had a small note; two cases of yellow fever had been found near the water front. Later another inconspicuous paragraph told how additional cases, the number unspecified, had come to light. Quickly the doctors declared there was no cause for alarm. This last was all that many knowing ones needed; that night hundreds left the city. Those who remained tried to show no alarm: "Won't be as bad as '32. . . . Another week, and it'll blow over." As the weeks passed, however, the number of people on the streets showed a great drop, and those who appeared had a worried look. Stores were raising their shutters; up at Natchez and Memphis quarantines were put in effect against "the Lazar city of the South." The port, by which New Orleans lived, became deserted. A few sails hung listlessly; the only sound was the slow creak of the ropes and the tread of red-eyed men with rifles, standing guard over holds filled with precious produce.

Myra watched the children with heightening concern. The number of dead grew with every day, and these were only the reported cases, as Eulalie noted; officials, believing it would "hurt business," were concealing scores of instances. As she came downstairs Myra saw Dieu-Donné slapping his feet with a powder. Grinning, he showed her it was sulphur and urged her to use it; it "hold off fever, sure." Eulalie handed them all cups of limewater. "I know it saves lives," she assured them. James Gardette shook his head; he could only recommend, as he did for so many of New Orleans' diseases, a simple set of remedies: cleanliness, good spirits, and rest.

September arrived, and the blasting warmth did not let up. From everywhere arose exhalations of death and decay. The always poor sanitation of New Orleans grew worse. Gutters clogged; in the thickening mud forgotten dogs and cats swelled and rotted, and green flies and mosquitoes swarmed about the carcasses. A Creole who kept a rooming place with ten men saw nine of them die within a week. A Spanish woman lost her husband, brother, sister, and five children; now she wandered about the streets, a mad, broken thing, asking passers-by if they had met any of them. Three of Eulalie's relatives died, and more were sick. Grand'mère Azéma, who had forbidden her room to Eulalie, finally sent word; would her grandchild come to see her? A day later Grand'mère was gone, and the Montagnets were re-united.

The intervals between the tolling of the bells grew shorter. Vehicles for carrying bodies were in constant use; cotton drays, carriages, and wheelbarrows were being commandeered. From her room Myra heard the ceaseless rolling of wheels. The sextons could not keep up with the demand; they were cutting long trenches, dumping the bodies. Vandals had begun to strip the corpses; men, women, and children were being thrown in, naked, indiscriminately.

As in other years, trying to do something to stop the disease, officials assembled piles of tar and pitch and set them afire on the corners, "purifying the atmosphere." Near Eulalie's a cannon blasted hour by hour for the same purpose. The nights grew hideous with noise, dim with acrid smoke. James Gardette went mechanically from one patient to another, working without letup. Then came dismaying word from Zulime's; the old sister Rose had been taken ill. James stayed with her for as many hours as he could spare. Gasping, Rose fought back with vigor, and slowly she recovered. Meanwhile Eulalie ran one night to Will, a new fear in her face; poor Dieu-Donné had fallen in the court-yard. When he saw the black man James shook his head. Still, they must leave nothing untried. Eulalie went to the bed of her tired servant, whose life since his birth had been given to the care of her family. For days she hardly left him.

Will and Myra stayed close to their room. Then one day, against Myra's protests, Will made a trip outside. "This letter just has to get off," he told her. As he gave it to the clerk and paid his postage he dropped his hand. His expression was puzzled. "I—I don't know . . . A little dizzy, I think." After interminable minutes in the withering heat he managed to halt a carriage.

When he alighted the familiar scene wobbled about him. To the side he caught sight of a big-boned man, leaning against the house next to theirs. A weedy lot separated the two buildings;

while Will watched, the fellow slid, then half collapsed in the thick grasses. With an effort Will made his way to the spot. When the man saw Will he gave a muffled cry. For almost a full minute their eyes held, until Will lurched away.

At Eulalie's doorstep Will's legs crumpled. Forcing himself upward on all fours, he scratched feebly against the paneling. Eulalie shrieked for help when she beheld him. By the time James arrived Will's eyes, tinged with yellow, appeared ready to burst from his head. As they watched, his skin grew mottled, and he twisted and groaned. Myra stared wordlessly. God, dear God, nothing must happen; Will had to live. Over and over he was muttering, "Fellow . . . fellow downstairs." He whispered what sounded like a name, but they could not make it out. To satisfy herself, Eulalie slipped to the doorway. She found nothing; it was the poor thing's delirium. In the grass the big man twitched and heaved, and the vomit was black. The sun beat upon his hot, half-open eyes, and a cloud of insects settled about his wet mouth.

During the night James and Myra and the others took turns with their patient. Will's lips were cracked, and he cried for water. At James's direction they covered him, rubbed his skin, applied warm cloths, anything to make him perspire. To himself James Gardette cursed; nobody knew anything about this hideous plague. All he could do was try one thing after the other— coffee, milk, quinine. As in so many other cases, James suspected that much depended simply on the strength of the body. Yet as Will turned himself James saw the deep cavity of the chest, the hipbones gaunt in their outlines; and the young doctor increased his efforts. Will, he realized, had never gained back his full health after that incident at the prison.

Hour by hour Myra stayed at her post in the stifling room, refusing food, asking how the babies were getting along in their separate chamber. In the middle of the night a moan came from below. Dieu-Donné had just died.

With dawn, Will lay more quietly. At the same hour, in the grass outside, that other man's mouth fell open, and he ceased to move. A mumbling crone, poking in the garbage, called a policeman. He knew the face; that was Blasco, the deputy sheriff. Will, who had also recognized him, had tried to save him.

Through the next day and the next Will's condition varied. During the third afternoon the sun gradually disappeared and the sky darkened. The clouds hung so low that they seemed to graze the cathedral spires. Myra had never seen so menacing a day; there was no single breath of air. Everywhere, in every crack, the heat remained; the birds that had been stirring about the courtyard had disappeared, and a hush fell over the city, as if all New Orleans were waiting for something. The only sounds were the incessant creaking of the death carts, and the cries: "Bring out yo' dead! Bring out . . ."

Myra went once to the window. The unending, stupid pound of the cannons sent smoke spiraling into the leaden sky; the neighborhood was alight with a lurid pink from the burning of the tar fires. As she watched, a dray rumbled by, overpiled with bodies. Men and women lay tumbled together, half clothed or nude, arms hanging over the edges, legs stretched stiff and blackening. A fat woman, further bloated in death, rolled from side to side with every movement of the vehicle. Before Myra, watching with horrified fascination, the form of a skinny child slipped off to the ground. There it rested, its yellow, bloodied face upward, eyes bulging toward the clouds. A starving dog leaped across the gutter; another spied the quarry and they began to fight over it. With a shudder Myra dropped the curtain and turned toward the sickbed.

Will turned his head and managed a smile. His breath grating in his throat, he talked. Myra leaned low; he frowned. "Not so close . . . Not too close." With an effort he strengthened his voice. "Bring babies . . . to door . . . so can see . . . Just see . . ." Myra complied. It was a good sign, wasn't it? she asked James Gardette. Look, he was interested again in things around him! Will succeeded in raising his head; his reddened eyes stared hungrily. Then he sank back, and James and Zulime removed the children.

After a few minutes Will looked at Myra. "I haven't—haven't done very well, have I? So far, they've stopped us." When she objected he shook his head. "But I didn't—didn't give you wrong advice. I know! I know!" His face twisting, he asked for water. When she brought it he rested, as if to regain his strength. His eyes sought hers again, and he tried vainly to speak. At last she could make out the rasping words: "Myra, Myra . . . what will you do now?" The rest was lost.

Her hand caught at her throat, against the wooden crucifix that had been her father's. Through the waves of heat she went cold. It couldn't—it couldn't . . . As convulsion shook him he tossed violently to the side; and suddenly Myra realized that the tortured breathing had ended. Zulime, who had been watching from the door, walked quickly to her daughter's side. In the next room the children were playing on the floor with the mahogany and silver music box that Josef Bellechasse had given her.

> Ah, handsome girl with hair so bright,
> From what forge came such warmth of heart . . .

CHAPTER XIII

THE newly dug grave was a black oblong against the softness of the enveloping snow. From the clear blue of the heavens, about the surrounding hills, the wind sighed through the elms. It lifted the thin hair of the minister as he opened his prayer book and let his eyes travel over the assembled family, and it tugged at the loose curls of Myra's hair as she stood, unweeping, next to Will's mother, her child Rhoda in her arms.

Will would rest in the earth that had nurtured him, forever apart from the overripe fertility of Louisiana. . . . During the long night that followed his death she had sat alone, staring in front of her. With dawn she arose, stiff and cramped, to advise Zulime of her decision. She would take Will home, where he belonged, where he had wanted to return more often than he allowed them to guess.

If he had had his way, at any one of several points, they might have come back long ago—and he would be alive. New Orleans, the Necropolis of the Nation, as some called it in irony —it had murdered Will. More than that, it was those damnable weeks in the prison that had weakened him. Once she had told R. J. Relf she would kill him if her husband died; but for the man she could now feel only a cold hate and loathing. And over and over another concern tormented her. Had it been her fault after all? Was she the one who had destroyed Will Whitney?

A small, inarticulate sound escaped her. The minister was droning on, and a word or two reached her: ". . . full return . . . proper payment." Was this her payment, her punishment? Perhaps, as some had said, she should have permitted the past to stay dead, its shame hidden. Who was she to act as God's avenger?

And the glint of wealth that had opened before her, those plantation lands, and that one third of all New Orleans, including Canal Street—she asked if this had taken too much of her thoughts. She didn't know, she didn't know. . . . Her hand touched the child, the plump, unblinking Rhoda, her blue-gloved fingers clinging to the fold of her mother's dress. No, it was for Rhoda and the other two that she had been fighting—for their names, their protection in the years ahead. Once more she was swept by alternating waves of fear and self-reproach; once more she clung to her child as to a tiny, solid rock in the angry seas.

A pause followed; as the minister stepped back the men of the family lifted the casket between them. Mrs. Whitney gave a long-drawn-out sob, and the other women wept about her. Myra, her eyes fixed sternly ahead, blinked back the tears. There was no call for them; she had cried too much already. Then she stood a moment beside the new mound of earth and tried to think of Will—Will who had carried his big frame with such assurance. They had not allowed her to see him again; and her heart turned when she thought of the misshapen object within the heavily nailed box. . . .

Back in her room at Whitney Place, beside the double cradle in which the younger children rested, she began again to unpack. Her hands passed over a broadcloth coat—the coat that Will had worn the afternoon that began their honeymoon. He had donned it, too, the night of their arrival in New Orleans. Sadly she dropped the garment. Her palm brushed against the cloth container into which she had dropped all of their legal papers; the touch made her jump to her feet. A few feet away the fire crackled. She tugged at the heavy bag and dragged it toward the hearth.

She was only a few inches from the flames when Rhoda toddled toward her. Perhaps it was the color that drew her, or the movement across the floor; but the child threw herself on the bag and clung to it. The face that looked up at Myra was oddly pleading. Myra hesitated. That expression in the blue eyes . . . Then she knew what it brought back; again she saw Will and heard his broken words: "But I didn't—didn't give you wrong advice!" Her fingers faltered; she dropped to her knees and threw her arms around the child. . . .

That evening Josuah Whitney pushed his bulk through her door, to be followed by his wife. For an hour they sat together with Myra before the fire in the unlighted room. The reflections lit up their faces—the sagging cheeks of the elderly man, the pinched lips of his wife, the musing look of their daughter-in-law. They talked of Will, his boyhood, his letters from boarding school, his last message from New Orleans. "It came only a few months ago," Mrs. Whitney reminded her. "He spoke happily of you and your life together. . . ." Her voice trailed off, and her hand touched the restless one of the girl beside her.

"Yes, he was happy." Josuah nodded. After a while, with a deep grunt, he lumbered off down the hall, while his wife remained with Myra.

Once more Mrs. Whitney spoke. "You must rest. We want you to stay here with us from now on; you know that. But whatever you think you should do, promise me you won't make up your mind too quickly." More than anyone in the big house, Will's mother knew the inner conflicts of the intense girl beside her.

"I promise." Myra nodded. Then all at once she could not suppress the question within her: "You don't blame me, do you— for what's happened?"

The face that turned upon her was compassionate. "How could I be so foolish? I wanted you two to go to New Orleans and work as you did." In the shifting light the eyes of the two women met and held. After a moment Mrs. Whitney added, "No, Myra. I thank you for what you did for Will. We know that you—you were good for him. And what you two did together, that was good. Don't be ashamed of it."

The next morning Mrs. Whitney was up at dawn, superintending the servants, inquiring after her other sons and daughters. With firmness she directed the servants as they shifted Will's clothes to an empty trunk in the attic; she hurried to the dairy and the kitchen. From the window of her room Myra heard her as she gave her orders. Around the corner waddled Josuah, the dogs racing about him; he tossed a stick and five of them ran barking after it. A sudden hurt rose within Myra. How could they? Will was their son; couldn't they pretend they cared even if they didn't? Swinging the curtains across the window, she dropped to the bed.

The next day she left her room and moved among the sisters-in-law and nieces and cousins; they smiled and spoke politely and, she understood, tried not to probe with their eyes. And still Josuah and Mrs. Whitney moved about, all calm and preoccupation. Her hands clenched, she turned away. From the library she saw a carriage roll off with the elder Whitneys; an hour or two later it drew up again, and she knew at a glance that the couple had been at Will's grave. With her first glimpse of their faces she was sorry for her thoughts. Will's mother and Myra exchanged a long look, and the older woman went to her room.

Carefully most of the Whitneys avoided mention of her case and of New Orleans as well; they talked of the children, Will and Julia and the sturdy Rhoda, now nearly four, who calmly superintended her playmates, marshaling them for games in which she impersonated a Chartres Street cake seller, a roustabout, or Eulalie Montagnet. When Rhoda referred to her Grand'mère Zulime and described a dish as *très chaud,* the Whitneys were convulsed. With a slight sense of shock Myra realized that the strongly American accents about her had taken on a jarring quality. Her ear had become accustomed to liquid French, the easy cadences of the Carrières. She discovered that her own voice had subtly changed; too, she used her hands whenever she spoke. With an amused shake of the head one of her brothers-in-law told her, "Myra, you've gotten like all those Frenchmen. Couldn't talk if your hands were tied." She smiled. "It might be hard, at that."

She walked for hours; she rode horseback whenever it was possible; at night her sleep was sounder. The hollows were disappearing from her cheeks, and when she stood before the mirror her eyes had lost the dulled look that had been theirs for weeks. She felt it a relief not to have to make decisions, to plan or arrange. During most of four years she and Will had been thus occupied, fifteen or sixteen hours of the day. Now, she assured herself, she could vegetate. Regularly, on balmy days, she took her brood to the water's edge, and while little Will slept in his blankets and Julia looked on, bright-eyed and curious, she and Rhoda sent improvised boats floating downstream, drifting anywhere the water would take them. That was how she felt; it was pleasant not to fight against the current.

Regularly there arrived letters from Zulime, chatty, informative. Her mother wrote carefully, choosing her words with skill and a touch of the elegant. Zulime's education had necessarily been meager; though she had supplemented it during her years with Daniel, gaps still showed. When Zulime puzzled over the spelling of a word she managed to use it twice, writing it differently each time; she would be right once. And, as she herself said, she wrote and spoke English in a French fashion. She was forever telling how someone had "made a marriage with" someone else, and how this one was a "friend to" the other. . . . Myra missed Zulime very much.

Samuel Davis's first letter was awkward. More than a year had passed since Marianne's death, he said, and he was only beginning to be himself once more. The note had a pensive quality; the old man had lost or alienated all his family, Myra, and finally Marianne. She could sympathize with him in his loneliness. Six months elapsed without further word from him, and then unexpectedly he answered her letter. He began and ended with almost a command—she must come to see him at Delamore Place; he had much to tell her. Several weeks later Myra and the children took a stagecoach to Wilmington, with one of the Whitney servants along to assist.

The colonel met her with a flourish, swallowing them all in his arms. As the carriage reached a curve in the road Myra gave a cry. There it stood, the house she had remembered, red brick walls, white portico with Greek pediment against the sky. The staff had lined up; though most of them were new, the matronly Phyllis stepped forward to plant a series of hearty kisses on Myra's cheeks. Cutting their greetings short, the colonel waved his hand. "Now, missy, off to your room. Company due in an hour."

Myra started. She had hardly expected dinner guests immediately upon her return. Yet wasn't that like the colonel? The children placed under the care of other servants, she hurried upstairs with Phyllis behind her, and they went to work at her toilette. Yes, Phyllis assured her, things were pretty much as ever here. A might quieter, but still helter-skelter, you might say. Colonel hadn't changed a whit. Poor Madame had gone off easy; Phyllis made the sign of the cross. Colonel had taken on bad for a while, like a man walking in his sleep; hadn't realized how much Madame had done, even from her sickbed, till he had to pass on things and look for his own handkerchiefs.

At her first opportunity Myra asked about D. W. Coxe. Well, after Colonel come back from New Orleans a few years since, they'd had a awful row. Colonel God-damned 'im, heavy and hard. You could tell, after, that they'd been real mad; they'd spit their tobacco all over the floor. For a while folks said Colonel and Coxe walked on opposite sides of the street. Lately, though, they'd made it up. Come to think of it, Coxe had been around twice the past week. . . . There was no more time to talk; Phyllis had her gown ready—the brocade that Mme. Camille of New Orleans had provided for her. Just before she left New Orleans, Zulime had treated it with a Creole dye that turned it a somber black. The last time, the only other time, she had worn it had been to that party of the Boisfontaines'. Could she have guessed then that it would be part of her mourning?

When Colonel Davis, pouring sherry from the decanter, lifted his head a few minutes later, he blinked. Myra, her skirts swirling about her, had a softened loveliness, a dignity he had never seen. Behind her eyes lay a glow, as if an inner light illuminated them. Her red hair, in ringlets at the side of her face, gleamed as if burnished; her lips, full and moist, had a hint of restrained humor at the corners.

Taking her hand, the colonel helped her to a place opposite him. His wide cheeks had a flush. "Myra, I've given a lot of thought to what I'm going to——"

As the doorbell rang the colonel swore to himself. In came a pleasant-faced couple, both in their middle years, both bespectacled, wearing varying shades of gray. Immediately behind them stepped a girl in blue lace, blond, shell-pink in coloring. "Mr. and Mrs. Jones . . . their daughter Sally," and the colonel leaned over to kiss Miss Jones's hand. With marked self-consciousness the girl looked from Samuel Davis to Myra; only gradually, despite Myra's efforts at light conversation, did she relax. No, Mrs. Whitney, she hadn't traveled much. She knew Mrs. Whitney had been in New Orleans. At that she winced, as if she realized she had touched a sensitive subject. Myra waved away the child's doubts, then suddenly halted herself, her hand in mid-air. The curtains had parted, to admit Mr. D. W. Coxe.

Involuntarily Myra rose, her fingers clutching her beaded fan. It snapped; as it fell to the floor Samuel Davis retrieved it and with a guilty stare whispered, "Please. Coxe was anxious to see you." In the mirror she observed that her skin was the shade of Sally Jones's white handkerchief. She forced a smile as the long, bowed figure of Coxe advanced upon her, teeth flashing, eyebrows lifted above gray eyes. "Miss Myra, a pleasure, a pleasure!"

"Good evening." The words were barely perceptible.

Before he turned aside he expressed his regrets. ". . . shocked at the sad news about young Mr. Whitney." Whirling abruptly away, Myra heard herself exchanging easy inanities with Mr. Jones.

At the table, as she began her soup, D. W. Coxe unexpectedly leaned toward her from his place across the table. "Henceforth I trust we'll be seeing a great deal more of you, my dear?" Silent a few minutes, Coxe began again: "Ah, then you may go back to New Orleans? We'd all hoped . . ." A flick of the hand ended the sentence for him.

This was all more than conversation; Coxe's pale eyes had grown intent. "Father." Myra glanced down the table. "Isn't it hard to realize that people are still so much interested in—in my plans?" She was being rude, she supposed; at least it was not what she would have preferred to do, which was to smash the long flower dish into Coxe's hated face. She did not hear Samuel Davis's reply, but she could not resist the impulse to ask him another question. "Have they been stopping you on the street again?"

The last was a shaft that even Coxe could not pretend to miss. As he applied himself to the turkey his face took on the same expression of angry frustration that she had seen the day Will had trapped him on the witness stand. Will, Will . . . Myra's face had a stricken look. Clearing her throat, Mrs. Jones hurriedly asked a question about pagan New Orleans.

Through the long meal, which now seemed needlessly elaborate, Myra tried hard to keep herself in control. After all, Coxe was her father's friend, a guest. Yet through the candlelight, over the mounds of the dishes, she saw him as he had testified. "Daniel Clark had no child called Myra." He seemed to sneer again with the malice of his uncalled-for words. ". . . this Zulime, nee Carrière, alias Des Granges, alias Gardette!" But, she observed through her misery, the colonel paid less and less heed to the two of them. He was giving most of his attention to the girl Sally: by accident Myra once intercepted a meeting of their eyes, and they looked hastily away. It was perplexing.

At last the evening ended. As the colonel escorted the Joneses to their carriage Coxe lingered. Firmly he took her hand, and the sly, polite smile returned. "If I have offended . . . It is difficult to express oneself in a court. . . ." Her face remaining impassive, he went on. "We know, of course, that young Whitney led you on in this unfortunate litigation. Certainly you must see that I have only sentiments of——"

Through a mist of quick tears she glared at him. "And I have only sentiments of disgust for you!" Her voice hoarsened. "I'll say this so even you can understand—I intend to leave the room the next time I see you here." Tearing her hand away, she slammed the door so hard that the glass panes rattled. A few minutes later the colonel found her in the library, biting her lip. Before he could start she wheeled upon him. "How could you have thought I'd welcome that—that person!"

He cocked his head, and his tiny blue eyes were bland. "But Coxe did nothing. I was angry at him, too, for a while. Still, he testified only what the lawyers made him answer, didn't he?"

"How can you say——" She checked herself. "Didn't he try to get you to lie?"

"Well . . ." Samuel Davis looked abashed. "I guess I misunderstood at the time. He apologized, you know."

It was hopeless; Marianne had always said that Samuel Davis would agree with anyone who worked hard enough on him. Then of a sudden he was talking of her case. Didn't she agree it would be best to forget all those ideas of hers and return here

—her home? He wanted her to take over in Marianne's place. Also he had another reason. He fidgeted and all at once he was asking, "How did Sally strike you?"

"An attractive girl." She saw that the colonel was blushing to his jowls.

Clumsily he made a new start. "I've been alone in this house nearly two years. The Joneses are very—very sympathetic. And I've asked Sally if she'd consider—consider becoming my wife!" He blurted it out in relief.

Myra could think of nothing to say. His eyes on the carpet, his face growing almost purple, the colonel went on. "I thought it'd be nice if you'd run Delamore Place. Sally's so young." After a moment he lifted his head. "How do you feel about the marriage?"

And what was wrong with it? she asked herself. What call had she, after all, to raise an objection to anything the colonel did? Everybody had a right to try for happiness on this earth. She nodded to him. "I'm sure you've made a good choice. . . . About the management of the house, though, let me think it over."

Several days later Myra took Rhoda to visit Marianne Davis's resting place. Following the lines of white crosses along the slope of the rolling ground, they sat together on a bench before the last grave. Though the winds were strong the sun gave a fine warmth, and Rhoda, well bundled, played in the grass. In the silence Myra's eyes passed from headstone to sky to leafless branch over her head. Now, in a flash, she realized what had been wrong in the colonel's house, why she had not felt at home in the echoing halls. Delamore Place without Marianne was not the home she had known. . . . Dark approached, and Rhoda complained of the chill. As they left, Myra cast a backward look; she would not see Marianne's grave for a long time.

A week later, as she brought the children downstairs in the morning, she kissed Samuel Davis and told him, "I think it's best for me to go back to the Whitneys, till my affairs straighten out anyway. You understand?" Though his expression showed that he did not, the colonel nodded slowly. When she bade good-by to Sally Jones she whispered her blessing. It would be odd to think of this child as her stepmother, or, more accurately, her foster stepmother. As she waved to them from the stagecoach her face was thoughtful.

Life with the Whitneys had become a routine into which she slipped without great difficulty. At times, despite her rejection of the colonel's offer, she felt twinges of alarm. Here she was, a woman with three young children. Besides the matter of finances, she had the problem of their guidance. Could she take Will's place while she also filled her own? Did she have the experience, the balance, to make decisions for them and for herself? Certainly she could not expect to spend all her life as a dependent of the Whitneys. But she could think of no immediate alternative and she was still tired.

Crossing the main street of Binghamton, Myra one day caught sight of a matron who several times had been a guest of the Whitneys. As Myra went toward her the other woman walked brusquely past. At home, when Myra mentioned the incident, Mrs. Whitney winced. She had hoped Myra would escape this. There were a few like her, only a few—narrow-minded, ignorant; they had heard of Myra's suit and chose to place on it an unkind interpretation. Myra nodded; it was obvious that the lady rejected her as a bastard.

Then Josuah Whitney called her. Easing himself into a big chair, he handed her a clipping. The *Evening Star* of New York City had devoted almost a full page to "this extraordinary case." After outlining every known circumstance, the paper concluded:

Here is an immense amount of property sold from Clark's estate by Relf, and no child, no legatee nor public institution has received it. No account has been rendered. It may be said this case is one of a private nature. Not so. It is one in which the whole country is interested—every citizen who makes a will; every husband, every father whose last thoughts and wishes are for the protection of his beloved. We shall be rejoiced if Relf and associates can place the matter before the world in a light so clear that not a shadow of suspicion rests upon them. Until then her cause should be made the common cause of all who love justice. . . .

The paper danced before her; several emotions clashed in her mind. Josuah Whitney now took out a packet of letters. They had arrived since the stories appeared; until tonight he had hesitated to show them to her. He warned her that some might be unpleasant.

The first made her lips tremble: "What kind of woman can you be, to wallow deliberately in the filth of your shameful birth?" The next was kindly: "As I sit before my hearth, my sympathy goes to one who, bravely and . . ." Another woman, who had little means, wished only to serve Mrs. Whitney for her board and maintenance. A mysterious note in a cramped hand hinted at "information of great importance, which I would provide if we agreed on a sum." From an envelope, sent anonymously, fell several bills; Myra must accept these in her fight for woman's rights in a world of men.

Myra shook her head. "I feel almost like an exhibit in a wax-works." It was strange to realize that so many people, whom she would never meet, were so much interested in her. With a smile Josuah Whitney patted her cheek and creaked off. She sat alone, the papers in her lap. Mrs. Whitney passed the door, looked in, then walked quietly away.

The snow was falling, steadily and monotonously. Her forehead against the windowpane, Myra wondered when it would stop. For two days it had let up only for short intervals; the two older children, their confinement irksome, had grown cross, until finally they fell asleep. She, too, found the situation irksome. It was the first icy winter she had experienced in years and even in an extra shawl she shivered. Only that morning Rhoda had asked, "Mama, when we going home, to see Grand'-mère and Eulalie? And get warm again?"

Home—where was it for her? During these past few weeks she had found herself missing things she had never known she valued: the dusk on the ironwork gallery at Eulalie Monta-gnet's, the sight of the roofs in the moonlight, a certain shrill cry of the crawfish women, the swarthy faces of the men who sold vegetables at the market.

Existence in Binghamton had lost its flavor. She knew to the hour what was happening. In town the stage had just arrived; the newspapers would be here within a few minutes; her sisters-in-law had finished their knitting. After a bored morning she tossed aside a book containing "nosegays of religious thought for milady"; after a while novels and histories also ceased to interest her. And always the Whitneys talked family and family traits. She sighed.

A servant handed her three letters, just arrived from New Orleans. The first she opened quickly. Zulime reported the family well. James Gardette was working hard, too hard; as a beginning doctor he earned very little of course. Judge Martin of the Louisiana Supreme Court was now completely blind, but nobody could get him to leave the bench. The financial panic had hit the city hard; businesses were closing; there had been several suicides in the river. Eulalie Montagnet, after a losing struggle, had given up her boardinghouse and was staying with relatives. Myra had heard vaguely of hard times that the new year had brought; until now it had all seemed remote.

A second letter came from Mr. Jensen, an attorney who had worked with Will during their last days in New Orleans. He hesitated to trouble her, but her case was still pending, and the other side demanded she do something about it or drop it. Slowly Myra put the note down, to take up the last one. It held only a newspaper clipping, forwarded by "A Friend." She read: "It is a matter of no small amusement that a certain wasp in human form, a notorious legal (or illegal) nuisance, has departed for good. The lady is one of somewhat informal birth."

They were stigmatizing her and her children again; and they were gloating that she had been run off! The papers slipped from her fingers; in a moment she was tugging at the lock of hair, her eyes brooding. For nearly an hour she stayed rigid in her chair. As the snow continued to drop in the blue-gray light at the window and the room darkened, she drew forth the cloth bag that contained the records of the case. She read, reread, sorted. Her eyes danced in growing excitement, and now and then she nodded quickly to herself. It was coming back, all of it: what Will had said, the way he had felt about this particular charge, the effect the other document had had on Relf. She and Will had only begun; they had laid the mere foundation for a decent trial. . . .

For months she had tried to keep her mind from returning to the case. Now she knew she had been wrong. For too long her life had been bound up with it; so, also, her children's. This was their case as much as hers. It must be a means of vindication and, beyond that, their bulwark against the winds of fortune.

Her mind worked rapidly. She had received a small inheritance from Will; part of her own money was left. She calculated, totaled figures in her head; at last she was satisfied. As she rose she remembered yet again the broken words that had been among the last that Will uttered: "But I didn't give you wrong advice!" He hadn't, he hadn't, and they'd all know it someday.

She recognized the footsteps of Josuah and Mrs. Whitney as they approached her door. She squared her shoulders. Clasping her hands as if to steady herself, she walked toward the door. What she had to tell them would not be easy.

"Chérie, chérie!" Zulime's throaty voice rang from the darkened landing. "It's been so long," her mother whispered, and Myra, through her tears, inclined her head; their few months together had made a bond that it would be difficult to break. Young James Gardette, smiling in his boyish way, steered them to a carriage. After blowing her nose Zulime chattered rapidly. Myra and the children must stay with them; to make room, James had moved up to the attic, where he would "roost the way the Cajun *petits garçons* do on the bayou"; everything was ready. Myra, looking all about her, smiled happily as she beheld the street lamps, cotton drays, crowds before the Chartres Street shops. When a dark *marchande* thrust a handful of flowers into the carriage she felt completely at home.

This was the place where she and Will had stood together against the rest of the world. She was taking up the burden again.

At the house on Rampart Street the beaming Aunt Rose and Aunt Sophie awaited them, with exclamations of delight, and coffee and hot milk. A little later, with the children put safely to rest, Myra herself consented to go to bed. A sheet drawn about her, she sat up and listened to the women's conversation. Hadn't she noticed the narrow line of boats at the water front, and the piles of unsold goods? But—— They caught themselves; they must talk of less depressing things. M. Jensen, the lawyer, would be around in the morning. Did she know . . .?

Myra's eyes grew heavier; despite every effort, her head sank to the side. Her mother made a motion, and the Carrières tiptoed to the door. Zulime loosened the coils of Myra's hair and pulled the cover tighter about her. A last look satisfied her that the children were comfortable; from above she caught the steady breath of her son James. Zulime's face had a light of new happiness as she went to her bedroom altar. Her family was about her.

CHAPTER XIV

LEANING back in his chair, Attorney Jensen permitted himself a frown. "There's a great deal, madame, that you'll have to pass on. I'm afraid that, after all, it would be wisest if you'd bow to the inevitable and——"

Myra's eyes, flashing angrily, stopped him. "I'm taking up the case just where we left off!" Mr. Jensen, an individual neither stout nor lean, whose noncommittal countenance was echoed in his neutral attire, looked falteringly about him. In practically everything he occupied a position between the extremes; only by watching his immense pair of salt-and-pepper eyebrows could she judge what he was feeling.

Gravely he asked her, "Have you considered the matter of costs—copying, translation, and so on?" His glance, sweeping over the plain room, made his meaning even clearer.

"How much would we need?"

After a moment he named a figure. Involuntarily Myra shuddered. The amount was about three quarters of all she owned. Mr. Jensen grew sympathetic. "Nobody can say you haven't done your best. Still, all things considered . . ."

Rising, she spoke quietly and evenly. "I'll go to the bank today. Everything will continue."

"But suppose the judge is as hostile as ever?"

"I expect that." Her lips were tense. "Isn't our hope, anyway, the Supreme Court in Washington City?"

"That *will* take money." Mr. Jensen's brow went far up.

"I'll find it!" Her cleft chin was trembling; discreetly Mr. Jensen withdrew.

A few hours later, however, she had a hollow feeling when she talked to Zulime. With the funds that remained they could live for perhaps twelve months. There was the property from her father, which Josef Bellechasse had given her; it was gaining in value with the years, and she had hoped to hold it in reserve. But now she would have to dispose of part of it. Zulime and her sisters had little; except for a few pieces of furniture, all that Daniel had given her mother was gone. Her face flushing with pride, Zulime pointed to her collection: a long mahogany sofa of exquisite design; four high-backed chairs; an armoire so massive that four men had trouble getting it through the doors. The pieces dwarfed the narrow rooms; Myra reflected wryly that the scale of their lives must likewise be constricted.

Leaving the house, she walked automatically toward a huddle of carriages. Halfway there, she went back; this would be her first saving. With a brisk upward thrust of her umbrella she started toward Canal Street. Before she had gone a few steps a dozen pair of male eyes were upon her in intent appraisal. Behind her she heard a low murmur, from one man to another. She sensed what it would be like to make her way on the streets without Will.

At the same moment she discovered where she was walking— along a cluster of bars and gambling houses, among them several of the city's fabulous bordellos of plush, gilt, and mirrors. From inside came a hum, the click of wheels, an occasional high-pitched feminine laugh. In a panic, she stopped short. Unexpectedly she heard her name called; on his way to the hospital, James Gardette had seen her. With a breath of relief she took his arm.

Just ahead a bearded gallant drew himself up. "Eh, madame!" Sweeping off his hat, he smiled and smiled. Myra felt young James's grip tighten on her arm. The other man gave a languid and outrageous gesture; his eyes opened in surprise as Gardette's fist struck his cheek. He dropped his cane, and the two began to exchange blows. A crowd formed swiftly, calling encouragement.

"Eh, watch the lil one!"

"But the other's got more weight. Look the way he's hittin' 'm in the belly!"

Myra cried to the men, "Please—please stop them!" She might have been speaking an oriental tongue. A number of proper gentlemen passed, heads high. She appealed to them; coolly they walked on. James and the stranger were now on the banquette edge, the latter astride the younger man, beating him heavily about the face. Biting her lips, Myra turned to a group of rouged and feathered girls from the houses. In desperation she caught their arms. "Can't you make someone separate them? He's only a boy." After a moment of indecision two of the women went to a group of their customers. At first the men shook their heads, but the girls, pulling at their coats, persuaded them to intervene.

Tearing the fighters apart, the men motioned James and Myra to a carriage, and two girls assisted them. Myra took the women's hands and thanked them; reddening, they fell back, and as the vehicle started off they watched with placid, wondering eyes. Myra thrust her bonnet from her face. The only people who had come to their aid had been a pair of harlots. James, nursing his jaw, smiled at her. "Another few minutes, Myra, and I would've had him!" She did not respond; her mind was elsewhere, on a day when another man had fought in her behalf on the streets of New Orleans.

A disappointment awaited her when she tried to dispose of her land. She found only one taker, for a small piece of it; and the bid was low. This, Zulime pointed out, was the worst possible time for selling property. Hard, slow days had arrived; almost every week saw an increase in the water-front beggars, the closed stores, the signs of want. The saying went that the only one who was not suffering was Judge François Xavier Martin, chief justice of the Louisiana Supreme Court.

She and Zulime were drawn yet more closely together in these days. They shared the knowledge of their successive losses, the certainty that the community about them was unfriendly, and— not least—a need for one another. They sat together in the Rampart Street garden, bordered by high fences and neighbors' brick walls; they took their places beside the children's beds; they talked over the young ones' ailments—Rhoda, approaching five, inquisitive, pert, with her many questions; Julia, not far behind her, bubbling happily; and Will, over two, chubby and ever hungry. With Myra at her side, Zulime told them Creole stories, of Bouki the monkey and Lapin the rabbit, and the way Lapin outwitted Bouki; she stitched dresses for them and she took them to the Place d'Armes.

Myra and Zulime referred only infrequently to the case. Myra was aware that the thought of courts pained her mother, yet now and then Zulime inquired about new developments. As she listened to Myra's excited voice she gave a slow smile. "Myra, this case means so much to you. Too much, perhaps."

But her daughter shook her head, saying, "No, not too much," and a familiar determination appeared in the line of her jaw.

"But"—Zulime hesitated—"suppose you meet someone else, and he wants to marry you? Your second husband's life wouldn't be this case."

Myra's chin raised. "I won't marry again." The corners of Zulime's lips lifted in a tiny gesture. She hoped, she told herself, that her daughter would not turn into a dull woman with a cause. Yet there seemed little likelihood of this. Myra had never appeared handsomer; though she had reached her thirties, she did not show it. Her cheeks had a soft bloom; her figure was as smoothly rounded as ever. Today Zulime saw a slight pensiveness about her eyes, a repose of the mouth that had not been there a year or two ago; the effect was not the less pleasing.

One explanation, perhaps, was the greater amount of walking that she did. She was finding a New Orleans that she had never known—a quiet, plainer city that she and Will had only glimpsed, the New Orleans of the French market, the smallest and least pretentious of the shops, the Cajun and Creole, Irish and German tradesmen. She went about it with Zulime or one of the other sisters; her eyes opened at the bargains that could be had by careful buying. After several trips Myra insisted on doing much of the marketing. She knew what to hunt: soup bunches, eight or ten vegetables tied with a string; big bags of shrimp, baskets of wriggling red crawfish which Zulime would transform into a rich bisque. As they used their clamps to catch up the gray-blue crabs the market people inquired after her children and gave advice about recipes, weather conditions, and babies' hives.

One day she wandered into an unfamiliar corner of the market and was greeted by loud shouts. It was Estevan Perez, of Terre-aux-Bœufs, and his brood, selling bayou produce. Estevan kissed her cheeks and summoned his neighbors to make her acquaintance. Meanwhile he asked her question on top of question: "People treat' you right, *sí?* You' enemy' still doin' bad on you? W'en you get married again?" Myra finally managed a query of her own; the answer came with a long sigh. "The old señora? She die, t'ree, fo' mont' ago. Funny, she remember you and Daniel right at end." With this, however, he looked as if he regretted what he had said.

Myra's face showed a flicker of fear. "Did she tell you anything more about—about my future?"

Estevan lowered his face. "Oh, she say lot' of thing' about ev'body. We t'ink she get kin' of crazy at the las'." But Myra's eyes made him go on. "Eh . . . She talk about mo' deat's, and big success fo' you, and then bad, bad time' some mo', and people usin' knife agains' you, and nobody know what all. Don' pay it no min'." Disturbed, Myra returned home and took care to mention none of this to Zulime.

Her mother was initiating her into the mysteries of the French Louisianians' *"petites économies,"* the saving of every item, an almost painful cleanliness achieved at low cost, the making of such dishes as boiled beef from the soup, served with a biting sauce as a second dish, and the use of bits of parsley, thyme, and peppers. They had no servant, and Myra wondered what the Whitneys or Samuel Davis would say if they knew the things she did—the daily rubbing of the furniture, scouring of the walls, washing of the floors with pounded red brick for the most thorough of jobs. At first she found the tasks irksome; after a time she grew not to mind. Every penny they did not spend they would have for the case.

A tentative knock sounded one evening, and Myra saw a well-beloved countenance, the plain, good face of Eulalie Montagnet. They stood in silence; then the Creole ran to the children and cried out her delight when they recognized her. After a time they spoke of the old days and the present ones. There had been a reconciliation of sorts between Eulalie and her family; she lived with Elégeas, on the last of the fund that had come from the sale of her house. And how did she like that? Eulalie lifted one shoulder. "It makes nearly a year and a half now since I am with him. In that time one should accustom oneself to almost anything." But whether or not she had accustomed herself to Elégeas she did not say.

Hours later, when young James prepared to escort Eulalie home, the guest took Myra in her arms again. "I have given myself more pleasure tonight than I've known for a long time! *Merci. . . ."* She went quickly out.

For weeks Attorney Jensen, his brow creased, had been relaying reports that something important stirred in the enemy camp. Then the blow fell. Mr. Jensen handed her a new document, just filed. "Peculiar," he mused. "Most peculiar." On this day of August 1838, a full quarter century after Daniel's death, Relf and Chew had at last taken steps to account for their administration of the estate.

She stopped at the opening statements. The two men wished to give their reasons for "not complying hitherto with the requisites of the law"; also they would explain "why a large amount of property in which Clark was interested was not included in the inventory taken shortly after his death."

She faced Mr. Jensen. "Why, they're *admitting* things I've been trying for years to prove they've done!"

Next came a greater surprise: Relf and Chew presented "articles of copartnership" between Clark and them. Myra's lips compressed. "Partners? They've never made any such claim." She read down the page for the date of such "articles." June 19, 1813. "Why, that was during Daniel's last illness, just eight weeks before he died. They're trying to say that, practically on his deathbed, Daniel handed them a two-thirds interest in all his estate. And they'd been little more than clerks. . . ."

Relf and Chew thus explained why they had made no inventory: the estate had been involved, difficult; they had been advised by their attorneys that they could delay in this way; they had acted with the approval of the attorney named by the court to represent Daniel's mother. Under such advice they had left out the "partnership property," including only what "appeared to belong to Clark individually"—about one third of the immense estate.

Attorney Jensen chuckled. "Now they say they didn't know what was 'partnership' and what wasn't. But shouldn't they, of all people, be supposed to have that information?"

For weeks, alone and with the attorney, Myra worked over the "accounting." Why this mystery, this complete lack of frankness, unless there were some reason for it? If these men had really become full partners of Daniel's, it was hard to see why they had kept that vital fact from all his heirs. None of them had been told that Relf and Chew were quietly laying claim to the biggest part of Daniel's property.

Excitedly Myra made her plans with Mr. Jensen. This gave them a new ground for her charges. If only Will had had this opportunity . . . The "accounting" had been filed in the state probate court, rather than before the federal judge who now had her case. When the day came for a hearing Myra and Mr. Jensen appeared in the state court.

Mr. Jensen rose, to offer Myra's objections to the "accounting." The judge, who had previously ruled against her, listened a moment, then slapped his hand down. "Your client has no standing here!"

"But, as Clark's daughter, she has an obvious interest in——"

"The court has already heard that matter and disposed of it."

A wave of anger passed over Myra. He was going to deny her even the opportunity of standing against this last-minute claim by Relf and Chew, this scheme to whitewash all of their deeds. Without realizing it she had leaped to her feet. "Your honor, surely you won't——"

"What? How dare——" The judge grew almost apoplectic. "Attendants," he finally gasped. "Another word from—from the lady, and you'll escort her from the room!" She sank back. All that she could see were the lines of Attorney Greer Duncan's heavy cheeks and the clam-white profile of the precise Mr. Relf; both seemed quietly triumphant. She was almost ill; helplessly she watched while the judge made ready to sign the papers brought forward by Relf. A noise at the back made her look up. A tall man with an air of authority was walking forward. The courtroom became still as he addressed the judge. "I wish to intervene here, to oppose these proceedings, as representing"—he paused—"two heirs of Daniel Clark's estate, Sarah Campbell and Caroline Barnes." Almost immediately behind him came two others, on behalf of property owners who considered themselves aggrieved. Myra sat up, fierce new expectancy in her face. So Daniel's sister and the girl Caroline and those others had at last waked up.

As court adjourned Myra strode to the new attorneys, hand outstretched. "Gentlemen, this court is locked against me. I think that, in this matter at least, we have a common cause. I'll

work with you in any way you say!" The three men looked
warily at her.

"This is somewhat unorthodox," the first began.

"It's an unorthodox case," she shot back. "Anyway, come
and see me when you're ready."

Two days later the attorneys were at her door. When they
left, hours afterward, there was wonder in their eyes. One,
lifting his hat as they parted, ventured an opinion: "A remarkable mind for a female."

The man next to him clamped down his beaver. "For a man
as well."

Late that summer the attorneys for the two absent women
filed formal oppositions to Relf's and Chew's "accounting,"
rapping out new charges that sent the Duncan brothers hurrying to their clients. Relf and Chew, it was declared, had nevei
really been partners of Daniel and were due no two-thirds por-
tion as they so belatedly claimed. The "accounting" was wholly
unsupported, shot through with errors and illegalities. Caroline
Barnes and Sarah Campbell denied they had ever approved what
Relf and Chew had done, or authorized anyone to approve it
for them. The two men, they observed, showed no dates on
which they claimed they paid out or received various sums; they
offered no vouchers to support these transactions; they had vio-
lated the Lousiana law at every turn.

The women proceeded to attack practically every transaction;
item by item they set forth amounts that had been kept from them.
Properties had gone for half or a third of conservative estimates
of their value at the time, under circumstances that raised serious
question—some for amounts so low as to make them giveaways.
One piece went to D. W. Coxe for four thousand seven hundred
dollars, when a proper figure would have been "upward of a hundred thousand." Another transfer of thousands of acres to Coxe
for a "debt" was called illegal; no such debt was due him. The
sale of Daniel's slaves to the Chevalier de la Croix should have
brought fifty thousand dollars, not a mere eighteen thousand.
Another man had paid seven thousand for a plantation, instead
of fifty thousand. . . . And one of the protesting creditors, in
his own peppery document, said that Relf's operation could best
be termed "alchemic experiments to turn *brass into gold.*"

The new developments brought a shiver to many New Orleans businessmen. Myra Whitney had fresh support for her side, and some of the statements had an unpleasantly convincing ring. That devil woman was going further and further. To upset things at this stage . . . Why, think of the hell it would cause to the financial structure of the whole state!

For Myra the change meant speculation on another matter. The girl Caroline, after ignoring all of Myra's letters, all her attempts to get in touch with her, had finally come forth against Relf and Chew. Myra wrote her once more; she asked Caroline's attorney if his client would not be willing now to discuss the matter with her. After a time, somewhat embarrassed, he brought the answer: Caroline Barnes saw no reason for any communication with Mrs. Whitney. Poor, drab Caroline, who had been hidden away in the Pennsylvania countryside for years, made to work as a child for her board, could not forget the stories that had been told about Zulime and Myra.

Myra's funds were running alarmingly low, and it was clear that, as in the case of everything connected with the litigation, the "accounting" would be drawn out indefinitely by the opposition. She and Zulime were watching expenses more and more carefully. Despite their attention, her black mourning dresses were wearing thin. Since almost two years had passed, Zulime suggested she go back to her other dark clothes, browns and greens. After a time these, too, showed signs of continual use. One day Zulime called Myra. "This will be another lesson, *chérie*." From parts of two frayed dresses they fashioned a single new one—sleeves and skirt of green, waist and lower fringes of black. Digging about the armoire, Myra found her last evening dress, the original red brocade from Mme. Camille, already dyed. "This will be a chic new street dress." Zulime smiled. When the scissors cut through the rich cloth Myra thought of the history of this garment.

As the bad times continued Myra sensed a further intensification of the hostility against her. Her friends at the market and the stores did not alter; but others, who had paid her little notice in the past, stood on the banquettes and stared. At one corner four or five middle-class housewives grew silent at her approach, following her with glaring eyes.

There was an explanation for the growing hatred. The land

she claimed had originally been owned by scores of persons; now it was in the hands of hundreds. Almost every parcel had been sold and sold again, sometimes seven and eight times. All of the owners had relatives; everywhere she turned someone was involved. How, she wondered, could she ever get justice here, when so many, related or connected by business and other ties, were lined up against her?

Yet she paid little heed until, one day, she was hailed by an old friend—Victorien Badeaux, heavy cake basket under his arm. "Jus' got back from Bayou Lafourche the udder day," he told her. "T'ings bad even dere; anyway, I got sick o' fish and molasses." Then, sobering, he leaned over. "Been wantin' see you and warn you. Some people stirrin' up folk agin you. In the business office' they tell the clerk' you causin' trouble, t'reatnin' an' all; and the clerk' go home and tell their fambly'." Myra, her eyes on the ground, started home; she had suspected something of the sort.

The next morning, as she neared the corner of the house, she felt an object splash heavily against her dress—a mass of soft, greasy mud from the roadway. A youth, perhaps twenty, jeered at her across the street; a crowd of younger boys had gathered behind him, hooting and laughing. She made a helpless gesture toward them; once more the leader reached down, and now he threw a double handful of the stuff. It struck her chest, spreading over her dress. She put up her trembling hand to wipe it away.

On the other side of the street several people came to a stop. The men watched with impassive faces; in the eyes of the women shone a hard glitter. Down the street another woman pushed open a shutter and leaned out to guffaw, violently and mirthlessly. Taking this as encouragement, the oldest boy yelled at her, "Bastard!" The rest took it up, and the word was snarled up and down the street: "Bastard! Bas-tard!"

Of a sudden the sport lost its savor; the boys broke into a run up the street. The men, who seemed ashamed, slipped off. Only the women remained, their eyes narrowed in contempt, bright with their hate. Myra walked back toward the house.

That week a letter arrived from the Whitneys. They must have heard she needed money; a tactful message enclosed five hundred dollars. Never had any amount looked so large to Myra. Much of the Whitneys' money was in real estate, she knew, and in these days of deflation values were still falling. They had done a generous thing.

With a care she would once have called penurious she worked over a budget—food, rent, children's expenses. It might be stretched over six or seven months to come. Firmly she gave the money to Zulime; she must hold it and apportion it, a certain amount each week. But before they started the new regimen Myra tucked a few extra dollars in her purse. She was feeling low, very low. She remembered a saying of Marianne Davis's that the surest way a woman could raise her morale was to buy a hat. She had not tried on a new one in two years or more. It would be a final small extravagance—an investment in her own well-being.

This time she did not consider the celebrated Mme. Camille. Outside the fashionable district Mme. Gouaux conducted her inconspicuous shop; Myra had made Madame's acquaintance at the market and now she went there. Two of Madame's customers were ahead of her; idly Myra watched. They were of the *ancien régime*, sparse and withered, in contrast with Madame, an overwhelmingly hearty, mustachioed female, with a figure roughly like that of a bull. As the white-haired customers spoke delicately to each other Myra caught a name, repeated several times: "Mme. Benguerelle . . . Benguerelle." Her back straightened; could this be the woman she had wanted so badly to find?

The Creole dames were startled when the Yankee woman approached them, talking her foreign tongue. They seemed to freeze, until Myra, realizing her mistake, switched to French. The Creoles melted; *une américaine* who knew the language of civilization, how remarkable! "But yes, it is Mme. Alcée Benguerelle we mean. Poor soul, she lives outside Opelousas in the Attakapas country. A mile down the road, a red brick house with a cow always in the front yard, a sign like a heart on his head. Jus' look for the cow!"

In a whirl of excitement Myra bade good-by a little later to Mme. Gouaux. Her selection of a hat, which she had wanted so much a few minutes before, had been perfunctory. She had a matter even more important on her mind.

Attorney Jensen wrapped his fingers together as her words tumbled out. "You must realize it," she told him. "Here's the only living person who heard Des Granges admit his bigamy! And she's very old. She might die before we reach her." Wetting her lips, Myra ran on. "I can leave tomorrow with Zulime——" Her voice weakened. That might have been the way before, but not now. Her eyes fastened on the attorney. "In any case we'll want a sworn statement. Won't it be best if you go? You can reach Opelousas in two days, partly by steamer, partly by wagon."

The sedentary Mr. Jensen winced. "We can certainly ask the lady to come here."

Myra grew firm. "How can we run the risk of delay—or ask a very old woman, a stranger, to make such a trip for us?"

After a while Mr. Jensen subsided. "Well, next week."

Myra shook her head. "I'll get the ticket for you right now, for tomorrow." Mr. Jensen could only swallow.

At home she and Zulime drew the money from its hiding place behind the mantel. Her heart lost a beat as she realized that this would wreck her financial schedule. She glanced at the children, Julia asleep in Rhoda's firm arms, Will curled up alone. For a moment she was about to put the bills back. Yet this was for their welfare, wasn't it?

A much creased Mr. Jensen greeted them on the boat's return. His weary smile reassuring them, he thrust a document into Myra's hand. Without hesitation Mme. Benguerelle had declared that Des Granges admitted he had another wife; also the elderly woman said flatly that Des Granges had eventually been convicted as a bigamist. Mr. Jensen made a tired appeal. "And now, Mrs. Whitney, may I go home?"

Soon they had funds for only a few weeks ahead. Young James, working at the hospital, received little more than board. Grimly Myra wrote Samuel Davis, and his reply brought several hundred dollars. He had news: he was a truly happy man, for he and Sally were expecting their first child. Again he urged Myra to give up this hopeless dream of hers; he still wanted her to take the management of his house. Myra sensed that her next request would be met on one condition—he would be glad to help when she came home.

Summer passed, and the winter advanced. The funds from Davis also approached the dwindling point. Returning late one day, Myra discovered Zulime's room stripped of its furniture—the carved armoire, everything that had been her reminders of Daniel. Zulime was in the kitchen, and a rich turtle fricassee simmered in the pot. "A very nourishing dish, this," her aunt Sophie told her solemnly. Zulime, peeling potatoes, was carefully expressionless. Myra, her heart pounding, touched her mother's shoulder. Through want and heartbreak and quiet happiness, for forty years, Zulime had managed to keep those dearest of her possessions; now they were gone.

Zulime's eyes, raising to hers, shone through her heavy black lashes. She thrust a small roll of bills into Myra's hand. "They didn't bring much. But it's worth it, to keep us together." Pressing Myra's hand, she went into the next room, where she knelt before the altar.

This could not go on indefinitely; Myra woke each morning with a growing fear. At last she and Zulime faced each other, and once again Zulime took the lead. A major expense, she pointed out, was house rent. Sophie had friends in the country; Rose's son-in-law could provide for her and also for Zulime. James would get a room at the hospital, while Myra could find one of the less expensive boarding places. They would join again, all of them, when things improved. Myra took her mother's hand and kissed it.

That afternoon, after a hunt, they settled on a tiny chamber on the third floor of a building at Canal and Carondelet streets, a former home fallen victim to business encroachment. Under a gas lamp a worn oak bed was crowded by two stiff chairs and a tarnished dresser. The carpet had been broken in several places; the fireplace was scanty, but it would do. The next day—they acted quickly to save an additional month's rent—the Carrière sisters waited together at the rail of their boat. As Zulime's face disappeared a sense of emptiness struck Myra, a dismay that was like an acute physical pain.

Doing her own marketing, she went beyond even Zulime's economies—poorer cuts of meat, slightly withered vegetables. The butcher, remembering her as one of his regular customers, slipped in extras. Her clothes, though not yet shabby, lacked their once modish touch. Yet Mme. Gouaux's bonnet wore well; when the feathers dragged lifelessly she ripped them off. Then came the grapes, then some of the braid. The hat still served.

The children missed their fertile garden. As often as she could Myra took them to the green Esplanade, but less frequently than she would have liked. A friendly woman down the hall, an elderly Kentuckian whose husband was a racing man, looked in on the children during her absence. Yet whenever she was out Myra worried about them. If the weather took a chill she had to keep them indoors all day, and they fretted in the dark little room. Her blackest moments came when they cried and asked about Grand'mère Zulime. Julia, who did not as yet understand things as well as Rhoda, was not certain Zulime would return. "Gone," she repeated. "Gone—like Papa?" Myra shook her head and tried to think of other things.

More and more she dealt with the Perezes and their neighbors from Terre-aux-Bœufs, whose produce sold at especially low rates. At length, cheeks flaming, she called Estevan to the side. Would he extend credit? "Ah, that all? If I couldn' do a t'ing like that for Daniel's chil', what kin' o' man I be?" Thereafter, week by week, she and the children lived mainly off the foodstuff from the Perezes. She learned that soup without meat could be nourishing; she boiled vegetables, she stewed them, they ate them raw. Now and then the two girls complained; the room grew hot and smelled always of food. No matter what happened, she managed to keep a few pennies aside for their milk.

A high-pitched cry stopped her as she hastened home, and the angular Harriett Smyth caught her in an embrace. This half-acid, half-tender little woman was a refreshing surprise. They went to Myra's room, where, despite Harriett's protests, she shared their meal. For several hours Harriett talked with energy; she puffed out her cheeks as she told of Attorney Duncan's snippy questions. "They didn't make me change a line, the rascals!" she boasted. "Duncan asked and asked, and I answered and answered, and they couldn't do a thing!"

As her tongue raced Harriett's eyes were also at work. She missed very little. Still chattering gaily, she left at the children's bedtime. The next day brought a message, with a substantial amount of money, dispatched just before Harriett's boat left.

Still the feeling against Myra increased. The number of un-signed letters grew with the weeks. Why didn't she go back where she came from? She and that Zulime, they were two of a kind, no-good whores. She knew, didn't she, what happened to people like her? . . . She destroyed such messages as they arrived; it was not so easy to forget them. One morning a woman on a gallery poured down a pot of slop, missing her by an inch. A few blocks farther on, as she went by, shop-keepers sitting in doorways smoked and exchanged comment. Behind her a gate opened with a creak; almost simultaneously a man who was moving toward her stopped short. *"Look out!"* All at once Myra realized he was shouting at her. She swung about, to find a middle-aged woman, her face distorted, almost upon her with a knife.

Automatically Myra put her hand up, and the blade sank into her forearm. Half dazed, she watched the blood running down her sleeve. Someone caught the woman from behind, but she shook him off and leaped forward again. Myra screamed; the blade glanced along her arm and buried itself in the flesh at the collarbone. As the crowd milled about, the woman was pulled away. Blackness closed about Myra; she heard a curse, a murmur of voices, then nothing.

CHAPTER XV

SHE would have to remain in bed for weeks. The doctor was cheerful. "You've lost a lot of blood, but it could've been worse. If you hadn't lifted your hand as you did . . . What you need now is rest and freedom from worry."

Her face was ironic as she pondered the last statement. Her lips pale, she managed a question: "The woman who did it?"

Her Kentucky friend from down the hall sobbed an explana-tion. "One of those miserable people they've been inciting against you. They told her you'd force her and her children into the street."

Myra inclined her head; she thought she knew how the poor

thing had felt. She whispered, "Tell them I want the charge dropped. She made a mistake, that's all."

The incident created considerable excitement. Some said their only regret was that the assailant hadn't plunged the knife in Myra's black heart; among others the reaction was one of sympathy. Dozens called to ask about her. Harriett Smyth sent more money; Victorien Badeaux sat for hours at her bedside; the Perez family came laden with food and material for poultices, which they were certain she needed most of all. Young James Gardette ran in, white-faced; with difficulty she made him promise not to tell Zulime. Her mother would want to come here, and that would not do. But it was Eulalie Montagnet who stepped forward, as on other occasions, to stand between her and the world.

On that first evening Eulalie arrived, hands shaking badly, decision in her manner. Quickly, her deep voice booming, she shooed out the awkward men, attended to the children, and prepared a *tisane* and bath for Myra. Then she dispatched a note to her own family; let them think what they wished, she would remain here as long as she was needed. "Now, Myra, all you have to do is sleep," she ordered her friend; to make certain she did as she was told, Eulalie added a few extra drops of the sedative left by the doctor.

Myra slowly regained her strength. Eulalie looked after her and the children, staying awake through most of the night, catching naps during odd moments of the day. When there were errands to be run she used Victorien or the Perezes; she cooked, cleaned the room, received visitors in the hall and scrutinized them before she admitted them. And she was with Myra one restless afternoon when a message arrived that left her sick friend strongly agitated. The Whitneys wondered if she were getting on well and urged her to rejoin them, if only for a few months. After, she could decide . . . Myra lifted her bandaged arm and gave Eulalie the letter. "If I go this time I don't believe I'll come back. But . . ." Her fingers traced a design on the cover. "What do you think?"

Eulalie Montagnet, a failure in her own single sustained attempt to fight convention, hesitated. For years she had watched Myra doing things she had never dared do. Eulalie's eyes followed the bad crack in the plaster, the smudge of smoke about the cheap gas jet. "I," she began, "I can give a dozen reasons why you should leave. But"—she stood up—"I won't. Hold on and see!" Myra did, and eventually was up again.

One morning when Myra came home a curious individual awaited her. He wore a bright yellow suit with a crimson-and-green cravat to match his waistcoat. Could Mrs. Whitney spare a moment of her valuable time? He was Zacharias T. Shober; he presumed she'd heard of his enterprises? When Myra shook her head his face fell. Well, anyway, he'd come here with a business proposition; he wasn't flattering her, he gave assurance, when he told her she had become one of the best-known women in New Orleans. He might say she was practically famous and —no offense meant, ma'am—a lady of beauty besides.

Mystified, Myra sat silent. Mr. Shober, embarrassed, finally blurted it out. What it amounted to was this—he wanted to add her to his list of attractions. Oh, nothing vulgar, nothing offensive. All she had to do was come on stage and tell her story. If she'd play piano or sing a song, so much the better. If not, he'd have somebody else do that in the course of the act. . . . Now, ma'am, no reason to take that attitude. Well, if she changed her mind . . . Tripping on the shabby stair, Mr. Shober shook his head; that damned woman could do with some money. A crazy world, all right.

As the winter holidays approached Myra felt a sense of terror. Eulalie called with toys for the children and several bills; the latter went quickly. Soon her purse held only three dollars and a few cents. She had not met her rent bill the previous month; as January 1 came nearer she knew she would again have to face the landlady, a stolid, green-eyed, straggle-haired Irishwoman, whose face had a suspicious expression whenever she beheld Myra these days. Zulime sent a box of New Year cakes; Myra and the children ate them for several days, but little Will found difficulty in swallowing the spiced confections.

Feeling the child, she discovered he had a fever. By noon, despite her precautions, he was tossing restlessly. She almost ran to the hospital. No, Docteur Gardette had gone to Mississippi to be with his family on New Year's Day. She managed to locate the doctor who had treated her for her stab wounds, and stood by nervously while he frowned over the child.

"Mm . . . This will bear watching." He scratched off a list, dismayingly long, of medicines. As he left, Myra made a hasty survey of the room; her eyes hit on her last few rings and the ornamented mahogany music box from Josef Bellechasse. Her strong hands resolute at her sides, she stood before a Spanish pawnbroker. He lifted her offerings and pried at them, then handed her a pair of bills. That was all; no, they weren't worth more, hardly worth that.

On the steps Mrs. Geohegan, the landlady, stopped her. Look here, nobody could stay if the rent went unpaid after the first month. She'd just have to have the money day after tomorrow. She was sorry about the baby, sure, but times were hard; she had to support her own children.

For hours that night Myra sat under the lowered gas jet. Will's fever was still high; and now she knew another dread. Where could she go? What would she do? From the window she looked down at a noisy crowd, milling at the corners. She had forgotten; it was New Year's Eve. . . . Her misery gave way to exhaustion. She woke a few hours later in her chair, her face creased from the folds of cloth against which she had slept. In the somber morning light the poisonous yellowish walls were more depressing than ever. Through the cold hours she maintained her guard over the child. The grate threw out only a feeble heat; she kept Rhoda and Julia in bed. Again had come the occasion of Creole calls, family to family, for *Le Jour de l'An*. Carriages rolled over the cobblestones, and clusters of people formed on the street. There had been that other New Year's Day, when she had suffered on the bed while Will hunted the doctor, then later quarreled with Colonel Davis outside her room. But surely her agony had been less than it was today. The sight of every family group, every smile from one party to another, made her more desperate.

She jumped as a pounding sounded on her door. Mrs. Geohegan, her face impassive, tossed out her words: "Man to see you." Myra stared. Someone else like that theatrical agent? Or a bill collector? She began to shake her head when Mrs. Geohegan, growing impatient, added, "Soldier, kind of important-looking, I'd say." Her eyes conveyed her conviction that Myra would do well to receive any caller, military or otherwise. She made up Myra's mind for her. "I'll bring him up."

A firm, light step approached. Myra waited beside the cradle, her fingers tight upon the wooden crucifix at the neck of her dress. Out of the gloom stepped an individual she had never seen before. They faced each other in silence, the one as curious as the other.

He was a man of lean, towering frame. As he stepped forward she saw that his skin, finely lined from exposure to the elements, was a sun-browned shade; the hair, part blond, part gray, was worn long in the Army style. His walk, the set of his shoulders, gave an impression of unabashed power. From a pair of snapping black eyes her visitor looked down with an expression that was frank and at the same time faintly humorous.

"First, my apologies for calling so informally." He bowed, gloved hand on the hilt of his sword. The voice, a penetrating one, betokened the Virginia gentry. "General Edmund Pendleton Gaines of the Army, at your service."

Foolishly she found herself unable to force out her words. His smile deepened, and his heavy brow lifted. With an effort she made some kind of reply. "Please . . . I'm at—at a disadvantage today."

He looked beyond her to the sick child; then he stepped to the cradle and his fingers rested on Will's restless head. "Poor little tyke. I have one of my own, some years older." Rhoda stood up in the bed to stare at the gold shoulder braids on the officer's uniform. As Myra indicated a chair to him Edmund Gaines faced her again.

"Several times I've thought of making this call. Then, today, I was at a New Year's party when a friend told me you were in —in some difficulties." The compassion in his voice made it impossible for her to feel offense; as he spoke she studied him. The nose was regular, rather patrician in its thinness, the lips kindly though also inclined to narrowness. The clean-shaven face had an engaging quality, full of a quiet strength. He was speaking again: "I think I have a right to be here. I knew Daniel Clark very well. Several times he extended his hand to help me, a younger man. I'm here to offer you any assistance in my power."

He stood up, his heels planted firmly together, and made a bow, the half-playful light again in his eye. "My sword and my purse—both are at your disposal." Then, with a sigh of relief, he sat down. "There! I've said it. Now we can talk more easily, can't we?"

Myra swallowed. For a moment or two she had been puzzled and suspicious. It might be a trick; was he a spy or . . . ? Then as she looked at Edmund Gaines she realized he spoke what he thought; the face was guileless. "But . . ." she started, and found she was weeping. Rhoda left her bed to climb into Myra's lap. In embarrassment her guest rubbed slowly at the side of his nose; then, gravely, he took out a large handkerchief and extended it. Rhoda, her mouth open in wonder, accepted it and passed it to her mother. The two of them together watched Myra.

"Blow," the officer commanded, and Myra obeyed. The sight of the others, regarding her so solemnly, brought a hint of a smile to her face.

"That's better, isn't it?" General Gaines asked Rhoda.

"Yes," said the little girl, her eyes intent on the bronzed countenance.

A few minutes later, when Edmund Gaines rose, he pressed an envelope into Myra's hand. "This is a loan—a return, and a small one"—he emphasized his words—"for the favors done me by your father. Call it a reinforcement from an ally." He wished to offer more—his advice for whatever it would be worth; in his earlier days he had practiced law. Now, though, he knew she wanted to rest. Moving toward the door, he suddenly grew constrained. "Some may misunderstand; it would be best to handle our future transactions through your attorney." He took Myra's hand, touched Rhoda's head, and left. Rhoda went to her mother. She couldn't understand why Myra put the man's handkerchief to her eyes again.

Myra's fingers, working at her throat, pressed the wooden crucifix. Out of the past Daniel Clark had come to her aid today.

During the following week Myra heard nothing from this new partisan. Tactfully he gave her time to adjust her affairs. Mrs. Geohegan was pacified. Climbing upstairs in a burst of friendliness, she looked at Myra in open curiosity; several times she seemed about to question her but thought better of it at the final moment. With her first opportunity Myra went to the pawnbroker. Promptly he handed over the rings; as he turned back her music box his fingers caressed the silklike wood and the bits of silver in the design. He pressed the catch to make it tinkle, and the Creole song rang out in the dusty shop. He cocked his head to the side. Would she be willing to sell? Putting her hand upon the box to silence it, Myra shook her head.

Little Will improved quickly; within a few days he was out of bed, running up and down the hallway, playing on the narrow edge of green beside the boardinghouse. She went to the market; when Estevan Perez spied her he ran forward. "You got good news. I tell it by your face." At first he refused to accept her money.

"You'd better take it." Myra laughed wryly. "The time may come when I'll need credit again." She could not believe such fortune would last long; in the past few years she had had too many disappointments.

Again she would allow herself a single small extravagance, a hat—a thing she had needed for some months. She would, of course, go to the establishment of Mme. Gouaux; that last visit had brought her a stroke of fortune. The madame, mustaches twitching, told her she had just what she wanted—a little green thing, practically bare, just eleven plumes on it. The feathers hung over her eyes as Myra walked forth, almost a new woman.

Her brow wrinkled as her thoughts reverted many times to Edmund Pendleton Gaines. The name was vaguely familiar. When she called on Attorney Jensen that imperturbable man for once showed emotion. "Gaines? Don't you know he's commander of the Army for this department, nearly half the country? You must've heard of him—'the hero of Fort Erie'—when he was in the War of 1812?" Myra frowned; it had been something in the history books, she remembered.

The lawyer had more to tell. "For years Gaines has been in line for command of the whole Army; he's missed it once or twice by a hairsbreadth, and some people—my brother for instance—are sure he'll get the job the next time." His eyes twinkled. "And Gaines's backers aren't satisfied with the Army for him. I don't know how anyone has missed the talk of Gaines for President!" As Myra looked more and more startled, Mr. Jensen continued. "For my part, I don't think he'll get either place. He's no politician, which may well be fatal. He's a curious chap; he's got a strong habit of telling anybody he doesn't like to go straight to hell. Most of the time they say he's easy to get along with—even to impose on; when he's mad, make for the woods!"

Gaines, Mr. Jensen went on, made his own way by his own rules. For over twenty-five years he had been before the nation as a military man; he had called tens of thousands as volunteers in his successive campaigns against Indians, Mexicans, Spaniards. Regularly his followers proclaimed him a shining leader; with almost equal regularity Washington officialdom fumed at him for his forthright, highly personal manner of conducting his affairs. "They've tried to court-martial him once or twice." Mr. Jensen grinned.

At home she learned more. Eulalie clapped her hands at the first mention of the man. "But who has to ask who Edmund Gaines is?" she demanded. "If he were not an American I would take him for *un grand maréchal,* so gallant, so *beau*— and lately a widower too!" Eulalie sighed. "I have seen him kiss a hand like a Parisian." More than that, Eulalie added, the general had become a wealthy man, able to act on almost any impulse that came to him. In recent years he had assumed a place as one of the great social figures of New Orleans.

As Myra listened she indulged her old habit of twisting her fingers about the curl behind her ear. General Gaines sounded a bit—well, unpredictable. Her musings were interrupted by a well-brushed young man at the door, who introduced himself as the general's aide. "The general's best wishes, ma'am; the general wishes to know if it would suit your convenience to attend a conference tomorrow morning with him and Mr. Jensen?"

The next day the general leaped to his feet at the sight of her and, while the clerks gaped, escorted her from the door to Mr. Jensen's desk. They all talked of Daniel Clark. "I was only a young sprout, on duty in the Southeast, when I met your father," the general told Myra. "It meant no advantage to him, but he went out of his way to do services for me. I've never forgotten." His bright black eyes softened; as he spoke he ran sun-darkened fingers through his hair. In a moment Myra discovered he was an intelligent listener.

"I confess"—he smiled—"that I don't know as much as I might about the case. Will you tell me about it?" His look en-

couraged her; almost before she realized it she was launched
on a recital of her story. She told of Bellechasse, Coxe, Des
Granges, Zulime; she left out nothing—the stumbling blocks in
their way, the trouble they had in finding certain documents.
The narrative lasted nearly two hours; only as she approached
the end did she discover how long she had been speaking. Edmund Gaines nodded quietly to himself, rubbing a thin finger
along the side of his nose.

"As I thought—even stronger. And they haven't made a
penny's return to you, these men?" Anger flickered in his eyes
as she shook her head. "Nobody can do a good job on short
rations. That's been one of your troubles." His eyes darted to
Mr. Jensen. "We'll take care of that from now on. This afternoon I'll place a sum in a special account at my bank, to be
drawn on by you, whenever you see the need. There'll be ten
thousand dollars for a starter."

Myra could only incline her head. She was just beginning to
sense the kind of individual who had found his way into her
affairs. She rose; she would need time to digest all of these
developments. They stood together for a moment, his tall figure
bent over hers. "Oh, but I've had my carriage waiting for you,"
he told her as she whispered her adieus; and he darted ahead,
opening the office door for her. Mr. Jensen turned back to his
desk; they had entirely forgotten him.

Crossing the banquette, Myra became aware of a stir. For
once no one was paying attention to her, because every eye was
upon the general. A group of dandies halted and stared in open
admiration. A trio of substantial-looking individuals, obviously
merchants, extended their hands. One appeared rather familiar
to her; then she placed him—the cotton factor, Ainsworth,
whom she had seen only at a distance since that disastrous evening at the Boisfontaines'.

Returning their greetings, the general bowed in Myra's direction. "Mrs. Whitney, gentlemen." He paused, his eyes passing
from one to the other, and added with emphasis: "The daughter
of my great friend, Daniel Clark." His tone let them understand that if they dared reply as many Orleanians would have
liked to do he was ready to run them through with his sword.
The three men mumbled something; the gray-haired, stooped

Mr. Ainsworth squinted in amazement, as if the general had suddenly presented him to a female giraffe.

They would have told him good-by, but the general, raising an authoritative hand, detained them. "Mrs. Whitney and I have been consulting her attorney. I'm satisfied she has a clear case." His listeners flinched. Ignoring their response, he made a final remark. "And I'm concerned in it as an admirer of Daniel Clark." They parted, and from the set of the three pairs of well-draped, middle-aged shoulders Myra knew their listeners were rushing to the business section to break this news.

At least once a week Myra and Edmund Gaines met with Mr. Jensen. Frowning at any inaction, the general was full of projects and suggestions, many more ingenious than workable. "Can't you file some more suits?" he demanded regularly. Mr. Jensen demurred: already they had appealed to Washington in their federal case. Edmund Gaines was unconvinced.

Myra, catching the general's puzzled expression, smiled. "The best defense is a strong offense, we know. But we'd better not scatter our forces, had we?" Her voice was firm; in a way that he could not find objectionable, she had scored against him.

Edmund Gaines grinned to himself and, as his gaze crossed Mr. Jensen's, he shook his head. "This little lady knows more than you'd think!" At Myra's startled glance he added hastily, "For a female, I mean."

At this she laughed quietly. "I'd rather have you say the first thing, sir!" He gave her a long look in which amusement matched his admiration.

A few minutes later the general was advancing a new plan. "Do you mind if I write my friends around the country and let them know the facts?" When Myra agreed he went on. "I want to tell some men in government offices, a few judges, and some lawyers"—he waved his hand—"Daniel Webster, Caleb Cushing, General Walter Jones, Reverdy Johnson . . ." He called off a dozen more, and Mr. Jensen's face took on a blurred expression; the man was calling a roll of the great figures of the American bar.

Then he asked Myra if she would mind dictating to one of the clerks, here, her own version of the affair. She complied, and as she spoke, rapidly, fluently, he marveled again at her grasp of scattered facts, her marshaling of a complicated narrative. "And now," he asked Mr. Jensen, "may I have about fifty copies made? I think I can prevail on my friends to read this and pass it to *their* friends; and my editor acquaintances will oblige too. This would certainly come under the heading of 'interesting intelligence' for their readers, don't you agree?"

Here was a new line of attack. Myra was convinced that Relf and Chew had used the New Orleans newspapers for their purposes. Now, with the general, she would be reaching out to the whole country. This kind of assistance might be almost as important as his financial contributions. Impulsively she put her hand on his sleeve. "Thank you," she told him in a low voice. "Thank you." She felt the muscles of his firm arm move beneath her touch, and she dropped her fingers. When they left, again they forgot Mr. Jensen.

Always, punctiliously, the general escorted Myra home. Almost always they were stopped by the general's friends, and more and more Orleanians showed varying degrees of surprise. Today, as the general's aide held open the carriage door, there approached a dowager in purple, her pompadour like a beacon above her full-blown features. The general kissed the grande dame's hand. "Mme. de la Villebeuvre—Mrs. Myra Whitney." The great lady drew into herself, and her nose lifted as if she had caught a whiff of an open sewer. Almost at once she excused herself, her skirts swinging angrily as she hurried away.

Seated beside Myra, the general gave her a blank look; he couldn't understand Madame's attitude.

"I can," Myra replied. "I'm claiming two plantations of hers." There was a moment of silence, and Myra added, "That would leave her only three." The general slapped his knee and shook with hearty laughter.

Unexpectedly Edmund Gaines's aide knocked. Could she meet the general within an hour at Mr. Jensen's? A matter of some importance; the carriage would await her. As her Kentucky friend took over the supervision of the children Myra dressed with fingers that shook. It could be only one thing—the overdue decision by the United States Supreme Court on her request that the Louisiana federal judge hear her case under equity rules, without restriction on testimony.

She almost ran into the office. Her first sight of the two men's anxious faces gave her the verdict. Sinking slowly into a chair, she read a stray sentence : under an act dating back twenty years, federal courts all over the country must act under federal rules, regardless of the state involved. These rules called for broad equity procedure in such cases. Obviously, the Supreme Court declared, the lower judge was not doing this in the present instance. . . . Yet, the decision went on, the record disclosed that this judge was proceeding with the case, no matter how irregularly he was doing it. Mrs. Whitney had not taken the proper action by appealing to Washington at this stage. She must wait until a judgment was rendered below, then appeal it.

"This says the judge is doing an injustice, but they can't do anything about it until he commits more injustices !" Myra's face flamed. "And they say he's proceeding; he *isn't*. He's doing nothing, nothing at all. He won't allow us to present our evidence, he refuses our requests and won't let the record show it." She was almost weeping. "Now Washington says we have to go back to him !"

Edmund Gaines had been watching in silence as she ran her hand through her heavy curls. For the first time since they had met she appeared defeated. He touched her arm. "Wait. . . . I happen to know the government's finally going to set up a full United States circuit court down here, as they have it in other states. Then we'll finally get two judges on the bench—not one, as in the past—and things will be different."

"How long will we wait ?" Her eyes were stony. "It's been six years already."

"If it takes another six we'll get it through." An encouraging grin on his lean face, Edmund Gaines rose. "And now it's time to forget the case for a little while." Head lowered, her shawl hanging loosely down her back, she let him lead her out. As they reached the door he gently adjusted the fringed cloth about her shoulders. Dusk had come; this time the ever-present military aide was gone. Edmund Gaines leaned toward her. "There's someone I'd like you to meet." She nodded, a question on her face, and he added, "My son." He called to the driver, "St. Charles Hotel."

Just above Canal Street, in the American section, they reached the celebrated new hostelry. Through the pillared "Ladies' Entrance," with its shiny placard, up the wide curve of the stairs, he escorted her to an elaborate public chamber. She thought it empty, until the general walked to one of the velvet-curtained windows beyond the range of the gaslight. A childish figure disengaged itself, and Edmund, taking the boy's hand, brought him forward.

In the bright light, as Myra first saw young Ed, she felt a sense of pity, almost of shock. Though he was about eleven, he appeared hardly taller than her Rhoda; the child seemed wretchedly pale, and his eyes were puffed and ringed with red; for a moment she thought he had been crying. The father shook his head sadly and, touching his finger to his own eyes, whispered, "Doctors say they're doing all they can." The boy extended a thin hand and looked up at her with a smile very much like his father's.

"We're going to like each other," she told him, and drew him against her.

Several times Edmund Gaines brought the boy to Myra's boardinghouse. With him young Ed always carried a box of soldiers with toy swords, miniature cavalry, and other accouterments. Rhoda was won to him at once, and Julia and Will quickly joined her. Preoccupied with his armies, Ed talked learnedly of troop movements and deployments over Mrs. Geohegan's dusty parlor carpets. With Rhoda he arranged assaults, emplacements behind chairs, and frequent troop inspections; the commanding officer, the tallest metal soldier of all, was invariably his father. "To battle!" he ordered in the general's name, and as Rhoda clapped her hands in delight the long files went out to die for the general.

The slender, nervous boy was alternately gay and listless. Again and again he rubbed his myopic eyes.

Myra stole a glance at the father as he watched; his face was kind, and sad. "Ed's always been sickly," he told her. "We've —I've had to watch over him. It's been one of my crosses. . . ." His voice died away and Myra knew that beneath his composed manner Edmund Gaines was an unhappy man.

Almost against her will she asked: "Crosses? You've had so much——"

"Everything but what I've wanted most!" The voice,

normally so easy, came harshly to her. "My career—a failure! Cheated, over and over, of the thing that should have been mine!" As the children looked up in momentary surprise he began to stride up and down the narrow room. Then, reseating himself, he apologized. The hurt look remained, however, and as Myra continued silent he spoke once more:

"Perhaps it was the injustice to you that first made me interested in your case." His thin, well-chiseled lips quivered. "How well do I know unfairness!" He spoke of his ambition to be commander of the American Army; of the way he had been deprived of the rank, partly because of his clashes with officialdom, partly because of the curious situation in which his career crossed that of another, a man of almost equal rank—General Winfield Scott. They had advanced side by side; they had offered nearly equal claims for the post; a few years ago, when a new commander was to be named, Edmund Gaines had been almost certain the place would be his. At the same time Winfield Scott had been at work, through dozens of highly placed friends. The result was a deadlock; some claimed that the President, as a consequence, had been forced to take a third man, a dark horse—"a fellow of minor talent, with far less claim for the office!" Edmund, his hand clenching, shot out the words.

Beyond that was the matter of the presidency. This, too, had seemed a good possibility; but once again the scales had shifted. In each case, she gathered, hope did not die; and there lay the continuing bitterness. Another time would come; would he miss again? . . . He lifted his face and spoke with difficulty. "You don't think I'm wrong, to feel as I do—or foolish?" He was especially afraid of that last word; people had laughed at him over his quarrels and sneered at his ambitions.

Myra shook her head. "No. They'll always laugh, and they'll always sneer. What does it matter?" Her voice had a caressing quality.

From the corner of the room, rubbing his eyes, young Ed gave a yell. "Fix bayonets!" and the four children crawled after their soldiers. When Edmund and the boy left a little later Myra walked upstairs with the children. For a long time she sat in one of the rigid chairs, her chin in her hand. Then she penned a note to Zulime, her third in a week. "You were right when you guessed," she began. "Now I know I've fallen in love again. But

I'm afraid. . . ." She compressed her lips. There were so many obstacles. He was older; he knew fame and honor, while in the eyes of New Orleans she was a woman about whom people whispered, with three children to support.

On their way from another consultation, a month later, Edmund paused at Myra's door. There was to be a special performance at Barrett's Theatre the following evening; the management had sent him tickets. He wondered . . . With a grateful smile she agreed.

Not until she was upstairs did she think of her costume. A long time had passed since she had gone to a function of this kind; her last evening dress had gone. Should she tell him she couldn't join him? Then she recalled his pleasure at her acceptance. Shielding the light against the children's eyes, she hurried to the armoire. In a heap at the back she found the rumpled brocade gown that she and Zulime had dyed and then altered to a street costume. Much of the material was in good condition, though the shoulders and waist had broken. Her eyes fell on a gray-green wrapper; why shouldn't she do as Zulime had taught her and turn the two into a single new dress? She had no headgear. . . . She searched until she discovered the last hat she had bought from Mme. Gouaux. The hat itself had lost its shape but the green plumes still looked fresh. Ripping them off, she placed them against her hair, then smiled and went quickly to work.

As Edmund Gaines took her hand the next evening his eyes swept over her in swift admiration. Her face, above her soft throat and her firm, bare arms, was alight; against her loose curls the feathers quivered in the breeze. As they approached the theater he told her of the night's event, the debut of Fanny Elssler, the danseuse who had come to America the preceding summer, to stir New York and every other city in which she appeared. For weeks Orleanians had been fighting for tickets.

Stepping out of the carriage, Myra heard the name of Gaines murmured all about them. Someone started a cheer; the general stood stiffly at attention, saluting twice, to the left and right. Her arm in his trembled slightly; he looked down with a protective air. Then, as the crowds parted, he led her forward along the carpet. The management had realized the value of a popular hero; in all the theater, she saw at once, there was no box so conspicuous as theirs.

As they appeared a hum arose from the tightly packed crowd. The general advanced to the side of the box and bowed as applause rose from the bejeweled women, their black-suited escorts, and the throngs in the upper seats. His face flushed, he returned to her and whispered, "I'm fortunate tonight. Every man here is jealous of me."

She resisted the temptation to say what occurred to her: "And every woman hates me." Perhaps that wasn't altogether true, but it became quickly evident, from their expressions, the inclinations of their heads, what they were saying. Was it really that Mrs. Whitney with the general? Malice shone unhidden in many eyes. To think that the woman had the effrontery to appear in this way in public. Momentarily Myra had an inclination to flee; in the shadow Edmund pressed her hand, and she quieted.

Lines of visitors entered the box, and Myra was introduced and reintroduced. Repeatedly they were invited to parties, to receptions, to suppers after the performance. The general refused all requests. "We have an important engagement," he assured them. Myra wondered but asked no questions. Meanwhile she made herself listen. It was the first such night the city had seen since the bad times, wasn't it? Beneath the excitement ran another note; New Orleans was withholding judgment. It had heard almost too much of La Elssler. Proudly the veteran theatergoers were telling each other that they knew the best; their city had had opera when upstart New York applauded vaudeville. They'd see. They'd see. . . . Myra felt a rush of sympathy for the woman they were to watch; how well she knew a merciless crowd!

At last the lights were lowered, and the orchestra struck up a lively tune; Elssler's first number would be "La Tarentelle." Out leaped a vivid figure. Like many others, Myra experienced a shock; the woman did not look beautiful; she was hardly comely. At first her movements appeared jerky, ungraceful. Could this be the female for whom the Yankees wrote songs and named hats? A heavy costume draped her legs, and the men were particularly disappointed.

Yet despite all this La Elssler gradually caught them. As much an actress as a dancer, she gained power in her movements; all sense of strain vanished, as Myra found her pulses racing, her lips parted. The Creoles and Americans cried out together. Singers and pantomimists followed; then Elssler appeared twice again, in a Spanish number and, as the Creoles had been demanding, in a classic Greek number, her form magnificently displayed. When she ended the whole audience rose, shouted, threw flowers; one Frenchman almost fell from his box. For nearly fifteen minutes it lasted, the dancer bowing, throwing kisses. Finally, with a half-laughing gesture of weariness, she blew them a kiss and the crowd gave up.

The manager escorted Edmund, Myra, and a few others to the great one's dressing room. Elssler reclined on a divan in a red wrapper. She looked exhausted; at close range Myra thought her little more than ugly. But the manager brought champagne; as she tossed her head back and burst into quick sentences the woman went through the same metamorphosis that had occurred on stage, growing lovely before them.

When the others prepared to go Elssler indicated that she wished Myra and Edmund to stay. Alone with them, she focused her shrewd eyes on the general. She had inquired about him in advance, and she had been well informed. She spoke easily, rather accurately, of his exploits; she mentioned certain soldiers of the Continent and what they had said to her. Then Myra was amazed to find the dancer discussing her case. Ah, but yes! She had heard of Mme. Whitney. This strange, wonderful America. She knew of no other country in which such a thing as Mme. Whitney's suits could be filed. Her hand took Myra's. "Please, my dear, don't let these men frighten you out of it." She laughed. "But I don't think they will. You have a certain look in the eyes—and in the jaw too."

At the door she drew Myra back again. "Would a little advice from another woman offend you?" She touched Myra's cheek; she had grown weary and lackluster again. "I meant what I just said about—about fighting for what is yours. Claw, kill if you have to! But remember, dear, there must be other things in life. Existence for a woman without joy, without love . . . nothing can be worth it." She gave a shrug.

In the carriage Myra asked Edmund about the other engagement he had mentioned. He was silent for a time, constrained; as the evening progressed she had sensed a growing unease in his manner. The driver turned toward the city's outskirts; the road lay quiet in the moonlight. She made out Edmund's long, straight profile against the glow from outside.

"Myra, I've been asking myself . . ." He swallowed, then caught her hand. "You need somebody to protect and—and help you. You have your children, and I have young Ed. . . ." His voice grew muffled; no longer was he the gallant of tradition. "We have the same interests, the same . . . Why shouldn't . . ."

Myra's voice was clear and sharp. "I realize all that, Edmund. But there's more than that. Don't you love me?"

Edmund Gaines's breath caught in his throat. What he replied she did not hear. Through the folds of her dress the steel buttons of his coat pressed hard against her; his mouth searched for hers. She, too, had planned what she would say: he'd hurt himself by any connection with her; she was strong-minded, she was used to her own way; most of New Orleans feared or hated her; certainly this wouldn't benefit his career. . . . At the pressure of his hands, the warmth of his firm lips upon hers, she forgot it all.

The driver flicked his whip. The horses jogged through the moonlight, beneath the folds of moss from the oaks, that caught at the top of the carriage as if they were the draperies of ghosts.

Part Two

MADAME GENERAL

CHAPTER XVI

THROUGH the figured curtains the early sun shone in pale beams. Beneath the mosquito net Myra stirred, then sank her head against the lace-trimmed pillow. The sound of a step, muffled by the carpet, and then a thin, scraping movement drew her back toward consciousness. She smiled; it was Edmund, shaving before his usual morning walk. Thrusting the curls out of her eyes, she glanced through the net at her husband's broad bare shoulders, the muscles working back and forth. He caught her reflection in the mirror and came to her at once.

When he bent over her he kissed her, long and fervently, first on the lips; then his mouth found the tiny scar beside her ear. He had quickly discovered the minor blemish; it was one of their private jokes. As they laughed together her thoughts slipped briefly to those other first days with Will Whitney. They had been different, the quick ardor of youthful bodies in union; yet her hours with Edmund were not the less joyous. It had been a happy month since their marriage.

With a sigh he returned to his dressing, and she began to check over her appointment list. Tonight a reception at the city home of the Valcour Aimeses, from up the Mississippi; in the afternoon the races with several of Edmund's Army friends, here for the carnival season. But the most important, he reminded her, would be their interview at breakfast. John Randolph Grymes, perhaps the most celebrated attorney in New Orleans, certainly the most highly paid, had agreed to consider their case. In the past few weeks Edmund had retained a number of additional lawyers, experts in certain branches. Myra had speculated over the wisdom—the extravagance, she suspected—of having so many. Edmund, however, had shown firmness: no battle was ever won without good officers. After a time she realized that this was one of the matters in which she must acquiesce.

As she adjusted Edmund's tie she reflected how understanding and how generous he had been in everything. Zulime had been overjoyed at word of their plans but, shyly, she had wanted to remain in Mississippi. At Edmund's urging Myra sent for her and her two aunts a few days before the ceremony. When Edmund met them he took the agitated hand that Zulime raised and began at once to talk of Daniel Clark. "Your husband"—though he gave no particular emphasis to his words, Edmund chose them with instinctive tact—"your husband was one of the finest men I've ever known."

As Zulime regained her composure he described his early years in the vicinity of Natchez and Mobile when he, a rising young officer, met the older man. Then, quietly, he turned to Myra's case. "I've heard your story, madame," he told her, "and I have complete faith in it." While Myra watched them she saw Zulime's tension slip away; her eyes took on a tender look.

When Zulime and Myra retired her mother took her hand. "How fortunate you are, *chérie*. A second husband so fine and so true! Perhaps *le Bon Dieu* is making it up to you for our troubles." Myra thought this a good moment to broach Edmund's proposal. Wouldn't Zulime come to live with them permanently, at the hotel? Her mother thanked her but declined. Myra and the general would be very much before the public; Zulime was unaccustomed to such things. Besides, there would be people, seeing her, who would gossip and ask questions; and that would not help Myra, would it? Reluctantly Myra agreed. A year ago poverty had separated them; now her marriage was doing the same thing.

Young James and Eulalie, the Carrière sisters, fellow officers of the general with their wives were present for the ceremony and the toasts in champagne and the cheers from a crowd that gathered on the street. Afterward Edmund had brought her here, to the room filled with blossoms in bowls and vases. Edmund's aide, she suspected, was responsible for the scattered profusion; for a moment, too, with a flicker of humor, she had wondered which of his male assistants had chosen the bed—a four-poster dominated by an overlavish pink-and-blue canopy on which fat cupids chased one another.

A few days later, catching her amused expression, Edmund agreed that perhaps the cupid canopy was a bit lush; and she made a replacement. She learned many unexpected things about this man. Though he was inclined to be cheerful, oversanguine in most things, a mere word or look could touch one of his underlying points of sensitivity.

He was the victim of moods and melancholy, when all his efforts seemed futile. Too, certain kinds of opposition infuriated him; having spent his life in the Army, he had acquired a habit of command. Now and then, Myra thought, Edmund did not comprehend that fixed obedience must not be expected outside the military realm. But a little tact and a minor concession restored him to good spirits; his face would break into a smile, and at once he was apologetic. Gradually she found herself looking after him with almost a motherly attention, smoothing the way, calming him.

As she had originally suspected, Edmund sometimes showed a certain gullibility—an inclination to believe whatever he wished to believe. A few days after their marriage a rat-faced individual in a checked suit sent word he wanted to see the general "alone and personal," on an important matter. A few minutes later, going to Edmund with a new message, she discovered him still with his caller, his purse in hand. "Look, dear!" he cried. "A sworn confession by that fellow Des Granges! Just what we've been hoping to get. Our friend here——"

The "friend" became suddenly restive. Murmuring that he had an appointment, he reached out for the bills that Edmund held. "Wait." Myra came between them and took the paper from Edmund. "The date says 1820. But this kind of paper came into use only three or four years ago. And this signature isn't faintly like Des Granges's. It's a crude fake!" As the man edged to the door Edmund Gaines's face tightened into a menacing frown; again Myra stepped between them. "You'd better go, quickly," she told the stranger. As the door slammed she turned back. "Edmund, you see . . ."

It took a little time to restore his spirits, but she succeeded. Sometimes she grew alarmed because Edmund was injecting himself so wholeheartedly into the case; he talked of it constantly, thought of ideas and schemes. But he was drawing the interest and—not less important—the sympathy of dozens of men and women who might otherwise be opposed to Myra; and without question he was enlisting powerful legal assistance.

Now Edmund leaned over for a good-by kiss; he would be back within an hour with Attorney Grymes, he told her. Drawing an embroidered wrap about her, Myra rang for her maid. The mulatto girl worked deftly as Myra ran through her mail.

It was of normal proportions, fifteen or twenty letters a day. She sorted out the invitations: two receptions, a grand ball, a party in their honor . . . Two more articles about the case, published by Edmund's friends, ten notes from men and women who had read them. The stories, reprinted widely, drew ever-increasing attention.

She found a surprise, a clipping from the Nashville *Republican Banner*. A Northern newspaper had inquired, not altogether pleasantly, what had happened of late to Edmund Gaines. The publisher replied:

The editor of the New York *Gazette* don't know that the General has won a field lately that has covered him all over with wealth and laurels—a field hardly fought and hotly won in the teeth of a hundred young, handsome and spirited gallants. General Gaines is in New Orleans—a conqueror of a fair widow's heart and the possessor of eminent wealth. Don't be cutting your shines about our Southern men. They don't bluster much, but when the tug comes, you'll hear from them.

Applying her perfume, Myra smiled. How different were the facts; and how differently had New Orleans taken the marriage! And over and over she heard the words she had expected—"old enough to be her father." But on the surface at least a vast change had occurred in the public reaction to her. The newspaper attacks ceased abruptly; instead the notes in the journals referred to "General Gaines and his lovely wife"; "the energetic, talented mate of the general . . ."

Turning back to her mail, she opened one that bore the mark of Binghamton. Mrs. Whitney wrote that they were happy at the news; it would have been unfair to Myra, and unnatural, not to expect her to marry again. . . . Myra whispered her thanks to the generous woman who had several times made her way easier. At the bottom waited a final message, from Samuel Davis. He stressed his surprise; he had heard good things of the general, but he hoped Myra had thought carefully before taking such a step, with an older man. Incidentally, he had news: Sally was about to have her second child. Myra smiled; there was less difference between her age and Edmund's than between the elderly colonel's and the childlike Sally's.

The maid brought three dresses, two of filmy white, the last honey-colored, trimmed in bows; she chose the third. As she placed a row of roses in her hair Eulalie Montagnet entered with the children, Rhoda marching steadily in the lead, young Ed bringing up the rear. How fortunate she was that Eulalie had joined them. Myra had known at once that she would need someone to look after the children, and she had worried until, riding along the street, she spied her old friend. In a few minutes she saw that Eulalie's discontent had sharpened. Elégeas had lost his position; now she was sharing a room with two crabbed cousins. Hesitantly Myra broached the subject; Eulalie accepted at once. The Montagnets were horrified: Eulalie was sinking to new depths, and at an American hotel too! None of Eulalie's family talked to her as she gathered her belongings, her altar, and her picture of Télémaque, and left to stay permanently with the Gaineses.

"They have been good today," Eulalie told her as the four children clustered about her. "Ed, he has fixed Will's shoes; and this week Ed has been eating everything he should." The older boy gave a nearsighted smile as Myra added her praise. It had taken him a bit longer than she had anticipated to fit himself to this changed life. At first he had been reticent, but Myra had taken particular pains to make things smooth for him, and now he responded more easily. Always "the general's son," the sickly boy had known few playmates. She was certain the companionship of the other children would be good for him.

Edmund himself, she reflected, had had no real problems with the other three. From the beginning the handsome soldier had charmed the earnest, sturdy Rhoda; bowing gravely before her, he consulted her wishes in many things. He carried the more wistful Julia on his shoulders, joking with her, telling her he had orders from "headquarters"—she was, like young Ed, to put on more weight, without delay. With little Will, Edmund had some slight difficulty. The boy, always Myra's favorite, raced in and out of the rooms, jumped on chairs in the hotel restaurant, and called shrill greetings to others of his age. Once caught, he would wrinkle his tiny nose and impish eyes, long like Myra's but not as full; he would nod solemnly and then be off again. "You've spoiled him." Edmund would smile, and she would agree.

As the children left, Myra turned her gaze, lightly curious, to Eulalie. What about this man John Grymes?

"Ah, *quel homme!*" The Creole's eyes twinkled. "What isn't he, that one? A great orator, a great liver, a great *farceur!* He's been here so long we think of him as a Frenchman, and doesn't he behave like one!" A Virginian, Grymes had come to Louisiana years ago as a young United States attorney. Before he was twenty-two the prodigy was holding his own in the courts, the saloons, at the gambling tables and dueling grounds; he had made himself a city character, about whom there was ever a new bit of gossip.

"Have you heard about the time he was attorney for those buccaneers, the Lafittes?" Eulalie lifted her eager face. During Governor Claiborne's time the grand jury charged the Lafittes, and what did those rascals do but turn around and hire Grymes, the district attorney, as their lawyer! Grymes resigned the office and took the case for twenty thousand dollars. The man who assumed his post pointed a finger—stolen money had made Grymes desert his duty. Ah, what excitement! Grymes challenged him to a duel and left the fellow a cripple for life. And he won the case for the pirates of course.

"Afterward, you know what happened? The Lafittes invited Grymes to the Mississippi mouth, their stronghold: they would give him his money and fete him properly. Grymes had a glorious week—every kind of pleasure, without exception, they say. Also they claim he insisted on gambling a bit, with the Lafittes and also with the planters of the delta country on the way back. Anyway, he came home with only an empty pocket and a heavy thirst; but he always said the week was worth it, and——"

This was curious preparation for the man to whom Myra might entrust her fortunes. Misgivings arose in her when the general entered, bringing an imposing individual almost as tall as Edmund himself, an elegant in skin-tight, pea-green pantaloons, claw-hammer coat, waistcoat in delicate shadings. John Grymes wore grandeur like one born to it; his well-defined features showed marks of long dissipation, but his blue eyes lighted up with a fresh and merry look.

"My dear Mrs. Gaines." The voice was musical, the words startling. "I salute the most hated woman in New Orleans—and the loveliest." Giving her no opportunity to reply, he went on. "They have cause for concern. Someday you may own 'em all!" He cocked his head. "Tell me, what will you do with your millions if we bring them to you?"

"I'll wait, sir, till you've brought me"—she halted—"justice."

"Ha!" With a Chesterfieldian gesture he gave her his arm. Edmund could only follow them down the curve of the stairs and across the lobby. The St. Charles of the early 1840s was regarded by many as America's most lavish hostelry. For the women in particular, it towered as an establishment of fabled splendor—great parlors and running water, a staggering array of obsequious servants, great ladies whispering behind lifted fans. From upriver and down-bayou arrived the planters—men of old families, their manner cold; the *nouveaux riches,* pleased to exhibit their flashy wives; men on the rise, determined not to show how impressed they were; men on the decline, begging a last advance from their brokers.

As they reached the dining room John Grymes took command. "We'll have, if Madame doesn't mind, a breakfast that the management—and I—recommend. Ham in wine sauce. Omelette with truffles, and see that Auguste is the one who prepares it," he directed. Myra was certain that if Grymes failed to recognize Auguste's handiwork he would at least throw the concoction to the floor. "And let's try Creole cream cheese to begin with; what do you say to fresh figs with it? Jellied oranges for the finish, with cream, the thick kind. Oh, and two pots of coffee."

Over the cream cheese he plunged into the case. "The main points look clear enough, though they may call for special effort here and there." He flicked a jeweled finger. Extravagantly polite to Myra, Grymes addressed most of his remarks to the general; there was no doubt that while he thought ladies admirable for certain places and purposes he did not regard them as partners in enterprises of this kind. "Now it will be easy to establish . . ." When he made an error in a date Myra corrected him; he bowed and went on. In a moment he slipped on a name and Myra noted it. Gradually the shrewd blue eyes shifted to her with new respect.

"I see," he said slowly. "You'll save me a lot of trouble, Mrs. Gaines. You'll be at my table during proceedings." Hacking off a bit of dripping ham, he leaned toward her. "You know, I never prepare a case!" He bellowed at her astonishment. "Ask arybody in New Orleans!"

Edmund pursed his lips. "I'm inclined to believe it, my dear."

Grymes gave an elaborate wink. "Sometimes if you know too much about a thing you can't argue it so well!"

In temporary confusion Myra turned to the creamy omelette. Then, quickly, Grymes concentrated his questions upon her. They were detailed, penetrating; he never took a note; he encouraged her to talk, asked what she suspected, what this one said when he refused to speak. She discovered that he remembered everything; analyzing, reanalyzing, his mind moved ahead of hers. He asked her permission to smoke; receiving it, he reached with a deft gesture into Edmund's pocket and took out two cigars, one for Edmund, one for him.

With some timidity Myra suggested he might wish her to call at his office. This brought another smile. "Mrs. Gaines, I have an office, but I can't remember when I was last there. That's what clerks are for. When my friends want me they know where to look—any bar, any café, any—never mind." He winked as he lifted his cigar. "And no matter what you hear about me—don't hesitate to believe it. It'll probably be true."

John Grymes shifted his gaze. "Ed, your wife has won me as much as her case has. I accept it for a down payment"—he stopped, as if in reflection, ever the showman—"of ten thousand dollars." Shocked at the figure, Myra did not raise her eyes. Then she heard the scratch of Edmund's pen and Grymes's grunt: "Good. That's just enough to repay my last month's gambling debts." As he folded the paper Grymes smiled sardonically. "Edmund, I hope you have change for the breakfast to which I invited you?"

As Edmund and Myra moved toward the hotel's ornate entranceway the following morning a feminine hand touched her furred muff. "Mrs. Gaines, please!" A rather familiar face smiled confidently into hers. Blinking, she placed it—Mrs. Ainsworth, the broker's wife of the evening at the Boisfontaines'. A wide, feathered hat covered the silky blond hair; sharp green eyes studied her with an ingratiating air. "I was afraid for a moment that you hadn't recognized me!" Mrs. Ainsworth looked expectantly toward the general.

A retort rose to Myra's lips, but she did not utter it: "I'm afraid I *have* recognized you." Those eyes had been cold as they abandoned Myra to her enemies on that last hideous occasion. But the woman bubbled on. ". . . how many times I've missed you at parties! I've wanted *so* much to talk with you"—she hesitated a fraction of a second before adding—"again. The last time, you know, we had *so* little opportunity——"

"I didn't think you were particularly anxious——"

"Oh, but I was!" The expression grew more and more suave. "I've spoken to a lot of your friends since then; we all think you're *so* brave." At last, flustered at Myra's expressionless face, Mrs. Ainsworth began to stammer, and her eyes went again to General Gaines. Edmund, always the gallant, pressed at Myra's arm, and she murmured an introduction.

"Ainsworth?" Edmund's pale eyebrows rose. "Albert Ainsworth? He once provided my office with cotton supplies."

Mrs. Ainsworth's voice trilled; quickly she recalled, or said she did, that her husband regarded Edmund as one of his old friends and, of course, one of America's great figures. Sinking her hands in her muff, Myra stared ahead. She came back to the present as Mrs. Ainsworth ended a question: ". . . next Sunday at six?"

"I'm sorry," Myra answered hurriedly. "That's the night Edmund has to review the troops."

"Why, no, that's Monday!" Edmund's face was entirely innocent.

"Sunday, then." Mrs. Ainsworth had a triumphant light in her eye. "We'll be honored. . . ." She retired in a swirl of perfume. Myra frowned as she worked at her gloves; oh well, the damage was done.

That Sunday night they drew up at a great white-pillared establishment in the rapidly developing American section. The elegance of the house seemed, somehow, freshly applied; and it was so overcrowded that afterward Myra recalled mainly a haze of names, platters of overplentiful food—and dozens of women who were spiritual cousins of Mrs. Ainsworth. Middle-aged, bejeweled, they clustered about her, elbowing each other in their eagerness to get next to her. Edmund, of course, drew a circle of his own; but many had apparently met him before, and Myra was the novelty. (Yet, she told herself sardonically, if she had not met Edmund, hardly one of them would have wanted to be found near her.)

When did she expect to win her case? "Oh, I'm not sure I'm going to win. I can only hope," Myra replied.

What would she do with her money when she won? "I haven't thought much. Pay my debts first."

The answer was honest, but the ladies clearly regarded it as quixotic. "But after that?" two cried at once.

"Well . . . I've thought of establishing a home for people in need the way I was—widows with children."

Glances were exchanged; this gave them a tidbit for future conversations. "How will you——"

A flurry arose at the door, and Myra was glad when half of the women began to slip away. Mrs. Ainsworth was leading forward a shuffling, elderly man; Myra's heart jumped as she recognized Judge François Xavier Martin of the Louisiana Supreme Court. Had Mrs. Ainsworth, remembering that last evening of their meeting, planned this to see what would happen? Myra managed to reach Edmund's side; her hand upon his arm, she faced the approaching figure.

The ancient judge looked toward them with the eyes of the totally blind.

"General and Mrs. Gaines," murmured Mrs. Ainsworth.

The justice's narrow lips tightened; the mane of white hair moved up and down. "General Gaines? I've had the pleasure— a glorious name, a glorious record." He appeared not to have heard the second name, and he turned to leave.

"And Mrs. Gaines," the hostess repeated.

Conflicting impulses showed themselves in the lined face as the judge remained in arrested position. At last he nodded stiffly and spoke in a half-audible voice. "Good evening, madame."

Myra sensed Edmund's surprise; it was impossible to miss the thrill of interest that shone in Mrs. Ainsworth's face. Then the woman *had* arranged it. A tide of anger rose within Myra. Perhaps she should pass it over, give the gossips nothing further to talk about. Then suddenly she told herself she'd be damned if she did. She spoke slowly. "Perhaps you don't place me, your honor. I'm Daniel Clark's daughter. Don't you recollect that you gave me some advice when we met?"

The judge's head jerked back; he was not accustomed to being caught up this way. "Indeed I do, madame!" He spoke in a furious rush. "And my advice still stands. You have no case;

you'd best forget this fruitless disturbance. It——" Then he checked himself and gave a cold bow. What little pleasure Myra had had from the evening had entirely gone.

The next day, partly as an antidote, she went with Edmund to the neighborhood of the old market and introduced him to her friends, Estevan and the other Perezes, Victorien Badeaux, Mme. Gouaux, and the others. Now and then, she told Edmund, she was inclined to feel that these were the only people whose attitude toward her had not changed. All except Victorien were slightly overawed by the general's repute and gilt buttons; the Cajun pounded his back, pumped his hand, and told him, "You done well, Gen'l, you done well wid dis lil wife, yes!" Thereafter she and the general walked regularly in the vicinity, and Edmund managed to call to the attention of several of the market people an opportunity or two to bid on small Army supply orders. But when he offered to suggest James Gardette's name to the military hospital authorities Myra's stepbrother smiled and demurred. "Thank you, sir." He smiled. "I couldn't be learning more than I am now, with my charity patients, and I'd rather do it this way." James, bless him, was another who would remain ever the same.

In the middle of a drowsy Sunday Myra heard a rap on the door. There stood James Gardette, his face dark with fury. He thrust a rumpled paper into her hand: "They're giving out hundreds of these, all over the city!"

Garish letters were splashed across the top: "HER OWN FAMILY HAS ANSWERED HER: HER FOSTER FATHER AND BROTHER DECLARE *MYRA GAINES ILLEGITIMATE!*" There followed the proceedings brought long ago by her foster brother, Horatio Davis, to get funds for Myra.

As Myra stared Edmund Gaines came in. Without further word he read the document from start to end. "There's nothing new here, is there?" he asked her at once. "Didn't Colonel Davis swear the word was used wrongly, without his knowledge?"

Myra nodded. "But to circulate it out of court this way, to discredit and humiliate me publicly!" Edmund, his chin set, went to the armoire; Myra caught a glint as he slipped his pistol into his pocket. "But we don't know who did this." She ran to him. "We've sued fifty, seventy-five people——"

"I may find out." His voice had grown metallic. "First I want to see Grymes." As he started off Myra quickly caught up her hat and shawl and put her arm through his. She waited in the carriage while he hunted for Grymes in the first bar, then the next, then in every café he could think of. Dusk had fallen when he returned, to sit beside her, dispirited.

"Let's try his office," she suggested. Edmund made a face; who'd ever seen Grymes there, even in day hours? When she persisted they sought out the place, only to find it closed and barred. Edmund took her arm, but she motioned him to silence, pushed open an alley door, and walked along it to a window. Her ear had caught the echo of a sound, and she rapped and rapped. At last the metal clasp opened and John Grymes looked out. His annoyance changed to chagrin.

"Trapped, at work!" he wailed. "Don't let this get around. I'll be the laughingstock of New Orleans."

Inside they discovered that he had been sneaking an opportunity to go over the case. Pushing aside lawbooks, wine bottles, and dirty plates, he made space for them. For a few minutes he mused over the circular. "So they're turning to new tactics," he said softly. "We have to face one thing, Myra. It's clear that your brother Horatio is well inside the enemy's camp. Don't you agree it's time to smoke him out?"

She shuddered at the thought of a family quarrel. But the matter had to be faced sooner or later, hadn't it? Finally she nodded, and they began to set out the facts as she knew them, for a public reply.

They did not have to wait long for a reaction. Not Relf and Chew, but Horatio Davis came back at them. His letter opened with pathos. "Myra! Did you write this statement? Are you the Myra I have so often lulled to sleep with all a brother's love, whose infant steps I have supported? . . . My father's authority is brought to bear against me, publicly raising a question of truth between us. Oh, shame, shame!" Finally Horatio struck a fresh blow. "From your infancy I never heard you designated otherwise than as the natural daughter of Daniel Clark. I believed you to be so, and I named you thus."

John Grymes rubbed his chin as he read Horatio's newest

words. "A curious document, this—saying much less than it seems to say." His light eyes were lost in creases of flesh as he broke into a laugh. "We'll see how well this Horatio holds the bridge."

When the case came to court again the courtroom was thronged as it had never been. General Gaines was present, sitting upright in his chair, pointed at, whispered about. John Grymes, making his debut in the case, dominated the proceedings. He swung from lawyers' table to the bench and back again, from document to statute book, always in motion, always pouring forth his stream of words. He was urbane, he was angry; he murmured, he thundered. Meanwhile he went regularly to his associates, for a name, a date, a place; a second's pause and he inserted it. More and more often it was Myra who whispered the information; gradually she was practically participating in the case. Had the showman planned it so obviously, bringing her directly into the foreground? She could not tell, but it was evident that the other side was raging.

Finally Horatio Davis stepped to the stand. Serenely the impressive, heavy-set attorney gazed at John Grymes. Quietly Grymes asked a question. The answer was given, brief and curt. Gently Mr. Grymes received it, almost lovingly he offered his next query. Then, without warning, a change occurred. Grymes's eyes flashed. "You say you never heard Myra called in your household in any other fashion except as the natural child of Daniel Clark? Who called her that?"

"Well, everybody. The servants knew it. Everybody did."

"Did your father use the term?"

"Well, that's my impression. He, among others——"

"When? Give us an instance." Grymes asked it very quickly.

"I can't think offhand of such an occasion. He may have more or less hinted——"

"But you just told us he said it."

"I didn't! I told you it was my impression——"

"Ah, that's different." Grymes had scored; he became one great, elegant smile. "Let's be more specific. Here I have a list of individuals." Myra had just put down the names of all persons she ever remembered in the household: servants, maids, grooms, friends. One by one Mr. Grymes called them out.

"Was it Phyllis who told you that?"

"Well, no. . . ."

"Then it was John?"

"I don't remember."

"Maybe it was Alice?"

The relentless inquisition went on and on. It developed that Horatio could recall no single person, no single occasion. Grymes shot a knowing look at the judge, then went on. "I have here a statement of your father's—a statement under oath." He read it: Davis had never called Myra illegitimate, and he denied he had led anyone to think such a thing. "What do you say to this?" Grymes's long face was thrust out suddenly at the witness.

"I"—Horatio Davis hesitated—"I don't know. My father's an old man. His faculties . . ." He made a deprecatory motion.

"But this statement was made some six years ago. I'm informed your father recently remarried, has had two children, and will soon have another. Isn't that so?"

"I've heard it."

"Would you say, then, that your father had really lost his— er—faculties? Or that he lost them six years ago and suddenly regained them since?" The blows were deadly. Horatio Davis flushed, looked ill, and remained silent. Grymes had calculated that this ultraconventional son would be touchy on the subject of his father's late new marriage.

Grymes pressed further. "Did you write that Colonel Davis gave you the grounds for your suit?" The witness nodded. Grymes brought forward Davis's own deposition and read it: Davis had been shocked when he learned what Horatio declared. He had told him to make no such statement, for the statement was entirely untrue, and he ordered Horatio to withdraw the suit. Grymes bore down hard. "Just how, sir, can you reconcile these statements?"

After a long silence Horatio replied, "I can only say that my father . . ." He paused, and Grymes took up the sentence:

". . . lost his faculties?"

Horatio contented himself with a look of loathing. Grymes went blithely on. "Here's a further statement by your father, saying that you conferred with Relf about all this." Grymes snapped a question. "Is that true or isn't it?"

"Yes, it's true. I did talk to Mr. Relf! Anything wrong with that?" The query had precisely the effect the lawyer wanted. Horatio, aflame, went on. "Mr. Relf has done nothing that any-body can——"

"Ah." Mr. Grymes grew gentle again. "Let me remind you, sir, that Mr. Relf has been accused of a great many things in this connection, and also that it was much to Mr. Relf's interest to have Myra stigmatized in this way——"

The Duncan brothers, almost purple, succeeded in having the judge rule out Grymes's last observation. Grymes resumed. "Then Relf knew this suit was being filed?"

"Yes. But he didn't want us to file it."

"So? Why not?"

"He said it might hurt the handling of the estate."

"Ah?" Grymes went back to Colonel Davis's deposition: "Relf said the estate was so unsettled, nothing could be done for Myra then, but when it was settled they might be able to do something for her." Horatio nodded. "So then—Relf did hold forth a hope that Myra might be given something?" Somewhat uncertainly Horatio nodded again. Out of his pocket Grymes brought another paper. "Yet here I have a statement of Mr. Relf, made years later. He claimed he knew nothing of Myra; he said he wasn't even sure she was Daniel's daughter, legitimate or illegitimate!"

Horatio shrugged. "I know nothing about that."

"But it's true *you talked with Relf about Myra's right to the property; and after Myra had been put down in the record as illegitimate, the suit was taken back?*"

Horatio could only answer yes. He stared at Grymes with heavy hostility; when the next question came he braced himself as for a blow.

"You're a good friend of Relf's?"

"I'm proud to say I am."

"You were a good friend of Relf's at the time the suit was filed?"

"Yes."

"But now you aren't on good terms with your father?"

"Well . . . we've had misunderstandings."

"Misunderstandings? Don't you know you haven't talked to

your father in years—that he hasn't exchanged even a letter with you in decades?"

"Yes." Horatio's face had active hate in it. The judge adjourned court.

CHAPTER XVII

AT THE mirror, as her maid put aside her velvet evening gown, Myra lifted her hand to remove the sumptuous ornament in her hair. Slowly, with a small smile, she ran her fingers over the design in silver and diamonds that had drawn such attention tonight at the opera.

She had wondered whether Edmund would remember the day, their second wedding anniversary; he had said nothing until, as they prepared for dinner, he reached into his pocket and placed the dark box before her. As she reached up to thank him her chin had trembled; it was, she knew, the costliest thing she had ever possessed, and the handsomest. These had been years of attentions, of deference and tribute. They enjoyed outings to the lake, trips to upriver plantations, an occasional visit to Washington and New York.

Yet neither of them, she suspected, was entirely content. Before her waited the case—always the case. Though John Grymes and their other attorneys worked earnestly, the opposition managed to delay their progress. The United States Supreme Court had ruled for her in one preliminary decision, declaring that the case, after all, must be heard under broad equity rules, admitting all evidence; and, equally important, that she need not present the fantastic array of documents demanded by the opposition. Yet still Relf and Chew threw up obstacles—technicalities, demurrers, objections. Would she ever get a full hearing? All they could do, as Grymes said, was grit their teeth and see that they stayed alive until a showdown came.

Edmund's interest in the litigation rose and fell; obviously he could not have maintained his original intense concern with it. His own goal proved equally elusive. He felt certain that if any change occurred in the office of the commanding general of the

Army the choice lay between him and General Winfield Scott; and disquieting reports reached him of the activity of his politically enterprising rival. There remained, too, the possibility of the presidency itself; his backers wrote him almost daily, making suggestions, urging strategy to be followed.

Tonight, from the next room, Myra heard Edmund arguing with one of these supporters and a merchant who had come along to talk over the general's thoughts on national policies.

"But we've got to have railroads!" Edmund shouted. "Steam power has created a revolution and, damn it, our Army is asleep. We have a border longer than practically any other country and we ought to be watching it. We need forts all over the West, with railroads connecting everywhere, East and South and West; and there's only one power can do it—the national government. We've got to overhaul our Army, reorganize our defense, and Washington has to provide the railroads to do it!"

Myra caught the word "socialism"—always a signal for intensified scorn on Edmund's part. "Hell, they use the word for anything they don't like!" he cried. "There's no other way to do this and do it right. It'll cut down unemployment, put money into circulation——" At this there came some further objection, and Edmund pounded so hard the rattle sounded through the walls. "Down here in the South we don't know what railroads are yet! One of the wonders of the new age—and we're letting the chance pass us by. . . ."

When Edmund joined her an hour later Myra was still at the window. She would tell him the thing that had been shaping in her mind these past few weeks. She spoke in a rush. "Edmund, what did Congress do with those last plans of yours, the defense scheme, railroads and the rest of it?"

He frowned. "Pigeonholed them, all of them." He had sent maps, blueprints, pamphlets, letters; a few speeches had been made in Congress, and then nothing had happened.

Myra rose. "Well, why don't you go to the country itself? These men keep saying you ought to keep before the public. Make a tour, talk just as you've talked tonight; and see what follows!"

Edmund was perplexed. "But wouldn't that hurt your case? How could we carry it on from a distance?"

"We'll find a way. Something will develop." As Edmund

watched Myra's determined profile, the scar below her ear flaming in a way he knew well, he had a suspicion that it would.

With his first speeches it became evident that the South was ready to turn out in heavy numbers to hear Edmund Gaines. His words fell like those of a prophet. The iron rail, marvel of the century—men's eyes were dazzled. Some, of course, grinned. "Aw, the general's been spending too much time in the hot sun with them Cree-oles." However, certain merchants, farmers, and planters were intrigued. They met in hotel lobbies, they exchanged letters, they sat about whisky bottles in their offices, talking, planning. Did you hear what they did yonder in Georgia last week? . . . The general's got it all drawn up, and he's ready to tell how it'll work. . . .

The tour gathered momentum. At their second stop the general and his wife were greeted with bands and banners. Veterans of his campaigns held parades; Edmund reviewed troops and spoke at banquets. The mayor's wife and the governor's wife had a tea for Myra, and she was pleased to find they knew a great deal about her case. Over the cups they managed to bring up the subject. Perhaps it was presumptuous . . . Would Mrs. Gaines mind? . . . Myra saw none of the covert hostility, the ill will that she sometimes felt. She cleared her throat; Mrs. Gaines not only did not mind, she was happy to tell whatever they wanted to know. As they listened the ladies put down their saucers and forgot to wipe the crumbs of cake from their dresses. She talked nearly an hour, and that week the newspaper had a long article on Madame General and her suits.

At the next town the scene was repeated. During breakfast, with a humorous look, Edmund handed her a message. The chairman of the committee in the place ahead had written in haste. Word had just gotten to them that Mme. Gaines was with him; as he knew, the lyceum movement was gaining everywhere; it had occurred to them that Mrs. Gaines might be willing to sit on the stage and say a few words too.

Myra began to shake her head, then stopped. At once she remembered the cheap impresario who had asked her to "tell about your life," with a banjoist or pianist as part of the act. Then she picked up the letter: "a few words on any subject she chose." Through her long lashes she gazed over at Edmund. "You're speaking on national defense. Suppose I talk about the way women look at war, and the need for defense to prevent it?" Edmund nodded, the suspicion of a smile about his lips.

In the next city it was raining heavily as the time for the engagement approached, and Myra grew so nervous she could touch little of the seven-course dinner spread before them by the town dignitaries. The chairman inquired if she were ill; quietly she told him no. The hall was already filled when they entered; the chairman observed, with a glance of surprise, that the number of women there was unprecedented. As Myra and the general advanced across the stage the audience rose. The general turned to Myra, she dropped a curtsy, and the crowd shouted. The general spoke first and when he finished he looked in Myra's direction. As she stood up a whole row of indignant females stamped out, shoulders twitching. They had come only to let the world know that woman's place was not on the platform.

Myra's hand, holding her notes, shook so hard that she buried it in her skirts. As she began, her voice seemed to squeak in her ears. "I know some will wonder that a woman dares appear this way before a mixed audience." Then all at once she was burning with rage against the resentful women who had protested against one of their sex, just as other women had stood against her in New Orleans. Her feeling crept into her voice; it deepened, booming through the hall. "True, a female's sphere should be domestic, hers the calm pursuits, man's the field of enterprise. But"—she extended her hand—"the hell of war is woman's concern as well. She, too, loses, and who shall say she loses less—the family she has held together, her sons, her husband . . ." Several times the crowd applauded. Coming to the end of her notes, she found she had more to tell; calmly she said it. A new feeling of power, of authority, possessed her. As she finally bowed the audience rose again, and several tossed flowers. She had found a new weapon.

After that Myra appeared always on the platform with Edmund. Her part was expanded to twenty minutes, then a half hour as the "double lecture" proved more and more pleasing. Larger halls were needed as additional requests arrived and the itinerary was expanded. John Grymes wrote jubilant letters; the more talk about her, the better for the case. Eventually they arrived in New York to resounding acclaim. Yet not all comment was favorable. The self-made aristocrat, Philip Hone, told his diary:

Lectures are all the vogue, and the theaters are flat on their backs. The Tabernacle, spacious as it is, is filled every night to hear the lyceum lectures. General Gaines and his wife have been making fools of themselves there. He has given a lecture, *secundum artem,* upon "National Defense," and she follows with most marvelous incongruity upon "The Horrors of War." "Jack Sprat could eat no fat, his wife could eat no lean." They began this ridiculous career of vanity and silliness at the South, and taking the applause for the novelty as a criterion of its merits, they came here as an itinerant Punch and Judy.

A few, like the *Onondaga Standard* of Syracuse, noted caustically that the general's lady was an even more popular figure than he was: "The General ought to look out for his pantaloons when he rises in the morning, or his 'better half' may get them on through mistake." When a "friend" coyly forwarded the clipping Myra took care that Edmund did not see it. Slowly she had come to realize that their speeches had disadvantages. Newspapers opposing the general printed violent attacks, while others held up Myra as an improper, shameless woman. The new weapon was one whose use required skill and restraint; it was a lesson she would remember. Besides, she was growing worried about the four children; it was the first time she had been separated from them, and her heart hurt whenever she thought of them. When a particularly vitriolic statement appeared she went to Edmund. "Don't you think our talks have served their purpose?" After some thought he agreed; thereafter they declined the offers of additional engagements.

When they returned to New Orleans and the hotel the children leaped forward to welcome them. They were attending school now, all except Will. It was a highly praised institution, and they liked it as well, Myra decided, as might have been expected. None of them, young Ed included, had been accustomed to formal schooling and the restraint that accompanied it. Rhoda, now almost eight and always set in her ways, was the most successful scholar. Ed, bright and alert, excelled in mathematics but had problems with his history. The winsome Julia, ever the quiet one, seemed bored; the child, Myra told herself, lacked the strong vitality that her brother and sister had inherited from

Myra. It was the impish, highly strung Will, however, who presented the greatest problem. Eulalie brought reports of the four-year-old's misbehavior about the hotel, a series of minor infractions of her discipline. However, Edmund's stronger hand now had its effect, and Will subsided.

Myra saw the children as often as she could, but at times she missed their old, hour-by-hour contacts. No longer did Rhoda come to her in her bad moments and caress her cheek; Myra's duties as the general's lady kept her from their rooms for longer periods than she would have wished. Now and then, in spare moments between her engagements, she sat with Eulalie Montagnet and remembered those excited, tragic-happy first days in New Orleans, and sighed.

The months went by. One night they found themselves in the uptown section, at a ball given for them by Major and Mrs. Cartwright, of Virginia. They were waltzing together over the polished floor; solemnly Edmund requested a second dance, and as they started forward again he kissed the back of her hand. A courier touched Edmund's arm. General Macomb, commanding officer of the Army, had just died in Washington. As unobtrusively as possible they slipped out; at the hotel Edmund worked for hours over a letter to the Secretary of War. He reviewed his career, his successive promotions; he expressed his belief that he deserved the post. Myra went over it, removing words, suggesting additions; when the messenger raced off she drew Edmund back into the chamber. How well she knew the agony of waiting that must follow.

At once editorials appeared in Edmund's behalf; every mail brought letters, including petitions from persons who expected him to receive the appointment. Then late one evening Edmund's aide came in with a letter. The general hesitated before ripping it open. In a moment his eyes turned to hers; the President had nominated Winfield Scott.

Edmund walked to the dresser, his ruddy face the color of putty. When Myra went to him he twisted away, bitter and incoherent. Then, apologetic, he took her arm and sank to the sofa. She stood beside him, her hands on his shoulders, while the curtains swirled about them in the wind. Myra must now be the comforter of the man who had come to her when her own world had seemed lost.

Next morning at the breakfast table he put down his glass. "I think it's best to resign from the Army."

Quickly Myra spoke up. "Why? That's just what they want! Instead you can stay and fight for what you think's important— the overhauling of the Army. And haven't you been saying, all this year, that you're expecting trouble in Texas? Don't tell me you want to watch others step in and take over everything you've prepared!" Moodily Edmund stirred his cup, but he listened.

Now she went to work with a new thought; she must keep Edmund's mind occupied, and off his Army problems. She and John Grymes talked with him, thrashed out difficulties of her case. Soon he had a suggestion for them: their great trouble was that none of the defendants, the seventy-five or more of them, would face the issue. If they could only persuade one or two to come forward for a fair trial . . . "Why not do something like this? Point out that it would be to everybody's benefit to have the matter settled; tell them if they agree to a hearing on the merits we'll make a good reduction in any amount the court may eventually grant?" Myra glanced at John Grymes. "It's somewhat unconventional," the attorney conceded. "But why not try it?"

In an open letter the general advised all involved that their interests were not the same as Relf's and Chew's; he suggested that for unprejudiced advice they consult attorneys having no connection with the two men. Several defendants came to discuss the case. Grymes, grinning, brought word that Relf and Chew appeared panicky; they were holding almost continuous conferences, demanding that all defendants "stand with them" and trust them with the whole case. But as week succeeded week Edmund's and Myra's hopes declined and they began to realize they would have to work at it the long, slow way.

Despite the opulent scale of her life, Myra could not forget her months of want. Passing the store of one of her market friends, she spied large tin children's banks; she bought four and then added a fifth, for herself. Thereafter she and Eulalie encouraged the children to deposit their spare pennies. On the first day she placed a silver dollar in her own bank; thereafter, when retiring each evening, she did the same thing. When she economized or found something left from Edmund's large allowance she added it. Over and over again she rejected Edmund's amused suggestion that she have the money transferred to their account at the bank. "I feel better knowing it's in the armoire," she told him. When her first bank filled she bought another and went on to a fourth and fifth.

Edmund's carelessness with money gave her twinges. She worried frequently over his expenditures on the case. "We can't omit anything," he assured her. Every bypath must be traced; he sent representatives to New York and Philadelphia to interview men who wrote that they "knew something"; agents searched tombstone inscriptions, checked registers, interviewed doctors. One day Myra asked Edmund how much he had spent to date on her suits. After a moment he replied, "About forty thousand." She dropped more dollars into her banks.

For the third time the United States Supreme Court gave a decision, this a perplexing one. Furiously Relf and Chew had insisted that the Supreme Court could not recognize Daniel's last will, as Myra asked, because they claimed the state probate court had exclusive authority over such a matter. The federal judges now gave an answer that seemed to beat about the legal bush. It was "a matter of serious consideration," they said, whether, if everything else failed, Myra might not someday come to them and request that the federal courts establish the will; at that future date they would go into the point. Then in the next paragraph they said something that made Grymes sit up quickly. If she wished, Myra might present her claim on another ground. Under Louisiana law, will or no will, a legitimate child was entitled to at least four fifths of her father's estate—as forced heir. Edmund rubbed his nose. "Looks to me as if the court's hinting to us to try that other way!"

Myra half rose. "Then I could go ahead, simply as Daniel's child?"

"Exactly," Grymes told her. "There's one consideration though. If we estimate that the property would be worth about forty million in these better times, one fifth is exactly eight million. Some people would think you were tossing that away."

She laughed. "To drop eight and receive thirty-two—that sounds like good arithmetic to me." Serious again, she faced Grymes. "I'm ready to sign the new papers as soon as you draw them up."

Eulalie Montagnet stood at the door. "Victorien Badeaux, he's downstairs. Says it's something you ought to know, right away."

In a few minutes the Cajun was before them. He did not sit down, he did not smile. "You remember those thing' in the paper, Gen'l, how you ready to give somethin' off to anybody what would face trial, yes?" Well, Victorien had a friend, owner of a property that was mixed up in all this. Victorien had been talking to him for months; finally the friend had come over to the cake shop. "He axing all kin' question', so I bring him right away, 'fore he change his min'."

At once he brought in the friend, Mr. Patterson, a gray-haired individual in a flowing yellow overcoat. After a bit of urging by Edmund, Charles Patterson removed his coat, folded it in his lap, and sat down. Behind his thick glasses his eyes seemed friendly but disturbed. "Well, it's like this," he gulped. "I got a little land, and wife and children too. I'm not well, not at all. Been worrying lately what would happen to the kids if something, so to speak, happened to me."

Myra reached over for her map of properties, and her face softened. This narrow parcel was worth a few thousands at the limit. Edmund's glance went to the frayed neckpiece, the shine at the knees of Mr. Patterson's suit. "We can assure you, sir, that if you meet us in fair trial your family won't suffer."

With great gravity Mr. Patterson shook hands. Myra felt a vein throb in her temple. As the little man left them she went to Edmund and clung to him. At last, at last . . .

For several years Myra had been hoping that eventually she would, in spite of everything, hear from her faraway half sister, Caroline Barnes. Though no reply came to her letters, Caroline's angry opposition to Relf's "accounting" of the estate remained on the books. Now Grymes brought disquieting reports: among the lawyers it was whispered that Relf had scored some kind of victory in connection with Caroline. Soon Attorney Duncan walked triumphantly into court with a brief motion. Relf and Chew has just conveyed "certain lands" to Caroline and Daniel's sisters; at the same time the women had agreed to abandon their opposition.

Myra looked at Grymes with a sick feeling. After Caroline

had made all those charges, going sometimes beyond Myra's! The lawyer gave a sardonic smile. "Caroline's been satisfied. I think we've heard the last of her." Promptly they discovered he was wrong; Caroline was far from finished. Again her attorneys went into court—with a suit against Myra, demanding she give up the land that Bellechasse had turned over to her. They wanted to take the only fragment of the estate that had come to her; also they wanted Myra to pay them twenty thousand dollars, which they said she had received in rent from the property.

"That—that figure's absurd," Myra told Grymes.

But Caroline had gone further than this; as Myra read on her eyes darkened in dismay. Caroline insisted she was herself not the child of Jerome des Granges, as Daniel Clark had declared in his will, but of Daniel himself. Zulime and Daniel, she said, had never been married, and she, Caroline, was the issue of their adultery. As for Myra, she was not Daniel's at all, but the child of another man, unspecified. Zulime, said her daughter Caroline, had "imposed on Daniel and deceived him" into believing Myra was his.

Caroline conceded that Daniel "did meditate" over a new will in 1813 and prepared "memoranda" regarding it. However, he never finished it; the witnesses who said so were lying. Caroline had been shocked when Myra brought her case, causing "dishonor and reproach" to Zulime and Daniel. ("But who has ever made statements so harsh as these?" asked Edmund softly.) Myra pushed the paper from her in revulsion. The strange, acid document lacked even consistency in its malice.

Caroline, with Daniel's sisters, was suing Myra in state court, and the matter required a jury. Myra grew alarmed; would it be possible to get jurymen who did not think she was a danger to New Orleans?

Myra went to the court with Grymes and Edmund. If she had hoped to see Caroline she was disappointed; her half sister was represented only by the attorneys. Before the matter had proceeded an hour, Myra knew trouble was ahead. The judge was a red-faced Irishman for whom the Virginia-born Grymes had scant respect; for two days they snapped at each other. At last, shortly before Grymes's turn came to address the jury, summing up the case, the judge spoke sharply to him; Grymes gave a short reply. When the judge shouted Grymes rose. "I'll have nothing more to do with this farce," he said, and stamped out.

Before Myra understood what had happened Edmund Gaines had asked permission to address the court. He requested that Mrs. Gaines, who understood the facts as well as anyone, be allowed to address the jury. Startled, Myra put out her hand to stop him. But Edmund led her forward, almost as if he were escorting her to a dance floor. Myra put her hand to her face; this would be different—how different!—from facing audiences during their tour. Out of the corner of her eye she saw that the court was crowded; word had spread that there was a new excitement in the Gaines case.

Trembling, she began. "I'm not a lawyer. But I know the truth, and I think you want it." Her brown eyes, earnest and pleading, swept the jurors before her, and their glances were curious, not altogether hostile. She left out all of the legal terms; she spoke without oratory. But the courtroom had quieted, and she received a silence that had not been granted even the illustrious Grymes. For two hours she talked, with hardly a break, her hands extended unconsciously before her as she begged for "understanding—simple understanding."

The judge appeared to grow more and more annoyed. At length he interrupted. "Madame, the document you mention hasn't been offered." His voice had a surly note.

"I don't understand——"

"You don't have to understand!" His anger snapped. "I tell you you can't talk about it!"

"And I know why you say I can't!" Myra flared, her Irish temper a match for the judge's. "You have an interest in this case. Didn't you represent the other side a few years back?" Now she had said the thing the attorneys had whispered, the thing she had been told she mustn't use; and she was glad she had.

The judge whitened. He glared at Edmund Gaines. "General, I expect you to control your wife in court."

Slowly Edmund Pendleton Gaines rose to his six feet three inches. In full panoply of his rank he took the stand of a commander of grenadiers. "May it please your honor, for everything the lady says or does I hold myself responsible, under law or rules of honor." His fingers touched the hilt of his sword.

The judge decided he had been affronted more than ever. "General Gaines, this court will not be overawed by the military!"

The general did not alter stance or expression. "Your honor may rest assured that when an attempt of that sort is made this sword will be unsheathed to defend your court."

Quieting, the judge declared it his duty to note Mrs. Gaines's accusation. He asked that she file an exception, requesting that he excuse himself; Myra said she was happy to do so right now. The judge called for her evidence; she produced a document, offered years earlier by Relf, bearing the judge's name as attorny. The judge admitted he had filed it, but only as a convenience for a fellow attorney, and he overruled her exception. Myra went back to the jurors and argued for another hour. They brought in a quick verdict—no agreement.

Wearily the case was tried again; this time she argued before the jury with even greater earnestness, and also with added experience. And now the jurymen came out for Myra! Angrily the judge declared that the verdict was not upheld by the law or the facts. Caroline appealed; and then Myra was confronted by the situation she had feared for years. The case went to the Louisiana Supreme Court, presided over by François Xavier Martin. Repeatedly of late it had been suggested by attorneys that perhaps the blind man should retire; his eccentricities had been growing by the year. However, Martin held on doggedly, dictating decisions, continuing to accumulate his fortune.

Edmund Gaines was less disturbed than Myra. "Since Martin's own property is involved, he'll have to excuse himself, won't he?" he asked Grymes.

"Of course." The Virginian frowned. "But is it possible that the others on the court won't be influenced—if not by him, consciously or unconsciously, then by the general prejudice against Myra in Louisiana?"

One bright spring day Myra and Edmund waited before the highest court in Louisiana and heard its decision. General and Mrs. Gaines "appeared to be strangers to the estate of Daniel Clark"; Myra had no right to even these parcels of land; she had to give them up and pay the twenty thousand dollars. In this contest between the two daughters of Zulime Carrière, Caroline was the victor.

For months Myra thought again and again of Caroline. Then one night a brief notice was delivered by a court messenger. Caroline Barnes was dead. . . . Myra would never see the woman who had hated her from a distance. Caroline had been always a dim figure on the edge of Myra's existence; now, as quietly as she had lived, she was gone. Perhaps, Myra told herself, she should feel anger or bitterness. Instead her emotion was closer to pity. Whoever had been responsible, Caroline had received shabby treatment from the world.

With a sigh Myra went to her desk. It would not be easy to give Zulime the news of this daughter who had turned upon her.

For Edmund, too, the cup was bitter. Until then the Army had been operated in two divisions, one under his direction. Now it was broken into nine departments; he would have eight others of equal rank to contend with. To a man whose life had been a military one, this was humiliation multiplied. When he came to tell her his face was tense with pain and he seemed to have aged ten years. Suddenly he exploded in vituperative rage; and for that she rejoiced. Again she argued and reasoned with him, and slowly his anger slipped away. He took up his new, reduced operations; he dispatched messages to the field, he reviewed his troops; in early evenings they sat together in their apartment. They talked only a little; her presence was the balm that he needed.

It was during this period that Mrs. Clement Clay, the senator's wife, visited New Orleans to find Myra a full-flowering celebrity. In the St. Charles dining room the newcomer was drawn by an unusual couple. Beside a military man with an air of dignity and vast command sat

. . . a very small young woman who hung upon his arm like a reticule or a knitting basket. Her hair was bright, glistening chestnut, her color very fresh and rich, and her golden-hazel eyes glowed like young suns . . . singularly searching, seeming to gauge everything at a glance. . . . Never did woman exhibit more wifely solicitude. She arranged his napkin, tucking it carefully into the V of his waistcoat, read the menu and selected his food, waiting upon him as each course arrived, and herself preparing the dressing for his salad. All was done in so matter-of-fact and quiet a manner that the flow of General Gaines' discourse was not once interrupted.

On a winter evening of 1845, in the sixth year of their marriage, the general gave a hearty welcome to a newly arrived couple at the hotel—Jefferson Davis, rising young politician, planter, and former soldier, here with his bride, Varina Howell, of the Mississippi gentry. Myra had heard of the union; there had been some surprise that the Howells, rigid Whigs of the ruling clans, had agreed to this wedding of a Natchez belle with a man not of the old elite and, moreover, a Democrat. Davis's party had yet to achieve its full place as the organ of Southern property.

Curiosity in her eye, Myra bowed to Jefferson Davis, a slim man, distinguished, with an air of remoteness about him. She found Varina as darkly beautiful as she had been pictured, with the slight hauteur expected of the plantation miss. The two women got on fairly well, but Varina had heard shocked comment regarding Myra's appearances on the public platform; and she blinked at Mrs. Gaines's forthright talk of Daniel and Zulime—after all, a somewhat delicate subject. When Mrs. Davis wrote her memoir of her husband nearly fifty years later she recalled the evening and Myra herself—"a laughing, brown-eyed little woman, unwhipped of social conventions, not because she did not understand them, but because she understood them and was naturally lawless." High barriers stood between a Varina Howell and a Myra Gaines.

On the hot sands of Texas guns roared suddenly. Zachary Taylor, Edmund's old friend, commanded in the field, and now Taylor was clashing with the Mexican Army at the Rio Grande. Across the long miles came word: in God's name, help was needed! Taylor faced massacre. . . . Quickly Edmund called on Governor Mouton of Louisiana, asking for infantry, artillery, anything that Louisiana could give. The state flamed with excitement, the Legislature voted one hundred thousand dollars to equip volunteers; at mass meetings men ran forward with fistfuls of money. In five or six states other military units sprang out of nothing, marching, riding, cheering, and shouting —on to New Orleans. Edmund, face shining, greeted them all and saw them off. Texas or bust!

From Washington arrived a message of a sort already familiar to Edmund Gaines. What authority had he had to call for troops? He must stop at once. Washington wanted anything but overt hostilities at this time; diplomatic exchanges were under way. Edmund, who never held a high opinion of diplomacy, broke into a fit of anger and dashed off a reply. As on other occasions, he gave his own estimate of armchair generals. In wartime, he let it be known, the soldier's job was to get there with the men; he preferred to act, then argue.

As quickly as riders could carry it came sharp protest from Washington. Edmund Gaines, his color rising, made sharper reply. At the end of a series of pointed sentences, he observed: "I carelessly submit to the reprimands, as they seem to be a source of pleasure to the War Department, and certainly inflict no injury on me." With a flourish he sanded the paper and turned to more important things.

Two weeks later Edmund walked into the room where Myra was reading to the children. The President had relieved him of his command, and he was ordered North for a court of inquiry. . . . Sending the children away, Myra talked to him in a low, earnest voice. Though he listened, he appeared to be hearing only a few of her words. In a little while she emerged, to give one direction after another: hand this to the hotel manager, see the school principal, find out when the next ship . . .

While Eulalie packed their belongings Myra took time for a hurried conference on the case with John Grymes. "No, I don't know how long we'll be gone, or if we'll return." Her voice sounded as if it came from far away. "I'll be with Edmund; that's what matters now." As she spoke her mind wandered back to the grim man in another part of the city, turning over his office to a successor. That night no crowd assembled to tell them good-by. For hours they remained in a corner of the deck, side by side, silent, in the mist that rose from the river and the levees.

At Fortress Monroe Edmund rose to defend himself. Through tense hours, her hands folded in her lap, Myra sat alone. At last, as Edmund stood stiffly at attention, the judges read their verdict. The general, they declared, had lacked authority to call for volunteers. But they had considered his long and honorable record, his motives, and what might have seemed the necessities of the situation to one far removed from Washington City. No

action was taken against him; Edmund Gaines was to assume a
new command, in charge of the Army's Eastern department.
It would be a quiet post, but at least he continued in his country's
service.

Myra was at her place near the door. At the first sound of the
familiar footstep she went quickly to the threshold and waited
for her husband, a firm smile on her lips.

CHAPTER XVIII

"ANOTHER party tonight?" Edmund ran his fingers through his
wiry light hair and stretched himself across the bed.

Working at her curls, Myra turned toward him. "And an important party at that. At least two Supreme Court justices, perhaps the President too."

Edmund sniffed. "Mrs. Fassnacht will have two feathers in
her hat instead of one." The judiciary of Washington ranked
as much more than secondary gods in this social heaven. The
court's members moved in a resplendent circle, above the Cabinet, above practically everything else. A hostess with a single
Supreme Court justice at her table could float for several sea-
sons on this triumph.

"Myra, would you want to stay indefinitely in this place?"
Edmund was yawning. Surprised at the question, she put down
her comb and crossed the room to his side. For nearly two years
they had been in the East, moving between New York and
Washington City. Poor Edmund! He missed his old friends,
his long-time headquarters in New Orleans; and he still felt
the pain of this transfer, at a time when Zachary Taylor and,
worse, Winfield Scott had won the glory in Mexico.

As for Myra herself . . . "I don't know how to answer," she
said softly. They were less comfortable here than in Louisiana;
Washington was a crowded, unfinished place. Frequently, too,
she grew concerned over the children and their schooling; Washington's best seemed inadequate to her. And, as on other occasions, she never quite realized the extent of her liking for New
Orleans until she found herself away from it. But now her case

had followed her to the capital city, and suddenly again nearly everything she did, everything she thought, was focused upon it.

She was attending tonight's entertainment primarily because of her case, she admitted to herself. At the beginning of her stay here she had gone mechanically through the "proper" activities—a few soirees and parties given by the wives of other officials; as Mrs. Edmund Gaines, it was expected of her. Then she discovered that her name and her case were known even to Washington. The first time an ambassador asked to be introduced to her she experienced a sensation of eminence, over which she eventually smiled to herself. Soon a card was left by the wife of a man she found to be an influential senator and attorney; at a tea she talked of her litigations with the daughter and the wife of two congressmen.

The women, it was evident, had much to do with the way affairs were handled. Washington remained a small town in many ways, much less cosmopolitan than Creole New Orleans. Certain of the women understood politics and played it; they passed judgments, they helped their husbands, they injured their enemies. A tight little social world, full of oddities, was crystallizing, and, by and large, the Southerners ran it. In most things Washington continued a Southern center; slaves darted about on errands, and the accents of Virginia echoed on the streets more often than those of Massachusetts. The place to which they were going tonight, for instance, was one of the Southern boardinghouses, a congressional mess as the term had it, where congenial legislators lived with their families.

Tonight she would see many of the capital's legal figures, lawyers and judges whom she and Edmund had first met while guests at the White House. "The Gaines Case" had emerged more and more as a topic of conversation in capital drawing rooms. At a later day Myra would have been called a propagandist of rare powers, the more effective because she did what she did simply and instinctively. She combined her story, when she thought it wise to tell it, with oyster pies and creamed soups; the cardinal rule, she well knew, was that she must not bore.

Within an hour or so, she reminded Edmund, they would meet some of the men who before long would be passing on her case. The matter involving the property of Mr. Patterson, the only one who had agreed to meet a trial on its merits, at last was coming to a head. . . . With a grunt Edmund rose and began to dress. When he beheld her in her new black velvet, diamonds in her ears, her tight curls surmounted by the splendor of her silver-and-diamond headpiece, he gave a little laugh. "Now I know this is a big affair. When you put on diamonds you're out for an impression!"

In a lightly falling snow their brougham awaited them. Along half-settled Pennsylvania Avenue they passed the endless alternations of unfinished Greek temples, broken shacks, ornate private mansions, and pigsties. Everywhere the eye met slush and empty distances; years must go by before the capital would look like anything but the beginnings of a city. It had none of New Orleans' air of tolerant quiet beneath surface bustle. But for her Washington was exciting; here the decisions would be made that would determine everything for or against her.

Early arrivals thronged the ballroom. As musicians played for the first dancers, caterers' assistants hovered about the punch and ices and jellies that formed a towering design. Mrs. Elizabeth Ellett eventually described the evening in her memoirs:

Mrs. Linn of Missouri and Mrs. Gaines, the distinguished wife of the General, presided as matrons. . . . Almost the entire *beau monde* was present, Senators, Cabinet and other members. . . . Mrs. Gaines bore her part with a kind wish to gratify all, and the enthusiasm of a noble and generous heart.

Myra found herself greeting Jefferson Davis, now senator from Mississippi, high in the counsels of the expanding Democratic party. The circles beneath his eyes were deeper, his mouth somewhat more set; he still carried himself with a dignity inclined toward stiffness. At his side, skirts billowing, walked his handsome Varina, missing nothing. A great deal had happened since the two couples had last met; again Varina gazed at Myra with an air of slight wonderment. Let others call Mrs. Gaines brave; on Varina's chiseled lips the word would still be "lawless."

An hour later, seeking a place to rest after many bows and five glasses of punch with as many senators, Myra heard her named called. She was taken to a tall, impressive man with a polished manner, Justice James Wayne of the Supreme Court.

He bowed; his long face, dominated by an almost hawklike nose, seemed kindly, with a marked interest; or was it, perhaps, mere curiosity about this woman, of whom he had heard?

For some years James Wayne had been the youngest member of the court. Though a supporter of the radical Andrew Jackson, he appeared the Savannah aristocrat from the tip of his light, curling hair to his carefully polished boots. With him stood his wife, a lively little woman with a friendly face. The three of them talked of Jackson, the war, the British writers currently visiting Washington. No matters of law of course; carefully they avoided the topic; but Mrs. Wayne looked as if she wished she could take Myra aside and ask her, womanlike, all about the case.

Then Edmund presented Myra to an oddly contrasted couple, a heavy man, rough-featured and stern, and a woman who might have qualified as a dowager duchess—Justice John Catron and Mrs. Catron. Unmoved by anything, the judge stared fixedly ahead; Mrs. Catron, beneath her elaborate ornamented headdress, peered majestically over the crowd. Myra found conversation with them difficult; neither seemed completely at ease. As she spoke Myra tried to recall what she had been told about Catron. Born poor, he had struggled against handicaps in the hill sections of Tennessee; despite hardships and ridicule, he had finally arrived. It was common talk that the woman at his side had obtained the judgeship for him. Some said Mrs. Catron, learning that the court's membership was to be increased, rode posthaste to Washington, found Andy Jackson in his dressing gown, and obtained a promise of the appointment before she left him. It might not be true, but, meeting the justice's wife, Myra could believe it.

Her eyes strayed from Catron's swarthy face to the smooth, composed one of James Wayne. It would not be long before these two men, so different in manner and background, would be judging her.

The day to argue her case arrived. That morning she called at the office of her chief Washington attorney, Reverdy Johnson, one of the capital's masters. A genial soul, with a body in the shape of a barrel, his enormous bald dome dominated any gathering in which he appeared; and when Reverdy Johnson spoke the courts listened. "Now," he told her soberly, "I can't promise you success; I'd be a fool if I did. This is a case with a lot of difficulties—points that might prejudice anyone who looked only at the surface. A narrow, self-righteous soul would rule against us, right off. We can only pray for a little human understanding; and that's a rare quality, isn't it?"

Edmund had been called to New York, and she walked with her attorney along the dark ground floor of the Capitol, to the entrance of the Supreme Court. She was disappointed; the place had none of the majesty that she associated with it. The chamber was a poorly illuminated little room with a sunken floor; she understood Johnson's jibe at this "national dungeon."

The crier lifted his voice, and an irregular line of black-gowned men filed in. Most of them were elderly, tired, and, she felt, bored. She strained her eyes to make out their faces; she caught James Wayne's clear bright eyes on hers, and he bowed pleasantly. From John Catron there came no response, and she could not be sure he had seen her. The court itself looked much less august than she had anticipated. Hearing cases that preceded hers, several justices left their chairs and wandered behind the bench. One leaned against a pillar, crossed his legs, and listened absently. As she watched, two of them sent an attaché for a sack of candy and munched.

Johnson, her attorney, stepped forward, bowed his great pink head; and at once she understood why he had won such respect. His powerful voice ranged from high-pitched excitement to almost sepulchral earnestness, yet there was no theatricalism, hardly an excess word. When he stopped Myra knew he had made a strong impression. Then appeared the opposition attorneys; they spoke coldly, scornfully; they made their case deliberately merely a routine answer to the pretensions of this misguided female. Myra grew less easy in her mind; they were making shrewd use of their ammunition.

As the lawyers argued her eyes went from one to another of the jurists. These ancients, so remote, so secure, how much did they know, or remember, of human suffering? She watched particularly the two to whom she had recently spoken. Which might be more inclined to favor her side—Wayne, the aristocrat, or Catron, who had fought against poverty? The opposition's arguments, without question, made a strong appeal to

those who favored the status quo; for many, she stood forth as
a threat to established rights. Staring at the faces of these two
men, she could not guess what went on in their minds.

Now for weeks she must hold her patience. It was agonizing,
and many times she told herself she could not wait. She went
out less frequently; with so much at stake, she had difficulty in
concentrating on idle talk. The children occupied more and more
of her time, and she was grateful for that, though she regretted
Edmund's absence in New York. Young Ed remained the most
tractable—thin, retiring, always handicapped by his eyes. Over
Myra's and Eulalie's protests, he read at all hours, in any light;
in vain they cited the example of old Judge Martin. Quietly Ed
would put his books away; a little later they would find him at
them again.

Rhoda, fourteen, had grown almost as tall as Ed. Sturdy and
determined, she was not as handsome as her mother but, as Eulalie pointed out, "she's you in everything else." The gentle, slim-
bodied Julia, who gained in pensive loveliness with the years,
had her intractable moments, when she stamped her feet and
fretted. As ever, Will offered the major problems—racing ahead
of the rest of them through the lobby, sliding down banisters,
riding roughshod over the others of his age in the building. But
when Myra saw his tiny nose wrinkling, his implike eyes twin-
kling at her, she generally lost her sternness. He would ever remain her favorite.

Leaving them with Eulalie for the evening, she met Reverdy
Johnson at a party, and the attorney whispered to her, "Court
took up your case today. Wayne's been talking a lot about it—
don't know if that's good or bad." A week later he called her
aside again. "Been some warm arguments among the judges.
Just heard Catron's sick; he won't take part in the decision.
Looks like Wayne may handle the ruling." So the aristocrat had
assumed the lead; the self-made man was lost to the case. Her
face had a troubled expression.

The night before the decision she tossed anxiously back and
forth. A note from Zulime told her her mother was thinking
about her and praying; thrusting it into her pocket, she left
early for court. Though the building was well heated, Myra's
hands were icy when she took her seat. As the room filled she

knew she was being pointed out. A placid man with a face that was curiously familiar advanced toward her. He said, "Henry Clay, at your service, madame. Your case is interesting, highly interesting." He talked at some length, but Myra was not greatly impressed; Clay looked and acted too patently the politician.

After him Attorney Johnson brought another whom she recognized in a moment. Daniel Webster gazed down at her, a dancing light in his deep-set eyes, which seemed to be saying, "So this is the woman that's caused all the rumpus. Mighty little, mighty little." His words were few, but, like his heavily furrowed contemporary's, they were very kind.

The judges walked forward. Her eye met Wayne's; graver than usual, he gave no hint that he saw her. Her face changed; was it a bad sign? Now the case was called. Wayne cleared his throat, and suddenly her heart was thumping so hard that she missed his opening words. Then they reached her almost like an echo.

The court was of the opinion that Jerome des Granges had been proved a bigamist. A slight tremor of excitement ran through the audience; behind her a newspaper correspondent was scratching over a pad of paper. But she could not give way to her own exultant emotion; it was only the first point, and she must pay attention to the next words. . . . The judge went on; Zulime's union with Des Granges, therefore, had been void; she had been free, all the time, to marry Daniel. Did she marry him? The judge took up the facts. A marriage must be established according to what would be proof of it in the place in which it happened. In Pennsylvania marriage was a civil contract; no publication was required, and this one had been performed by a priest in a private home. A marriage could be proved by any person present: Zulime's sister Sophie declared firmly that she had been there. The other sister, Rose, told of Daniel's proposal of marriage and of a letter from Philadelphia declaring it had occurred. Boisfontaine, Harriett Smyth, and others told how Daniel himself said he had married Zulime.

The judge paused. There was nothing under the law to prevent Zulime from marrying again the moment she learned of Des Granges's bigamy. But from an understanding of Daniel's pride and temper, it seemed natural that he would want the announcement withheld until a formal sentence of annulment was obtained by Zulime. Returning to Louisiana, Daniel rose higher in political affairs; he held off disclosure of the wedding, they quarreled, and Zulime was told she could not prove the marriage had taken place. After that had come her ill-considered union with Dr. Gardette. Here the judge looked up. He would not try to gloss over Zulime's errors, but this third connection could not affect her marriage to Daniel. She remained Mrs. Clark.

Meanwhile Daniel had grown fonder and fonder of his daughter Myra. He advised four or five people of his plans to establish her rights in his new will. On his deathbed, when "his time was near its end, and eternity looked him in the face," he spoke of Myra as his proper child. A single witness, De la Croix, claimed Daniel called her his natural daughter. But De la Croix's remarks could not outweigh the overwhelming testimony of the others. Also, De la Croix's statements had differed in several details and should therefore be "received with great caution." The judge halted again. "Besides—for there must be no disguising the facts—there is in the record a money relationship between De la Croix and the estate of Clark which, unexplained, does not leave a favorable impression of his impartiality."

As to the specific matter at hand—the sale of land to Mr. Patterson through Messrs. Relf and Chew. Here the judge took on new sternness. It was illegal. Relf and Chew had made the sale long years after their terms as executors had expired; the court had never approved the sale. The defense, of course, said this was legal because Relf and Chew had a power of attorney from Daniel's mother. Mrs. Clark—the judge frowned— could have given them "no power to dispense with the law."

She had won! As the black-robed justices filed out Myra remained standing. She had been crying silently as Judge Wayne said the things she had hoped so long to hear; in her hand she clasped the crucifix that had been her father's.

Now the crowd swirled about her; men shook her hand, women acquaintances kissed her. Reverdy Johnson, pushing his heavy frame into view, beamed as if this had been his first successful case. Asking for a carriage, she had herself driven to the telegraph offices, to use Mr. Morse's new invention. Her messages, though almost incoherent, managed to convey what had happened. She asked John Grymes to seek out Zulime and give her the news; on impulse she added, "And tell her her daughter loves her very much." She wired the Whitneys, Samuel Davis, and, of course, Edmund Gaines. Poor Edmund . . . The world looked very bright to her; for him there continued the gnawing unhappiness of his military situation. She must try more than ever to make it up to him.

The clerk stared at her signature. As she headed for the door he motioned an assistant. "Good Lord! Millions rolling in that woman's lap. Just holds out her hands and gets rich, like that!"

The same evening Myra's full celebrity burst upon her. In poured letters, cards, bouquets, then callers—woman with high-pitched cries, men with wide smiles. Eulalie Montagnet hurried the excited children to their rooms, then restrained her own tears of joy as she poured tea and sherry for their callers. The manager burst in, to whisper, "Would you want to move to our biggest suite, Mrs. Gaines? I thought——"

"No." Myra frowned. "We'll be comfortable here." Edmund might have said yes; she remembered too well the days when a dingy room was welcome security. Interrupting them, a woman thrust a pad at her for an autograph. With a firm hand she signed *Myra Clark Gaines,* and then, eyes darting, took it back and underlined *Clark.* She had full right to use it now, and use it she would! The ostrich plumes on the caller's hat tickled Myra's nose; her eyes lifted and she smiled. Hereafter she could afford, at the least, a lot of new headgear of her own.

At the railroad station she clung to Edmund, her fingers digging into his uniform, her face against the rough cloth of his coat. "There now," he comforted her. "I know. I understand." The newspapermen crowded about them. How did she feel? Had she really expected to win? One gruff-voiced individual informed her she would soon be the richest woman in the country, maybe in the world. Forty million, maybe fifty!

"But you must understand," Edmund interposed. "Mrs. Gaines really hasn't received anything yet. The decision says she is the proper daughter of Daniel Clark, but it applies, strictly speaking, only to Mr. Patterson's little property. Unless others give up, it looks as if we may have to go back and sue them all, one by one."

"But, seeing how firm the court was, won't most of them

surrender?" This was the common opinion among Washington attorneys.

"We hope so," Myra responded. "And now, gentlemen, if you'll excuse us . . ."

She and Edmund would be alone for the first time in months; declining a half-dozen invitations, she had arranged a quiet evening for the two of them. At the hotel entrance she was met by a group of women, bearing books for her signature. Before she had finished, a senator bustled up; a group of Washington citizens were planning a banquet for them, and he had to discuss the details. Upstairs two magazine representatives were waiting; Eulalie, not knowing what else to do, had asked them to come in. Finally a stranger knocked and announced in a foreign accent that he would not object to waiting until the others finished; what he had to say was very confidential. Two hours later Signor Pestalozzi was opening his hands in voluble explanation. He proposed a "grand tour" of America, with Myra and the general on the platform. The sum he mentioned was staggering.

"I'm sorry," Myra told him. "We wouldn't——"

Without blinking Signor Pestalozzi doubled the figure. Edmund stood up. "If you doubled it a second time, sir, we wouldn't want it." Ten minutes later, against his near-hysterical objections, they bade good-by to the signor. As they were closing the door two attendants walked forward, arms filled with letters and packages. Myra answered Edmund's amazed look: "My mail. It comes twice a day."

Edmund chortled at several of the clippings—long stories of Myra's life, with details enlightening to both. Here were two magazines, drawings of her on the covers; one had the general, too, though the uniform was wrong. Edmund handed her clippings from England and France, reprinting accounts from New York papers. Sighing, Myra put five notes into a separate pile—requests for appointments by other lecture agents. Edmund hooted at the next—from an individual who proposed to become her manager, guaranteeing a safe, conservative handling of her fortune. Yet another, who had presumably not heard of the general, asked to marry her. Enclosing a daguerreotype, he pointed out that he had had three wives and promised he knew a great deal about "female nature and character" and would be very gentle.

The next morning her fame crowded upon them again. Over their omelette they glanced at a variety of new projects. The gold rush to California was getting under way; three men had plans to talk over with her and, of course, the general—plans that could not fail. Then there was a filibustering scheme involving Latin America; a revolution would be raised in any specified time. Elaborate drawings accompanied the next proposal, a scheme to run engines with water instead of oil—"at a large saving in cost." As they left the table a woman with incredibly yellow hair, in an orange dress, rushed up. She and her father ran a publishing house in Boston, and they were anxious to have Myra write a book, the story of her life. . . .

The days went rapidly now; Myra seemed very close to a realization of everything she had contended for; she had her family, and she had Edmund. In her room, kneeling at her *prie-dieu*, Eulalie Montagnet told her Télémaque that things were going very well.

When news of the court's decision arrived in New Orleans the first reaction was incredulity. It must be a mistake; the woman couldn't have won. Then, as the meaning grew clearer, there came a momentary inclination to panic. Plantation owners, pulling at their mustaches, stepped aboard steamers for the city; boards of banks called special meetings. At the St. Louis Hotel men looked glumly into their frosted juleps. "This—this is a blow to the institution of property itself!" "If the court does a thing like this, what'll happen to the Constitution, the country?" Hotheads termed it "a stinking Yankee trick." "But," the less excited pointed out, "the decision was given by a Southerner, and concurred in by other Southern justices." There was no answer to that.

Holders of land scheduled for development ordered the work delayed; advertisements of sales were canceled, expansions curtailed. Her critics could declare with truth that something of the normal growth of New Orleans and its environs was being halted. One or two talked of compromise, to close the whole matter. Then Relf and Chew, after long sessions with their attorneys, sent out word: they intended to fight, harder than ever. After all, the decision covered, directly, a single property; if she wanted the court's opinion to have any effect she'd have to carry her suits against every other person, one by one; and they'd be ready for her.

On a winter day in 1849 Edmund received instructions to return South, to take his old post at New Orleans. "I'm glad—for you and all of us," Myra told him. For months Washington had been dull, a tasteless place of which she was thoroughly tired; but until this moment she had not permitted herself to realize how much she longed for home—New Orleans.

Through her tears she spied her mother at the wharf; quickly she ran down the gangplank to Zulime and the Carrière sisters. Zulime looked older; her face had additional lines, but there was a serenity that had not been there before. Myra knew at once that the decision of the court had meant as much to Zulime as to her.

They all spent the evening together. Over and over Zulime returned to Judge Wayne's decision. "And what did he say then? How did the people act?" Myra brought out the clippings and read at random: ". . . the mother, whose marriage to Daniel Clark was recognized beyond question . . . Zulime Carrière's story has now been accepted. . . ." Her mother wept.

Spring arrived. The days were balmy, with breezes from the Gulf dispelling the light mists that swirled in from the direction of the bayous. Summer came early; for a time they spoke of going to one of the Gulf resorts, Grand Isle or Isle Dernière. But the children had just been re-established in school, and they delayed from week to week. The hotel remained a pleasant place.

On a hot June afternoon in 1849 Myra came back from a drive to discover Edmund tossing restlessly in a fever. Quickly she called James Gardette; one look and her half brother compressed his lips. The children must be kept away, and it would be best if Myra went to another room. "I'll stay," she said, shaking her head, and when he tried to argue she silenced him with an angry glance. An army cot was brought in for her, and for days she did not leave the chamber. Edmund moved back and forth on his moist bed, muttering in discomfort. At dusk of the fourth day he relaxed and began to talk quietly to her. At his opening words her hand clutched against the bedcover.

"I'm not afraid, my dear." His voice thickened, and she had to lean close to understand him. "I've had a full—a full life."

She sent a hasty message for James Gardette; turning back, she attempted to soothe him. He tried to lift his hand but found he could not manage it. "I've done the best I could. . . . Now they'll have to recognize you, won't they? Won't they?" For a long time he was silent, and then abruptly he spoke again, of his childhood in the fields and valleys, the flaming defense of Fort Erie against the British, his Indian fighting in Florida. Then he shuddered for the last time.

At noon, while thousands waited outside, the official party gathered in the hotel parlor about the tall figure in the casket. Edmund Gaines lay in his uniform, sword buckled at his waist. With Myra sat Zulime, her arms about her daughter. A little apart from them, stiffly, awkwardly, stood representatives of Army and Navy, city and state authorities. The minister spoke, but Myra heard little of what he said; her mind was elsewhere. She was thinking of the shabby room to which a lean soldier had come on a New Year's Day.

The drums started their muffled beat. A fife sounded a sorrowing note, and the men in uniform assembled in a long file. As the party moved forward guns went off, one by one at long intervals, in salute to Edmund Gaines. Along the way Myra saw men and women crying on the corners. Young Ed, who had been silent at her side, turned suddenly and dropped his face against her shoulders. Rhoda, earnest and methodical in all her actions, sat between Julia and Will, her hands holding theirs. The youngest of the group, Will, had a look of perplexity on his intent face; he had been too young to recall anything of his own father's passing.

At the wharf the body was transferred to the steamboat that would take them to Mobile, where several of the general's relatives lived. From the shore, as the vessel moved off, the artillery fired its last salvo. The guns, raised against the bright blue of the sky, were the final sight that came to Myra through her veil. They seemed to be signaling the end of a phase of her life.

Part Three

MYRA

CHAPTER XIX

LIFTING the window shade with a determined gesture, Zulime went to her daughter's side. Stretched on the sofa, in the square of sudden sunlight, Myra stared blankly about her. For the past two weeks she had left her room only for an occasional hesitant visit to the children down the hotel hallway. Messages went unanswered and letters were piled high on her desk. She did not cry; she lay silent. Later she might be able to turn back to the world, to force away this pain that held her like a hand pressed upon her throat. But it would be a long time from now, she felt certain.

She remembered Señora Perez of Terre-aux-Bœufs, and her prophecy: Myra would win, yes, but only after agony and loss. . . . How much more agony, and how much more to be lost? . . . For ten years she had enjoyed a protection such as she had never known. The strong hand of Edmund Gaines had supported her in a hundred ways. He had given her a great deal more—his firm love, the backing of his name, and, in some ways most important of all, his faith in her and her case. Not for a moment, as far as he had let her realize, had he questioned the story that she was trying to prove; not once had he doubted she would win. Now, suddenly, it was all gone, and she waited, half dazed, unable to think ahead, not knowing what she would do and caring less.

Zulime touched her arm, startling her from her reverie: "Chérie, I must disturb you. Mr. Grymes is downstairs again, and he says it's very important."

Wearily, her eyes devoid of expression, Myra sat up. "Couldn't I sign the papers, or whatever they are? I can't think about—about anything. . . ." Leading her to the dresser, Zulime handed her a comb. Mechanically Myra prepared herself.

When John Grymes came in and sat across from her she felt as if he were frowning at her from a distance. She barely noticed the alert, handsome, younger man, a mustachioed Creole who appeared very friendly. She heard Grymes give his name:

"Philippe d'Abadie, my new associate." She nodded, and after a moment a word or two caught her attention: ". . . new evidence . . . They might change the case overnight." She began to listen. Relf and Chew had been working harder even than before; their attorneys must have talked to several hundred new people. Her case against the two men themselves was finally coming to full trial; Relf and Chew had suddenly grown confident that, with their fresh material, whatever it was, they could get the Supreme Court's decision overthrown. Grymes's face was graver than she had ever seen it. "It'll be a hard fight, and we'll need your help from now on."

As Grymes continued Myra was fully attentive. For some time his health had not been good; Philippe here was taking over part of his practice. Also Grymes had in mind a young lawyer over in Mobile, John Campbell, who had created quite a stir in cases going back to the colonial days; it would help immeasurably if they retained Campbell. Her brows contracting, Myra nodded again. For once Grymes appeared uncertain how to proceed; he cleared his throat. "I'm afraid I have more bad news. I've been checking into Edmund's estate. Well, Edmund was no businessman, you know; things are pretty involved——"

"What is the news?" Myra interrupted, her hands pressed against her temples.

"There's only a little left." Grymes's expression was pitying. "A few thousand, more or less."

"But——"

"Edmund spent practically seventy-five thousand dollars on the case."

The room swam before her. For the first time she understood the full extent of what this man had done, out of his love and his confidence in her cause. Now, abruptly, the old specter rose before her: she might yet lose the case.

She raised her head. "How much will we need to retain this man from Mobile?"

"About half what you have left."

An uneasy silence fell upon them. Myra's eye traced the rich pattern of the carpet; her foot tapped nervously. Then she stood up, and her voice was a trifle louder, as if she were defying some inner doubt. "I'll sign a note for him now." As she started toward the desk she added more quietly, "Tomorrow we'll begin meeting regularly. The way it was before."

When the two men left she spoke quickly to Zulime; together they pulled out a pair of heavy trunks and drew forth their contents. At the bottom of one of them they found the tin banks into which she had dropped her dollars. With hands that shook she broke them open. Nearly eight hundred dollars. Edmund had scattered that much or more in a day's time.

First a new place to live. As Zulime packed Myra left the hotel. No carriage this time; she walked a few blocks up St. Charles Avenue, tried several boardinghouses, and eventually, at Lafayette Square, selected two rooms on the top floor of an old house. It had enjoyed more prosperous days; well, so had she. Back at the hotel, she realized it would be hard to carry out some of the decisions she had just made. After the funeral young Ed had remained with Edmund's Mobile relatives; now she must ask if they could continue to look after him. She had come to love the boy very much; yet what could she do?

Eulalie entered. Her face was composed, but there was a look of concern about her eyes. "You have no further need of me," she said. "I'll find someplace . . ." Myra went at once to her long-time friend and supporter; as long as she kept a roof over her head there would be a place for Eulalie. Again the door opened and uncertainly, almost timidly, the three children came in. Myra held out her arms.

The next week she went to John Grymes's office; in his later years the attorney had succumbed to conventionality in this respect and met his clients like anyone else. His associate, the Creole Philippe d'Abadie, brought forward a young man of rather unimpressive demeanor: "Mr. John Archibald Campbell." The Mobile lawyer stood stolidly before her, tall, long-faced, with beetling brows and high forehead. He had little to say; it was clear that this intent legal scholar saw scant reason for social non-essentials. As he listened he frowned and scratched at his chin. Then in a few minutes he demonstrated a tight grasp of the case. Cutting to the heart of the matter, he spoke quietly, unemotionally:

"One thing's clear. Their main attack will be through your mother. If you don't mind my saying it"—his face remained cold—"she's their logical target. She'll remain here, of course, so we can call her to the stand?"

Myra exchanged a quick look with John Grymes. This time Grymes was firm; it might mean everything for them to have Zulime as a witness. Myra hesitated; for years Zulime had feared that Relf and Chew would force her to appear. They had thought that this, at least, was over.

"Well," Myra said, "let's go see her."

When they entered the dark little hotel room Zulime came forward. As she listened her mouth trembled. "Oh no, I couldn't! Myra"—her heavy-lidded eyes appealed to her daughter— "Myra, you know the things they'd say!"

The Creole D'Abadie went to Zulime's side; patiently he spoke to her in French. His olive skin flushing slightly, his dark brown eyes warm in sympathy, he spoke with friendliness and understanding. He answered her arguments, he tried to reason away her doubts. "You understand, madame, the other side can still call you in a moment. . . . The only reason they haven't is that you might hurt their case. . . ." Finally he persuaded her to accept a suggestion of his: she would attend one of the opening sessions, so that she might know the scene she would face. After that, he was sure, Zulime would agree with them. As the callers prepared to leave, Myra watched Philippe d'Abadie with a heightened respect.

There was something about D'Abadie that seemed vaguely familiar. The Creole's manner, that slight lift of the lip that made the mustache bristle, the strong, aquiline nose . . . She had it, of course. He was the man who had come to her that day—how long ago it seemed!—when her carriage stopped and she had appeared to smile encouragingly at him. She could see again the mark of her hand across his surprised face. Then, afterward, they had met for a moment at the Boisfontaines' party, and he had looked at her in discreet amusement. Now his glance intercepted hers, and he gave a little laugh. "I was wondering how long it would take you to remember!" For the first time in weeks she was able to smile.

In an atmosphere of heightened tension, before a courtroom thronged beyond capacity, the case reopened. The newspapers ran stories of unprecedented length; one enterprising editor arranged to issue the full record in booklet form, "complete and unabridged." The conservatives shuddered; what was the world coming to, when such scandalous goings on were considered subjects for reading in public journals? On the second day Zulime arrived early, alone, and slipped into a seat at the back. Her face hidden beneath a veil, her hands clutching a rosary, she focused her nervous eyes on the attorneys.

The moment was ill chosen. Lucius Duncan waved a hand and shouted: "What kind of mother are we considering? A mother who discarded two infants, Caroline and Myra, and never showed the slightest interest in their welfare. They might have starved for all she cared! A mother who stands convicted of adultery, on the case her daughter Myra seems to make, *before* the pretended marriage to Daniel—and then *afterward,* says the loving daughter, of bigamy!" Zulime cringed. "At one time she had three living 'husbands.' Three husbands, mind you—one on the French plan, another on the American, the third on any old plan!" Handkerchief to her mouth, Zulime fled the courtroom.

That week the Duncan brothers came out with the "sensations" that they had promised. Rising, Lucius remarked that he had several documents to offer. Philippe d'Abadie's dark eyes flashed a signal to Myra.

Duncan brought out, first, an ancient, much-folded piece of paper—"proceedings instituted against Geronimo des Granges for bigamy" back in September 1802, before the vicar general of the church at New Orleans. Slowly, as Myra listened in amazement, he read. Des Granges had come back from Europe, with the woman Barbara Jeanbelle d'Orci; shortly afterward he was arrested on a charge of bigamy. The D'Orci woman testified; she had known Des Granges in the East about twelve years earlier, had intended to marry him but had never done so, because he wanted her first to go with him to New Orleans. Later she married someone else, she said. No, she had no record of that marriage, but she remembered the witnesses were M. and Mme. Bernardy.

Des Granges also had testified, to much the same story. He had recently met Barbara again in France; it was a mere coincidence that they returned on the same boat. It appeared that rumors had been circulated about him and yet a third woman,

Marie Yllar, also recently come to New Orleans and staying at the house of the leading citizen, Bernard de Marigny. Des Granges insisted that he had no connection with her either. "And now"—Attorney Duncan's eyes flashed—"here is a signed statement from Zulime des Granges herself, part of the same record!" Zulime declared she had gone North the previous year to investigate a report that Des Granges was married to another woman; there she learned only that he had courted Barbara without marrying her. She was satisfied that he was not a bigamist. As a result a decree was made by the vicar general: "Not being able to prove the public report and having no more proofs for the present, let all proceedings be suspended, with power to prosecute them hereafter, and let Des Granges be set at liberty."

Triumphantly Duncan stared over at Myra. She whispered to her attorneys, "But that doesn't sound at all like the government's criminal proceedings against Des Granges. This 'church hearing' was supposed to take place *in 1802;* all the witnesses say Des Granges was convicted by the state, not the church, and *late in 1803!*" Also Myra's representatives had hunted for months in the church files, as well as the state records, and nothing of this sort had been found there.

John Campbell's thin lips twisted. "It's a curious document, all right." Myra saw that he had filled three pages of notes with questions to be asked about the "proceedings."

Exhibit Two, announced Mr. Duncan—"the civil court record of a suit brought in 1805 by Zulime des Granges against Jerome des Granges." The man had returned for the last time to Louisiana; she went to court to demand he pay alimony. Des Granges did not answer, and she won a judgment by default. Exhibit Three was dated six months later. The opening pages were missing, but clearly, said Duncan, it was another civil action for divorce; and now Zulime obtained it. Mr. Duncan had acid in his voice: "Here was the lady getting a divorce from husband number one—three years after her daughter says she married Daniel Clark, husband number two!" A wave of guffaws broke over the room.

Before the feeble fire in the boardinghouse Myra's three lawyers faced Zulime. Her arm about her mother's waist, Myra patted her hand. An hour before Zulime had been close to hysterics; now, with an effort to maintain her composure, she was answering their questions.

"That 'church hearing'—it's false from start to finish! I never appeared before anything like that, and I never signed anything! How could I have said those things? I had already married Daniel; I myself was going to the criminal authorities and demanding that they put Des Granges in prison!" Her voice broke.

John Campbell pulled at his chin. "I have faith in your story, madame, for several reasons." His precise mind was at work. "The document has all the marks of a forgery, made up by somebody years later, to destroy our case. I've never heard of 'church hearings' of this kind. The thing's contradicted, too, by every piece of evidence in the case. What motive would you have for exonerating a man who, as half the city *was* certain, was a bigamist? Up in the East you'd found a witness to Des Granges's marriage to the D'Orci woman. If it was claimed you were still Des Granges's wife, how could you have been called on to give evidence in a case involving your husband? A wife can't testify against a husband. If this 'hearing' was really a legal one, how could Des Granges have been called to testify against himself?"

Zulime, encouraged, went on to the two later proceedings in civil court, to obtain recognition that she was no longer Des Granges's wife. These were true documents. After escaping from Louisiana, Des Granges had suddenly returned. At once she went to her attorney, asking that he take some legal step to make Des Granges declare he had married the D'Orci woman. At first the attorney brought proceedings, asking alimony; Des Granges could not afford to pay, the attorney said, and this would make him come forward with the admission that he had never been her husband. "I never asked the lawyer to file action for alimony: I was surprised, in fact, when I saw what he had done," Zulime explained.

In any case Des Granges entered no plea but fled a second time. Within six months, at Zulime's insistence, the lawyer went into court again, and this time, as Zulime urged, he made a direct plea for annulment. And then, finally, she had won; her marriage with Des Granges was officially recognized as void from the start.

Grymes bent forward. "The other side is trying to make it look as if your second action, too, was for alimony. The opening sheets, the petition itself, have been removed; or perhaps they merely fell away." His expression made it clear what he thought had happened. "So the record itself doesn't give the reason for action. But the very contents prove that the grounds *must* have been Des Granges's bigamy. If you'd been seeking alimony, or a simple divorce, you would have been described as Mme. des Granges. Look, the request is in the name of Zulime Carrière, not Des Granges. And you'll notice that the attorney carefully gave the full certificate of the 'marriage' with Des Granges. There was no reason for him to do that if you were only trying to end a legal marriage. In a suit for *annulment* you had first to show that the form of a ceremonial had been followed, then prove it wasn't valid."

Philippe d'Abadie's eyes widened. "Then by introducing this last document they've given us one of the best pieces of evidence for our side!" They looked at one another, hope returning to their faces.

The next day the lobby outside the courtroom was packed with middle-aged and elderly men. With the first witness the opposition's purpose became clear. Etienne Carraby, a slight individual with a walrus mustache, smiled brightly. "Mme. Zulime des Granges? Her reputation was bad. Yes, she had an illicit connection with Daniel Clark. M. Clark himself? A man of spotless reputation, sir—too high-minded to contract marriage with his paramour."

Zenon Cavellier, red-faced, harassed, spoke nervously. "I always knew Daniel as a bachelor—a man of good reputation, the lover of Mme. des Granges. Ah, *non,* he could never have married the woman he kept; he had too much delicacy of feeling for that!" M. Cavellier's next answer, however, made Attorney Duncan start. *"Oui,* I knew the fellow Des Granges. He ran away when it was discovered he was a bigamist." This had been a piece of miscalculation on the part of the opposition, and Grymes made the most of it. As quickly as he could Mr. Duncan got the witness off the stand and called his next one.

"Was Daniel Clark generally reported to be impotent?"

"I heard so." The witness blinked innocently at the audience. "The women I visited myself told me that." The audience stirred in delight at the new tidbit; Myra's head dropped at this gutter-snipe approach.

The imperturbable Campbell whispered wryly to Philippe d'Abadie, "Strange stuff, eh? They're passing up no chances; but I'd call *that* grasping at a straw!"

On and on went the elderly men, angry, coy, bitter, bland, twenty or more of them: "Mme. des Granges was a light woman." "Daniel? an upright, honorable man; he would have had her only as his woman, never his wife. . . ." From all of them, however, Grymes and D'Abadie obtained admissions. No, they had no proof that Daniel had never married Zulime. No, they could give no direct evidence that Zulime was immoral; people just said it.

Repeatedly Campbell asked: "This bad reputation you claim for her—just when did it arise?"

"Oh, 1803, 1804," came the answer. Or "Around 1803. . . ."

"Didn't it grow, then, out of Daniel's connection with her, and nothing else?"

"I suppose so. . . . When they saw her on the street, every-body said, 'There goes Daniel Clark's woman.' "

Campbell nodded. "And if we prove Daniel and Zulime were secretly married all the time, then you couldn't call her what you did?" The opposition attorneys jumped up in anger; Campbell thought he had made his point.

Horatio Davis took the stand for Relf and Chew. Turning carefully away from his foster sister, Horatio reached into his pocket and with his usual dignity handed forth a letter. Daniel's sister in Liverpool had sent it to Daniel in 1806. She had just finished fitting up a toilet set for him; somehow, she wrote, she had the idea it would soon go to "Mrs. Daniel Clark." Would he let her know if her suspicions were correct? Six months later Daniel replied, and Horatio identified this message as well. " 'I assure you,' " he read, " 'it would have given me infinite pleasure to offer the set either to Mrs. Clark or any person likely to become Mrs. Clark. But this will not be the case for some time to come, for so long as I have the misfortune to be hampered with business, so will I remain single.' "

John Grymes probed: "You've heard of secret marriages?"

"I suppose I have."

"Wouldn't a fairly vital part of such a marriage be its secrecy?"

"Well, yes."

"Would a man, wishing to keep such marriage secret, tell all about it to a curious woman relative?"

Lucius Duncan prevented a reply, and Grymes bowed.

A heavily veiled widow was led forward. Her family had owned a house on the bayou near Daniel's, she said. About a year or so before his death Daniel started to call regularly; he was paying his addresses to her sister, "evidently with a view to marriage." She understood at the time that he was engaged to her sister, but the marriage was delayed on several occasions, for "reasons I did not particularly comprehend." Then Daniel died. John Grymes, raising an eyebrow, asked no questions.

Two women relatives of Beverly Chew stepped up. A prim pair, they cast resentful glances at Myra, then looked promptly away. Chew's niece, an angular lady, all laces and ribbons, described a visit to New Orleans as a girl of eleven. Yes, she saw Daniel daily; he developed quite an affection for her. At the next question the lady's head tossed. "I *know* he wasn't married! My intimacy with him was such that if he'd been married he would have told me." She almost spat out the words.

Grymes had a single ironic query. "Despite this—er—remarkable intimacy between you, at eleven, and Clark, in his forties—suppose Daniel thought proper to marry privately? Would he have told you of a secret marriage?"

Her look was heavy with venom. "No, I suppose not. But, anyway, he was courting my aunt!"

Now came the aunt, slightly taller, slightly more angular, no less belaced and beribboned. Yes, she'd been there at the same time. "Daniel gave me every proof he wasn't married that a gentleman could give to a lady. The nature of my acquaintance with him necessarily"—her lips tightened—"precluded the possib-il-ity."

Grymes had decided it was time to be sharp on his own account. "Madame, another lady just testified she thought Daniel was courting her sister at this identical moment."

"Ridiculous!"

"When did Daniel ask you to marry him?"

The lady turned a coral shade. "Well, on no particular date. I understood——"

"I amend the question. *Did* Daniel ask you to marry him?"

"Well, it wasn't so specific." The lady was becoming more and more flustered. "In a little while, I think . . . That is, I understood from small things . . ."

"Did he or didn't he say he wanted to take you to the altar?"

"Well, not directly."

"Thank you, madame."

Joining her niece, the lady glared at Grymes and Myra with impartial contempt and whirled out. "Truly an ardent family!" Grymes grunted. The Duncan brothers had grown highly uncomfortable, and the Virginian enjoyed their expressions. "They seem to be tripping over their own case. First they say Daniel was incapable of marriage, and then they have him proposing to two women at the same time!"

And again Myra remembered the statement that Daniel had made to Harriett Smyth: "I won't give Myra a stepmother." No matter what had happened, no matter what others said, the fact remained that he had never done so.

Philippe d'Abadie, after hours of hurried preparation, called a small line of witnesses to refute or temper some of the opposition's evidence. The first was the priest who had charge of records at the cathedral. Yes, he had found the proceedings of the "church hearing." How? He had received a request from the attorneys to look for it. No, he had never seen it before. No, he had never seen a record like it, ever before, in any of the Louisiana church documents.

Philippe d'Abadie pressed forward. "Father, did the Church have authority at that time to hold a hearing on a criminal matter like bigamy?"

"That, my son, I do not know."

"But have you ever heard of such a 'hearing' being held here in a case of bigamy?"

"No, my son."

Next came Jules Manouvrier, lithographer and engraver for twenty-five years. He was brisk and tart-tongued. D'Abadie presented to him a document signed by Zulime in 1796 and with it the "church hearing" containing her supposed signature.

"Is the writing that of the same person?" the Creole attorney asked.

"They're entirely different. One of them is forged. Counterfeit!" M. Manouvrier shrugged, then looked over the courtroom as if to defy anyone to deny it. A stir resulted.

Philippe d'Abadie handed him other samples of Zulime's writing. "From a study of them all, which would you say is forged?"

"The writing on this one—the 'church hearing.'" M. Manouvrier's voice was firm.

Philippe d'Abadie reached out again. "I'm handing you a marriage contract between Zulime Carrière and Jerome des Granges, which was *found and presented* as an authentic document"—he emphasized the words—"by the opposition. Now look at the signature supposed to be that of Zulime Carrière. Does it appear as if it were written at that date, 1794?"

"It certainly don't!"

"Why not?"

"For one thing, it's much too dark, too fresh-looking."

"When would you say it was really written?"

"Oh, about forty years later!" The witness ignored the new excitement he was creating in the court.

"Is there anything else odd about this so-called signature?"

"Yes, one thing." M. Manouvrier's eye twinkled. "It was written—or at least freshened up—by a steel pen. And steel pens weren't being made back at that time. Nobody used anything but quills."

CHAPTER XX

THE next morning, as Myra worked at the collar of her dress, James Gardette entered, puffing, a heavy box under each arm. In opening his new office a few days ago he had done something he had long promised Zulime; throwing together all his father's old papers, he had brought them to her to look over.

James and Zulime bent together over the dusty packets, untouched for years. Patients' bills, letters—James smiled at the conglomeration. This one was in Latin, a notation of some kind of religious ceremonial: "*Sacerdos Catholicus . . . Ecclesiae S. Patri Apostoli . . .*" Two names made him swallow suddenly:

"Jacobum Degrange et Barbara M. Orci." Des Granges and
that other woman! Quickly he translated it aloud:

"Greeting in the Lord. I, the undersigned Catholic priest and
apostolic pastor of the Church of St. Peter the Apostle, make known
that on the sixth of July, 1790, I conjoined in matrimony . . . Witnesses were John O'Connell, Charles Bernardy and Victoria Bernardy. . . . In testimony of which things I with my own hand have
written and signed and confirmed by seal. September 11, 1806.
William V. O'Brien, pastor."

Zulime's eyes bulged. "St. Peter's—that was the church
Sophie and I visited when we tried to find the record of Des
Granges's marriage! The old priest wasn't there at the time,
and we were told the register of earlier marriages was missing
or destroyed." She went on with a rush. "Then—then this *proves*
Des Granges's bigamy, doesn't it? But why, James, didn't your
father tell us he had this certificate? The date it was given—look,
it's some time before Daniel and I broke up." She turned to
Myra. "Daniel and Dr. Gardette had been friends. I suppose
Dr. Gardette had the priest make the statement for Daniel, then
never had the chance to give it to him." She frowned. "A year
or so later I married Dr. Gardette. He always tried to persuade
me not to talk about the matter or think about it; he saw how
upset I became. Perhaps that was why he said nothing about
this. . . ."

When a knock sounded Myra almost ran to the door. John
Grymes and Philippe d'Abadie, after glancing at the document,
talked excitedly. "This might change the whole case," Grymes
cried. "Still, it needs support—affidavits taken at the scene.
With the trial in full swing, though, I'd be afraid to ask for a
recess."

The Creole D'Abadie, eyes shining, disagreed. "It'll be at
least twelve days before it ends. Somebody could leave right
away, work at full speed . . ." He pulled out his watch. "The
cars for New York start in an hour——"

Grymes laughed. "Somebody? It's you. Young man, you're
on your way to New York right now!"

As Myra entered the courtroom again an elderly man was
taking the oath. For a moment she did not recognize D. W.

Coxe; he had aged greatly since their last meeting at the dinner table in Wilmington. Soon she was hearing the familiar, soothing tones and watching him glance slyly about the court. The long, pale face nodded; like practically everyone else at this trial, Coxe wanted to introduce something new, a "few letters" he had found in checking over his files. They turned out to be no less than seventy-five messages that passed between him, Daniel Clark, Relf, and Chew. The alert John Campbell reached out for copies and retired to the corner to study them.

Meanwhile Coxe went back to the story of Zulime's first visit to Philadelphia. Everything the Carrière sisters said about it was untrue, he insisted. The girl Caroline was not born late in 1801, as they testified, but in the spring of 1802. Daniel was in Philadelphia, alone, for a few months early in 1802, but then went back, about April, to New Orleans. Shortly afterward Zulime arrived, with a letter of introduction from Daniel to Coxe. "It told me confidentially that the woman was pregnant by him, and asked me to make provisions for the child's birth," Coxe said. "Well, she had the child; then in July Daniel joined her in Philadelphia for a brief time. Within a month Daniel had gone to Europe and she had left for New Orleans."

Myra and Grymes looked quickly at each other. This was an entirely different story from the one Coxe had told before! Grymes made a signal to her; they'd give Coxe a good length of rope and see what he did with it. When Attorney Duncan sat down Grymes went to the witness. "Here, sir, is a copy of one of your earlier statements. At that time you swore you removed Caroline from her mother 'on the day of her birth.' And then you said that very soon afterward, as quickly as Zulime could travel, she left Philadelphia. Yet today you tell us the child was born in *April* and Zulime remained until *August*. Now which version is correct?"

Mr. Coxe coughed. "Checking through my correspondence, as I've done, I've refreshed my memory, and I recall the facts more clearly now."

"Then Zulime *didn't* leave so quickly, but stayed several months?"

"She stayed, yes." He spoke slowly and carefully.

"But you still contend you took the child from her the very day it was born?"

"I most certainly do!"

"Well now. The first time you testified you made no reference whatever to a 'letter of introduction' that you claim Zulime brought. How was that?"

"Simply a matter of defective memory, sir. I must apologize." The smile that spread over his face was disarming.

"May I see that 'letter of introduction'?"

"Ah, I don't have it. It's my impression that because of its nature I destroyed it. Or it may have been burned in a fire that took my countinghouse a little later."

"Still, you seem to have saved a lot of other letters, haven't you?"

"Some escaped, fortunately." Mr. Coxe had grown bland again.

"And some didn't—unfortunately for some of us."

Benignly Mr. Coxe blinked. "Unfortunately for all of us."

Grymes lifted an eyebrow. "You now say Daniel remained in Philadelphia till shortly before April. Immediately after he started back Zulime appeared with this letter. Didn't it strike you as odd that she would have brought you a letter of introduction announcing such a personal thing, from a man who had just been with you? A man who'd seen you much later than he'd seen her?"

"I don't know." Mr. Coxe's light gray eyes seemed hurt.

"Well . . . So Daniel *wrote* you he was the father of the child. Then, seeing you face to face, months later and for several months, he didn't discuss the matter with you at all?"

"I've said that already." Mr. Coxe looked unhappy.

"You mean that Daniel wrote the letter for Zulime, traveled fifteen hundred miles to Philadelphia, saw you daily for months, and didn't once mention to you that Zulime was coming? Then Daniel left, Zulime came those fifteen hundred miles and gave you the letter Daniel had written those long months ago?"

"I suppose so." Coxe's unhappiness was increasing.

From the corner, having finished his study of the letters Coxe had offered, Attorney Campbell walked up. Almost apologetically he began: "You've said the lady brought you a letter of introduction in 1802? I presume you're certain of that year?"

Mr. Coxe nodded. Campbell continued. "But among these letters you've brought forward I find an inconspicuous sentence from you to Daniel : 'Mme. Carrière and sister handed me your letter of introduction.' And the date is *1807!* How do you explain that?"

"I won't try to explain it. It just happened."

"Is it customary to write two letters introducing one person to another?"

The opposition attorneys managed to stop the question. The calm Mr. Campbell, however, was not yet finished. He read from another of Coxe's earlier statements: "Didn't you say you and Daniel were on terms of 'most unlimited and confidential intimacy'?"

"Exactly so!"

Campbell made a grimace. "Then how do you explain this letter written by Daniel to Relf and Chew, at the very time he was in Philadelphia in 1802, when he married Zulime?" He read: " 'When you write me on private matters, let your letters come directly to Mr. Earle, as things will often occur which I wish only to see. Forward me the $2000 I wrote you for, in one or two good bills, that I may have some funds at my disposal, without calling on Mr. Coxe for trifles. *This must be a matter kept to yourself.* ' "

A snicker came from the back of the room. His vanity touched, Coxe blushed painfully. "I can only say there might have been matters . . ." Tightening his lips, he did not finish.

"Yet you'd have us believe Daniel trusted you enough to write such a very private letter about a supposedly illegitimate child of his? And that he put it in writing *before* he saw you, then saw you for months without mentioning the matter, and then Zulime came forward with the letter?"

Mr. Coxe spluttered, until his attorneys came to his rescue. Grymes and Campbell nodded that they were finished with him. But Coxe, it developed, was not through with them. "If you don't mind, I have one more thing that might interest the court." Catching a well-remembered gleam in the man's light eyes, Myra listened intently. Back in 1842, he said, he had heard that one of the city's leading attorneys, Stephen Mazureau, had certain information about this case. Coxe had talked with Mazureau; then, returning to Philadelphia, he decided not to rely on his memory of what they said. He wrote Mazureau, and he now offered Mazureau's reply.

According to the document, Mazureau said that Daniel had once consulted him to find whether a will, of which Daniel had made a rough sketch, would be legal. Mazureau went on, in his message to Coxe:

The will thus intended stated Myra to be his natural child and instituted her his universal heir, leaving to his own mother an annual rent of, I believe, $3000. On asking Clark the name of the girl's mother, he answered: "You know the lady; it is Madame des Granges." "But," I said, "that woman was married, and Des Granges was alive when the girl was born." "Yes," said Clark, "she was married, I know; and what matters it? The ruffian had deceived that pretty woman; he was married when he courted her and became her husband, and, as was reported, he ran away afterwards from fear of being prosecuted. So, you see, this marriage was null." "That may be," I replied, "but until so declared by a competent tribunal, the marriage exists, and the child is of such a class of bastards as not to be capable under our laws of receiving by will from her father anything beyond what may be necessary for her sustenance and education."

"What shall I do, then?" asked Clark. "Sir, if you have friends in whom you can place your confidence, convey them some of your property or give them money for the use of the child, to be given to her when she becomes of age." "That I'll do," said Clark.

Grymes, his face an angry pink, stepped toward Coxe. "Is Mazureau alive?"

"Alas, no. As everybody knows, he died a few months ago."

"Yet he wrote this letter to you eight years ago! You held it all that time without offering it, when he could have been brought to court for questioning about it and the circumstances. Now that he's gone . . ."

This, of course, the judge overruled. But Grymes and Campbell had much more to argue. These were the unsworn recollections of a dead attorney, about an incident that had happened thirty years earlier; there was nothing to prove it occurred as Mazureau had said. The lawyer's claim that Daniel called Myra a natural child was contradicted by Daniel's own statements to many others. Then, too, Clark's marriage to Zulime was a secret at the time; would Daniel have blurted it out to a man who was not one of his close friends? As to Mazureau's statement that Zulime's marriage to Des Granges remained in full effect until

a court ruled officially—that was only his opinion, and an errone-
ous one. Why, the United States Supreme Court, in this same
case, had ruled otherwise. Legally Zulime's union with Des
Granges had been void from the start. And here was a signifi-
cant passage: Mazureau had been an attorney for Relf in one
of his cases against Myra. Wouldn't that place a question beside anything the man had said?

Into court came Charles Patterson, against whom Myra had
won the Supreme Court decision. He had been summoned by
Relf and Chew, and Myra had been warned of their purpose.
Mr. Patterson let himself carefully into his seat, folded his big
overcoat in his lap, and looked politely at the Duncan brothers.
For an hour they worked upon him, hammering their theme:
the case against Patterson had been fraudulent, a fixed contest
arranged by General Gaines to cheat the other defendants.

To each furious question Mr. Patterson made a mild answer,
maintaining his position. That was right, sir, he hadn't had to
give up his little parcel of land, even though he lost the case;
General Gaines had assured him, all along, that he wouldn't
suffer. But, every time, the general told him he wanted to make
as strong a case as he could. " 'The stronger the better,' them
was his words. He told me to bring in every bit of evidence I
could find. You know, I introduced the whole record of the
previous trial." Mr. Patterson reached into his pocket; here
were the sworn statements of his attorneys, describing in detail
how hard they had labored, and denying any suggestion that they
had not done their best. . . .

"But what did you think of something so secret—so clandes-
tine?" Mr. Duncan pointed a shaking finger.

"Secret?" Mr. Patterson frowned. "It weren't so secret. The
general told me he talked to a lot of landowners, personal, with
the same idea. He even went to Judge Martin of the supreme
court, with the same proposition; if the judge would agree to a
fair trial in federal court, the general would see he didn't suffer.
But Mr. Martin wouldn't go in on it."

The judge and all the attorneys looked startled. Myra had
known nothing of this, nor had anyone else. The hostile, can-
tankerous Martin of all people in Louisiana! How indiscreet
Edmund had been; and yet how like him, rushing ahead in his
own fashion, directly toward his goal. Poor Edmund; what

hadn't he tried to do for her? She wiped her eyes as Mr. Patterson left the stand. The brothers Duncan were perspiring.

The last witness of the day was one brought in by John Grymes, to Myra's surprise. With a twinkle the attorney had declined to tell her what was pending. Peter K. Wagner, a chubby old man with red cheeks, explained how he had frequently visited his good friend Daniel during the latter's last illness. A minor money transaction once came up.

"Oh, I have no change," said Daniel. Until then Clark had been in the habit of making payments to Wagner by drafts on Relf and Chew, whose firm he controlled.

Mr. Wagner therefore told him, "Give me a draft on Chew."

And now Mr. Wagner testified, "Daniel said, 'That fellow Chew is such a damned rascal, I don't even speak to him.'" To the Duncan brothers Mr. Wagner turned a firm face. "Oh yes, I'm certain he said the words—'damned rascal.'"

The case neared its close. A brief but encouraging telegram arrived from New York; Philippe d'Abadie had uncovered several good leads. A little later they had another message: he would be there within five days, God willing.

Two more days passed. The judge was growing restive. Grymes talked more slowly; he raised additional points; but still the time did not go fast enough. At length Grymes informed the judge that D'Abadie was due soon with vital evidence.

"I give you thirty-six hours," the jurist grumbled. "If he hasn't arrived by 3 P.M. tomorrow I close the case. Till then, court adjourned."

Philippe was expected at ten the next morning. Myra went early to the station, and Grymes joined her. The clerk yawned; train due at ten, yes, but that usually meant noon. At noon the clerk remained undisturbed; oh, sometimes she came five hours late. Myra found it impossible to leave the station; she paced back and forth beneath the soot-laden rafters, her face reddened by the wind, while Grymes sat moodily before a potbellied stove. Two o'clock, now two-thirty. Even if Philippe did arrive soon, how would he have time to compare his notes and check his findings with them?

Shortly before three Grymes left her; he hated to face that judge. But when he advanced to the bench he spoke long and earnestly. Lucius Duncan interposed bristling objections. Grymes was afraid to stop talking; he argued, he cited precedents, anything to hold off a definite action by the judge. Then his sensitive ear detected a faint echo of a whistle—the New York train. He set to work with increased vigor, pulling forth lawbooks, riffling the pages. Frowning, the judge took out his watch.

At the station, as the train chugged in, Myra ran along the coaches, causing other women to turn looks of piercing disapproval upon her. When she caught sight of Philippe she waved frantically; he was off the steps before the car came to a stop. She took his arm, and together they ran toward a carriage. Travel-stained, unshaven as he was, he must offer the material at once if he was to offer it at all.

The judge struck the bench a sharp blow with his palm. He was sorry; he couldn't allow the court—— John Grymes paid him no heed. Myra and Philippe were racing down the aisle.

The Creole addressed the court in a low voice. Here was a certificate made before his death by Father O'Brien of New York. It told how he had married Des Granges and Barbara d'Orci in the year 1790. Here were sworn statements by relatives and associates of the dead man, proving that the writing was in his peculiar style. The document was one of many similar certificates that Father O'Brien made out when interested persons asked for them. And here were statements by the niece and other connections of the dead priest, explaining how there was great confusion in the church's formal records, due to fire, accidents, and other causes. For many years there were no records in the church's possession for the period before 1800; many persons had tried to find them, but in vain.

The niece knew, from her mother and others, that a ceremony had been held uniting Des Granges and Barbara d'Orci; the girl recalled hearing of it especially, because one of the witnesses, Mrs. Bernardy, had been dressed so oddly they all talked about it later.

Here Philippe exclaimed, "This bears out all our contentions about Des Granges's previous marriage! Zulime's sister told how she and Zulime, strangers to Philadelphia, looked in vain for the record; here is confirmation that the original documents were in a very confused state. Eventually, though, a native of Philadelphia, Dr. Gardette, found the priest, conferred with him, and had him sign a certificate that the marriage *had* taken place."

The Creole paused, amusement playing at the corners of his mouth. "And here's a curious fact. In the record of the so-called 'church hearing,' which the defense claims 'exonerated' Des Granges, the D'Orci woman is made to tell of a marriage about 1790, in which she was supposed to have married *another* man." He picked up that document. "She says 'Mr. Bernardy and his wife were witnesses.' Lo and behold, the priest's own certificate shows that in 1790 a marriage did occur, with Charles and Victoria Bernardy as witnesses. But the woman actually married Des Granges himself. By this little slip they've been betrayed!"

The defense jumped forward. That priest's certificate—it meant nothing. Why, it wasn't in regular affidavit form; why hadn't the priest sworn to it before an attorney? . . . Myra smiled to herself. A little earlier the other side had offered a letter written by the attorney Mazureau, who had been paid by Relf to represent him against Myra. It, too, had been unsworn. Now they objected to a certificate from a priest!

Grymes and Campbell stepped up to take over the argument. Philippe d'Abadie rubbed his tired, bearded face and stepped out. Myra hurried behind him; in the excitement she had forgotten to take his hand and thank him for the service he had done her. Wearily he smiled; he was sound asleep before his carriage was halfway home.

The same evening Philippe d'Abadie sat with Zulime and a notary. After some consideration, as a final effort to complete their case, they had decided she must try to answer written interrogations. Philippe would question her in French; the familiar language and a familiar presence might reassure her. Zulime knew, however, that she faced a rigid cross-examination from the other side. Hands locked in her lap, she waited. Gone was the childlike person whom Myra had first met; her throat working, eyes staring before her, she looked like a tired old woman.

She began in a muffled voice, then she faltered. Names, dates whirled in her mind; and always she seemed to be afraid of something. That man Duncan and the words he had used against her in court a few weeks ago . . . What was that last question, please? Well, it had been in 1803—no, 1802 . . . A moment, so she could think . . . She had to make another start and ask the notary to reread the last paragraph. Her voice faltered and Philippe concluded that they had gone as far as they could; another few minutes and she would have broken.

The puzzled notary extended the document to Zulime to sign, and her moist hand made a smudge across the ink. In the hall outside stood Myra, Grymes, and Campbell. They read it over, then looked at one another. Slowly John Grymes shook his head to the notary, who shrugged and left; and then the attorney tore the sheet into small pieces.

Myra went inside to her mother.

CHAPTER XXI

AT THE window sill, Myra leaned forward, her eyes on the strolling figures in Lafayette Square. How tall the three children, walking beside Eulalie, had grown—Rhoda, seventeen, Will and Julia just behind her. Poor things—it wasn't much of a life for them, was it? In and out of hotel rooms, living from trunks, their companions chance acquaintances . . . She had had to change their school several times; each institution was a less prepossessing one. But now their education offered a problem of finances again.

Regardless of what happened, she must keep Will in his classes. During the past year and a half, with Edmund's restraining hand gone, the boy had presented increasing difficulties for her. He was nervous, he was moody, alternately belligerent and tractable. At times he appeared to be a little old man, and beyond doubt he had a wisdom beyond his years; again he acted like a lovable, intensely affectionate child. His trouble, she felt sure, lay in his high spirits and in a certain lack of stability. He quarreled frequently with his playmates, whom he must dominate in everything; and then he would stay alone for hours at a time, sulking and resentful.

Will thought more about the case than either Rhoda or Julia.

Occasionally Myra found him boasting to his friends about the "big, big fortune" that would eventually be theirs; and she tried to persuade him that it was not good to talk of such things. Will, she was certain, suffered more than the others from their sudden drop in affluence. He grew fretful when they had milk instead of cream and when the quality of his garments appeared inferior. Still, she told herself, it was only natural that the boy would not understand. She would never cease to love him with a special affection.

Young Ed Gaines, Edmund's boy, who had been at her side for ten years—she wondered about him, as she often did. Could she somehow get him back with them? But at once she told herself that this would be impossible.

Sighing, she turned back to her mother. She and Zulime had asked the children to take the sun for a time, so that they could be alone for an appointment. The previous week Myra had realized that less than seventy dollars remained in her pocket. Gradually she had pawned everything—first the sparkling silver and diamond headpiece that had been Edmund's anniversary gift; then her rings and brooches, even the mahogany music box from the Bellechasses. James Gardette, of his own volition, had begun to make contributions; but the amounts were limited, for James had married and had a household to maintain.

Month by month her funds had declined. Suddenly, too, she needed money for the case. It had gone again to Washington; to her chagrin she learned that Relf and Chew had retained Daniel Webster. The eminent elder lawyer was taking even fewer cases than before; her opponents must be paying a staggering sum. With so much new evidence offered by both sides, the struggle there would be a hard one. In this crisis she had remembered some of the many letters that had come to her a few years earlier, from organizations that offered loans. Then, when she had not needed them, they had almost begged her to accept their resources. Quickly she wrote. All but two of her letters were ignored; one had brought a note of polite regret, the last an agreement to talk over the matter today.

At a sharp knock she and Zulime composed themselves. Mr. Bostick, a heavy-jowled man, holding his bowler hat firmly in his hand, took a seat and came promptly to the point. Just when did Mrs. Gaines figure she could repay the money and what did she have in the way of insurance, property, jewelry? His cold brown eyes, which seemed almost yellow in the bright light, explored the dragging curtains, the marks of wear on Myra's costume. She found herself uncomfortably on the defensive, offering explanations and apologies. Her voice died; Mr. Bostick showed hardly a flicker of response.

Then, to Myra's astonishment, Zulime slipped forward and deftly took the dealings out of her hands. No longer was she the cowed, hesitant woman; her lips came together firmly. "Well, what will it be, monsieur? My daughter has told you the situation, and we'd like a decision now. Another person is calling within an hour with his proposal. This is a business matter with us as it is with you."

The man's expression altered as Myra watched; he was inclined to doubt that part about someone else, but . . . "I'll lend four thousand at four per cent a month."

Myra's breath caught; they required more than that for the case alone, and what a rate he was proposing! She opened her mouth, but Zulime's fingers closed against her leg, and her mother snapped, "Seven thousand, at two."

"No." Bostick moved his head slowly from side to side.

With a gesture of impatience Zulime rose. "Already we've had better suggestions than that."

Bostick, his yellowish eyes quivering slightly, did not get up. "We can't do no better than that. We got risks."

"You offered better rates last time."

"Things've changed. Mrs. Gaines had just won her case. Now . . . Well . . ."

"You know what we want." Her skirts rustling angrily about her, Zulime headed for the door. If he left this way, thought Myra, what would they do?

"Well . . ." Bostick hesitated. "Well . . . Five thousand at three."

Her hand on the knob, Zulime faced about. "Six thousand at two!"

"Six at two and a half, and that's final."

"We'll take it."

As Bostick left, slamming the door, Zulime tossed her head. "I've had dealings before with that kind of—vulture." Giving her mother a quick kiss, Myra hurried out to send a telegram to

Washington. As she walked the grass of the square seemed greener, the city happier than it had been in months.

On her way home Myra sensed that someone was staring. She turned her head; as she did so the other woman tried to look away, but it was too late. Mrs. Ainsworth, wife of the broker, came forward. "Ah, Mrs. Gaines. It's been awhile since we met each other, hasn't it?" Since the day of Edmund's funeral Myra had seen or heard nothing of the woman. Mrs. Ainsworth's smile was less effusive than heretofore. "And how are you, dear?"

"Well enough. My children keep me busy—and my case, you know."

"Oh yes." Mrs. Ainsworth started at the mention of the litigation, as if Myra had brought up a subject that ladies did not discuss. "Of course. And now, my dear, I really must be going. You *will* let us hear from you, won't you? Good-by." It was evident that she had not wanted to be seen on the street with Myra. There were many, Myra knew, who felt the same way. As the wife of the commanding general, she and her suits had been titillating subjects. But now . . .

To save money she delayed her departure for Washington until the last minute. She picked an obscure, fairly clean boardinghouse in the capital, and she used the hacks only when absolutely necessary. For a time, between visits to her attorney Reverdy Johnson and others connected with the case, she lived much to herself. As she sat alone in her room her thoughts turned back to New Orleans, to the family, and, unexpectedly, to Philippe d'Abadie. He had called before she left to tell her he would be at her disposal in the case whenever she wished; still, he knew of her finances, and there appeared to be no further need to retain him at this time. Here was a true friend.

Then one morning on Pennsylvania Avenue a senator's wife waved her umbrella and stopped her. "No, you're coming with me. I ought to be hurt that you didn't let me know you were here." The welcome was warm and honest; a few hours later Myra let herself be persuaded to remain for a reception, where she met a dozen others who remembered her at once. Women hurried across the room; two dowagers took places at her side. "How is the case?"

"I heard the other day . . ."

The crowd and its quick interest stirred something inside Myra. Her face glowed again; her eyes were grateful. That same week a flow of letters and invitations began; still wearing her widow's black, she accepted a few, for the more subdued events. Once more she was pointed out; as the case approached a new climax newspaper correspondents called for interviews. Most observers were certain that this decision would settle the subject, one way or the other. For a little while, at the parties and dinners, Myra relaxed; but as the day of the decision came nearer she found herself more and more often forgetting to answer a question from her partner, or gazing absently away, her mind upon the black-robed men of the court.

Reverdy Johnson brought word that did not reassure her. The justices were bickering over the matter, and there were signs that worried him. Catron, of Tennessee, whom she had met that evening years ago, had been ill the last time and had not passed on the case. Now he was arguing against her at the deliberations. On the other hand, Wayne, who had already ruled so strongly for her, stayed firmly in their camp. The two men, never close, had clashed several times. Two justices, because of illness or other reasons, would not take part. Wayne and Catron were working hard on the remaining five.

How curiously events were working out! Wayne, the aristocrat from a plantation region, ruled by a privileged caste, favored her case though it offered a threat to propertied interests. Catron, who had risen despite prejudice and social pressure, sided with "established order." Which view would win? She stared by the hour at the pattern on the faded brocade curtains in her room. For years afterward she would be able to trace the design of leaves and flowers.

Once again she entered the gloomy basement room of the Supreme Court. As if from a far distance, a stranger watching a performance of other strangers, she saw the justices file slowly in. The case was called; with her shoulders tensed, her back held firmly against the dais, she waited. Wayne gazed ahead, his lips set more tightly than usual; Catron, his eyes narrowing in his heavy face, appeared almost defiant.

"The decision will be read by Judge Catron." Then she had

lost! Catron had swung four of the judges to his side, giving a decision against her. Through the pounding of her heart she heard his first words. Regardless of the way the court had previously ruled, John Catron declared that Des Granges had *not* been a bigamist and that no marriage had ever been performed between Daniel and Zulime. Myra Gaines therefore became— —his voice grated harshly—"an adulterine bastard."

The judge, speaking hoarsely, cast aside everything said by Boisfontaine, Bellechasse, Harriett Smyth, and the others to whom Daniel had acknowledged Myra; and he declared D. W. Coxe entitled to complete acceptance. As for Zulime's sisters, "they are not worthy of belief"; his lips curled slightly. He took as entirely true the "church hearing" that Zulime and others called a forgery.

Her cheeks flaming, Myra listened with astonishment. Catron was giving his own version of the story, making error after error in dates and places, even changing those presented by Relf's and Chew's witnesses. Accepting contradictory statements, omitting a fact here, inserting another there, he had developed an account different from that offered by any other person. Through it all ran a thin line of snobbery. Repeatedly the judge noted that Daniel was a man of means and acclaim, whereas Zulime had known want; she was not "a lady of Clark's own rank." The justice was zealous in his attitude of protection toward the class into which he himself had newly arrived.

Myra gazed down. There had been no need for these biting words, this reaching out in all directions for terms almost of abuse. Now Wayne cleared his throat to offer the minority opinion. At first his light eyes were calm, but soon his voice, like that of the other justice, quivered with feeling.

Myra, he insisted, had proved that Zulime and Daniel were able to contract marriage and had done so. The majority decision was given against Myra on material "altogether unadmissible under the rules of testimony." With a sharp look the judge went on. "In all my experience I have never heard of witnesses so assailed and upon such illegal testimony. Witnesses are said to be 'unworthy of belief' "—this was a direct blow against Catron—"in their testimony concerning the marriage and Myra's legitimacy, when they are confirmed by other, disinterested witnesses to whom Clark admitted both."

As to D. W. Coxe, "to demonstrate how little reliance can be placed on his memory," Judge Wayne cited his many contradictory statements. Daniel's own letters, regarding his presence in Philadelphia, tended to confirm the statements of Zulime's sisters. Coxe could not show that the couple were not married; he could only say he thought they were not. Regarding the "church hearing," the defense had yet to prove it was authentic. Yet even providing it were, it could not be offered if a witness involved was within the court's jurisdiction and could be called for questioning about it. If the defense believed the "hearing" was not a false one, why hadn't it summoned Zulime? Pausing a moment, Wayne lowered his voice for a solemn conclusion:

"Those of us who have borne our part in the case will pass away. The case will live.

"It shows the hollowness of friendships formed between persons in the greediness of gain. It shows how carelessness in business and secret partnerships with others may give to the latter its spoils, and impoverish those whose capital alone gave consequence to the concern. It shows how a mistaken confidence given to others by a man who dies rich may be the cause of diverting his estate into an imputed insolvency, depriving every member of his family of every part of their inheritance.

"We learn from it that long-continued favors may not be followed by any sympathy from those who receive them, for those dearest to our affections. It shows that if a ruffian takes life for the purse which he robs, a dying man's agonies, soothed only by tears and prayers for the happiness of a child, may not arrest a fraudulent attempt to filch from her her name and fortune. . . .

"I, the Lord God, am a jealous god, and visit the sins of the fathers unto the second and third generations. . . ."

Seldom had such passionate words been uttered regarding the men who were her opponents; not often had so fervent an indictment been made against them. And yet Judge Wayne had lost to Judge Catron by several votes. The line of justices rose, but Myra did not see them. Men and women crowded about her to extend their sympathy; mechanically she bowed, hearing nothing they said. "I want to be by myself a little while," she told one of the men who hovered nervously about her. They left, and she remained in her seat, alone in the wide, dim room.

From outside the window came the chirp of a bird. "I the Lord God . . . sins of the fathers . . ." Was she to know now, and for the rest of her life, the penalty of the sins of Daniel Clark? She and her children, and her children's children?

An attendant with a mop moved across the chamber. "Court closin', ma'am," he told her. "You want me to call somebody for you?"

She stood up. "I'm all right." An hour or so later she discovered that she was still walking alone on the street. The day turned gradually worse; it rained but she paid no heed. Through puddles of water, the drops trickling down her neck from the feathers of her hat, she kept on and on. At last, without knowing how she had come there, she stood before her boardinghouse and crept up the stairs to her room.

She had heard of people who did not know where to turn; now she understood how they felt. Somehow, in all her concern over the matter, she had never really prepared herself for such a verdict. Her case was ended—wiped out. Over and over, as she pushed her face against the pillow, she told herself that; still, somehow, she could not believe it.

But when she called on Reverdy Johnson he shook his great pink head, compassionately yet with firm decision. "If there were a single possibility I'd advise you to try it. There isn't. If he'd set out to do it, Catron couldn't have succeeded any better in blocking every path before you."

Myra quoted Wayne's opinion: "Errors of fact . . . disregard of all accepted rules of evidence . . ."

Johnson shrugged. "Granted. Errors galore—but the errors of the majority." He dropped his hand, and the slap of his palm against the oak of the desk had a sound of finality. A kindly light in his eye, he leaned forward. "You're an uncommonly handsome woman—and still in your early forties, aren't you? The fact that you're intelligent shouldn't be too terrible a handicap." He grinned. "I have a little advice from an old man. Take a good rest—and forget this. Go about with others; your life lies ahead."

She could manage a smile. "The marriage block?"

"I wouldn't put it so baldly, but . . ."

She drew on her gloves. "Whatever I do, I don't think I'll marry again." Extending her hand, she found she could not speak. Reverdy Johnson stood staring after her as she descended the stairs.

As she entered her room again she had a feeling of panic. Whatever followed, her place was no longer here but in New Orleans. Hastily she scratched off letters to her particular friends; and then she boarded the train for the long and sooty trip. Through the glass of the window she saw the familiar outlines of government buildings sliding past. Would she ever return to this place in which she had known her highest triumph, her worst defeat? As she tried to sleep against the hard cushion her eye was caught by the oil lamp, just above her head, rocking slowly back and forth with the motion of the cars. When dawn came she was still watching it. So much motion, nothing accomplished, round and round in the same unending circle. How like her life! And now no circle, even, in which to move. . . .

At the station waited James Gardette, looking grave and mature, with the children beside him. He explained that Zulime was ill and Eulalie Montagnet had remained at home to watch over her. He had a suggestion: Myra and the rest of them must stay with him and his family on Burgundy Street; by shifting things about James had provided two extra rooms. Myra's eyes conveyed her gratitude.

Zulime, propped against her pillows, called to her. "Ah, *chérie, chérie!*" Suddenly she was weeping, her body shaken by deep sobs. "It's my fault, all of this. If only I'd lived my life differently . . ." Myra was shocked. How haggard Zulime had become! Eulalie murmured that her mother had hardly rested since the bad news arrived from Washington.

With difficulty Myra soothed Zulime. "Things will be all right; you mustn't worry. Don't worry. . . ." At last she slept, and Eulalie called Myra aside.

Affairs had not gone too well. As Myra might have suspected, they had been forced to discontinue the children's schooling during her absence. They had had a little trouble the night word came that the case was lost. A crowd formed outside, screaming and throwing bricks. Fortunately for them, Philippe d'Abadie got wind of it and came running over. He talked to the mob and persuaded them to go quietly. Philippe had been helping them more than Myra realized. That brought Eulalie to one more matter. She'd been thinking for an hour how to tell Myra. Her deep voice hesitated.

"It's something about Will?"

Eulalie nodded. "He's gotten into the habit of staying out late; and then when we ask where he's been he's furious. Not that I say he's been in wrong places . . ." Eulalie was anxious not to alarm Myra unduly. "But he ought not to be so—so careless. And he's getting a little saucy." Eulalie had come close to tears, and Myra, recalling all that Eulalie had been to her and her family, felt ashamed. Yet Eulalie had more. "Just a week ago Philippe d'Abadie saw Will around the water front. He didn't like the look of the boys with him and brought him home. Will sulked—and he cursed."

Later Myra summoned Will. He began before she did. "I wasn't doing a thing that day, not a damn——"

She stopped him with a finger across his lips. "Certainly, Will, you know boys who don't talk that way?"

"Who do I know anyway? Who do I have a chance to know, that has a decent home, a nice place——"

She reasoned, she pleaded, she obtained promises from him. For hours afterward, however, she remembered his reproaches. What opportunity *had* there been for Will or the others to develop stable, lasting friendships? And she'd accomplished nothing, with all her struggling over the case—worse than nothing, a name officially placed upon her by the Supreme Court. "Adulterine bastard . . ."

That week she called on John Grymes and Philippe d'Abadie. The elder attorney caught both her hands. His Creole associate, his narrow, sensitive face brightening at the sight of her, bowed and waited respectfully while his superior spoke. At once Grymes proceeded to discourage her. "Myra, take the advice of one who was cursing over the law before you were born," he told her gloomily. "You'll break yourself and end up a vinegary old woman, a shrew. No, my child. The case is *fini.*"

She rose in silence and started toward the door. Philippe, striding after her, stopped her there. "Somehow," he told her, "I just can't accept what Grymes says. I can't believe it. We've worked too hard on all this. . . ." Withdrawing her hand from her muff, she made a tiny gesture of hopelessness. Almost absently the Creole shook his head. "There has to be a way."

For the time being she had to concentrate on other problems. After a debate with herself she wrote apologetic letters to the Whitneys, to Colonel Davis, and finally to several of the Gaines relatives. Would they lend her whatever they could afford? Meticulously she made a record of each amount; someday, she promised herself, she would pay them back.

Zulime improved, though slowly; after several weeks she was up. Determinedly Myra set to work to lift her mother from the mood of despair into which she had fallen. Gradually Zulime regained much of her spirit. Eventually she and Myra walked together along the familiar, balcony-hung streets of the ancient French section on their way to the market. As they reached the Place d'Armes, now rechristened Jackson Square for the hero of New Orleans, Zulime looked up shyly. "It's a little like old times for us, isn't it?"

Myra nodded. It seemed as if they needed adversity to unite them. Her hand tightened against her mother's; this time they would not be separated again. She'd see to that. Threading a path among the drays and cotton floats, she and Zulime shopped, as before, for shrimp and crabs and vegetables. One day they encountered Estevan Perez of Terre-aux-Bœufs, his family, and several friends.

"You all remember Myra, what was Daniel Clark' daughter, what married Mr. Whitney, what married General Gaine'?" he demanded. "This still her, this pretty lil thing!" At the same time Myra recognized a fellow customer, Mme. Gouaux, her hatmaker for years; Madame twitched her mustaches, dropped her basket, and embraced Myra. In a moment someone spied Victorien Badeaux. The Cajun, heavier, more settled-looking, hitched his cakebox over his shoulder and smiled.

"You married again? Why not? Me, I 'ave two wife' and half since then, yes!"

For a half hour she and Zulime enjoyed the conversation of her still loyal friends. Tactfully none referred to her case; by common consent they pretended it was still going on, and for this she was grateful. As they parted Victorien called after her,

"Don' you forget you' promise from long time 'go—I be you' pastry cook when you get rich!"

When she got rich! She and Zulime were silent on their way home; the trip had revived memories. They sat together, as they often did in these days, at the window of James Gardette's living and dining room. From their chairs, as they stitched over the children's garments, they listened to the sounds from James's office. His clientele was increasing; people came early and late —market fishermen with swellings of the jaw, *bonnes femmes* bearing their chronic ailments, oystermen whose hands had been torn at their work.

Zulime was staring at an old drawing of Daniel; she had come upon it that morning, inside a book. "It's a good likeness, the best I ever saw," Zulime told her quietly, a note of happiness in her voice. Placing it on the mantel, she spoke slowly: "When I die, Myra, can't you—place me beside Daniel?"

Myra, startled, faced her. "Come now, you're too young to think about dying!"

"But—do you think I could be buried with him?" Her brown eyes showed her deep concern.

"Yes," Myra answered, "yes." Quickly she changed the subject.

Soon they were joined by James's wife, a good-natured girl, who was half Irish, half German. "Is everything all right?" she asked, and nodded pleasantly when they smiled. The younger Mme. Gardette was not one to agonize over fate. If she sometimes became curious about the odd history of Myra and Myra's mother, she did not show it. She gave her time to her two children, her household, and her husband.

It was a placid life for them all. With Myra to keep a check upon him, Will was managing better. He appeared less restless, less tense. Julia was a handsome girl, though still a trifle moody and inclined to sickliness. The capable Rhoda, redheaded and firm-eyed like her mother, seemed one of the older generation; she, too, helped look after the household affairs.

Only occasionally did Myra suffer a particular twinge—when a birthday came, or an anniversary; or when the sight of a familiar lawyer's face reminded her of her case. In these days New Orleans paid little attention to her. Seeing her on the street, some wondered briefly what she was doing, then went on to matters

of more immediate interest. Once, turning a corner, she heard a
matron whisper to a friend, "Myra Gaines, just behind us. . . .
You can't help feeling a little sorry . . ." She blinked back the
tears, and soon the hurt was gone.

Zulime, waiting at the door for her, had a letter from Philippe
d'Abadie. John Campbell had just been nominated to the United
States Supreme Court. The young attorney, Philippe pointed
out, had had a sensational rise in Washington legal circles; it
had been her case that gave him his first real introduction to that
audience. It was good to know that she had had a part, at least,
in the making of the bright new career.

Zulime started across the room toward her; halfway she
stopped and her hand clutched her throat. Before Myra could
reach her Zulime had slumped to the floor.

James worked over his mother until finally, his hands dropping
helplessly to his sides, he motioned to Myra to follow him into
the garden. "A bad stroke," he told her. "She can last only a
little while. No," he answered her unspoken question, "there's
nothing to be done."

When Myra returned to the room Zulime appeared to be wait-
ing for her. Though she could not talk, her anxious eyes sought
her daughter's. Then they shifted to the mantel and Daniel
Clark's picture. Her mother's broken words rang in her ears:
"Can't you place me beside Daniel?" Her face fixed on Zulime's,
Myra nodded.

As the night advanced Myra sat beside her mother for hours,
her nervous hands clasping the tiny, whitened one that lay still
within hers. A little before midnight the older woman managed
to turn her head slightly, and she seemed to smile. She sighed
once and then she was still; worry and anxiety had left her forever. Myra closed her mother's eyes and went into the moonlit
garden, to be alone.

Shortly after daybreak Myra walked into the cemetery. The
sexton, standing before the half-crumbling tomb of her father,
sucked at his lips. "M. Relf have charge, madame. Pay' for out
Clark estate, *oui;* but M. Relf the one that have say-so." With
that, he walked away.

A little later James set out from the house. He would be a

less offensive emissary than Myra. Relf had won; surely he could relent a bit now? Standing beside the frail form in the casket, Myra tried to comfort the two bent Carrière sisters who had arrived from the country. As Zulime lay there the resemblance between her and Myra was greater even than in life. The deepened lines of the past few years had softened; the long eyes and the full red lips were Myra's. In her mother's hands she had placed the crucifix that Zulime had treasured, as Daniel's prize gift on the day of their marriage. At her own throat Myra wore its counterpart, given her by the old Señora Perez.

The door opened, and James came to her, his face cold. He would never tell her everything that took place during his interview with Relf; James said only that he had offered to sign an agreement, declaring that Zulime's presence in the tomb meant no recognition of her relationship to Daniel. The inscription, James had proposed, would call her only Zulime Carrière. He had failed.

As she stood there the blood surged to Myra's cheeks. For the rest of her life she would remember this moment. Of all the things for which she hated R. J. Relf, this would not be the least.

CHAPTER XXII

THE slow days had begun again. She helped look after the Gardette household; with Eulalie she did the marketing; and she economized. Still, they could not live upon economies; and one day, when she saw how near they had come to the next date for payment on her borrowings, she blanched. Two years had passed since the decision against her in Washington; she had only a few dollars left. She must, she told herself, resume her "begging" —her letters to the Davises, the Whitneys, friends of General Gaines. But the same morning, as she walked through the French section, she found she had left untapped a source that had never suggested itself.

At the corner, hobbling upon a gouty foot, John Grymes raised his gold-headed cane to catch her attention. Much heavier, his face sagging, he still maintained the manner of his great days.

Linking his arm in hers, he escorted her to his office. There he took both her hands. "Now out with it!" When he had heard her story he puffed out his lips. "As usual I'm broke. But I may have resources."

Rubbing his chin, he glanced at his watch. "Well! A client, one of the Canal Street merchants, will be here in a minute. Sit quietly in that corner." She obeyed, and soon a resplendent popinjay stepped in.

"Not ready yet, Grymes? The case comes up in a few minutes!"

Grymes ran his hand across his face. "I'm afraid I can't go today, Breckinridge——"

"But the judge is mad enough already. He said he'd rule against us, right off, if you delayed any more!"

"I know, but something very—very personal has come up." Grymes was growing more lugubrious by the minute. "I'm about to be seized as a debtor. The sheriff's man is on his way."

"But they can't. . . . A man like you!"

"You don't understand, Breckinridge, just what kind of man I am." The blue eyes took on a crafty look. "This has almost happened before. Never so close though. . . ."

The client's face indicated his belief that this was none of his business. Grymes remained swallowed in gloom. He sighed, played about his papers; it was clear that with such a weight upon him he could not concentrate on so minor a matter as a lawsuit. The minute hand moved on; the merchant proposed a series of schemes; Grymes rejected each with a groan. At last Breckinridge, rising, demanded, "Damn it, how much do you need?" When he heard the figure, twenty-five hundred dollars, he almost put his purse back. But Grymes, reaching out, pulled the money from his hand.

On their way out Grymes called to Myra, "Madame, when the sheriff arrives give him this—and spit in his face for me!" Then, to her astonishment, Grymes leaned over, kissed her brow, and murmured, with a frown, "Myra, in your time you've trapped me in several acts unbecoming my reputation. Don't let this part of it get around. *I'm* the one who always borrows!"

A few weeks later Philippe d'Abadie was knocking at the door. She must excuse him, he told her. John Grymes had been discreet, but Philippe had gathered that Myra was in need. He was embarrassed; normally a Creole did not discuss these things with a woman, widowed or otherwise.

Thanking him, Myra declined. "You're kind, but we'll manage." Her eyes, not entirely serene, wandered to her tall son, lounging in the garden.

"That reminds me," Philippe began. "I've had an idea. . . . What does Will want to do for a living?"

Her eyes flew open. "I'm not sure." The subject had been giving her concern. Because they held a somewhat anomalous social position no form of employment had suggested itself to them; and Will, she had to admit, showed little pronounced interest in working.

Philippe spoke his mind. "The boy needs discipline, something to steady him. Would he want to start as a clerk under me, in the law office?"

Myra jumped to her feet, grateful at once. She called Will, and the youth, looking diffidently at Philippe, slumped into a chair.

"Clerk," he repeated when she used the word. "Me—a clerk?"

"Why not, young man?" Philippe's dark complexion colored. "Daniel Clark himself, I might remind you, began as a clerk."

Hastily Myra intervened. "Please, Will—M. d'Abadie has a place in which you could advance yourself. You could study for the law if you wished."

"Well, it's worth trying, I guess."

To cover his lack of enthusiasm, Myra went to the boy. "You'll see, Philippe, how well he'll do. Won't he, Will?" She squeezed her son's shoulder. Will nodded, and the arrangement was made.

Returning at the end of his first day, Will tossed his hat on the chair and reported the work "easy—practically a joke."

Myra, who had waited for him, was not entirely pleased. "And who are with you—the other clerks?" she asked.

"Oh"—Will made a grimace—"nobodies, people you never heard about. One's a grocer's son, and then there's the youngest boy of that greasy Perez who sells at the market. A fine thing, eh?"

Myra looked over sharply. "Do you realize that all of us

might have starved, several times, if it hadn't been for the Perezes? They're good people. And every man's entitled to show what ability he has, even if he's a grocer's son——"

"All right!" Will said. "You think that way if you want. I don't have to pretend I'm one of them, do I?" Not pausing for her answer, he walked out. Myra remained at the window, watching him as he sauntered up the street. A young dandy hailed him from a carriage and Will climbed in. She turned away; when Eulalie called her to supper she could not eat.

Two weeks afterward Philippe d'Abadie, his brown eyes somber, was there again. She guessed his errand. "It didn't work out—Will at the office?"

He shook his head, relieved that she had spared him a recital of the story. "He's—well, too young perhaps. After a while he should see things a little differently." Should he tell her that the boy had tried to shift the burden of his work on others, had quarreled and played the petty snob—and then arrived drunk several times? He could not bring himself to it; already he saw too much pain in Myra's face.

A little later Rhoda, her red hair dancing about her, ran through the parlor. "A job—I've got a job!" she cried. "They'll let me teach at Miss Andrews'!" It was a school that she and Will and Julia had once attended. "Please, you'll let me take it?" she begged. "It'll help a little anyway." Myra exchanged glances with Eulalie Montagnet; her friend's eyes were as proud as hers.

The thin-faced, sensitive Julia, nearly eighteen, had seldom given her cause for worry. But now, during a damp winter, Julia began to suffer a series of chest colds. The moisture-laden New Orleans climate had never been kind to her; for weeks, this year, she had had to be in and out of bed. As usual the shy girl kept largely to herself, reading or knitting or walking in the garden. Early one afternoon Myra came upon her, sitting alone under a pecan tree. At her first touch she knew Julia was ill once more.

James cautioned them that Julia must be careful; she had to stay in bed, watch her strength, and take more nourishment. Myra remembered one of Zulime's recipes for beef broth; Eulalie hurried to the market for the ingredients, and they went to work. Still Julia continued to languish. Tonics, drugs, schemes to spur her appetite had scant success; the girl lay silent and tired. When Myra asked if anything was troubling her she shook her head.

From James's air, Myra gathered that he thought the case hopeless. "She isn't fighting," he told her. No! Myra cried to herself. She wouldn't let it happen. Not Julia, after Zulime and the others. Sobbing, she caressed the girl; she and Eulalie redoubled their concentration; she drew her chair to Julia's bedside and did not sleep for days.

The girl lapsed into delirium. For the first time Myra realized the full effect of the unsettled life they had led, the transfers from place to place, the overturns in their fortunes. Julia cried of her anxieties, her fear of what might happen if the case were lost. An asylum, a poorhouse—the words ran through her mutterings. And once Myra caught a whisper from the depths of Julia's suffering: "No, it's not the truth! Mama isn't—isn't that!" She understood now that her children, at school and at play, had had to contend with the contemptuous stories about her, passed down from their elders.

With all of the family about her, Julia died early on a June afternoon; and again Myra spent bitter hours by herself in the garden behind the house. Near Zulime's resting place, in one of the long files of receptacles, another niche was opened and sealed. As they left the cemetery they passed the tomb of Daniel Clark. Myra hardly recognized it; the structure had been elaborately restored, plastered, and painted. A line shone in gilt upon the slab: *Amicus Amico,* A Friend to a Friend. Over the objections of her children, she stopped to ask about it. The helper explained, "Ah, *oui,* M. Relf have had it done. Wasn't it nice how he remember M. Clark, eh?"

Philippe had asked permission to call during the ensuing week; he was due that afternoon. For days Myra had wandered about the house, from bedroom to kitchen, garden to office, her eyes taking in nothing of what occurred about her. Eulalie, her deep voice uneasy, proposed to James's wife that this might be a good time for a long-deferred, thorough cleaning of the house; soon Myra, a towel about her head, her dress pinned up at her ankles, was working with them from room to room. Last came the attic, where she had stored the two large trunks that held the records of her cases. During the morning Myra's hands moved among the dusty documents, untouched for nearly three years. As she reached over to brush off the top one her eyes stopped.

It was an early ruling of the Supreme Court, dating back about fifteen years. The court had noted that, if she wished, she could sue as "forced heir" of Daniel Clark, entitled to at least four fifths of his estate, regardless of Daniel's will. Well, she'd done that, and lost. She read on: *it was a matter for grave consideration, if every other effort failed, whether a lost will might not be established from the evidence.* True, it was added, the Louisiana law said nothing about the way to get a lost will probated; in such a case a judge might act according to the needs of the situation. Myra blinked. Did that mean it would be possible, after all, to go back to the Louisiana courts and ask them to accept the lost will?

Neither she nor her attorneys had paid much heed at the time to these passages; the Supreme Court had seemed then to be pointing so strongly in another direction. But why not take the court at its word and see what happened? Long ago she had given up thought of the law in Louisiana. But her old enemy, Chief Justice Martin, was dead. The federal court had turned against her. Could she try the state again?

Clutching the papers, she clattered downstairs. By the time Philippe arrived she was waiting nervously at the threshold. As she thrust the records into his hand she blurted out her plan.

"But didn't the judges say, the last time, that they could recognize no will they hadn't seen?" he asked her. "What would we have to show them now?"

Reflectively Myra tapped her lip. "The will that our witnesses *remembered!* Let's put it down the way they told us it read— and show that to the courts."

Philippe hesitated. "It wouldn't be the will. . . ."

"It would be the nearest we could come to it. Have it as they recalled, with some whereases and such things. . . ."

Sinking into a chair, Philippe sat silent for a long time, looking from her to the document and back again. He rose; he wanted to spend a few hours with his lawbooks. Before dusk he was back, his eyes big with interest.

"It's a gamble," he said, trying to repress his own excitement. "Most lawyers down here would tell us it's crazy. But look, I found several cases in American law—one, even, in Louisiana—that indicate we'd have at least a fighting chance. Law is changing; judges, especially younger ones, lean toward broader interpretations. We'd bring the case on a different basis. Still, it would be a risk to——"

"I've taken risks before!" She smiled, and he marveled at the change in her face.

"And it'll stir up a lot of—a lot of feeling."

"And I'm used to that! How soon can we file, and where? What judge . . . ?"

When word spread of the new steps she had taken the immediate result was disbelief. That woman must be going crazy; the matter had descended to burlesque. . . . But some grew anxious. Philippe, meeting her a month or so afterward, admitted with a grin that he was coming in for his share of attack. John Grymes was in virtual retirement; as her principal attorney, Philippe had acquired a new status. Also, he discovered, two of his cousins were landowners whom Myra had sued! As a consequence—so ran the Creole gossip, retailed by Eulalie—he was being denounced as an enemy of his own people.

Like Myra, Eulalie appeared to become younger as the case went into action again. The Creole listened intently when Philippe called with news; she chatted in her deep-pitched voice over the developments; she relayed reports picked up on the streets. It was Eulalie who came to Myra, her lips white, with the rumor that Philippe was about to fight a duel over the case with a relative.

Myra threw on shawl and hat and rushed to Philippe's office. She found him at his desk. He gave her a disarming smile. "A gross exaggeration, my dear. There was—well, some possibility of it. He was a younger cousin, a hothead. Both of us reflected a bit; that's all." His eyes, a quizzical light in them, darted over her face.

"Well . . ." She hesitated. "You've got to promise you won't endanger yourself in anything like this."

The Creole bowed. "Your concern makes me happy." Impulsively he lifted his head again. "My mother's been asking me about you. She's practically a recluse, you know. Could you come see her with me? Good! Why not now?"

The carriage rolled over Esplanade Avenue toward the tallest building in the vicinity, a three-storied brick structure with iron-

work over the front. In the dim parlor—really two rooms, the
sliding doors opening between them—an elderly woman rested
in a thronelike chair. At her first glance the careworn face
lighted.

"*La!* It is Mme. Gaine'! I would have recognize' you from
your picture' in a moment." The voice was rich and gentle. Mme.
d'Abadie had known an acclaim of her own, first as a young
Creole beauty, then as a successful matron. After a steamboat
tragedy had taken her husband she had turned her back on the
world. Fingers that once glittered with diamonds were bare, and
her face had a sadness, as if she understood some secret at
which others might only guess. In a moment she had Myra at
her ease.

She hoped her guest would not be offended, but Mme. d'Abadie
must tell her that her forthright course seemed strange to women,
like the madame herself, who had lived entirely under the control of their families. She remembered, years ago, how shocked
her own *maman* had been when she proposed that she and her
sister go alone to a reception, a single square away. "She tol'
me, 'Suppose someone sees you? They will conclude the worst;
I have become careless with my children. And what mother
would then regard either of you as a *parti* for her son?' " Mme.
d'Abadie's eyes lost their temporary merriment. "*Ma chérie,*
she did not exaggerate!"

Now the elderly woman became meditative. "Yet the world
has changed. I cannot but believe you do right to fight for
what should be yours." Myra, silent, thought it curious that
this secluded woman, of all she had met, should be sympathetic.
Mme. d'Abadie continued: "Sometime' I feel sure our generation would have been a bit more 'appy if it had been less—what
is the word you would use?—submissive." She spread out her
tiny, plump hands and shrugged.

A young man and woman entered, the youth a less poised,
equally handsome Philippe, the girl a radiant *jeune fille* of sixteen, her figure well matured. Philippe's children shook hands,
then looked in frank wonder at the guest. They realized who
she was; she found their questions amusing. Finally, when she
rose to go, Mme. d'Abadie took her hand and kissed her cheek.
None of the others heard her whisper, "Courage, courage!
Come see me again."

As she entered the state court once more, after so many years, Philippe tried to caution her. If they did win here it would be only a first step. "But a big first step?" she demanded. He nodded. "I'm ready for anything," she told him with firmness, and the small scar along her cheek suddenly stood out. It was like the old days, she was telling herself. She had spent half her life in and about the courts; now she had come back again.

Before the case was an hour old she was convinced she would at least have an unhindered opportunity to offer proof of Daniel's second will. The judge, J. N. Lea, gave her none of the scowls that she had come to know; repeatedly he assured the attorneys he was uncertain of the law's exact application. In closing the hearing, he admitted he would need time to digest the matter.

Months later Judge Lea ascended the bench, and his air was grave. In the case of this will, he said, the reasonable inquirer would naturally go for information to those who had been most intimate with Daniel during his last years, and beside him in his final hours. This was precisely the testimony that Myra had produced. He had no question in his mind that Clark did make the will of 1813, fully recognizing Myra. Daniel died believing it in existence; the will was there "until a short time before Clark's death, if not afterward." Myra pressed forward, her mouth half open. This was the first time a Louisiana judge had conceded so much.

The man on the bench continued. Despite all this, he was afraid the Louisiana law would not admit the will. To prove such a document, two witnesses must swear they recognized it as being written in Daniel's handwriting, *as a result of having often seen him write and sign during his lifetime.* True, Myra's witnesses declared they knew the will was entirely written by Daniel; yet nowhere did they say they *had often seen him write and sign.* . . . Then, too, the document must be dated. This one had only a month, not the day of the month. She had reached within a hairsbreadth of her goal; the judge conceded her the whole case except the final verdict!

Philippe shook his head when he saw her stricken face. "We'll appeal today to the Louisiana Supreme Court. We've only lost on a technicality. Next time we'll really win—you'll see."

Less than a year later the highest court in Louisiana gave the citizenry one of its greatest surprises in a long history. It agreed with Judge Lea's convincing statement of the facts and with his careful ruling, in all details short of the last one. True, it added, Mrs. Gaines had not offered proof of the will within the strictest letter of the law; but justice meant more than a narrow application of technicalities. If the law said that under circumstances such as these a lost will could never be proved, it would place a premium on scheming relatives or friends. No, they must take the spirit of the law. In a word, the court declared that Daniel Clark had made Myra his heiress.

In admitting the will, the judges admitted also the executors whom Daniel had wished to administer his estate. Only one of them remained alive; and he was one of Myra's sternest foes, the Chevalier de la Croix.

The opposition, of course, would appeal to the Supreme Court in Washington. She must wait again for months, perhaps years. Then, at the age of eighty-one, De la Croix came out of retirement to fight back at Myra. A note in trembling handwriting told her he had no intention of performing as her executor; he did not accept the outrageous decision. In walked the ancient, tottering on the arm of his son, himself in his late fifties, to file his own suit, insisting that the recognition of the will be canceled. De la Croix, who had been first to demand in court that the will be produced, now declared himself convinced that Daniel had never made such a testament.

The same month Eulalie brought Myra a newspaper with the story of how R. J. Relf had died in the night. The *Crescent* called him "one of our oldest and most exemplary citizens, a model for the rising generation." When his remains were placed in his tomb, two lines were engraved on it:

> Blessed are the pure in heart
> For they shall enter the kingdom of heaven.

Was it a reproach to her and her charges, or mere generalized piety? She would never know. But of this she could be certain: the man who stood at the heart of her troubles had given up nothing. Through the years, disdain in his chill blue eyes, he had watched her struggle. For a time she had won; then he had witnessed her humiliation. She had a consolation: before he died, he must have understood that she was fighting forward again. Her head rose; and before *she* died she would have the record changed in *her* favor!

It was the late summer of 1860 and the time approached for Myra's return to Washington. New Orleans appeared to have lost much of its interest in the case. The bitterness between North and South was growing rapidly stronger; in Louisiana, as over most of the country, men were abandoning talk of compromise or readjustment. Didn't everybody know, cried the orators of Canal Street, that if that black Republican Lincoln got himself elected there'd be just one way left for the Southland—secession! The newspapers gave their columns largely to "Developments at the North," to furious attacks on Yankees and Yankeedom. Like many about him, including planters, merchants, and brokers, Philippe d'Abadie stood against secession. "It can mean only one thing for us—ruin," he told John Grymes.

The aging cynic nodded. "You're perfectly right, Philippe. It's madness, suicide—and soon we'll all be leaping happily into it, you included!"

Yet prosperity filled the air. New Orleans had never looked more thriving—cotton and sugar in piles along the levee, steamboats puffing arrogantly downstream, men with rolls of bills in their pockets strutting about the hotel lobbies. This boom period, in fact, made it possible for Myra to continue the suit. Among the moneylenders the odds in her favor had changed again. Now, as during the previous period when her prospects were improving, they approached her. She remembered Zulime's technique and, standing firmly against the table, she argued back. She need not pretend, this time, that she had several alternatives; she was really bargaining among them. Flushed, a bit breathless, she ended with enough to support her for several years. When she thought of the interest rate she felt almost sick; but it had to be this way.

At once she sought out Rhoda. "Look, dear, there's no need for you to teach. You can——"

"But I want to teach!" Rhoda was firm. "I like it, Mama. Maybe you've set me a bad example. You know I couldn't be content to sit around a parlor and play the lady!"

Myra's face grew troubled. "I want to provide you with the means"—her words tumbled together—"like other people——"

Rhoda took her mother's hands. "We're not *like* other people, and I'm glad of it. We're ourselves. It won't hurt me to earn a little money."

"But"—Myra bit her lip—"you'll have no chance to——"

"To meet people?" Rhoda lifted her eyes. "I'll manage. Will isn't having any trouble!"

Instantly she was sorry she had said it. Will, alas, was meeting too many people, and the wrong kind—elegants of the gambling places, youths who frequented the bars along St. Charles Street. Rhoda, with a hug, left her, and Myra walked slowly to Will's room. He was adjusting his cravat, a brilliant purple one.

"I've been thinking, Will," she started.

"Not another lecture?" Though the words hurt, his smile removed some of the sting.

"Not entirely. Just this. I have a little more money now. I might be able to start you in some business, a little firm——"

"But the case—it's going to be decided up at Washington City, and soon, isn't it?" His slim figure leaning against the sill, he regarded her with a slightly raised brow. He was so young; he looked, she told herself, like a child wise beyond his years.

"Don't you think you'll really win this time?" he persisted, and his eyes suddenly brightened. "I'll—we'll have a lot of capital after a while, something worth giving time to. You don't get anywhere these days by starting small."

"Still, meanwhile?"

"I can wait." He worked at the buttons of his flowered waistcoat. "For God's sake, dear, don't be so tragic. You enjoy hard work; you've spent your life at it. Things are different now. I have friends who know their way around. There's money to be made, right here, for a man with cash and common sense."

"What do you mean?"

"Haven't you been listening on the streets? The war's coming; we just can't get away from it. There'll be a blockade, but some people will be able to break through it. Cotton'll be worth more than gold. Don't you see?"

Myra shook her head. "It doesn't sound quite right, Will."

"It's legal." His face darkened. "Of all people, you ought to understand about the law. What's the law? Whatever a lawyer gets a judge to say it is!"

Myra flinched. "I've felt that way from time to time, yes. But there's more to it than that. I've made my whole fight because I've thought it was more than that." Suddenly there seemed nothing else to say; she felt very tired.

At the door, his hat in his hand, Will turned. "Another thing. D'Abadie—what's his game?" Myra's startled expression made him pause, but only for a moment. "He doesn't have to be around you all the time, the way he is. Why's he coming this afternoon? That's why you're all dressed up, I know!" He had a final word: "I hope you won't be taken in. You'd make him a nice match, with the case coming your way again. A fortune for the picking!" The boy appeared suddenly to regret what he had said. He hesitated, then went out, banging the door behind him. Myra stood looking after him, for once too angry to feel resentment.

When Philippe came later he went quickly to the thing that was worrying him. "Myra, I hope you're not expecting too much of the case." His face was clouded. "To expect the Supreme Court to reverse itself yet again—first one verdict, then the opposite, then back to the first . . . The more I think of it, the less optimistic I am."

"I'll be prepared for anything it does."

"Good. There's something else," he started, clearing his throat. "This is as good—as good a time as any. Maybe you've guessed the way I feel about—about you. I've been a widower a long time—too long. I don't have any great fortune—a few properties here and there, but enough. . . . What I mean, damn it, is that I want to marry you!"

His long, cool fingers touched hers and closed upon them. Her head averted, her eyes passed from the crepe myrtle bush to the garden bench outside and then back again. Her answer came less easily than she had anticipated. "Philippe, I've thought of it several times. I'm sure you know the way I feel too." At this he drew closer, but she shook her head. "There'd be gossip, malicious gossip. It wouldn't be fair to you and your family. And if I lost, what would you have? A heavy debt——"

"And—and you! That's enough for me. I'm not afraid of

talk, and a lot of Creoles understand what debt is." His arm
went around her waist.

Hurriedly she drew away, close to tears. "Still . . . your
friends, the people you've lived among all your life. They
wouldn't approve; that duel, you remember? And the children,
yours and mine. It would be too hard for them, for all of
us. . . ."

They talked a long time without coming to any decision. Finally she told him she wanted to think about it a while longer.
She would wait until after she'd been to Washington City before she gave him an answer. At the door he kissed her hand,
then suddenly her mouth, and walked away in the dusk.

CHAPTER XXIII

MYRA found herself almost a stranger in Washington City.
The town had spread; everywhere ornate new buildings were
filling the gaps between the Greek temples and hogpens of early
settlers. She had hardly left the railroad station before she
sensed a further change in the atmosphere.

As she ordered a carriage she heard men arguing; on the
way to her hotel room she felt the increased tension. A friendly
senator hailed her when she emerged from the building. How
was she? How were her family? Then, almost without pausing for her answers, he went on to "the situation." The election of 1860 was approaching its climax. "Do those fire-eaters
down there really mean what they say against Lincoln?" he
asked. And he plunged on with his own remedy for curbing the
Southern lords.

Two women caught Myra's arm as she started across the
sidewalk. "What a surprise! We heard you were coming, but
we thought the political troubles . . ." Promptly they, too,
switched to the absorbing topic. "Don't these crazy Yankees
know the South will never stand for it?" Myra tried to say
what she, as one who moved between the two regions, thought.
Slavery had to end; it had gone in most other civilized nations; yet wasn't there a way to end it without slaughter? Her

words made little impression; when she left them a few minutes later they were still expounding their own attitudes.

At his law office the bald-domed Reverdy Johnson rumbled toward her, welcoming her with a look of amusement. "So you got those Louisianians to admit there *was* a will!" he laughed. "I never thought you'd do it. I wish, madame, I had half your determination." He spoke of the litigation for a few minutes; then he, like the others, shifted to the election. Only by firm effort did she bring her attorney back to her own affairs. "I can assure you"—he frowned—"that your case hasn't been forgotten. Every now and then Judge Wayne, especially, refers to it. But none of this, of course, may mean anything if there's shooting. There mayn't even be a court once the country splits." His gloomy outlook was contagious, and she left him with a heavy heart.

As she waited fury hovered over Washington. Abe Lincoln was elected; one by one Southern state conventions were called, ending with formal withdrawal. The inept President Buchanan occupied his last days in the White House by wandering about, talking, proposing, failing. On February 4 Louisiana's senators rose to bid good-by to their colleagues. With several other women Myra listened to the normally suave Judah Benjamin, earnest and grim-faced for once as, in Louisiana's name, he defied the North. She shuddered at the frenzy of screams and applause that greeted his words. Women broke into hysterics; men shook fists across the chamber. But here and there a few cried quietly when they saw what was happening. They had been born in the years when the government of the United States was being born; now they looked on as it seemed to be dying. Only then did Myra know with certainty that for her a race was on between a decision in the courts and the inauguration of a mighty struggle. If she didn't obtain a ruling before long, she might never get one.

February ended, and still the matter hung on. Two weeks difference might determine the issue for her. Meanwhile, like half of Washington, she was wondering what stand the Supreme Court justices would take in the matter of final secession. To the two who had shown the greatest concern with her case, these were days of withering uncertainty. In the early months of 1861 the Southerners Wayne and Catron had to make their choice. Would they go with those among whom they had begun their rise, to whom their sympathies were naturally closest, or should they look to the oath they had taken to uphold a united nation?

One winter day Major Harry Wayne of the United States Army called on his father in the justice's office. He had re-signed his military commission to return to Georgia. The judge, graying but still firm and erect, told his son he could not dis-approve of the decision. "But I have to stay. My place is with the Union. . . . I expect some people will misunderstand; I'll leave that to the future." After an hour the son walked silently out, to join a cause that would call his father enemy and traitor.

And from the paneled office of John Catron, of Tennessee, the grim, dark-visaged jurist let the word go forth. He, too, would stay. So, Myra reflected, her chief supporter and her chief enemy would remain to judge her again. To Reverdy Johnson came reports that made her tremble. Wayne was argu-ing in her behalf as usual; but Catron was denouncing her with increasing bitterness. The vote would be very close; a shift by one man, or two of them, might change the result.

Alone in her room, Myra spent sleepless nights. When she did doze off she woke with a groan from dreams that terrified her—great accomplishments turned into disaster, trips through the clouds, ending with heavy falls into bottomless caves; and always, peaceful interludes with Marianne Davis, whom she had first known as her mother. Sitting beneath the gaslight, she clenched her fists. She *must* win this time. She couldn't face the towering burden of her debts—unpaid bills to the moneylenders, unpaid attorneys' fees, court costs, borrowings from twenty or thirty friends and relatives. Nor would she be able to lift her head again to a world that would truly laugh at her now. She re-quired the money for another purpose. She had to get Will out of the atmosphere into which he had drifted, away from the friends he had made. More and more, finally, Myra's thoughts centered upon Philippe. She needed his help—and she wanted it with a new urgency. Suddenly she felt tired, more tired than she had ever known herself.

Below her, from the street, came a hum of conversation. Men were standing together on the corner, and their talk revolved, as ever, about the war. Would Philippe be in the struggle? He

belonged to one of the Creole drill companies; of course he'd
be going! Then she knew that she wanted, as much as anything
else in life, to be with this man for the rest of her days.

On a day in mid-March of 1861 Myra sat next to Reverdy
Johnson as the justices marched slowly in. John Catron cast a
truculent look in her direction; was it a good sign that he
appeared to be furious at her? James Wayne's long fingers
tapped on the desk ahead of him; he seemed impervious to
everything about him. The clerk spoke: the decision would be
given by Judge Wayne! Then the thing had happened that they
told her could not happen. She had won. The court had overthrown its previous decision, just as that decision had overthrown the one before it!

The Georgian cleared his throat. With his first words he
pointed out that the present case presented the controversy in
a new light. Mrs. Gaines came with a support she had previously
lacked—the probate of her father's second will, now recognized
by the Louisiana Supreme Court. Then, turning to the "church
hearing," the so-called vindication of Jerome des Granges from
charges of bigamy, he proceeded to demolish it. Investigation
made it clear, he said, that in 1802 and 1803 no religious group
in Louisiana, under rules which the church itself recognized,
had power to try such cases. He went far back into the history
of the Inquisition, the relations of church and government. As
early as 1770 the Spanish king had returned bigamy proceedings
to state courts; under such regulations in Spanish Louisiana no
churchman could have acted as this paper claimed one did.

Yet, even if it were accepted as genuine, by its very terms it
did not exonerate Des Granges; it declared only that the matter
was left open for further inquiry. From all the evidence, the
judge was certain that actual criminal investigation took place
later and that Des Granges was then declared guilty. Therefore,
he concluded, Myra was the proper child of Daniel and Zulime
Clark. There was a burning dissent by Catron: Myra had already been ruled an adulterine bastard; nine years ago the court,
with him as its organ, had given a decision that all had accepted
as final. To change it now meant gross injustices; men would
have property taken from them, investments based on the
earlier decision would be wiped out. . . . Myra's eyes sharp-

ened. Again Catron had set up her rights as a human being against those of property and made his choice. And still she had won.

Men and women clustered about her; absently she smiled and nodded, and waited until they left. In the empty hallway she took a position near the door from which James Wayne would emerge. After a time a lean figure came out. Wayne looked at her, his expression hesitant. She extended her hand. "I wanted only to give you my thanks, and my children's." Her voice weakened, and she could think of nothing more to say.

He smiled a moment, and then his face regained its gravity. "It wasn't an easy decision to make. I believe it was the right one." With a bow, he moved away. They would not meet again.

In the twilight she walked down the long flight of steps. Below her the lights blinked on; in the soft hush that had fallen on the world before her it was difficult to realize that men were planning for war. Back at the hotel crowds awaited her. She thought not of her triumph but of Rhoda and Will and then of Philippe. Until today she had been afraid she would burden the Creole with the weight of her disappointment, her final failure that would mean only a lifetime of never-to-be-realized expectations. Now she knew what she would do.

At the telegraph office, she wrote across the paper, in her firm script: "Mr. Philippe d'Abadie, No. 31 Esplanade . . ."

A clerk touched her arm. "This came for you a few minutes ago. Thought I'd save you time." The message was from Philippe. By the time she received it, he told her, he and his men would be on the march from New Orleans; God bless and protect her. . . . She drew a long line through the sheet before her.

At her elbow the correspondent of the New York *Herald* was scratching out his story: ". . . against difficulties, delays, combinations, and reverses that very few men would have had the moral courage to face, she has achieved one of the greatest legal triumphs of this century. . . . Decision creates profound sensation . . . absorbing subject of conversation in every circle . . . Mrs. Gaines is undoubtedly the richest woman on this side of the Atlantic, and, if wealth could give it, ought to be the happiest."

Within a month, on April 12, a force of Confederates under the command of a saturnine, mustachioed Creole fired on a federal relief ship in the harbor of Charleston. The boom opened the war.

The tramp of troops woke her in the mornings; at night she watched the torchlight parades; daily she studied every paper that would tell of developments in Louisiana. Into Washington City poured men from every nearby locality, dirty and bedraggled, neat and suave, men of grim visage and men of smiling unconcern. Soon after the decision, as she started out of Reverdy Johnson's office, she came upon John Campbell, who had thus far remained in Washington with the other justices. As she talked with him she sensed a more serious expression than usual in his pale face. When they parted he took her hand and said softly, "We may not see each other for a long time." Then he went quickly away.

John Campbell was the only justice to leave the bench because of the war. After only eight years on the court, at the beginning of a brilliant career, he went back to Alabama late in April.

The losses of other friends saddened her; and increasing bitterness touched her with the passing days. Being closely related to both North and South, she was torn between them. Her Northern connections, knowing of her long years in New Orleans, thought of her, as a matter of course, as a Southerner. A New York woman inquired, "Why, may I ask, aren't you with your traitor friends?" Similarly, to the Southerners, she appeared to be a rank Northerner.

After a time a number of rabid Washingtonians decided she was a "Southern spy." She discovered she was being trailed, her papers rifled. Annoyed, she pinned a note on her desk when she left her room: "To Whom It May Concern: After searching here, please put my records back in neat piles." Eventually a soldier met her at the door and took her to intelligence headquarters. Before an officer she spoke swiftly: "If you'll only call my friends, Johnson, Eustis, Mrs. Allen . . ." An hour later, her attorney at her side, she walked out.

"It won't happen again," Johnson assured her. "You'll be left in quiet."

"But I don't want quiet!" she fumed. "I want some action in my case."

"There's nothing to be done here. Whatever happens next, it will be in New Orleans; and that's in Confederate hands. We can only sit still."

Myra was hardly one to accept so quiescent a view. In May she picked up a paper, to learn that the Confederate Congress had voted to move its capital to Richmond, less than a hundred miles away. Avidly she followed the reports; at last the Confederates were in their new quarters. That day, in heavy traveling attire, a parcel of carefully wrapped records under her arm, she descended upon Johnson. She spoke casually: "I'm on my way to Richmond."

His eyes darted to her face. "In the name of God, what good will that do? And how do you think you can get through the lines?"

"I know a lot of Southerners; and the way to find out what I can do is to go to the scene." Patting his arm, she sailed out.

Astride a horse, Myra jogged forward day after day. She had her story ready: "urgent sickness" in her family, just a few miles farther along. With her she carried several letters from properly selected Washingtonians, vouching for her. For a time these worked; soon, however, she had to use other methods. Twice she slept in the woods, then spent a tense night being led through a forest by a Negro whom she persuaded to help her. When they were suddenly fired on she and her helper threw themselves in a ditch. After a time, at Myra's insistence, they started again. At dawn her guide shook his head; she had to go the rest of the way alone. Wet with perspiration, she pushed ahead. All at once a file of Confederates stepped from behind a ledge, and she faced their guns.

"What the hell are you doing here, ma'am?"

Summoning every bit of conviction at her command, she tried to explain. The lieutenant remained unmoved. "You certainly act like a damned spy to me. Come on." What to do with her at the camp became a problem. A captain called her; again she went through her story, but he was less impressed than the lieutenant. "They just caught a federal agent near the next camp; shot him this morning," he told her. For three days she stayed in a hot, dirty cell, fed on bread and verminous meat.

At last, when a pair of tight-jawed officers arrived for further questioning, she realized she was in a perilous position. At that moment she recalled one of Edmund Gaines's sayings: "When in doubt, get to the highest officer you can find."

"I demand to see your commander," she cried.

"Commander got no time for things like this."

"That's his office over there, isn't it?" She pointed to a building a hundred yards off. They said nothing, but their eyes gave her the answer. Bracing herself against the window, she opened her mouth. Out came a wild, almost maniacal scream, then another and another.

"God damn it, ma'am! Shut——"

Still the screeching went on. When the younger officer put his hand over her lips she bit; as the other came for her she kicked him in the knee. A few minutes later she sat opposite Colonel George Benson, a young man with a sardonic light in his eye. As soon as she could talk she gave an account of herself, mentioning General Gaines, Daniel Clark, every Southern friend and connection she could summon; finally, by accident, she hit on John Grymes. "My father was mighty close to him," Colonel Benson conceded. "How do I know, though, that you're not making this up?"

On the right trail at last, Myra pulled from her memory every fact she knew about the reprobate, every story she had heard. Though Colonel Benson chuckled, he was not entirely convinced. Finally, after a long silence, she recalled the breakfast at which she and Edmund had first met Grymes, and the conclusion, eminently à la Grymes, when he made Edmund pay for the breakfast to which he, Grymes, had invited them. The major gave a sigh. "That's Grymes, all right. And I guess you're free, madame."

She had never felt more grateful to anyone in her life. As she thanked him she smiled. "I'm going to reward you in my will!"

"I'll try to remember that, madame."

"You will."

A few days later Myra rode up to one of the principal hotels of Richmond. Before she removed her soiled garments she wrote a dozen messages to friends in the city. The next morning she went to work. In the soft air of the new capital she struggled day by day, waiting in the offices of the authorities, pleading for appointments, calling on wives to enlist their interest. For more than a week she tried unsuccessfully to see the Confederate attorney general, Judah Benjamin, whom she had met casually in New Orleans. It was not until then that she learned what she should have known before: one of Benjamin's closest connections was with Duncan Kenner, Louisiana planter and Confederate congressman, a man against whom she had filed one of her suits.

Nowhere did she get a definite reply to her inquiry as to how she could obtain her rights in New Orleans. Of one thing, at least, she was certain. By letter James Gardette advised her it would be wise if she stayed away from Louisiana for the time being; she was hardly a popular figure at the moment. Meanwhile she attended one of Varina Davis's levees, in a white-porticoed Richmond mansion. The President's wife spoke pleasantly enough to her; and once more Myra mused over their varying fortunes. For a moment she thought of appealing for help to Varina Davis; almost at once she knew it would be hopeless. From the party, however, Myra gained something—a whispered word that within a few weeks Confederate courts would be established in New Orleans.

She had the peg she needed. To get the benefit of the new ruling in her behalf, she would almost certainly have to sue every man who had her property. Well, why shouldn't she start now? From Richmond she wrote a New Orleans attorney who had once represented her; she wished him to file proceedings at once against two hundred and forty persons whom she named. The result was that when the Confederate district court opened there the first cases offered were those of Myra Gaines.

Citations went out, in New Orleans, up- and down-river. Usually they were ignored; some people displayed them as souvenirs. So the woman had her decision from the Yankee capital, did she? Well, let her see what good it did her! Once the war ended and permanent Southern courts were established, they'd listen to her whistle for her money. The few answers that came in were identical: the lady possessed no standing in these courts; she was nothing less than an "alien enemy." The judge hesitated, and nothing happened.

A tense summer passed in Richmond. Occasional letters reached her from New Orleans; they only contributed to her concern over young Will. He had caught pneumonia and almost died, she suddenly learned; but he was recovering. Intermittently mud-stained messages arrived from Philippe in the field, and these did not increase her ease of mind. In the Confederate city Myra watched the electric exhilaration that followed the defeat of the Union forces at Manassas; she heard the roars that greeted the Northerners' call for a half-million more volunteers. The South could whip 'em all, practically without lifting a hand! Gradually, however, the elation dissipated. Bad news flew back—defeat at Roanoke Island, Nashville, Shiloh . . . the frightening word that the federals had reached the line of the Mississippi at New Orleans.

The Creole city fell. For a slow month Myra bought every newspaper, searching nervously for items from the deep South. Finally her finger stopped at a little note: federal courts were to be re-established at New Orleans. Now, at least, she could see her children again and, perhaps, Philippe. That evening she slipped out of Richmond. Her face was set; by this time she understood a bit about dealing with the military.

Her cheeks haggard, streaked with grime, Myra almost wept when the familiar spire of St. Louis Cathedral lifted itself along the river. Under a gray rain the city lay chill and dispirited. Few walked the streets; along Canal she caught the smell of burned or soured produce. In a frenzy of hate and despair the city had set its treasure afire to keep it from the Yankees—hills of cotton bales that had reddened the wharves, hogsheads of molasses that broke and sent the liquid gurgling into the gutters.

James Gardette opened the door with caution, then threw it wide. Rhoda and Eulalie, with James's wife and their small children behind them, ran to her. Through the doorway she saw that Will lay in bed, and she sped to his side. His eyes looked lost in his shrunken face; obviously he had been very ill and had not yet recovered.

James tried to be cheerful. "Will's on the way back now. Nothing to worry about, is there, boy?"

The youth nodded listlessly. After a time the others left them alone. Even then she found it difficult to talk with him; he seemed devoid of all spirit. Eventually he lifted his head. "Things didn't turn out very well for you, did they?"

"What do you mean?" Her eyes widened. "I won."

"What good has it done?"

"But the war, Will! We have to wait——"

"Wait! That's all we'll do, all our lives, all our lives!" His pale face flooded with color, and he began to cough. Appearing quickly, Eulalie thrust a brown mixture into his mouth and forced him to lie on his back. As he gasped she led Myra to the door.

In the adjoining room the two women faced each other. "Myra, poor Myra," the Creole whispered in her rumbling voice, her plain face pitying. "Try to understand. Will was disappointed, so disappointed. He didn't realize the war would come as soon as it did; he believed you'd get the decision in Washington much earlier, and he had made plans." She paused. "Me, I don't know about these things, but it had something to do with cotton and shipments. From little remarks he made, we know he thought he'd make a lot of money. Then"—she opened her hands—"it didn't come."

"But—but what happened?"

"He stayed away from home for a month. Then James found him in the city hospital. He—he hadn't been caring for himself."

Myra dropped her head in her hands and remained silent for a long time. Then, returning to her son, she stayed with him for hours. Late that night she went to bed; by early morning she was up, calling on her lawyers. All of the cases, brought under the Confederates, would be filed anew, according to federal law. Let those two hundred and forty defendants think of new arguments now! After some thought she drew up yet another suit, one whose preparation gave her a special satisfaction. In it she demanded that the Chevalier de la Croix be made to give her back the full value of the slaves he had obtained from Relf and Chew. She listed the Negroes, by their names and ages at the time of their sale; she set down their valuations as of that date, and the best possible estimate as to how long they lived afterward and how much their labor was worth to De la Croix. Having no way of determining how many children these slaves had, she also estimated this, and she did the same with the slaves' children's children, and also approximated their valuations and labor. Originally there had been seventy-five slaves; "more than three hundred" others must have been born of "the female slaves aforesaid." Totaling it all up, she sued De la Croix for one million dollars. Five hundred thousand of it was for interest. He had taken the slaves for eighteen thousand.

As she hurried about the city Myra was startled. New Orleans, the commercial metropolis, had lost its commerce. The port had become a place of empty sails, of dead cargoes and battle vessels. James told her that, regardless of their complaints, most of his patients suffered from a second trouble—lack of food.

Myra now went back to the people she had known best, her friends in the market area—the former butchers, operators of stores and shops. She found them in a state close to desperation. Of the money she had borrowed, she had more than fifteen hundred dollars left; on it she had hoped to support herself and the children for some time. Now, with a sigh, she dipped into it. She could not pass the children of people who had reached out a hand to her in her days of want, and see hunger in their eyes. Victorien Badeaux was a regular recipient of her help; stouter now, less agile, he mumbled his thanks and kissed her hand. Then there were old Mme. Gouaux, the Perezes and their neighbors, and, among others, Myra's two aunts in Mississippi, feeble, their needs hardly less than the Orleanians'.

Word spread of her contributions, and the petitions increased. Soon she was making a daily round of visits. Often she called at a great, decaying residence, in which descendants of the builder huddled in a single room. Furniture and jewelry had been pawned, a marble fireplace ripped out in the night and sold to a merchant for a few dollars; now that money, too, was gone. As she walked away from the house she realized that the address seemed somehow familiar. Then she knew—it was one of the properties that Daniel had left; years ago it should have gone to her. Somehow she could not feel so certain now about justice and her rights. In some cases she would be creating more injustice, denying the rights of others who were not responsible. Confused, she returned home.

Will was beginning to sit up, though his system remained

greatly damaged. It would be a long time, James made clear, before the youth had his full strength again. Will's spirit, like his body, was coming back only gradually. What had happened had been a hard blow to his self-esteem—too hard a blow. Will, she knew, had little of her own resilience, her ability to fight back. Yes, she told herself, he was weak. But was that his fault? Was it, instead, some failure for which she was responsible? Whatever she did, she told herself, she must make it up to her son for these years.

For months Myra's few comforts were the intermittent letters that came from Philippe d'Abadie. He had been assigned to a new company; this last one had been ripped to pieces. Shaken, she read on: would she, please, see his mother and his daughter for him? The son was away in the Army, near Atlanta. Myra called on Mme. d'Abadie, now confined to her bed. The old woman smiled gratefully when she saw her visitor; thereafter Myra read to her. They never discussed the subject, but Myra grew certain that Madame wanted her to accept Philippe; long ago Myra had decided that she would do so at their next meeting. Meanwhile Mme. d'Abadie stirred in agitation as she spoke of the war. No Anglo-Saxon Virginian hated the Yankees with greater fury than this retiring French Louisianian.

During the following winter Myra had to bring her bad news. An official message carried the tidings that Philippe's son had been killed in battle. It arrived when Myra was about to leave the D'Abadie house; the mulatto servant, her eyes fearful, asked Myra what to do. With the slim Odalie, Myra returned to Mme. d'Abadie's bedside; and as the three women sobbed together another fear grew within Myra.

For nearly a year they had received intermittent letters from Philippe; then these stopped. Rhoda knew the reason for her mother's taut face and the unshed tears in her eyes. The fortunes of the Confederacy rapidly worsened. Grant cut deep into Georgia; suddenly Lee had put down his arms, and in Richmond the government packed its belongings. In a few more weeks everything would be ended; and all over the South women groaned in bitterness, then gave thanks to God that it was over.

A creased, much-delayed letter came to her. Holding it
against the edge of her desk to steady her hand, she read that
Major d'Abadie, after having been missing for months, had
been located. He was still recovering from serious wounds, but
it now appeared he could be sent home. The major had given
her name. On the eighteenth he would arrive at the station;
would she be able to meet him?

Early that evening Myra and Rhoda stood side by side at the
station. At a signal from a distance the crowd pressed ahead.
Myra found herself among harassed wives and children and
aged men, each waiting for a glimpse of a remembered face.
As the line of coaches came to a stop tired men began to step
off, looking lost or saddened or stolid with the defeat that they
carried like an extra burden. Nowhere could she discover
Philippe. The file slackened, the last soldier stepped down; several halted and turned back. Men on stretchers were being assisted out.

All at once Myra recognized a white face with burning eyes
that were almost those of a stranger. Philippe sat in a wheelchair that was being lifted to the ground. As he raised his hand
in an attempt at a greeting the shawl in his lap slipped down.
Both legs had been amputated just below the hip and his slumped
body seemed oddly shrunken. Her low, involuntary moan was
lost in the noises about them.

Rhoda helped her move the wheelchair to a corner of the
crowded place, then left her for a time with Philippe. Holding
himself rigid with an effort, he looked sadly at her, but she spoke
before he could. "Philippe, I'm sure you understood from my
letters . . . Can't we have the wedding right away? I'm ready
right now."

His deep-lined face lighted up, then quickly became grave
again. He half whispered his words. "You know I'd like that,
more than anything else." For a moment he lost control of his
voice, then he went on. "But you'll want to think about—about
this. I'm not the man who proposed to you. A hopeless cripple.
So much, so much has happened. . . ." The carts rumbled over
the cobblestones; a short distance away a young woman cried
out in her joy at the sight of her husband.

CHAPTER XXIV

MYRA and Eulalie Montagnet faced each other across the table. Between them lay records covering every property that Myra could claim. Quickly she flipped through them, making two separate piles, one considerably larger than the other. Finally, with a quick gesture of decision, she slapped her hand down.

"Yes," she told her friend. "It's the only thing to do—the only fair thing." Then she smiled. "I feel better about it already."

Solemnly Eulalie nodded. *"Le Bon Dieu* will thank you for doing it." A few minutes later Myra lay in bed and asleep; the struggle of the past hour had left her exhausted.

The next morning, shortly after seven o'clock, she set out to follow a lengthy route that she had outlined for herself. She went to the humbler area below the limits of the old French town, the river-front fringes above Canal that were becoming known as the Irish Channel, and other places equally unprosperous. The houses showed the effects of the bad years—broken gates, weather-worn windows, galleries that sagged. The poor, who had suffered most in the war, also suffered most in the peace that followed.

Myra knocked briskly at the first place. As the door opened and a suspicious woman stared at her she spoke rapidly. "I'm Myra Clark Gaines. May I come in?" After a long wait the listener stepped back. "I want to tell you this myself, so you'll be sure of it," Myra added. "I have no intention of taking this property from you. It's yours."

"But they told me if you won——"

Myra shook her head. "I'm a widow myself. Could I rest at night if I did that?"

As the woman started to cry Myra turned and went down the street. For the rest of the day, and for several days after that, she pursued her schedule. Some, with dull hostility or puzzlement in their faces, were not inclined to believe her. Usually, as she told Eulalie, she got at least a cup of coffee or a glass of Creole sugar and water. Then, returning to her quarters, she worked over the smaller pile of papers. These represented another kind of property owner, the prosperous and the arrogant ones.

From them she would demand her due. For a time, in her hopeful moments, she thought that some, at least, would finally recognize that the courts' decisions must apply to them. But she had to go to the law again in each case, renewing her charges and, frequently, amending them. Often death had intervened; often sons or nephews or grandchildren were in possession. Several times she discovered she was changing her complaints a third time, starting on yet another generation. The years were going by. . . .

She had won her case, but . . . The words beat in her ears. First came the problem of postwar lassitude, the slowing up of all normal processes, delays in the functioning of the Louisiana courts. Political upheavals—killings on the streets, violent shifts in government—played their part. In many cases records were lost; files had been burned during the war, affidavits and letters removed. Yes, she had won, but . . .

She welcomed the driving labor that sent her to bed muscle-weary, mentally fagged; there were things she did not want to think about. A wave of misery and longing came to her whenever she remembered Philippe. Why hadn't she accepted when he first asked her? She had denied them what might have been at least a brief happiness. Over and over that ghastly hour at the station returned. Philippe and his mother had gone to a small plantation near New Iberia on Bayou Teche. From time to time he wrote: he was improving, he thought; things at least were quieter there than in New Orleans. Another worry, she realized, bedeviled him; from the long lines of foreclosures in the papers, she learned that the D'Abadies had lost their last properties in the city. As she sat at her desk she found herself listening for that light, familiar step. Then, catching herself, she dropped her eyes. She wondered if she would ever see him again.

Now Will was helping with the case. Regularly he accompanied her on her calls. With him beside her she felt a sudden pride and then a sadness. Long ago she had moved about New Orleans with his father, and they had talked of the children and the future they would win for them someday. Could she have thought that she would still be at the task more than thirty years later?

Slowly she had come to realize that one of her great cases, or collection of cases, was that against the city of New Orleans. Daniel had owned a wide acreage near old Bayou St. John. Then it consisted largely of outlying wood and swamp, a ridge or two, and a dreary stretch infested by alligators and crawfish. Gradually settlers had advanced toward the marshlands. Back in 1821, after Daniel's death, Relf and Chew sold the ground for five thousand dollars. By 1834, the year Myra made her first formal charges, the municipal government purchased it for twenty-five thousand. At that time Myra informed the city of her rights; it ignored her and proceeded to cut streets, drain the place, and then to sell most of it. Today the area was worth millions.

Myra had sued for the bayou land, and also for every penny of rent and other profits that had come from it during the years it should have been hers. Step by step she was carrying the matter forward. The record of the litigation had reached staggering proportions. It covered eight thousand pages; the cost of printing came to almost thirty thousand dollars. This matter of the bayou property was now approaching a climax. Finally Myra thought of John Campbell, back in private practice in Mobile. As she wrote him, she wondered how he would feel about appearing as an attorney before the United States Supreme Court, on which he had sat as a judge.

Campbell's reply came at once; he looked forward to working with her once more. She had her papers ready for him. The impassive attorney permitted himself a smile at the familiar sight. "Wars and presidents may come and go, Myra; you and your case go on." Campbell had aged considerably; his narrow face seemed to have contracted further. At the corner of his mouth and in his light eyes, however, she saw a new sympathy, a hint of softening. Glancing across the desk, she reflected on their two lives. Each had had his greatest hopes realized; then each had watched triumph fade away. But she was winning back. John Campbell, no matter what happened, could never hope for the place which he had once had in Washington.

Before they had gone very far into the case there was a

sound outside. She pulled open the door, knowing who would be there. His wheelchair in the hands of a Negro servant, Philippe d'Abadie sat smiling at her. "Did you think you could keep me away?" His face, leaner than before, appeared rested, and his eyes shone. As he took their hands he exclaimed happily, "When do we start? . . . But first, Myra, haven't you become Creole enough to want some good black coffee?"

Picking up his documents, John Campbell made a discreet excuse. As he left they were smiling over the steam from their cups, and Myra felt five years younger.

They must fight forward, as ever, from one court to the next, and pray for a minimum of delay. Counting over her bills one morning, she frowned at the total. What was she doing—mortgaging her children's future? Returning from her schoolwork, Rhoda found Myra close to hysterics. Her daughter blinked at the amounts, but her face remained calm. "We've been through worse," she coaxed. "Remember the day we were about to be put out of the rooming house? And the way everything seemed ended when Judge Catron swung the court against you? Now you're upset because our debts are high!"

Rhoda succeeded in her purpose. As they put the records away she suggested that Myra walk with her to Jackson Square, to clear her head of the cobwebs. En route Myra grew pensive. "I wonder if I did the right thing with you children, from the beginning? After all, should I have taken you to the Whitneys or Colonel Davis?"

Rhoda stared. "And given up the case? You'd have been the unhappiest woman in the world, and we'd have suffered with you! When I think how well you've managed . . ." Her daughter's expression changed, and she looked away. They sat on a bench near Jackson's statue; after a minute or two Rhoda said, "There's another thing I've wanted to talk about. . . . You know, if it hadn't been for the case, I'd never have met Jim Christmas." The name off her lips, Rhoda lost part of her constraint.

Myra smiled; she well remembered Jim, the tall, goodnatured son of a Mississippi planter, introduced to them some months ago by one of Myra's attorneys. Myra had liked the red-haired, trimly built youth from their first meeting; his clear blue eyes had candor and intelligence. As a Confederate colonel he had won considerable local repute; since then he had gone to North Carolina to look after several farms. Until today Myra had not realized that Rhoda had any particular feeling for the boy. Now her daughter went on:

"When he asked me, I told him it was best to wait. He ought to settle down a little more, I think. And then, our affairs— your case . . . I ought to be with you. . . ." In the dusk the cathedral bells chimed across the square, and the lights went on, one after another, in the double row of brick apartments on each side.

Myra frowned. "You're sure about him, Rhoda?"

"Oh yes. Still, wouldn't it be better if——"

"It wouldn't!" Myra caught her arm. "Don't make the—the mistake I made!" The two sat motionless; a passing soldier peered curiously at them. "Why don't you let Jim know our plans?"

As they argued over the bayou property before the lower judges the city's attorneys suddenly tried a new approach. They bore heavily on two contentions. The whole estate had been insolvent; therefore Relf and Chew had sold it simply to pay Daniel's debts. Also, even if the court did recognize Daniel's second will, Myra could take only what was left out of a final third of the property. Relf and Chew, they said, had been Daniel's full partners, entitled all along to two thirds of everything. While they were alive the two men had not stressed that last claim; the city of New Orleans went back to it. It was on these grounds that the next case would be decided in Washington.

The capital was another city in this spring of 1868. Residences went up everywhere, with the wooden gimcrackery ornamentation that was currently sweeping America. The circle of neglected military forts remained on the outskirts; as always after a war, the Army clung hard to its powers and prerogatives. In the White House the unhappy Andrew Johnson waited for the end of his term. Northern businessmen were masters of cotton and cane; America was changing before Myra's eyes. The Supreme Court was housed in new, more magnificent quarters.

As Myra walked into the courtroom she suddenly felt lost. James Wayne, her great judicial advocate, had died in the heat of the preceding July; Catron, too, was gone. After a moment's reflection she whispered to her attorneys that five of the nine justices were entirely new to her; and not one of the men survived who had sat on the bench when her case was first heard. She had outlived them all.

A silence fell when John Campbell rose. Hardly ever in the history of the Supreme Court had a former justice returned to argue before it. Gravely, with quiet deference, Campbell addressed the jurists among whom he had sat a few years ago. As word spread men and women hurried in to see and hear. Campbell gave no hint that he realized what was happening. When he finished he wiped his face lightly with his handkerchief; it was his only sign of emotion.

Afterward word leaked out that some of the justices had shuddered when they glanced at the record of the case. How could they be expected to absorb all the thousands of pages? "We've got another enemy," Campbell had told Myra, "lethargy. If only the judges will take the trouble to get to the facts . . ."

And now, as so often before, she saw the judges file by on decision day. The opinion would be given by Justice Davis, plump and bearded, a man who looked like a younger, more jovial Lincoln. With an easy gesture of his hand he began. The city said it bought the bayou land "in good faith." But this was not so. Mrs. Gaines had put forward her charges at the time; she had already sued Relf and Chew. Though well warned, the city had gone ahead nevertheless. As to the claim that the estate was insolvent—this was simply not so.

Then the judge turned to the statement that Relf and Chew, as "full partners," were due two thirds of everything. The justice called it "extraordinary" that everyone else who was most concerned should have remained in ignorance of the "partnership" for twenty-five years after Daniel's death. "During this time it was equally concealed from creditors, purchasers of property, and the court." Year by year Relf and Chew had sold the property but avoided any claim that they were acting as partners. "Why was not title asserted when the estate was inventoried?" the judge asked. "Why was it not shown on the conveyances of property? Why were creditors not informed? And when Mrs. Gaines attempts to unkennel the fraud, this 'partnership' comes to light for the first time. No reasonable explanation can be given of the conduct of Relf and Chew."

And then, as Myra held her breath, the judge spoke with deep solemnity: *"No reasonable mind, from the evidence in the case, can doubt that Daniel Clark's testament of 1813 was purloined and destroyed."* For the first time, directly, the United States Supreme Court was on record as declaring that Daniel's will had been stolen. Here was vindication of the strongest of her accusations—the thing she had been trying to prove for most of her life!

Shortly afterward Myra sat by herself in a Washington church and heard Rhoda exchange vows with Jim Christmas. The Mississippian, his small red beard incongruous against his youthful face, accepted the circlet handed to him by the nervous Will Whitney; as Myra watched she experienced a glow of quiet happiness and then a touch of pain. Her thoughts shifted to New Orleans and Philippe d'Abadie. For a moment she felt all alone, more alone than at any other time in her life. But then she caught herself, for she still had Will near her.

Now she would take a step that she had planned for a long time: on the way back to the hotel she told Will of it. Several times he had spoken of his wish to have a business of his own. Well, though it had been a struggle, she had borrowed yet again, on the basis of the latest decisions; and she had a working capital for him. Will's look of surprise gave way to warm gratitude. "You'll be careful with it?" she asked him after a moment.

"Very careful," he told her, and leaned over to kiss her.

A few days later Will came back, his face flushed. "I've found it! Two men in the War Department—one knew the general—are putting me next to something. Contracting—providing supplies. There'll be a fine profit."

Myra nodded quickly. "Good. Then you can start as soon as we get back to New Orl——"

"Oh, it'll have to be up here!" A tiny incoherent sound escaped her; then she would be losing Will too. He barely noticed her change as he sped on. He'd deal in roofing materials and lumber. Already he had a place picked. Absently, as she made signs of agreement, she reasoned with herself. Shouldn't she have looked for something like this, sooner or later? She couldn't have expected her son to be tied to her forever.

During her final weeks in Washington she accepted most of the invitations that were showered upon her, including one to President Johnson's farewell evening at the White House. Recently she had bought back several of the jewels that Edmund Gaines had given her; now she took out the glittering diamond headpiece. The fete was attended by Washingtonians old and new; and Mrs. Elizabeth Ellett wrote:

Mrs. Gaines, radiant as ever, wore a pearl-colored satin trimmed with black lace, with a light dress bonnet decorated with a large aigrette of costly diamonds. "She must have been successful in one of her ejectment suits," said one. "Oh," replied another, "every now and then they send her a million as a sop to keep her quiet." [This, alas, was as untrue as most of the things they said about Myra.] Her features are regular and she is beautiful beyond criticism. Full of life and animation, with manners cordial, piquant and winning, she had a court of gentlemen about her wherever she moved.

Few realized that Myra was now over sixty, for later at Grant's inaugural ball she drew similar attention.

It was at this hour of social triumph that Myra had a much-publicized encounter with another, rather different celebrity, "Mrs. Dr. Walker." Mary Walker, an accredited physician, had labored for years in behalf of women's rights. Long before this, she had reached a conclusion that women's costume was unhealthful; she wore full masculine garb, men's street clothes in the daytime, men's evening attire after dark. A humorist called her a "self-made man." Mrs. Walker always took care to display a full head of curls, "to show everybody I'm a woman"; but it was a matter of record that at least one hotel attendant was fooled on seeing her advance to the door of a woman's dressing room.

Walking one day with a group of friends, Myra approached Mrs. Walker. At first neither was certain of the other's identity. Halting her, Myra asked, "May I give you a little advice?" The doctor nodded. "Please discard those pantaloons," Myra urged.

"Why?"

"Because they shock people. The world isn't made for you or me alone. You place our sex in a false position, to be ridiculed. I've had to struggle for my due too; if I'd taken your garb I'd never have won the sympathy of people all over the country." Smiling, Myra added, "If your object is imitation, don't imitate man—something that God has made only half as perfect as woman."

By this time Mrs. Walker had regained her tongue. "Why do *you* dress as you do, in these laces and flowers?"

"If somebody told me my costume was against public taste I'd change it right away. Feeling more or less young, I dress accordingly. When I feel old I'll dress that way."

"Who *are* you, madame?" The tone was belligerent.

"Mrs. Gaines."

Mrs. Walker's eyes widened. "How is it you seem so much more youthful than you are?" (This remark appeared not entirely unfeminine in its import.)

"I have a secret." Myra's head tossed. "I'm not bitter; I feel kindness toward practically everybody around me." There came a pause, during which the two eyed each other.

"I dress this way for my health."

"That can't be. Day and night I'm continually exposed to the weather, all kinds of weather. And I might say I look younger than you!"

With this stroke the interview ended. Mrs. Dr. Walker strode off, her trouser cuffs flapping in indignation, while Myra, with a backward look, rustled away in her silks.

Crossing the street one day, she halted. A man with a curiously familiar face was walking toward her, led by a woman of his own age. Myra realized in a moment that it was Edmund Gaines, her stepson. They had exchanged many letters but it was the first time she had seen him in nearly twenty-five years. At her first glance she knew that what she feared had happened; Edmund was entirely blind.

After the excitement of their greeting Myra took the couple to the hotel with her. The young woman was his wife. They had been in Washington for some time; Edmund had had to give up his position when his sight declined. Soon it was evident that they were in need. Poor Ed! The years had not been good to him. His sensitive face was calm and gentle, and suddenly their

days together came back to Myra in a wave of warm memory.
How many times, in the years that followed the general's death,
had she wanted young Edmund back again! Quietly Myra
pressed several bills into the girl's hands and obtained a promise
that she would keep in touch with her. As they said good-by
Myra pledged herself to see them again whenever she came to
the capital.

On Myra's return to New Orleans, Philippe d'Abadie
awaited her at the station. Frowning, he gave her the latest
development. The city administration, much disturbed over
her Washington victory on the bayou lands, was planning to
carry its fight even further against her.

She blinked. "But I've won! Isn't everything settled?"

"Not exactly," Philippe sighed. "Its a pretty complicated
situation. The Supreme Court has said simply that the city
obtained this land through improper means. You have the right
to it, and all the rents and profits that have come from it
through the years. But the next question is: Who's to pay you
—the city, or the people who eventually bought most of the
land? These people say they didn't know about any flaws in
the title; they insist that, as a routine in such transactions, the
city guaranteed them full protection. Now the city is trying to
wash its hands of the affair."

"What happens now, exactly?"

"A federal master inquires into it; and meanwhile we keep
on suing the city *and* the people who have the land. Somebody's
responsible, and we'll pound at them till we find out."

Her face set in discouraged lines. Would she spend the rest
of her days in waiting? Philippe took her hand, and his words
were the same ones his mother had once used to her: "Courage,
Myra, courage."

As the struggle against her took a new turn the opposition
to her began to crystallize in the city administration. Sometimes,
fuming, she swore at New Orleans itself—this cursed place
and its cursed people, hostile, always hostile. But each time she
quickly softened. The little group of scheming politicians were
not the people whom she had come to know through her years
of good times and bad. For the real New Orleans she had a

growing affection and sympathy; as for the politicians—her lip curled—she'd keep after them to the end.

Gradually the owners of small tracts in the bayou property began to call on her. Caught in the clash between her and the city, they chose Myra. Among them were a number whom she had already agreed not to eject no matter what happened. They had only their plain homes, unpainted, unimproved; in these postwar years they found trouble even in meeting tax payments.

It was difficult to see all who came to her. One day, as fifteen men and women crowded into her narrow room, jostling Dr. Gardette's patients, she came to a decision. Later that week, for the first time in the city's history, a woman opened an office of her own. In busy Exchange Place Myra rented a room and filled it with her records. That day the disapproving had something new to chew on. Outside she heard an intermittent scuffling; men were coming down the hall just to look. What would females try next!

In the long run, Myra was certain, she would win against the municipal authorities. But would she be in her grave before the final decision? She called Philippe and talked over a new scheme. Suppose she offered a compromise? To save everyone from long litigation she would settle for—she considered—four million dollars. That night she went to the Cheramies and the Whalens, two families she had known in the war days. They could help her, if they would, by talking with their neighbors and asking the city administration to accept such an agreement.

Early in the following year, with the fervent Cheramies and Whalens in the lead, a band of two hundred and twenty-five individuals marched to City Hall with their petition. Council members scurried about, alarmed and impressed. The mayor promised that the matter would be referred to two disinterested attorneys for their opinion.

Before long Philippe had his servant roll him to Myra's office. He grew almost white with excitement. "The city's changing its stand!" A meeting was quickly announced by the council, and a crowd of nearly a thousand gathered at City Hall, women with children in their arms, men on their way home. Entering with Philippe and Eulalie, Myra received shouts of greeting.

"Don't let 'em fool you this time, ma'am," called a grinning Irishman.

"*Eh là-bas!*" cried several Creoles.

The lawyers rose, and quietly they gave their advice that the city government accept the compromise. The law was clear, they said; the city had been guarantor when it sold the land, and eventually it could not evade the necessity of full payment to Myra Gaines. Not only was the municipality failing in its pledge; it was injuring itself. "One thing is certain." The elder lawyer tugged at his beard. "Before this is over the city will have lost in taxes, which would otherwise have been collected, and in money spent for lawsuits, double the amount for which the matter can now be settled." For decades all of New Orleans had suffered; the city had seen the growth of whole sections seriously retarded.

"You're damned right!" declared one of Myra's supporters.

Benignly the mayor promised "full consideration." Word went out that the compromise would be adopted without delay. As the gavel fell, men and women ran up, shouting and applauding. A crowd thickened about Myra, to thank her and to congratulate her on getting the matter settled. The Whalens and Cheramies brought friends forward, one by one, and Mrs. Cheramie burst into tears of joy. There were tears, too, in Myra's eyes; as she stopped along the stairs that led from the high pillars of the hall the stars gleamed across Lafayette Square.

Again the months went quickly by. Good tidings came from North Carolina, where Rhoda was soon to have a child. Myra's heart beat quickly at the news; so she would be a grandmother! Will, too, appeared to be in excellent spirits. His contracting firm was prospering; and then he had more news for her—he had met a girl from Pennsylvania, and they would be married by the time his letter arrived. At first Myra was upset; couldn't he have let her meet the girl? Then she reasoned with herself. It was Will's life to lead. How many times had she rejected the wishes of her elders? Eventually a note from Rhoda reassured her; Jim and Rhoda had passed through Washington and found Will's wife a quiet girl with an almost matronly air. "Almost exactly what Will needs, I guess," Rhoda added. And Myra was satisfied.

Absorbed in other affairs, Myra gave little attention to one of New Orleans' periodical and, as ever, turbulent elections. A new administration was chosen; still she paid no heed until Philippe came to her, a hard light in his eye. The new officials had decided not to accept her compromise! They had chosen to spend the money in fighting her again. They would go the limit to win.

He bent his head. "I don't understand it—to turn suddenly so pigheaded . . ."

Myra's jaw set. "I do. They're in the pay of one clique of landowners, the wealthier ones, who have brought pressure!" Sick at heart, they could only wait developments.

Then into the Louisiana courts walked seventy-five of the larger property holders. They demanded that the courts reopen the whole matter of Daniel's last will of 1813. Nearly fifteen years ago the Louisiana courts had finally accepted it; the opposition now claimed that a mistake had been made. And they wanted the will annulled.

"Can they do it?" Myra appealed to Philippe.

Philippe's brows knitted. "I wouldn't think they could get away with it. But . . ." He had no need to tell her what most Orleanians were saying at the moment. The courts of this day were among the most venal in the history of the city, which had long known corruption in its politics.

Early in the winter of 1873 Myra again went before the Louisiana Supreme Court. The last time she had been there the justices, rejecting the technical objections of the opposition, declared she had proved her father's second will. Now a completely new group of men occupied the bench; on the narrowest of technical grounds they reversed that verdict. The judges pointed out that two witnessess must swear that they were familiar with Daniel's signature, *because they had often seen him write.* Her witnesses had not said that, although they had implied it.

Myra felt an almost uncontrollable impulse to cry out, quoting the previous remark of the same court. No one, for or against her, had bothered to ask these witnesses—Daniel's most intimate friends—that routine question. Certainly they would have sworn it! The presiding judge droned on. Since no one had seen the will during Daniel's final sickness or after his death, they must presume that *Daniel himself destroyed it*.

But what, she asked herself, of Daniel's own words, as he lay dying, his appeal to those about to deliver the new will?

Suddenly, as the full import broke upon the crowd, it yelled its approval. Men beat their feet and laughed; one stood before her, shaking his fist in derision. Philippe's face was a mask of pain. Myra rose and walked unsteadily through the door.

CHAPTER XXV

OUTSIDE the court she stood for a moment at the banquette edge. Then, without knowing how she got there, she found herself on a bench in Jackson Square, near the general and his horse. A pigeon swung down and pecked at the wood near her. Heedless, she stared at the ground, her hands clenched so tightly that the whites of the knuckles showed. What was left for her? In God's name, what lay ahead?

A short distance away, beyond the wharf, rolled the Mississippi. She had always liked to watch the oily tan water, sweeping past New Orleans. Heedless of the jostling women with their market baskets, she now walked forward along the wooden wharf. The fresh, cool scent struck her, with it the pungency of tar and coffee. She moved toward the edge, above the eddying current. Below her, caught in one of the swirls, danced a scrap of paper, part of that morning's newspaper. When it disappeared she continued to study the spot.

Here, at least, lay escape. Her children could now care for themselves. What had she left except the memory of frustration? The wharf was empty; only a few feet of space remained between the edge of the weather-worn piling and the peace of the water. She moved forward tentatively.

From a shed behind her came an exclamation. A stout man limped in her direction. "Mme. Gaine'! Mme. Gaine'! Haven' see you since who know' when!" Victorien Badeaux, old and tired, a basket of cakes under his arm, was waving at her. He spoke without pause. He had thought he recognized her; it brought back so many good times. . . . He led her to a seat along the wall; when he offered her a cake she took it and managed to chew it.

"How you' case is, *hein?*" His small eyes squinted.

"I've lost it just now." She forced out the answer; then suddenly a stream of angry words rushed from her lips.

After a time Victorien raised his hand. "Ah, she don' soun' too good, all right. But jus' one *de*-feat! You done take a lot of 'em in you' time, *hein?* When you gon' hit 'em back?" A grin spread over his wrinkled face.

She blinked. "I don't think——"

Victorien interrupted. "You got all those big friend' in Washington, ain' you?"

He took it for granted that she would strike back again. But hadn't the Supreme Court in Washington made it clear that it based all its actions on Louisiana's acceptance of the will? Then her thoughts shifted. Four—no, five—times now the Washington court had given rulings that grew out of that acceptance. Nothing new had been produced; did the Louisiana courts, without further evidence, have a right to reverse themselves in this way? Why couldn't she find out?

She jumped to her feet. Her hand, when Victorien took it, was not the icy one he had touched a few minutes before. He stayed there, leaning against the wall. Poor lady! She didn't know that, from the beginning, he had been watching her in the shadows of the wharf. Poor lady . . .

On all sides the conviction grew that Myra had lost irretrievably. *L'Abeille* declared almost gleefully: "The last sensation here is not President Grant's message, nor the news from Sandringham, but the announcement that Daniel Clark's pretended will of 1813 has been revoked, and that after all the case of Mrs. Gaines is now decided completely against her." The matter was taken up in most of the legal journals; the *Gazette* of London, more charitable than some, said: "It would seem as if the poor little lady has had her underpinnings knocked away, and was finally gone, hook and line."

Overnight a new fury broke upon her. Almost everyone to whom she owed money wanted it at once, with interest. The professional moneylenders wrote acid letters, demanding, threatening. They charged her with devious practice; she had deceived them all into believing she had well-grounded expectations. They would go to court, expose her as a charlatan, seize everything she possessed. Usually she asked them merely, "What do I have now that you can take?"

Suits accumulated in court, for five, ten, and twenty-five thousand dollars. A hotel owner in Washington refused to send down her trunks; he would hold them until she paid him. As before, when her fortunes fluctuated suddenly, people who had been pleasant to her swept by, chill and disapproving. It was this treatment, she told Philippe and Eulalie, that really revived her spirits. "I get so mad every time I think of it"—she smiled—"that I forget to feel sorry for myself. I'll show 'em yet."

The holders of the smaller plots of land did not change; the Whalens, Cheramies, and their neighbors remained her allies, no less fervent than before. Philippe called regularly, and Eulalie and the Gardettes found ways to lessen some of her worries. Rhoda and her husband, Jim Christmas, sent her a fair-sized check; they offered to come to her whenever she wished. At the same time Rhoda confided that a second child was on its way. Myra's eyes brimmed; she longed to drop everything and hurry to her daughter. That, however, was out of the question. The cases were under appeal now. Will Whitney wrote, and she was buoyed by his words. Will appeared more and more stable; his wife Hattie had had her first child and expected another. Four grandchildren . . . In some ways God was still good to her.

She had to give up her business office. She had discovered the new boon of the poor, the horse-drawn cars; for five cents she could reach almost any part of the city. Purchasing a heavy black umbrella, she walked through rain and sun and wind, alone or with Eulalie. Always, in these days, she carried a big dark bag to hold the records she would need for the occasion. Streaks of gray threaded her thick red hair, and there were growing shadows about her eyes. But her complexion remained unimpaired, her figure still slender and erect. Practically never ill, she spurned ladylike vapors and such goings on. But she was completely feminine, dressed in garments that did not show their wear and stayed in style with slight alterations through one season after the other. Let her have a new hat twice a year, she said, and she was ready to face anything.

Again she was fighting for survival; if she could only hold on, keep her cases going, until the court in Washington acted again . . . She went to the pawnbrokers with her last jewels, including the diamond headpiece and too the silver-decorated mahogany music box from the Bellechasses of Cuba. As before, a few women friends found ways to leave money behind a clock or beneath a pillow. In each such case, discovering the gift, Myra entered a record of it under "loans."

Unexpectedly another change occurred. James Gardette had an offer to take a country practice in the sugar region above New Orleans. The Godchaux family learned that an aging practitioner wanted to retire; one of the Godchaux boys had known James. When Myra urged him to accept the opportunity James sold the house on Burgundy Street. Only then did Myra realize what a wrench this would be for her, for her stepbrother had been generous beyond measure.

On the day they said good-by Myra and Eulalie went to the stores and came back with a great box of toys for the younger children—cheap, sturdy things, big dolls, unbreakable soldiers. Myra had come, necessarily, to appreciate durable values. It was a poor return, she told herself, for all the Gardettes had done for her. Someday she might manage more. Someday, always far ahead . . . She kissed all the Gardettes a last farewell, and she and Eulalie returned to the room they found in an isolated boardinghouse.

Still her need grew. She saw Philippe less often; she did not want him to know her real situation. He had very little himself in these days. Her previous economies had been trifles in comparison with what she must do now. For a time, at least, she had to give up even the horsecars.

Meanwhile Eulalie looked after Myra's hours of rest, her digestion and her mental outlook; she was ready with her advice, whether it was a prescription for a root tonic or the need for a week end in bed. Regularly, when a visit to court was necessary, she marched firmly beside Myra to "protect" her from insult or to cope with any other emergency; though what assistance the little gray Creole could give was questionable.

Searching one day through her purse, Myra frowned and said, "For the next few months, Eulalie, we've got to live on fifteen cents a day. That's all there is to it." Finding a small food

stand on Canal Street, she made an arrangement for both of
them. They breakfasted on a cup of coffee and two pieces of
bread, had a bowl of soup at noon, and more coffee and bread
at dusk. "On that we can survive anyway," Myra told her
friend. Eulalie knew a trick or two to make the way easier.
She paid frequent calls on old Creole connections; from such
visits she often returned with a napkin of food for her "sick
companion at home."

Suddenly they could no longer pay for even their meager fare
at the Canal Street establishment. Now Eulalie intervened. For
a nickel she purchased a bunch of bananas; with another two
pennies she got a loaf of bread, slightly stale. For nearly a week
they lived on this. They toasted the bread; they fried the fruit
or ate it raw. After a time they had difficulty forcing the rich
pulp down their throats.

At the end of this crucial week an impressive letter arrived.
A group of capitalists, joined in a syndicate, had a plan in
which Mrs. Gaines might be interested. Could their representatives call on her?

The representatives, an attorney and two businessmen, had
imposing exteriors and impressive words for her. This was
purely a business affair. Investigating the matter of the bayou
property, they had concluded she had a fair reason to expect
a favorable action in the United States Supreme Court. Individuals in such cases were often sorely embarrassed by the law's
delays; the syndicate members were willing to assume a risk.
Their proposal was this: they wished to buy her rights to about
half the property in question and plan a businesslike development of it for the time it would be released by the courts. If
she signed with them she would receive, tomorrow, eight hundred thousand dollars.

"If I sign, what will you do?"

"Once the court acts, take possession of course."

"But some of the people who live there . . ." Her face
showed her anxiety. "The city really ought to protect them
financially. I've been hoping——"

"That, madame, is not our concern. We'd follow the law."

"Meaning you'd put them on the streets?"

There was no reply. Myra felt a pounding in her head, and
when she finally spoke her voice was calmer than she expected.

"Gentlemen, this is a lot to offer a woman who's living on anything she can borrow. But my answer, I'm afraid, will be no."

Myra went back to the moneylenders and now she was more successful. Another year went by, and then another, and matters still dragged in the courts. For a time no letters came from Will; from others she learned that his contracting firm was failing. It had never succeeded quite as well as Will had indicated; the Army friends, of whom he had expected favors, had failed to carry out their promises. When a sudden appeal came from him for several thousand dollars, Myra could only tell him that even a hundred was beyond her means. She was heartsick, but what could she do? After a while Will wrote that he had found a place as a government clerk; and his words were tinged with bitterness at his situation.

Rhoda remained her major solace and support. Cheerfully her letters described the children's progress, Jim Christmas's success with his farms. By now Myra had six grandchildren, three by each child. As she sat with Eulalie in their dark room she thought of this new generation. Her son and daughter were far away, so far away. Someday, when all of this was settled, they must be together. More and more tightly she clung to this determination.

Another winter passed, and as spring approached word came that at last the Supreme Court would act on the annulment of the will. It would be almost impossible for her to go there this time, she told Eulalie. But things worked out differently than she planned. One March evening in New Orleans, as she walked toward her boardinghouse, she saw a carriage waiting before it. Eulalie stood beside it, her face drawn. In the dimming light Philippe d'Abadie thrust his head forth, and his Negro attendant stepped out. The door was opened for her, and mechanically she slipped inside. She and Philippe looked at each other in silence, and she spoke first: "It's something bad."

He nodded.

"Tell me right away." Her voice came hoarsely.

"Rhoda——" he began, and her hand dug into his sleeve. A message had just arrived; Rhoda had died very suddenly. Taking her to him, Philippe whispered what comfort he could give.

From the funeral Myra and Jim Christmas and his three children went to Washington City to take up residence, at least temporarily. Myra wanted her grandchildren near her. Then, too, the time had arrived for the Supreme Court's ruling.

The evening before the scheduled court session she kissed the grandchildren good night and went to her room. She would not attempt to go to court; she asked them to bring her the message at the earliest possible moment. Through a chill, rainy night she sat up in her chair, her shawl wrapped about her. When dawn came she had bathed and dressed, but then she could think of nothing further to do. By noon she was pacing the floor. Could the lawyers be delaying the word because it was against her? Downstairs the bell rang; when steps sounded along the hallway she threw open the door. The note that Will handed her slipped from her agitated fingers; for a moment or two it eluded her trembling hands. Then she saw the words.

The justices had ruled for her. The Louisiana courts could not, so summarily and without new evidence, throw out the will they had already recognized. Myra felt her way back to her chair and lowered herself into it, crying softly.

Several creditors apologized; two new moneylenders offered any amount, within reason, that she wished. Everyone assured her that her worries at last were over; there remained only the quibbles, the final rear-guard actions. . . . She had been fooled too many times to be entirely satisfied.

But at least some of the litigation was really over. The city was ordered at once to pay her one hundred and twenty-five thousand dollars for tracts of the bayou property still in its possession. Myra went to the offices of her Washington attorneys, and there was quite a little ceremony, ending, as she had been warned, without her having a penny in her possession. Her creditors, moneylenders, lawyers, and others, had made claims for far more than this amount; all the "representatives" —sprucely attired young men with hard eyes—were there. She reached out for the check, fingered it, and then let it go. Quickly the amount was divided in twenty or more directions; one by one the "representatives" placed the checks in their pockets and walked out.

Myra turned to Will Whitney and Jim Christmas with a

slight smile. "They didn't even thank me." She added, "For five minutes I felt rich."

The verdant Washington spring settled about them. Jim Christmas wanted to return to North Carolina, but Myra asked him to remain, "just a little longer anyway." She reminded him that he needed someone, in any case, to look after his three little ones. With Hattie, Will's blond young wife, she watched over these children of Rhoda's, giving them their milk, taking them to the parks. Will's three children also drew her to their playroom, where she sat by the hour. How like his father was Will's youngest, the Puckish boy with the deep dimple beside the mouth; and young Rhoda, earnest and unendingly gentle, helped supervise the younger ones in the same way her mother had first done back in the courtyard of Eulalie's house. And now and then Myra spent a day with young Edmund Gaines and his wife. Her stepson's wife had found a small position; with contributions from Myra, they were managing better than before.

Moving to a boardinghouse on I Street, opposite Franklin Square, Myra asked Will and Jim Christmas if they would be willing to take rooms there with her. She wanted to be near the children and also, though she did not say it, near Will. Her concern over him had increased again; he had become heavy, almost gross, and his face bore marks of continued indulgence. Discontented with his job, he had grown nervous. As soon as she could Myra had called Will's wife aside; the girl admitted that Will was drinking frequently, missing work for days at a time.

Philippe dispatched a surprising message from New Orleans. Certain of the property owners were approaching him. Would Mrs. Gaines agree to compromise, ending the matter, case by case? Immediately she wrote Philippe that she would accept; he could negotiate agreements at thirty or forty or fifty per cent, with payments to be made in any way feasible.

Before long Will came to her, haggard, his manner awkward. "Look," he began, "I've heard of a good chance for a man with a little capital. Friend of mine in the wig business is about to move away." Reading her eyes, Will spoke more rapidly. "I know. I failed before but that was different. It wasn't my fault. This is my chance, my real chance."

She hesitated, her finger playing with the hair behind her ear. "Will, I've worked very hard to get the little I now have. Suppose we lost that?" Pacing the floor, Will argued for nearly an hour, anxiously, desperately, until finally, setting her back firmly against the chair, she told him, "All right, I'll make a bargain with you. I'll set you up as you want—provided you give me your pledge you won't touch liquor; and then I want Jim Christmas as your partner." When Will's face clouded she explained. "Jim's had more experience in things of this kind. It's something I'll insist on."

After a pause Will agreed. At her bank she drew out three quarters of her reserve. Only to Jim Christmas, however, did she explain the full situation. When her son-in-law protested she stopped him. "Jim, I expect your help with Will. If there's a risk it's mine, isn't it? And it's worth it for me."

The venture started well. Will's spirits were rising, and the figures that the two men brought to her were encouraging. In New Orleans Eulalie and Philippe, exchanging her letters, told each other they had never known Myra to be happier.

Then gradually, after some months, Will grew taciturn and silent. "What's wrong?" Myra demanded as she met him in the hallway.

"Nothing, nothing." Sullenly he walked away.

In tears, Hattie motioned to Myra. "He's been this way all week. He claims Jim Christmas is trying to get on your good side and force him out. He and Jim have had quarrels at the office, you know." Myra sighed. She remembered Will's unreasoning jealousy of Philippe d'Abadie. But that had gone. She would talk to Jim, ask him to make allowances; this would pass too.

It did not pass. One morning as Myra entered the living room for breakfast Will cursed at Jim. "You're scheming against me for Mother's money. I know it, damn you!" The two men argued, until Will shouted, "You make one more false step, you bastard, and I'll let daylight through you!" At that he turned away and rushed from the house.

Upstairs again, Myra lay on the bed and tried to sleep. When the bell rang for luncheon she rose. From the hallway she recognized Jim Christmas's step on the stairs. Suddenly the front door slammed; Myra looked up sharply at the sound of hurried steps, and then came the crashing report of a pistol.

At the foot of the stairway stood Jim Christmas, a gun in his hand, a circle of silent men and women about him. Will Whitney had run through the door at him, and he had defended himself.

For nearly a month Myra remained to herself. Hattie Whitney brought down word that she stayed day by day in her chair; she did not cry, only stared ahead, twisting her handkerchief between her fingers.

So her last child was gone. Myra's mind went to that morning of her suffering, when Eulalie had called Will and told him that at last they had their boy. Her husband's tears had come as he bent over her and the child; and they had planned for young Will—bright hopes and shining projects that seemed so easy then. But Will had failed completely; or had she failed him?

Certainly she had worked to provide him and his sisters with security. Yet had she, in doing so, helped kill her son? Because of her case he had never been able to enjoy a normal childhood; always before him as he grew up, it had offered the gleaming prospect of life without struggle, without labor. And then, ironically, such a life had become an impossible hope; they had seldom received what they expected. As she looked, white-lipped, at the floor, she saw her life spread out before her.

What bitterness she felt toward Jim Christmas was subsiding. She could not bring herself to see him, for a while anyway; but what had happened, she knew, was not his fault.

Hattie entered, a letter in her hand. Recognizing the writing, Myra tore it open quickly. Philippe d'Abadie told her he had only a few things to say. He reminded her that he, too, had lost his only boy, in the war; he understood her anguish. He, Philippe, had also cried out against the world. But time would remove the sting; there would be consolations. The boy, Will, she must know, had been good at heart; Philippe reminded her of the day when he had come to them to offer the small treasure of a handful of dollars that he had saved, as a sacrifice for his

mother's cause; he recalled the boy's defense of a weaker play-
mate, mistreated in the park. Philippe ended: "We do our best;
we can do no more. *L'homme propose; Dieu dispose.* There is
the future—and there are your grandchildren."

The letter dropped to Myra's side, and she lifted her tired,
lined face to the light. Could she have done anything but what
she did? She could not have lived a "quiet life." ... . She
paused, and the old feeling of strength returned. Even if she
didn't get another dollar—she hadn't lost! She had wiped the
blemish from her mother's name, and her children's, and their
children's.

She walked to the door. Things would be better now.

The last years brought a contentment, an inner serenity that
she had never known. She visited the courts, she wrote letters,
she waited. To an ever changing New Orleans Myra Clark
Gaines had grown into a legend, a living one, yet a legend
nevertheless. She was still the central figure of a hundred tales,
but where once she had been inevitably the villainess, she now
became the heroine. The faces of those to whom she was pointed
out were curious but kind.

She remained ever alert, ever absorbed in her case—and in
her grandchildren. As she talked she reached into her bag and
handed about pictures of the new generation, daguerreotypes
made at her request. At times she lived in Washington, again
for long stretches with Jim Christmas and Rhoda's children in
Brooklyn. Always she came back to New Orleans.

Here, late on a December day, she was caught in the rain. By
the next morning she had a cold, which settled in her lungs. On
Christmas Eve of 1884 the bell rang many times, and a group
gathered about her bed: Eulalie Montagnet, officers who had
served with Edmund Gaines, women friends, Victorien Badeaux, two children of the Perezes from Terre-aux-Bœufs.
Philippe d'Abadie was home for the holidays with his family on
Bayou Teche. Several times, Eulalie thought, Myra's eyes
seemed to be seeking him. At Myra's insistence, the apprehensive Eulalie set up a diminutive Christmas tree, and it threw
a cheerful reflection. Eventually, as Myra grew tired, Eulalie
signaled to the others and they left.

During the next week Myra's condition varied little. On New

Year's Day, the Creole *Jour de l'An,* the door opened and a black man pushed in a rolling chair. Philippe smiled as he moved toward her, but his lips tensed as he saw how quickly her breath came, how fevered her face appeared.

He took her hand. From outside came the noise of crowds, the echo of laughter, the rumble of voices as families made their holiday calls. Into the sickroom penetrated something of the luster of this Louisiana day of days.

Myra spoke. Did Philippe remember the morning they met, when big John Grymes brought him to her? And that furious trip he made to New York? He asked how he could forget them. . . . They were quiet again, each with his thoughts. Philippe's eye was drawn by a box beside the bed, the gift of Josef Belle-chasse in Cuba, long ago. The silver ornament shone in the late sun. "It was a bird of good fortune, they told me. . . ." Her eyes had moistened. "Many's the time I wondered. Still, when I think back . . . life hasn't treated me too badly, has it?"

Her glance strayed about the room. "Maybe I'd have lived more happily if I'd never heard of all this. But I *had* to fight back, once I'd heard." A hint of a smile crossed her lips. "I was Daniel Clark's daughter after all!" She stared at the blanket and shook her head. "I'm sure of this. Today, if I had to make the choice, I'd do the same thing all over."

Her hand sought Philippe's again, and she anticipated him: "I have one regret, yes . . . one regret." Lifting her fingers to his lips, Philippe kissed them.

Late on a January evening, as the family sat about her bed, she raised her head, half annoyed, half amused. "What's the matter? Nothing's going to happen to me." She gave a thin laugh. "I'm tired, that's all. Philippe, I've been thinking. When the city comes into court again . . ."

As her voice trailed off a shudder ran through her fragile form. She opened her mouth but the words did not come. She smiled, as if to ask pardon, and her face sank to the side. Slowly Philippe's head lowered, and Eulalie began to sob. In the gaslight Myra's white hand lay tightened about a small object, the crucifix that had been her father's.

Passing through the iron gates of the St. Louis cemetery, the men halted with their gray box before a tomb just above the ground. The minister spoke, his voice rising over the wind. A wordless cry came from a woman at the front, and then a hush fell. Myra Clark Gaines rested beside her father, in the city that had become her own.

A handful of green leaves fell from the overhanging tree, scraping lightly across the marble. A balm was in the air, and several red birds swept by in careless flight. Spring, which is always quick on the heels of the new year in New Orleans, was not far away.

Epilogue

IN DEATH, as in life, litigation followed Myra Gaines.

During the last five days of her life, her family was never away from her for a moment. On a Monday in 1885, with great difficulty, she had made her will as the family wished it; on Thursday she died.

A few days later, as the family prepared to file her will, an agitated woman appeared beside them. She, too, had Myra's "last testament"—a different will, leaving a good part of the estate to the lady herself! It was dated two days later than the family's document.

The individual who asserted herself so dramatically, Mrs. Marie P. Evans, had been close to Myra some years earlier. Myra had befriended and assisted her, then "lost confidence" in her, and they parted. As far as anyone knew, the two women had not met for years.

Angrily Myra's family recited these facts. Mrs. Evans had an answer: secretly Myra had long been planning to "reward" Mrs. Evans for her help. True, Mrs. Evans hadn't been able to get to Myra at the end; the family had ordered her away when she approached. But that hadn't been necessary. Mrs. Evans had walked up the front steps the day before Myra's death, and a woman "in shabby black, with a black veil tied on her head" had opened the door and slipped into her hands a paper wrapped in a handkerchief. And there, Mrs. Evans told the court, was the will!

She was never able to identify the mysterious lady with the black veil; but she had the will, signed in a careful handwriting that looked exactly like Myra's. And Mrs. Evans produced a procession of witnesses who told how Myra, over a period of time, had confided her intention to leave a great deal of her property to Mrs. Evans.

And thus again the courts had to pick between two varying wills, with a large sum in the balance. The matter hung on for about ten years. Mrs. Evans's attorneys proved very dexterous; and she appeared to have at least a small point or two. Testimony was offered that Myra had been extremely reluctant to make the will when the family urged her. Finally she agreed to sign the document only at the insistence of those about her. The doctor held her weakened hand in his and pushed the pen across the paper. Thus Mrs. Evans denied that Myra had really signed at all, charging coercion, undue pressure, and so on.

Mrs. Evans had a final argument. The will that the family presented, she insisted, was technically defective. Certainly, of all people in the world, Myra should have known how to make a proper will.

The Louisiana courts agreed with Mrs. Evans's last point. They rejected the family's will because it *was* defective. At the same time it refused the Evans will. There things rested, though only briefly.

Myra had maintained a legal residence in Kings County, Brooklyn. Both sides rushed to Brooklyn to offer their wills there. This time the family won and Mrs. Evans's will was thrown out. She appealed to the higher New York courts; pending their action, the Brooklyn court named a Brooklyn official as "special administrator" of the estate. And now Brooklyn had a "Gaines case" of its own.

The "special administrator" bustled down to Louisiana with his credentials. Certainly New Orleans would recognize Brooklyn. New Orleans would not; the Brooklynite had to go twice to the Louisiana Supreme Court before the judges would admit his presence. Meanwhile the indefatigable Mrs. Evans was scurrying about, trying to get the other side, one and all, cited for "contempt of court." She called herself "the second Myra Gaines."

Eventually the highest New York court ruled against Mrs. Evans, calling her "will" a forgery in its entirety. Thereafter the "second Myra" slipped away. But now there came a schism among the members of the family. They filed contesting claims, and *this* situation brought further complications, delayed matters for additional years, and further reduced, through court costs, the extent of the estate.

And exactly what did the family get at the end? Myra had died with the expectation that at least two million dollars would be netted from her suits against New Orleans over the bayou property. A few years afterward the United States Supreme Court gave its truly last decision on all phases of the litigation. Though it upheld her, it reduced the amount to $576,000, plus interest. (The lower courts had declared her due not only the profits which the city collected, but other amounts it would have obtained had it exercised good judgment and management. This was too uncertain a basis, and the highest court cut down the figure.) Still, the interest that accumulated reached nearly $350,000; and thus the figure came, on the final day, to $923,788.

On a July day in 1892 the *Daily Picayune* presented a story which began:

"As far as the City of New Orleans is concerned, the Gaines case is a thing of the past. On Monday, W. W. Whitney, the administrator of the estate received

A CHECK FOR $923,788

in full settlement of the city's indebtedness. . . ."

At once Myra's debtors pressed forward—lawyers, heirs of lawyers, agents, men and women who had advanced sums to her. One attorney demanded $180,000; others offered claims of $50,000, $25,000, and similar amounts. Claims immediately recognized against the estate totaled $340,000; but there were others. It would seem that when the unrecorded settlements and adjustments were made the heirs obtained several hundred thousand dollars.

Edmund Gaines, the son of the general by an earlier marriage, received $25,000; Myra had taken care to remember him. A $10,000 grant went to Colonel Benson, the young officer who had saved her from a possible firing squad during the Civil War. She had never forgotten him either. Her grandchildren received the bulk of the remainder.

How much did Myra herself actually collect? That will never be known with any degree of certainty. She made various settlements out of court; compromises in her lifetime brought undetermined amounts. Some have claimed she received millions; others have put the figure at several hundred thousand. In any case it all went in two directions: first, to help pay off her ever mounting burden of debt from her case; and then to carry on the many suits themselves.

Well had Justice Wayne called her case "the most remarkable in the history of the American courts." At a later date Justice Davis observed that the matter had been "pursued by the complainant through a third of a century, with a vigor and energy hardly ever surpassed, in defiance of obstacles which would have deterred persons of ordinary mind and character, and had enlisted on both sides, at different periods, the ablest talent of the American Bar."

The latter judge underestimated the full length of the litigation. In all of its phases it remained before the courts from 1832 to 1896—a little less than sixty-five years. No case in America has had such a course. It went to the United States Supreme Court on seventeen separate occasions. And in the end she had done what most observers were certain she could never do; she had obtained recognition for a will never really produced in a court, a will which several aged people had remembered seeing long years earlier!

During her lifetime she had made others wealthy while she lived for years in a state close to poverty. For some she had brought ruin, for others the key to renown and fortune. With her lawsuits she helped create great names; through them she destroyed the reputations of others.

"She died without having seen the promised land," one of her attorneys wrote. He was wrong. Myra Clark Gaines had achieved the thing to which she had given her life. The world had recognized her; she had forced it to do so. She never received all she had hoped for; complete fulfillment evaded her to the end. But all matters considered, that was unimportant.

Today a few elderly people still speak of her, a vivacious woman with red curls, hurrying about through rain and sun and heat, good times and bad times, smiling, talking, arguing; hailing friends on the streets of New Orleans, catching their hands and telling them the story that she had to tell—the story that she made them accept.

NOTES AND ACKNOWLEDGMENTS

FIFTEEN years ago a friend first called my attention to the strange tale of Myra Clark Gaines. Since then, more or less regularly, I have gathered materials regarding her. During periods of intensive research on other subjects I kept this book in mind, seeking out elderly men and women who remembered her in her later years, studying files of newspapers and magazines, collecting data in other forms. Meanwhile, with the assistance of attorney friends, I familiarized myself with much of the almost staggering collection of legal volumes on the subject—the records of her cases.

From the first it seemed to me that the novel was the most effective medium for telling this story. The litigation itself is incredibly involved, sometimes fantastically interconnected—best handled, I think, in simplified form, stressing a number of major points, subordinating a great deal of the more technical material. Also, as I see it, Myra the woman became gradually more important than her lawsuits; she, rather than her litigation, becomes the predominant interest.

It has been difficult at times to choose between varying narratives and anecdotes in a life as full as hers. She spoke often; she was quoted—or misquoted—on frequent occasions; men and women, admiring her or hating her, set down conflicting impressions and conflicting sequences of events. I have tried to select the more probable versions, or those that appear the best documented.

In a number of instances I have exercised the novelist's privilege of foreshortening events, making transpositions of unimportant scenes or incidents, offering a composite personage in place of several others. Eulalie Montagnet and Philippe d'Abadie, for instance, are composite characters. It has been necessary, of course, to eliminate most of the dozens of attorneys who represented Myra Gaines, many of the minor episodes in her career, and some of the more imaginative "occurrences" for which truth has been claimed. In various instances I have presented in the form of court testimony statements made in other forms by the witnesses. Essentially, however, this is as true an account as I have found it possible to give, after a study of the documents and traditions about Myra Gaines.

Two large collections of volumes dealing with the cases are available at the Howard-Tilton Library of Tulane University and at the Louisiana State Bar Library in New Orleans. These include briefs in the case, upon which attorneys long dead have scrawled their comments, often ironic, sometimes sulphuric. Records of the litigation which followed Myra's death are available in Kings County, New York. United States Supreme Court records have also been consulted.

Particular thanks are due to Eleonora Waldman Wharton, Tess Crager, and Frances Bryson for their assistance in reading and checking over the manuscript; to S. Sanford Levy, Trist Wood, Joseph Carroll, Hoyt King, of Chicago, Nolan P. Harmon, Jr., of New York, and Dr. James W. Silver of the department of history, University of Mississippi, who made available to me his thesis on Edmund P. Gaines.

Appreciation is due Dr. Garland Taylor of the Howard-Tilton Library; to Marguerite D. Renshaw, Mrs. Mary Bell Herndon, Mrs. Audrey Godefroy, Mrs. Margaret Hughes, Mrs. Elizabeth Shannon, and Muriel Richardson of his staff; to Dr. Edwin Adams Davis, archivist of the department of archives of Louisiana State University; to Mrs. Ruth Campbell, curator of the Louisiana Room, Hill Memorial Library, Louisiana State University; to John Hall Jacobs, librarian of the New Orleans Public Library; George King Logan, assistant librarian; to Margaret Ruckert and others of that staff; to Mrs. E. D. Friedricks of the department of archives of the city of New Orleans; to Leonard Oppenheim, librarian and assistant professor of law, Tulane Law School; Cecelia C. Macfarlane, librarian of the United States Circuit Court of Appeals at New Orleans; to Mrs. Eilleeñ M. Kean, law librarian of Louisiana State University; to the staff of the Louisiana Supreme Court Library in New Orleans; to Josie Cerf, librarian of the Louisiana State Museum in New Orleans; to Essae M. Culver, executive secretary of the Louisiana Library Commission, for her general assistance in the field of Louisiana research.

Alexander A. Lawrence, of Savannah, author of the authoritative biography of Justice James Wayne, assisted me with answers to many legal-historical questions; and Mayor Walter Chandler of Memphis, author of the excellent monograph on Justice John Catron, also helped me along the way.

Acknowledgments go, too, to F. H. Price, librarian of the Free Library of Philadelphia; Gertrude Brincklé, librarian of the Historical Society of Delaware, at Wilmington; Mrs. James E. Powers, librarian of the Washington Memorial Library, Macon, Georgia; Paul North Rice, chief of the reference department of the New York Public Library; Martha L. Ellison, McClung Historical Room, Lawson, McGhee Library, Knoxville, Tennessee; Jane F.

Walsh, corresponding secretary of the Columbia Historical Society, Washington, D.C.; William D. Hoyt, Jr., assistant director of the Maryland Historical Society of Baltimore; Mrs. John Trotwood Moore, state librarian and archivist of the department of education at Nashville; M. Christine Stokes of the National Archives, Washington; Winifred Ver Nooy, reference librarian of the University of Chicago; A. F. Kuhlman, director of libraries, Joint University Libraries, Nashville; Harland A. Carpenter of the Wilmington Free Library, Delaware.

Also to Charles Rosen, of New Orleans; George S. Gaines, Columbus, Mississippi; C. G. Stokes, Meridian, Mississippi; Rhoda Christmas, Washington, D.C.; Mrs. Erma Shepherd Griffith and Alice Doubleday, Binghamton, New York; Kenneth VanderHulse, Gainesville, Florida; Josephine Packard, Baltimore; Mrs. M. D. Martin, of Houston; Alexander Allison, of New Orleans; Miss Louise Allison, of Houston; A. P. Harmon, of Vicksburg; Mrs. C. Overstreet, Pascagoula; Mrs. C. A. E. King, of New York City; Mrs. Ralph D. Steele and Mrs. Helen Worth, of Brooklyn; E. Ridgley Simpson, of Baltimore; Stanley Faye, of Calumet, Illinois; William H. Connor, of the Wilmington *Sun;* Roger Baudier, editor of *Catholic Action* of New Orleans; Margaret Dixon, of Baton Rouge, Louisiana; Mrs. Angele Gaines, of New Orleans; Mrs. Paula Coad, of Savannah; Rees Stith, of Washington, D.C.; Hudson Grunewald, of the Washington *Star;* Eugene Stanley, of New Orleans; Mrs. Mary P. Gibbs, of Warrenton, North Carolina; Howard F. Jones, editor of the Warrenton *Record,* Warrenton; Anna Marie Kane and Florence Kane Reynolds.